TO ALL THE THEATER DWEEBS OUT THERE.
THANK YOU, PLACES!

# CHAPTER ONE

I get about as far as "Dear Millie Price, we are delighted to inform you" before I emotionally black out like I've just been whiplashed by a rainbow and drop-kicked into a river of glitter. I slam my phone down on the nearest table, jumping to my feet.

"It's *happening*," I gasp.

"Can it happen somewhere else?"

In my defense, I forgot I was in the library. But also in my defense, Oliver Yang would be annoyed with my existence in any room in this school, and likely every dimension hereafter.

Sure enough, he is fixing me with the same patented Stage Manager Scowl I've watched evolve since we first started mutually irritating the hell out of each other freshman year. In the beginning it was far more pronounced—all furrowed brows and tight lips, aimed with the intent to burn. But after three solid years he's adopted a much more impassive micro-scowl, either because he's too cool for a full one or because the two of us get on each other's last nerves too often to warrant it.

I grab my sheet music off the copy machine and glide over to his table, brimming with the kind of excitement that even he and that irritatingly handsome face can't puncture.

"Finals are over," I say, jamming a finger down on his open physics textbook.

He pulls it closer to him, out of my reach. "I'm taking this one late. I had to sit in for all of the auditions."

Ordinarily he wouldn't spare so many words for me, but there's a slight warning in his voice—a reminder that he'll be helping make the casting decisions and it would be in my best interest not to pester him any further. But he's spent the last three years pestering *me*, so it only seems fair to get in a few last jabs now that my theatrical fate is safely out of his hands. Some of the casting decisions our theater teacher has made for me over the years likely have less to do with me looking the part of "Townsperson #7" and more to do with Oliver holding a Millie-shaped grudge.

"Well, I'm done with finals," I tell him cheerfully, sitting on the edge of his table.

"Woo," Oliver deadpans without looking back up.

"And with this school."

"If only."

I toss my hair back behind my shoulders, fully aware that the swoosh of curls is every bit as much a good comeback as any verbal one. But Oliver isn't looking at me, focused on closing his physics textbook and jamming it into his backpack. I scoot myself off the table as he heads out.

"You're not even going to ask *why*?"

Oliver sighs. "I have a feeling you're going to tell me whether I want you to or not."

I twist my lips shut. The thing is, I really shouldn't waste this kind of news on Oliver, who prides himself on his ability to pretend I don't exist. But I'm in what my aunt Heather calls one of my "Millie Moods," when everything is just *so much* that it feels like it's going to spill out of me if I don't find a place to put it. And unfortunately for Oliver, it's the last day of school, and he's the only person within a reasonable radius.

"Fine. I won't tell you, then," I decide.

Oliver pivots toward the exit of the school. "Oh no," he says flatly.

I follow him out onto the sidewalk, where he's crossing the street to get to the science wing of the school. To be clear, it's not that I *want* to continue to have him in my line of sight, but getting on Oliver's nerves is a cherished pastime of mine. And if this really is the last time I'm going to see him, I want to leave an impression. I want him to look up at my face on a Broadway marquee five years from now and remember exactly what it was I said to him before my big bouncy curls and Heather's old nineties mom jeans walked into the West Village and out of his life for good. I want him to remember my—

"*Millie!*"

Oliver's hand wraps around my elbow and yanks me back just as a taxi whizzes past, close enough that I let out a yelp at a volume extremely embarrassing for a native New Yorker. Even more embarrassing, though, is the fact that I am now pressed chest-to-chest against Oliver. Worse still, when I open my eyes, I discover that my face is buried directly into his neck.

We both step back at the same time, his face as red as mine feels.

"What the hell were you thinking?" he demands.

My brain is too busy trying to delete the firmness of his bicep and the smell of his shampoo to formulate a worthy response.

"Thanks," I mutter, crossing my arms over my chest to hide the fact that I'm shaking.

Oliver stands there for a moment, his weight shifting between his feet. "Fine," he relents. "What is Her Majesty freaking out about?"

And just like that the panic about my fleeting mortality—and the fact that I expressly forbade him from calling me "Her Majesty," along with a slew of other unflattering nicknames—is all but forgotten. "I got into Madison Musical Theater Precollege,"

I exclaim loudly enough to stun a flock of pigeons into immediate flight. "Partial scholarship. I'll start next semester for senior year, so I can finish up high school and start getting college credit at the same time."

I'm not exactly expecting him to congratulate me. So far his highest praise of my performance ability was when I overheard him saying to our teacher, "I guess she's the only one who can belt that high G," during sophomore year. But I'm at least expecting a little more than a head tilt and a "Huh."

"'Huh'?" I repeat. "Did finals really eat up your last brain cell?"

"No," he says drily. "The glittery disco pants you wore auditioning with 'Super Trouper' took care of that."

"That was insurance," I tell him. "Donna or bust."

"We're not doing *Mamma Mia*," he sighs for approximately the eighteenth time this month.

Oliver is sworn to secrecy on what the school picked for the fall, but I have my sources. Namely that Mrs. Cooke's been humming "Money, Money, Money" in the hallways way too often for it to just be a consequence of the public school system underpaying its teachers. That, and *Mamma Mia* is closing its limited Broadway run next week, which means the rights will finally be up for grabs again, three long years after Oliver crushed my dreams of doing it.

See, freshman year we lost the rights to the other show we were planning to do at the last second. As it is my responsibility as someone with excellent taste in both music and cuffed overalls, I suggested *Mamma Mia* as a replacement. I had more than half the theater kids on board, but before I could so much as say "Voulez-Vous," Oliver convinced Mrs. Cooke we didn't have the "resources" and talked her into waiting another year.

Which is, of course, when the Broadway revival was announced, and all our hopes of getting the rights went out the window right along with my last few shreds of patience for Oliver meddling with my plans.

"You're just mad that you're going to have to teach someone to train a spotlight on me for 'The Winner Takes It All.'"

"You're that confident you're gonna get a lead?"

I raise an eyebrow at him. Even with Oliver's scheming against me, we both know there's no way I'm not in consideration for a lead. My occasionally overblown ego aside, I'm the best singer this school has.

Or had, I guess. Because I'm out of here.

"I don't need confidence. I've got a three-octave range." I wrinkle my nose. "Not that it matters now."

Oliver shakes his head, letting out a breath that may or may not be a chuckle.

"What's so funny?"

He stops just outside the building, his eyes grazing me—the jeans, the floral combat boots, the hand-cut crop top. The immaculately styled eyebrows and cherry-red lip balm and meticulously heated curls. I know I look good, only because I'm in the business of looking good. My rule is to never leave the apartment unless I look and feel like a rock star, because the thing I learned about living in New York before I fully understood what it meant to be a New Yorker is that things are different here than they are everywhere else. There's this nonstop hopefulness, this weird charge that never leaves the air, like anything can happen. Like your destiny is constantly right around the corner. And I'll be damned if I'm going to get caught in the same old pair of black leggings and white sneakers everyone else owns when I meet mine.

But Oliver is decidedly not appreciating that sense of destiny when he looks at me, because all I see when his eyes meet mine is a faint smirk.

"Just thinking about the stuff the theater department will finally get done with all the peace and quiet."

"Ugh," I say, throwing up my hands. He's been a lost cause since day one. "See you *never*, Oliver."

He seems unconvinced of this but still says, "Fingers crossed."

I let him have the last word only because I am feeling generous. After all, my future just got set, and his is being stuck here chasing after props backstage and busting the stagehands for smoking pot in the rafters for another year. Meanwhile I'll be rubbing elbows with future Broadway stars and getting the kind of education I'll actually *use* in the real world, full offense to algebra and all the other genres of math.

He disappears into the building, and half a second later, I take off. Sprinting in the late June heat with the cement hot enough to cook an Instagram influencer's entire brunch plate is admittedly not the brightest move, but I can't help myself. I'm in the full grip of the Millie Mood now. I scramble up the four blocks to my apartment and take the stairs up to the fifth floor two at a time, pausing only to bang on Teddy's door across the hall.

"What?"

He goes to a fancy private school, so he's been out for summer vacation for the last week. Odds are he is on his couch eating his infinitieth bowl of Reese's Puffs in iced coffee, the kind of lawless behavior only a kid with two extremely busy award-winning brain surgeons for parents can get away with.

"It's happening!" I call through the crack in the door.

I hear the telltale sounds of Teddy hoisting himself up from his parents' absurdly large couch. "Which it?"

"*It!*" I exclaim, turning to my own apartment door. I wedge my boot in the bottom of it and lift the knob up with my palm to get it open without unlocking it, a habit that drives my aunt and dad nuts. But I don't have time for keys. I leave the door open for Teddy, sweeping through the front hall of the apartment, which my dad has dubbed "The Millie Hall of Fame." The color of its walls is constantly changing depending on whatever mood my aunt is in, but the rest has stayed the same: wall-to-wall photos of me from infancy to present form, from pudgy baby Millie to hammy toddler Millie to stage-hopping teenage Millie, only briefly interrupted by the 0.2 seconds during puberty when I was shy.

Right now the walls are a charming turquoise, which does nothing to make me want to gag any less. It's not that I don't appreciate my dad's enthusiasm for my antics. It's just that I am committed to fully reinventing my image every six months, so I have no greater enemy than my past selves, each of them reminding me of the lesser version I was before.

"Dad Dad Dad Dad," I call.

Any other parent would hear the calamity of me knocking the door open and running through the hall and immediately assume there was a fire, but my dad just glances up from his laptop with his usual mild-mannered smile.

"How was the last day of school?" he asks, adjusting the glasses that seem to be perpetually dipping down the bridge of his nose.

You would think that being the youngest of the dads in my cohort would mean that Cooper Price had one iota of cool, but that, it turns out, is something I must have inherited from my mysterious mom. At thirty-seven years old, my dad is somehow as Dad™ as it gets, complete with a wardrobe of half-zips and khakis, a tech job that he's described to me and Heather a thousand times without either of us understanding what he actually does, and a book about golf that for some reason lives in our bathroom even though I've never once seen him play.

"The *last* last day of school!" I crow. "Look."

My dad squints down at the phone I've just thrust in his face. "What's this?" he asks. "Did you get a part in the school show?"

"No, better." I fully hand the phone to him, hopping on the back of the couch and tapping my foot against it impatiently. "Read it, read it, read it."

It's about then that Teddy wanders in, his hair a big floppy mess, his sweatpants far too large for his skinny, overly tall frame. He has to wear a uniform to school, so during the summer he rebels by becoming a full-time Muppet.

"Which it?" he asks again, and it's clear by the rough edge to his voice that we are probably the first sentient creatures outside of the geocaching app he's hooked on that he's spoken to all day.

I grab him by the shoulders, shaking him back into full consciousness. "Madison. Pre. College."

Teddy's eyes widen. "Oh," he says, his breath decidedly smelling of peanut butter, chocolate, and coffee.

A second later, my dad echoes him: "Oh."

This is marginally better than Oliver's "Huh," but still not cutting it.

"So?" I prompt him, releasing Teddy fast enough that despite being a full eight inches taller than I am, he stumbles into the couch.

"Mills . . ." my dad starts.

The door to my aunt's room creaks open. Heather's messy topknot bun emerges first, followed by the rest of her, blinking at the commotion. "What is occurring out here?" she asks, her hands wrapped around a steaming-hot cup of tea despite it being a bajillion degrees outside. To be fair, she works late, so this is basically breakfast time for her.

"I got into Madison," I squeal.

Her eyebrows fly up into her bangs. "No shit?"

"Not one!"

"You knew about this?" my dad asks, turning to her.

"I didn't know she applied, I just know what it is," says

Heather, padding over to us in the ratty old Ugg slippers we both have to match. "The school in Los Angeles, right?"

"Yup. All musical theater, all the time. Singing core, acting core, *dancing* core . . ."

I begrudgingly put some emphasis on that last one, because despite all my efforts, I don't fully qualify as a triple threat. I may have pipes that can match pace with Megan Hilty's and the kind of acting ability to bring strangers to tears, but my feet could definitely use some work.

"But it's across the country," says my dad. "And it's—basically college. So you'd have to live there."

"Well, yeah. But it's okay, I just need parental permission," I say, grabbing my phone back from him so I can show him the school website.

But then my dad looks at me with an expression I very rarely see but immediately recognize: the one that means I have flown too close to the sun.

"And you're gonna give me parental permission . . . right?"

My dad runs a hand through his hair, glancing back down at his laptop like something's going to pop up on the screen and give him a way out of the conversation. I should probably give him some room to think, but that's not necessarily my forte.

"I didn't just get in. I got a partial scholarship," I add. "So it's not even that expensive."

"It's still a lot of money."

"So I'll pick up more hours at the Milkshake Club," I say, my tone more chipper than a flight attendant's. "Or get a part-time job."

"Los Angeles?"

"So I'd have Grandma and Grandpa out there," I press. Admittedly not my finest argument, seeing as they ditched New

York for a farm in Oregon the year before I was born, but it's still technically on the same coast as LA.

But my dad shakes his head. "It's not just that. . . . We're not gonna . . ."

He looks helpless, like I just shoved him into the Hudson in a boat without a paddle.

"We talked about doing dance classes over the summer," he offers.

It's like trying to trade me a marble for a diamond. I look at Heather, hoping to find an ally, but she's already furrowing her brow in that way she always does before declaring herself Switzerland.

"You have to let me go," I tell him, trying to keep my voice measured. "Like—this is the kind of opportunity that could change my whole life. This is my *destiny*."

I'm fully aware of my own melodrama, but not enough to curb it. This *does* feel like my destiny. What were the last seventeen years of aggressive jazz hands and late nights watching bootleg Lea Salonga videos and openly weeping to the *Dear Evan Hansen* soundtrack for if not *this*?

In the end, my dad talks more to the floor than to me. To be fair, he's not the best when it comes to discipline. But to be *more* fair, I hardly think this situation qualifies.

"I really wish you'd talked to me about this," he says. "When did you even apply?"

Several months ago, with some extreme subterfuge and a sprinkle of lies about study groups that may or may not have existed. The truth is, I knew before I even started looking into it that he probably wouldn't be on board. But I thought maybe if it were already a done deal—if he saw that I'd actually defied the bajillion-to-one odds and gotten in—it'd be enough to sway him.

"I didn't wanna jinx it," I say instead.

It turns out, though, I already did. Because if destiny really is something that's constantly around the corner, apparently I just slammed into mine like a traffic accident.

"I'm sorry, Mills," says my dad. "My answer is no."

# CHAPTER TWO

"Be on my side," I whine, wedging myself into Teddy's couch cushions, which are just deep enough to make you feel like you're being swallowed whole. I hike my knees up and prop Heather's laptop on them, staring at the sea of open tabs with determination.

"I am on your side," says Teddy through a mouthful of popcorn. "I can be on your side and on my phone at the same time."

I jostle Teddy's shoulder with mine, peering at the open chat app on his phone. "How's your girlfriend?"

Teddy rolls his eyes. "She's a fellow GeoTeen, not my *girlfriend*."

I sidestep the fact that the word *GeoTeen* makes them both sound like underage superheroes in a poorly animated eighties cartoon series. "You told her about your deep-seated fear of pigeons," I remind him.

"They're demons with wings."

"*And* your middle name—"

"If only my parents' first date hadn't been to see *Toy Story*—"

"And even told her your cross streets. That's like the New York version of a Social Security number, so. I feel like she is close to girlfriend status, if not officially there."

Teddy pulls the kind of face that is less of an expression and more of a gymnastics routine. "She'd probably want nothing to do with me if we met in person. We just share a love of finding random useless objects across Manhattan and annoying MTA employees by poking all over their stations. It's hardly a love connection."

I know better than to believe this because I know Teddy better than I know my own self—which is saying something, considering how many hours I've clocked practicing for auditions in front of mirrors. We've been best friends since I was six months old and he was two days old, after my dad heard him crying across the hall and just about tripped over himself to make friends with fellow new parents. (Apparently getting an infant unceremoniously dropped at your door when you're a coed—which is, incidentally, what happened to my dad—can be a kind of isolating experience.) By the time Teddy and I could walk we were simply poking our heads into each other's apartments like we lived in both. Neither of us has any genetic siblings, but Teddy and I have been brother and sister since before we knew what those words meant.

"Maybe it would be, if your usernames weren't all anonymous and shrouded in dweeby mystery." I squint at the first open tab. "I could be a Postmates delivery person."

"With what car?" Teddy asks. "And what driver's license, for that matter?"

I close out of the tab. Only twenty-seven more to go. "A preschool is looking for summer help."

"You'd turn all those kids into show tunes—belting monsters. Their parents already have to deal with two *Frozen* soundtracks, don't make them deal with *Wicked*, too." Teddy sets his phone down and takes in the chaos of Heather's screen. "Do you really think getting a summer job to help pay for this is gonna change Coop's mind? It seemed like a pretty hard no."

"A no *for now*. But between my savings from the Milkshake

Club and the scholarship and a part-time job, I can definitely pay the first semester. And saying no would be like, illegal."

"I don't think that's how parenting works." Teddy reaches over my shoulder to click out of the next tab, which reads "Personal assistant to chill male exec!" I turn to glare at him, but it jostles the computer, pulling a tab out from the bottom of the screen.

"How do you have this many unopened emails?" Teddy gasps.

"This isn't my email, it's Heather's," I say, about to minimize it again. But just then a new email pops in, the caps lock in the subject line seizing my retinas: OMG I THINK I FOUND YOUR LITTLE BRO'S OLD LJ IM CRYING.

It's from Heather's ex-girlfriend Jade, who's currently couch-surfing through Europe and apparently still very much up in the Price family's business. I make a mental note to slide in a passive-aggressive comment about this at the dinner table, then click into the email.

The regret is almost immediate.

"His username was *middle-earthling83*?" Teddy exclaims. "Even I'm not that nerdy."

"Your app history begs to differ."

"Click it," says Teddy.

"I'm in pain," I protest.

"Click iiiit."

"I swear, you're always warning me not to be a busybody, but *you're* the nosy one here."

That said, of course I click into the LiveJournal page, because the universe wouldn't dangle something this absurd in front of me if it didn't intend for me to do just that.

And there, lo and behold, is a profile page that is so unmistakably the twenty-year-old version of my math-loving, *Lord of the Rings*–guzzling, computer-hogging dad that it feels like the ghost of Cooper Price Past just walked into the room and caught us in the act. The whole theme is done up in images of the Shire, and the banner on the top reads ALL THESE WORDS MAKE NO SENSE, I FIND BLISS IN IGNORANCE.

"Uh, dark much?"

Teddy types the line into his phone. "It's from a Linkin Park song."

"Cooper was an emo mathlete!" I gasp.

"Cooper contained multitudes," says Teddy, putting half of his tall self into my lap to continue to scroll down the page, like one of those Labrador retrievers that still thinks it's a puppy and never reevaluated personal space after growing into a dog.

It gets worse. Edits from *Lord of the Rings* movies. Some sort of meme-ish-type thing with a cartoon bunny that says "not listening" on it. Sappy playlists titled things like "autumnal jams." It's like it was trying to be a Tumblr page before anyone respected the true meaning of the word *aesthetic*.

"Oh my god, he was super into this Beth lady," says Teddy. "But also someone named Fedotowsky? Wait, are these actual *journal* entries?"

"Don't click," I squeal, slapping a hand down on his.

"Too late."

I skim what appears to be a very long post waxing poetic about a friend of his, and then I genuinely do start to feel something adjacent to guilt. "Okay, okay," I say, clicking back out to the main page.

"The 2003 is hurting my eyes," Teddy moans.

I pause. "Wait, did you say 2003?"

"That's what the time stamps say. Almost all of them are October."

"Uh . . ."

I do some quick math, but Teddy does it quicker, his eyes widening.

"Could one of them be your mom?"

I yank the laptop away from him, scowling at the screen. I'm a July baby. As gross as it is to have to think about how I *became* a July baby, this is the closest thing I've had to insight in all sixteen years of my life.

"Holy shit."

And that's how the complete and utter evisceration of twenty-year-old Cooper Price's privacy begins. I scroll down until we hit what appears to be the first entry from October, then click it open and start reading it out loud.

"'I don't know why I'm even writing this, nobody's ever going to read it,' yada yada yada," I mutter to myself, skipping through a few paragraphs of existential ennui to get to the juicy bit. "'I know it's super cheesy, but I'm going to give her the mixtape and tell her how I feel about her. I just feel like it's the right time. She's one of my closest friends, but it feels like we've been something more than that for a while,'" I read.

"For the record, if you ever fall in love with me, *please* don't express it with a mixtape," says Teddy through a mouthful of popcorn. "I've had enough of your Broadway nonsense inflicted on me."

"Noted," I say, even though my heart's beating so fast that it feels like it's thumping through the couch and down to the floorboards. I click back out, and there's a post a few days later of a "jams for beth" mixtape, with a link to some file-sharing website that is more than defunct by now. It's riddled with love songs—"Yellow" from Coldplay, "I Don't Wanna Miss a Thing" from Aerosmith (but specifically, from the *Armageddon* soundtrack), and, of course, "Many Meetings" from the score of

*The Lord of the Rings*—and at the bottom is a note: "Sooo she liked it."

My jaw drops. "Oh my god." The somewhat life-scarring implication of that "Sooo" aside, I might be, for the first time in my entire *life*, reading words about the woman whose DNA is half of me. "Oh my *god*. This is my mom."

"Not so fast," says Teddy, clicking back out and scrolling up. "October twenty-fifth looks like a sad one."

Sure enough, there's just an empty post that says in tiny lettering under it, "current mood: melancholy." Teddy keeps scrolling past a few mopey band lyrics to another post on October 28 that's titled "!!"

We both speed-read through it, the two of us so in sync that we end up reacting to everything in the same beats:

> Fedotowsky and I got so drunk last night. I don't even know how it happened, but it happened. I was upset about Beth and she was upset about Roger and at some point we just . . . ugh. I mean, she doesn't want to "make a thing" out of it. But it felt like a thing to me. At least enough of one that we should talk about it.

My eyes linger on the screen when I'm finished reading, until I feel Teddy's square on me.

"'Make a thing,'" I repeat. "So . . . I could have been the 'thing.'"

"Yeah. I guess," says Teddy.

He's a little less gung ho now, a new somberness in the room. Like we found a shiny new race car and hit the accelerator before figuring out what road we were going down. I feel kind of queasy as I click out to the main page of the

LiveJournal again. There's only one more journal entry left in that time span, dated November 1, titled "what the hell is wrong with me."

I'm in too deep now to not click. Still, I wait for an extra second, taking a breath before it loads onto the screen.

> So hungover. So confused. Farrah came back from some audition and dragged us out to a Halloween party and I woke up next to her on the floor. Not the bed. The FLOOR. I need to get my shit together. At some point I'm going to run into Beth and her "ex" boyfriend, and I don't want to look like a total idiot when I do. Logging off now. Going to study. No more distractions. No more feeling sorry for myself. And definitely no more Smirnoff Ice.

There are a few beats of silence after that, and then Teddy extricates himself from me, typing something into his phone. I stare at the screen like I've just fallen into it and I don't know how to pull myself back out. I don't even know if I wanted to know this. I certainly wasn't *supposed* to know it. But it's like the option of not knowing was gone before I even realized I had an option at all.

"Hey," says Teddy. "For what it's worth . . . I think I found them."

I blink the screen out of my eyes, turning to him. "What?"

He's got the Facebook app open on his phone. "They're all still mutual friends with your dad. People with those names in his year at NYU, at least."

The blood is roaring in my ears. "How did you . . ."

"It's human geocaching," says Teddy.

"No. No, it's obviously a *Mamma Mia*," I realize, sitting up ramrod straight.

Usually Teddy groans at my musical theater references—particularly the ABBA-related ones, because his mom is so obsessed she owns their entire discography on vinyl—but he chimes in without missing a beat. "It's a *Millie* Mia. Here—"

"No," I say, pushing the phone back toward him so fast that it stuns us both. I stare down at it like it might burst into flames. "I . . . I shouldn't. I mean—it just feels kinda—wrong."

Teddy hesitates for a moment before putting the phone down. "You sure?"

I'm not. It's going to take at least three hours of melodramatic belting in my room and some of Teddy's Reese's Puffs to be sure, if even then.

The thing is that I need someone to talk to about it, but there isn't a someone I can. My dad has always sidestepped the topic like he's allergic to it, and my aunt says my dad never actually told her who my mom was. I took their cues growing up and never discussed it much either. Not even with Teddy. The secrecy aside, it just always kind of left a bad taste in my mouth to think about, let alone say out loud.

"Yeah. I'm sure." I click out of all the tabs in that window, bringing my mountain of jobs back up. And then, without necessarily meaning to, I add, "She didn't want me. It'd just be a waste of both our time."

It's not like I haven't had the thought before. I know the shape of it. I've followed it through. But as Teddy shifts away and closes the app on his phone, the thought does something it's never done before—it reaches out and it tugs, and I'm not sure how to let it go.

# CHAPTER THREE

LiveJournal deep dive aside, I know precisely three things about my mom. The first is that she knew my dad in college. That's something I don't really remember anyone telling me, the same way I don't ever remember being told about my mom situation in the first place—it was just something I grew up already knowing. The second thing is that she didn't tell my dad about me until I was well and fully born, at which point she showed up to the apartment with me in a stroller with only my inherent baby cuteness and a *very* surprised twenty-one-year-old Cooper Price to keep me alive. (At least, that's how my dad tells it.)

The third thing I know is this: she is, in some way, a theater person.

Scratch that. There's a fourth, somewhat related thing. She *royally* screwed me over in seventh grade.

Because here's what happened: my dad, bless his ridiculously well-intentioned parental heart, took a video of me playing Jo in *Little Women* in our middle school's junior version of the musical. It was my first-ever lead, and I was showered with both praise and a milkshake larger than my head, so it was safe to say I was drunk on the attention—enough so that I sat by my bedroom door just in case my dad and my aunt said other nice things about me after I went to bed.

And they did. I was happily soaking it in like the vain little sponge that I was (okay, am) when there was this pause, and my dad said something to Heather along the lines of "I guess it's in her blood." Heather, in that supportive big-sister way of hers, was like, "You can't sing for shit." At which point my dad was like, "No, her mom . . ."

I couldn't see him, but I could still feel the vague gesture he made as he trailed off. By then my ear was so close to the door I was in danger of falling through it.

"Let's just say this theater thing was inevitable," he finally said, with this sigh at the end that made it clear he hadn't meant to say anything at all.

Have you ever been distracted by a shiny thing and not noticed a full-fledged avalanche is coming down to bury you? Because that's what happened to me, metaphorically and emotionally speaking. I was so busy hoarding that shiny nugget of information that I fully zoned out during the *next* part of the conversation, in which my dad said he was going to post the video to YouTube. Had that actually registered in any meaningful way, I would have forbidden him—even at twelve, I had a precise plan for my future social media image, and it did *not* include a video of me in braces and a training bra screltching at the top of my tiny lungs—but baby Millie was so distracted by the mom comment that she let it happen.

In 99.99 percent of cases, that would have been the end of it. It would have gotten twelve views—one from my grandparents and eleven from my dad—and died in internet obscurity like every other precocious theater preteen's YouTube performance. But because I was born under a particularly weird star, instead it got shared to a Reddit page, and then in some private Facebook group for theater students, and then tweeted out by Sutton Foster, a.k.a. Jo March from the original Broadway cast. It went the theater-kid version of viral.

And it has haunted me every day since.

Up until then, I'd had some modest success auditioning in the city. I'd played kid roles like Baby June in *Gypsy* and a Lost Boy in *Peter Pan* in respected off-Broadway theaters and was starting to get callbacks for Broadway productions and generate interest from agents. But "Little Jo" cast the kind of shadow I couldn't shake. For weeks, any time I went on auditions in the city, I was "Little Jo." I was cooed at and complimented and hair-ruffled, but I could sniff out adults patronizing me like an FBI dog. I watched the video and understood: I was plucky, I was adorable, but I also was *bad*. No twelve-year-old should have been attempting to scream out the notes to "Astonishing," and it showed. The song's strong beginning did nothing for the end, which was so excruciating that I'm surprised my dad was able to use a spare hand to record instead of covering his ears.

All this was embarrassing enough on its own. But the most embarrassing thought came a few weeks later—that if my mom really *is* a theater person, there's a chance she might have seen it, too. Which would mean the only real impression she'd ever have of me was one that the internet mercilessly mocked.

Within the year I dyed my hair a darker shade of auburn, and the first of my routine Millie transformations began. The first was admittedly ill-advised—I had a six-month punk phase, abruptly followed by a six-month hippie phase and subsequent athleisure, fifties vintage, and full VSCO girl phases, leading into the nineties grunge one I'm about to finish when I figure out whatever's next. I maintain that I've looked mostly decent in all of them, but that wasn't so much the point as it was to be completely, utterly, and thoroughly unrecognizable as "Little Jo."

I've come a long way since then. Practiced enough that nobody in my school can match me vocally. Spent every single night rehearsing monologues in mirrors and watching YouTube videos of the greats. Stood in every rush ticket line to see not just Broadway stars, but every single one of their understudies, absorbing all their tiniest movements and micro-expressions and vocal tricks to try to search for my own. Never let myself get distracted while my dad was filming anything he might be senseless enough to upload, and did my best to shove the whole mom comment out of my mind right along with the rest of it.

But most importantly, I've avoided auditioning for the main stages in the city ever since. I need enough time to pass to scrub the memory of the old me out of everyone's brains. When I throw myself back into the ring, I'm going to do it so fully reborn that nobody will ever utter the words *Little Jo* within a mile of me again.

I'm almost there. I just need this precollege to whip me into shape, and my absurdly long mission will finally be complete.

Which brings me to the next part of said mission: getting Heather on my side.

"Mint chip or cake batter?" Heather asks, holding up an ice-cream scoop.

"Both."

She raises an eyebrow at me. "Bold combo, but I respect it."

Usually Heather isn't the one scooping the ice cream and shoving it into one of the endless blenders at the Milkshake Club, since she's the owner of the all-ages music venue, conveniently located at the bottom of our apartment building. But tonight is an exception, since it's doubling as a goodbye to my dad before he leaves for his annual two-week-long business trip out to his company's main headquarters in Chicago. It's always a bummer when he goes, but they also let him work from home the other fifty weeks out of the year, so I guess we're not in any real position to complain. Especially since he'll get back the day before my birthday, so we'll still have plenty of time to celebrate (read: subject him and Heather to the movie musical of my choosing).

Heather gets to fixing up my cake batter mint chip monstrosity and a strawberry chocolate shake for herself. She doesn't start the vanilla with toffee bits one for my dad quite yet, so I know I have a little time to get to her.

"So you already knew about the precollege?" I ask.

The smirk is already squarely on her lips before her eyes meet mine, so I know I've been about as subtle as the sound check of the metal band that's supposed to play later tonight.

"I am aware of its existence, yes," she says. "Why ever do you ask?"

I should have waited until I had ice cream in my mouth to try to navigate this. "It's just . . . don't you think it'd be a good opportunity?"

She shrugs. "I mean, yeah. But so is, y'know. Finishing regular-kid high school."

"Heather," I whine.

She tops off our milkshakes with the customary absurd amount of whipped cream, sprinkling hers with Snickers bits and mine with Andes mints. Then she pushes my milkshake over to me and comes around from her side of the bar to sit next to me on one of the bright pink sparkly stools that match the rest of the club, which essentially looks like it was jointly interior decorated by Barbie and the Powerpuff Girls after they got fast and loose with a confetti cannon.

"I mean, what's the pull here?" says Heather. "Are you telling me you'd really rather live on the West Coast?"

I wrinkle my nose. "It's nothing to do with where it is, and everything to do with *what* it is."

"Well, if you really want to get your dad on your side, let's think about it from his perspective. Why he might say no."

I narrow my eyes at her. She has half a psychology degree from before she sharply pivoted to business, but she sure does try to milk it for all it's worth.

"Because he wants to ruin my entire adult *life*?"

Heather makes a noise that is a frankly terrifying impression of a game show buzzer. "Try again."

I sigh into my milkshake. "This program is so selective. I worked really, *really* hard to get in," I tell her. "And they didn't just choose me. They gave me money. They *want* me."

The words rub me in a way I didn't mean for them to, flashing back to what I said to Teddy about my mom earlier. But this has nothing to do with that and everything to do with my future. With the very thing I've had my heart set on since the first time I opened my mouth to sing.

"But you're kind of obligated to stay there for four more years if you go for precollege, right?" says Heather in that measured, rational way of hers that I love as much as I hate. "And you had all these other places you wanted to audition for. NYU. BoCo. Carnegie Mellon—"

"And those are all great options, but this—*this* would get me up to speed even faster. I'd be able to start auditioning again, and college probably wouldn't even be an issue anymore. I'd be eighteen and able to work without legal ramifications and raring to go."

"Like, talent-wise, maybe. But human-wise?"

"*Human*-wise?"

"And besides, who's to say a few dance classes wouldn't get you where you needed to be just as fast?"

I scowl at her. "No, no, no. I'm trying to get you on *my* side," I tell her. "You're not supposed to try and get me on Dad's."

"I'm just being objective!" She takes a thoughtfully large sip of milkshake. "But I know what you mean. If you're looking for me to dissect his reasoning on this, I haven't talked to him yet, so I really don't know."

This is a rare event. I've essentially been co-parented by my dad and my aunt from the start. When my grandparents peaced out and neither of their kids opted to go with them, they left Heather in charge of my dad, which by the transitive property of accidental parenting left Heather semi in charge of me.

"What I *do* know is that maybe we should all take a breather on this. They don't need a yes right away, right?" says Heather. "Maybe we just . . . simmer a bit. Come up with a list of logical reasons to let you go. Crank out a PowerPoint or something."

What she's hedging around with this advice is that she wants to avoid one of everyone's least favorite Millie Moods: the kind where I come slightly unglued. And I include myself in that "everyone." I don't like it either. But trying to control it is like yelling at the ocean to stop making waves in shapes you don't like. Sometimes I feel every bit as powerless to stop myself as everyone around me.

I mope into my milkshake, taking another sip. I don't want to concede to this idea, because I'm not exactly a logic-based individual. I've always been one to follow my heart and let my brain catch up. It's messy, sure, but it's me. It's why I'm good at what I do, and why when I make friends, I make them for life.

Oof. And there comes a pang I can't ignore. I have a lot of friends at school, barring Oliver. Kids I've known for years. It'll be hard to leave them. I'll have to put in an extreme amount of effort to make sure we all stay in touch. But it still isn't enough to stop me, even if there's a part of me that wishes it were.

I'm so preoccupied in both my milkshake and my thoughts that I don't even notice my dad arrive until Heather kicks up the blender to start making his vanilla one. He settles in the stool next to mine, looking as absurdly out of place in this Hello Kitty wonderland as he always does, and bops me on the shoulder.

"I've been thinking—"

"About the program?" I ask.

"About summer dance classes," my dad says patiently. "I know you had a few in mind. Maybe tonight we take a look at them all before I leave?"

I purse my lips. "Orrr maybe we could take a look at the precollege program?"

Heather passes him his milkshake. My dad isn't really a "sweets person," so he claims, but he humors us with our never-ending reasons for ice-cream rituals regardless.

My dad does that close-lipped, Clark Kent-y smile of his. "I've taken a look."

This is probably where I should take a beat to strategize my next move, but instead of doing that, I blurt out, "*And?*"

He fiddles with the straw of his milkshake, glancing over at Heather, like maybe she'll be able to form the words he clearly doesn't want to say. The disappointment is already settling in my bones before he gets that far.

"I just . . . you know I believe in you. You've got a rare gift. But I just don't think this is the right move—at least not right now," he says carefully.

But I'm anything but careful, the words spilling out so fast that I can feel Heather wince. "Do you know how low their acceptance rate is? Do you know how hard it was for me to get in?" I demand.

I mean, I'm sure he does, but he also doesn't. He must have figured out the application fees I fronted and the effort I put into rehearsing, sure. But he doesn't know about the terror I felt through every single one of the *six rounds* of auditions that led to this. The second-guessing every sixteen- and thirty-two-bar cut I chose, every outfit I wore, even the angle and thickness of my eyeliner. He doesn't know the sheer panic of doing a dance call in a room full of legitimate dancers, or the exhausting hour-long personal interview they put me through, not to mention the weeks and weeks and *weeks* I had to wait before finding out

I'd made it through each stage to the final one. This has been a part of me for so long that it feels impossible to extricate it now, like it's leaked into my bones.

"You're only sixteen, Mills. You have a whole wide future ahead of you—"

"Any other parent would be proud of me," I say.

This lands harder than I thought it would, his eyebrows raising so fast that his glasses slide down almost comically fast in unison. I hadn't meant it to be a reminder that he was just one parent, but he clearly took it that way. And for a moment, I'm almost glad he did. It isn't fair that he gets to be the be-all and end-all on this. That I don't have another parent I can appeal to, anyone who might make him understand what this means to me and get him on my side.

I know that's not his fault, it's just him, but if anything, that only makes the frustration worse—knowing that I can't justify it. That it has no real place to go.

"Of course I'm proud of you," he says, so quietly I can barely hear him over the din of servers setting up for the night.

Heather grazes a hand on my shoulder. A warning. But I can barely feel it over the swell of everything else. "Then why are you holding me back?"

"I'm not—if I thought this was holding you back, I would never—"

"My mom would want me to do it. She'd be all for it. Wouldn't she?"

I say it all in a rush, in that same witless, gut-driven way people in crime dramas pull a gun on someone. Heather's hand slides off my shoulder. My dad's entire face goes gray, turning to Heather and then to the floor, like he doesn't know where he's supposed to land.

The guilt feels like it's crawling up my throat and strangling me. I should say something to make this right, but I can't.

"Yeah," he says. "She probably would."

The response is so unexpected that my next question is more out of curiosity than any actual malice. I can't help myself. It's like the shiny thing all over again, and this time my dad's feelings are the avalanche I don't want to see.

"She's a musical theater person, too, isn't she?" I ask.

"She . . ." My dad's mouth twists. "Yeah. But . . ."

He gets up from his stool.

"But *what*?" I persist.

Then whatever it was I felt tugging at me earlier is less of a tug and more of a pull. I've never asked about my mom, maybe, but I always just assumed I'd get some kind of answer if I did. Now that it's clear I might not, there's some irreversible part of me that has to know why.

"Millie," says Heather lowly.

His eyes are misty. My dad's kind of an easy crier—the type who tears up during the big climaxes of Star Trek movies, or when he's telling one of his patented Dad jokes—but I don't remember ever being the one to *make* him cry. It's rattling enough that I don't need Heather's warning. My heart starts beating out warnings of its own.

"But she's not here," he says. "And I am. So. I'm sorry. But that's what I think about it."

The words are so riling that I can't think of any way to respond except to hack through his happiness the way he just hacked through mine.

"Why *isn't* she here?" It's lava pouring out of me. The questions are so immediate that I know I've always had them—that I've been waiting until the moment felt right, for us to feel ready. Now that it seems like we might never be, they're brimming to the surface so fast I feel like I'm choking on them. "Where is she, Dad? Why don't you ever tell me anything about her? Is it to punish her, or to punish me?"

"Hold up," says Heather, easing off the stool onto her feet.

But it's too late. I've said it, and I can't take it back. Not the words, or the way my dad looks like I've just slapped him across the face.

"You want the truth?" he asks. "I don't know where she is. I wish I . . . but I don't."

Whatever thread he was following, he lets go of it just as quickly. He may be telling the truth, but he's not telling the whole truth.

But it's clear from the way his voice breaks on the next words that there's no way to ask him for the whole truth without getting a whole lot else. "I'm sorry about that," he says, not looking at me.

I know he is, but I don't trust myself anymore. I've hurt him and I don't like it, and if I stay I won't be able to *stop*. So I tear out of the Milkshake Club, up the five flights of stairs, up to Teddy's front door, and slam my entire body on it. If I don't have the answers, and my dad can't give them to me, then maybe someone will.

Teddy opens the door so fast that I almost trip into it.

"What are you—"

"I want to find them," I tell him. "Her, I mean. My mom."

"This is escalating very quickly," says Teddy, clearly recognizing the full magnitude of the Millie Mood I am in. "Are you sure?"

This time I am. I walk in, shoving his door closed behind me, and hold out my hand for his phone. "Amanda Seyfried walked so Millie Price could run."

# CHAPTER FOUR

The apartment is so quiet the next morning I feel like I'm haunting it. My dad's already left for his early flight, Heather will be asleep until at least noon, and Teddy will probably spend the morning sleeping off a post–Reese's Puffs hangover. There's nobody to tell me that I'm completely out of my mind when I decide to trespass into a major talent manager's office before breakfast in pursuit of Potential Mom #1.

I haven't decided what my next Millie phase is, so I settle on wearing one of my audition dresses with Heather's boots and stuffing a notebook and a pen into a tote bag my dad got for subscribing to *The New Yorker*. Then I power walk the twenty blocks up to Check Plus Talent, using the adrenaline rush to pump me up for the admittedly harebrained thing I'm about to do.

It's one of those stagnantly hot days, so I'm already sweating bullets when the security guard in the lobby lazily waves me up, saying "tenth floor" before I even open my mouth. It occurs to me that he must think I'm the "talent," and that little buzz carries me up all those floors and straight into the waiting room.

For a moment I forget what I'm actually here for, soaking it all in. The plush royal green seats and the blush-pink walls. The gold accents on the round glass table, stacked with *Playbill*s and copies of *Variety*. The wide windows with an open view of the city below. I've never been in this room before, but I've seen it a hundred times. It's all over the Instagram stories of Rob Yaghutiel, Broadway's current Phantom in *The Phantom of the Opera*, and Elizabeth Benson, who just took over for the lead in *Frozen*. You have to be somebody to get in this room.

And right now I'm in it.

"Hi there, how can I help you?"

I suck in a breath of surprise, and there she is, sitting at the front desk in a bright pink dress and a perfectly poised smile: Stephanie Fedotowsky. I recognize her from the Facebook photos Teddy pulled up for me last night, a mix of candids on rooftops sipping wine with her friends and old headshots, all broad laughs and big curls like a model from a vintage ice-cream ad. In person she's even more arresting, her eyes so wide and blue that they stop me on a dime.

"I . . ."

*Wonder if we have the same color eyes. Wonder if I am going to be that beautiful when I grow up. Wonder if I am quite possibly the kid you ditched at my dad's front door almost seventeen years ago.*

I clear my throat. Stephanie's smile doesn't falter in the least bit. There's this innate warmth in it that I'm sure would make me feel at ease in any situation other than this.

But I came prepared. Well, *ish*. She's the executive assistant here on and off when she isn't acting in theater roles all over the city, so I spent nineteen of the twenty blocks it took to get here deciding that my "in" would be pretending I wanted to interview her for a school thing. I had it all mentally rehearsed, but for the first time in recent memory, I've forgotten my lines. In the space where the words should be there's just this inconveniently enormous cavern filling up with unhelpful things like, *Does she recognize me? Does she think I'm cool?*

"What are you *doing* here?"

I stumble back, looking decidedly *un*cool, my eyes flying to the left of me to meet none other than Oliver's.

I blink at him, sitting in one of those fancy green chairs, dressed in a perfectly pressed button-down tucked with a belt into a pair of dark-wash jeans with his hair swooped in a way I've never seen it. I might concede that it's a good look for him, if I weren't so suddenly preoccupied with wanting to murder him for intruding on what just might be the most important moment of my life.

"What are *you* doing here?" I shoot right back.

He's clutching a folder like it's his lifeline. "Don't tell me you're—"

"You must be interviewing for the paid summer internship, too," says Stephanie.

I turn back to her, my cheeks on fire. This is the part where I'm supposed to ask to interview her, so I can go home and figure out a string of totally impersonal but just personal enough questions to gauge whether or not she is, in fact, my mom. I'm counting on the fact that she won't be able to see through this extremely precarious lie of mine so I can see it through to the end.

But Oliver can smell my bullshit from a mile away. And the *last* thing I need right now is an audience of one who actively hates me and is a human lie detector to boot.

"I'm Georgie's assistant, Steph," she says. "Do you have a résumé I can file for her?"

My brain continues to short-circuit. I am simultaneously aware of Steph's kind eyes and Oliver's blazing ones, both waiting for me to formulate some kind of response.

"I . . ."

The phone at Steph's desk starts to ring, saving me from verbally face-planting. "Just a sec, honey," she says, shaking back her curls so she can pick up the phone and press it to her ear. "Check Plus Talent, this is Steph speaking, how can I help you?"

I'm about to let out a breath and try to regroup, but Oliver interrupts.

"You don't want this internship."

He says it through his teeth, his expression stiller than a ventriloquist's. I take a step over to where he's sitting, putting both hands on my hips.

"Excuse you?"

His eyes flit over to Steph. I can see him calculating the pros and cons of engaging me on this—the biggest con being that unlike him, I have a long history of not being afraid to make a scene.

"It's all management-focused. You're, like . . . completely on the other side of this. You need manag*ing*."

I slide into the seat next to him and hear him take the kind of breath that is clearly intended to become a sigh, one I've heard a hundred thousand times before. Like when I have notes about his lighting transitions (in my defense, they were blinding the ensemble on stage) or the timing of the fight calls where we rehearse tricky choreography before each show (he always wants to do them as soon as possible, but you have to do it *after* warm-ups, or everyone's going to be all tense and blow it, obviously), or whether we should spring for the expensive face paint for the actors (he has *zero* appreciation for proper skincare). Oliver has moaned so much about the "time he'll never get back" that it's probably only a matter of time before I turn his hair gray.

But for once, I really have no incentive for annoying the daylights out of him. It's actually oddly calming, having him here. We may be so at odds that fellow theater kids flee for the hills when they spot us in the same room, but at least we know where we stand with each other.

Where I stand with my dad's beloved "Fedotowsky" is about as clear as the plot of *Cats*.

"Maybe I want to learn about the business I'm about to commit my entire life to," I say idly.

"So read a Wikipedia page."

I scoot closer to him, keeping one eye on Steph, who is thoroughly distracted by whoever is on the phone. "Sounds like someone's scared I'm going to beat them out," I say lowly, close to his ear.

Oliver bristles but doesn't pull away. His eyes meet mine like we're playing a game of chicken that he's determined not to lose. "No. I'm obviously more qualified for this than you are." His fists curl and uncurl over the knees of his pant legs. "But I know you."

"Do you, now?"

He turns the rest of his body to look directly at me, glowering. "You're going to pull that stupid Millie charm."

The edges of my lips tug upward. "Are you calling me charming?"

His scowl deepens. "It's not going to work. Georgie Check is a total hardass, and she'll see right through you."

There are approximately two things in this world I can't stand: Oliver Yang, and the concept of failure. This rubs both of them so aggressively that for a moment I forget the entire purpose of this little drop-in.

"To what?" I ask.

Oliver is a little *too* ready to answer that. "To the flighty, overly dramatic, unnecessarily loud—"

"I'm ready for the first applicant."

Oliver's face goes slack. My back is turned to whoever just walked out of the back office, but his big Millie scowl was, for a moment, aimed directly at her instead.

"After you," I say graciously, feeling the smirk curl on my face.

Oliver is on his feet so fast that he looks like a toy soldier in our ill-fated ninth-grade production of *The Nutcracker*. (Apparently trying to add modern dance and Billie Eilish songs to a historical classic is a no-go among the boomer grandparent crowd.)

"Yes, uh—I'm Oliver Yang. Hi. Thank you for . . ."

I turn to catch a glimpse at whoever just inspired the light to die in Oliver's eyes, but her back is already turned to head into her office, and Oliver is bolting to keep up. I watch until the door shuts behind him and leaves a merciless silence in its wake.

It's just me and Steph. Just me and a woman who might know more about me than I've ever fathomed knowing. I watch as she deftly types something into her MacBook Air, then shakes the curls off her shoulders again in a gesture that seems so familiar to me that I can't *not* account for it, like I'm peering at some potential grown-up version of myself through a microscope.

"Don't let Georgie scare you," says Steph, pointing a thumb at the closed door.

"Oh, I'm not . . ."

*Here for the interview,* I'm going to tell her. As fun as it was to endure a bonus round of Millie versus Oliver before pirouetting out of his life forever, I have no desire to run around a talent management firm and watch *other* people's dreams come true while I'm still trying to manifest my own.

But she's watching me so intently that I realize right then that if she really is my mom, I need time to think. To dig. To understand why she did what she did. I'm not going to be able to interview her and leave it at that.

Plus . . . she said *paid*. Which means if I play my cards right, this might be a two-for-one deal: I get to dig into the inner workings of Steph Fedotowsky on my own time *and* potentially make enough money to pay for the first semester at Madison to boot.

The decision is made before my brain can even fully process that there's a decision at all.

"... scared of much," I finish.

Steph smiles conspiratorially at me. "Good answer, hon," she says with a wink. Then she leans back in her chair. "To be honest, when you walked in I assumed you were a client."

My ego was already swollen enough from the security guard, but now it might burst. "Yeah?"

"Sure," she says. "I've been around long enough to sniff out a fellow actress."

I scooch to the edge of the cushy chair. "You're an actress?" I ask, as if I don't already know. As if Teddy didn't help me pull up YouTube videos of her professional reel, where she played everything from a chokingly hilarious Kate Monster in an off-Broadway production of *Avenue Q* to a heart-wrenching Ilse in a community theater production of *Spring Awakening*.

But even if I'd only seen one of them, I'd know she's talented. Like, mega-talented. Talented enough that I'm still confused about why she's working in a talent agency when she should be on stage making angels weep.

"When I can be," she says, with this dainty little shrug.

"Did you go to school for theater?"

She bites at her lower lip, an old habit of mine that used to have my dad buying a new Lip Smackers lip balm every month of the year. "I did," she says, seeming amused at my interest. I guess most of the people who come through here aren't exactly chatting her up about it. I continue to stare, prompting her to say, "I went to NYU."

"Tisch?" I ask, referring to one of the performing arts schools there.

"You're thinking of applying?"

I mean, yes, duh, since I was old enough to use Google and immediately searched for the top musical theater schools in the country (even at six I had a plan). But I suppose that's off the table now—even Tisch can't beat out Madison. The precollege may be a much newer program, but it's turned out so many new Broadway elites in the past few years that there's no way to justify *not* going.

"Yeah," I lie anyway, because I'm already ten steps ahead of this conversation, wondering which buttons I can press to get her to talk about my dad. "What was it like?"

"Oh, man. Hell," she says, with this kind of affection that I understand all too well. You have to be a certain degree of masochistic to survive in theater. "But also just so great. The training there—it'll turn you into a whole different person."

I'm already a pro at reinvention, but I keep that to myself.

"And also just—the friends you make there? You make them for life. We're all still in a group text. It's wild where everybody ended up."

There's this wistfulness in her voice then, and it rubs me in this way I don't love. Like I'm feeling sorry for her. That's not how I want to feel about her, how I want to feel about this person who might be half of me.

"Where do you want to end up?" I press. I need to know that there's something in her that still cares about this, because there's something in her that *did*.

Only then does Steph look over at me, mildly indignant. "I'm thirty-seven," she says. "This is where I've ended up."

My cheeks burn. "I didn't mean . . ."

She recovers faster than I do. "I just mean—performing makes me happy. I'm lucky to do it when I can. But statistically speaking, not everyone's going to make it."

I'm not sure whose disappointment I'm feeling in that

moment, mine or hers. "Well." Shit. I try to figure out how to pivot this conversation back to NYU, back to my dad, without further making an ass of myself.

For once, Oliver does something useful. That's the exact moment the office door all but spits him out. He stands there for a moment, looking like he's just walked out of a trench.

"Uh—she's ready for you," he finally tells me.

"Right now?"

Steph nods her head, clucking at Oliver sympathetically. "Georgie moves fast. I'd hurry it up."

"Got it," I say, walking toward the door before the last nerve ending of my brain committed to common sense can wake up and stop me.

The office I walk into is somehow more staggeringly beautiful than the room I just left, with chairs in deep purples and dark maroons, windows almost as high as the walls, and an old mahogany desk big enough for my entire friend group at school to eat lunch at. Behind the desk is a woman typing something furiously into a laptop, dressed in a sharp navy blazer and enormous jewelry, her strawberry blond hair in unrepentant, wild curls.

She glances up at me, except it feels less like a glance and more like that time as a kid when I walked straight into a glass door. I can count on one hand the number of people who stop me in my tracks—like, Barbra Streisand, *maybe*—but for some reason I know to be on top of my game with this woman before she opens her mouth.

"Oh," says Georgie. She doesn't even give me an up-and-down. Just shakes her head once. "No."

I'm used to brutal rejections. It comes with the territory. I once got typed out of a call for young Cosettes and young Éponines and sent packing before I even opened my mouth to sing.

But I'm pretty sure it's illegal to type someone out of an actual job interview.

I sit down in the chair in front of her desk. "No," I repeat, forcing her to elaborate.

Georgie gets up as if I haven't spoken, attending to the coffee that is steaming out of the bottom of a sleek single-serve Keurig on her desk: a splash of half-and-half, exactly one sugar packet. She takes her sweet time. I can hear the fancy white marble clock on her desk ticking, the sounds of cars honking and braking below, the entirety of New York swelling up beneath us. When she does sit down with it she glances over at the chair where I'm sitting with some mix of ambivalence and mild surprise that I'm still there.

"You want to intern for me."

Insofar as it will grant me automatic proximity to a woman who may or may not have given birth to me.

"Yes," I answer, a defensive edge in my voice.

She doesn't miss it, her eyes raking me with new intention.

"I don't hire actor types." She gestures at me, and before I can protest, she says, "Look at you. Your eyes are basically screaming 'squeeze me in between the Equity auditions.'"

It's not my fault getting a union card is so impossible that newbies have to scramble to get seen. I shift my butt in my seat, trying to sit up straighter and seem less like a teenage girl who had a month-long pie-baking phase after seeing *Waitress* and more like a force to be reckoned with.

"Yeah, well. You hired Steph, and *she's* an actor type," I blurt.

She raises one perfectly groomed eyebrow, and something surges in me—like I'm not just defending myself, but Steph, too.

"So you did some research."

"That I did." Kind of.

"That still doesn't mean you'll be of any use to me," says Georgie with a dismissive wave of her hand.

"How do you—"

"You show up without a résumé, without any kind of elevator pitch, without seemingly any experience in this field—"

"I've got an elevator pitch," I tell her, which is a total lie until, miraculously, one starts falling out of my mouth. "You want an intern to help you with your clients. With your prone-to-melodrama, unpredictable, needy *actor* clients. Who better to help you anticipate their ridiculous needs than one of their own?"

She sets down her coffee cup. Her expression doesn't change, but just enough of her posture does that I know I've got an in.

"You have thirty more seconds to make your case."

I lean in to her desk, propping my elbows on it, fixing my eyes on her as unflinchingly as hers are on me. "I never do anything halfway. I *am* an actor type, and I'm a *great* actor type. Not because I was born talented. But because I fought for it. Because I fought tooth and *nail* for it, and practiced harder than everybody else, until I was the best. I throw myself into everything I do with a vengeance, and this would be no exception." I can feel it then—the fire that's always been in me. The one that has chased me into every audition room, soaked up the light on every stage, quivered in my bones. "You hire me, and you'll get my best. My absolute best. And my best is something to be reckoned with."

Georgie's eyes narrow just enough that I can tell I've gotten through to her. "Why do you want this?"

She means for the question to be damning, but I'm ready for it. "The same reason you do," I tell her. And in that moment, it doesn't matter that I have no idea who she is, or what this internship actually entails, or what the hell I'm even doing here. What matters is the truth—and that, at least, is so solid in me that it feels like I've been waiting my whole life to speak it. "I want to be the one in control. The one calling the shots. And the only way for me to do that is to learn every angle of this business inside and out."

Georgie doesn't say a word. She juts her chin out and stares at me. I stare back. Enough seconds pass that I'm certain anyone else in their right mind would have looked away, but it feels like a challenge—and I have no intention of losing.

"All right," she finally says. "You're dismissed."

I stand up sharply, without saying a word. Some gut instinct tells me not to protest, to go quietly and powerfully, leaving everything that poured out of me in my wake.

Oliver is still talking to Steph when I walk out, my face flushed, my body electric. He glances over at me and I can feel his smugness—his interview was short, but mine was shorter. He must think he's won it.

But then Georgie follows me out, and the blood just about drains from his face.

"Here's what I've decided. You'll both intern for me for two weeks. Then whichever one of you earns it will get to stay for the rest of the summer."

Oliver's jaw drops, and it's more satisfying than the time Mrs. Cooke told him that he would be in charge of the quick-changes for the kids double-cast as Bird Girls and members of Whoville in *Seussical*. He was pulling glitter out of his crevices for months.

"Do you agree to these terms?"

I answer first. "Of course."

It takes Oliver a moment to recover. "Um—yeah. Okay."

"Good. I'll see you both at nine A.M. tomorrow."

We both stand there, mouths ajar. The door to Georgie's office closes behind her. There are a few beats of silence, and then Steph says, "Do either of you need a drink of water?"

"No," says Oliver faintly, "but thanks."

She hands us some paperwork to fill out then, with pre-addressed envelopes to send to their outsourced HR. Oliver turns to leave. I hesitate, lingering by Steph's desk. There's still so much I want to ask her. But at least now I've got time.

"See you tomorrow," I tell her.

She smiles at me widely, shooting me another wink. Like she's proud of me for pulling this off. My chest feels warm in this way that it probably shouldn't, because even if she is my mom it's not like she stuck around long enough that any of her feelings about me should count.

Then I hear the *ping* of the elevator arriving and wrestle myself out of that particular tailspin and back into the hall.

Oliver does a very poor job of suppressing his shudder when I pop up next to him just before the doors close. We sail back down to the lobby in total silence, his entire body so tense that I'm half expecting him to burst into flames. He walks out of the lobby and into the street fast enough that it's clear he's trying to shake me off, so for once, I let him—except then we hit the sidewalk and he changes his mind, whirling around to face me.

"What do you want?" he asks, gesturing up to the tenth floor. "Why are you doing this?"

I keep walking, so this time he's the one who has to keep up. "I could ask you the same thing."

"Seriously. This is too much. I get enough of you during the school year, and now I'm getting handcuffed to you for half the summer?"

"Why do you hate me so much?"

"I don't *hate* you, Millie," Oliver exclaims, throwing his hands up in a very un-Oliver-like gesture. It appears that after all these years, I've finally found his last nerve. If it weren't so insulting, it'd be kind of fun to watch. "I'm just *exhausted* by you."

I don't have a retort to that, but for some reason I stop walking. For some reason those words hold me there like a stun gun, and I can't wake up my muscles fast enough to wriggle out of them.

He lets out a breath, and weirdly, there isn't any meanness to what he says next. He just says it like it's a fact that he's come to terms with. "You're just—you just need people to like you. Like, all the time." Before it can fully land, he adds, "And you're good at it. You're good at making people like you."

Usually being annoyed with Oliver is more recreational than not. But this just pushed it somewhere ugly.

"Obviously not," I mutter.

"And that's fine, for what you do. For what you want to do. But I want to do *this*," he says, evidently not even realizing how hard his words hit. "And now you're using your Millie witchcraft to butt in on it. Is there really no other place for you to intern this summer?"

I dig the heels of my boots into the steaming-hot sidewalk. "Did you ever consider the world doesn't revolve around *you*, Oliver?"

He actually laughs out loud at this. "Sorry, sorry," he says. "It's just—hearing that—from *you*—"

"Laugh all you want." I'm back now, and in full motion, all of me swinging—my hair, the bag, the sleeves of my dress, the too-long laces of these boots. This outfit may not fit into any of my Millie phases, but it feels like there's an extra *oomph* to me, like I get to blow past him twice. "We'll see who's laughing two weeks from now."

Oliver catches up to me in an instant, likely because people on the sidewalk are giving us a wide berth. "So you're really doing this."

My nostrils flare. "I'm really doing it."

"Fine," he says. "It doesn't matter anyway. You're not going to last a week."

I turn to him, and I can tell from the way his eyes widen that he wasn't expecting me to look as steely-faced as I am. "Wanna bet on it?"

"Betting implies that I care, and I don't."

"Good. That makes two of us."

He stops again, and then so do I.

"Aw, loosen up, would you?" I say. "Maybe this could be fun."

I reach up and mess up his hair, unleashing it from its swoop. I meant for it to be annoying, but there's this moment where my hand's on his head and his eyes are on my eyes and we both go so still that other people have to weave past us like we're a mismatched two-person island.

Then he reaches up and takes my wrist, pulling my hand down with this measured kind of gentleness, like he knows exactly how his hand will fit there and exactly how little pressure he needs to move me.

"Good luck, Millie." His eyes are gleaming. He knows you're not supposed to say "good luck" in the theater world. It's a jinx. "You're gonna need it."

# CHAPTER FIVE

"So here's the plan," I say, laying upside down on the ratty old armchair that, legend has it, has been in my family since my great-grandparents bought the place. It certainly smells like it, at least.

Teddy throws a Twizzler at me from the couch, where he is currently splayed like an oversize, sweats-clad starfish. Heather has already headed down to the Milkshake Club to work out scheduling with Carly, the booker for the venue, so we've got the place to ourselves.

"What *plan*?" says Teddy, his words gummy from chewing. "You walked in there to meet a potential mom and walked out with an internship. That feels like the opposite of a plan."

I take the Twizzler, which landed conveniently in the crook of my elbow, and yank off a bite with my back teeth. "The plan is to get to know her while I'm at the internship."

"So you think she's the one?"

I stop chewing for a moment so I can chew on that instead. I don't want to think about it too hard, because it gets close to thinking a thought I've been trying to avoid. I should probably just *know*, right? Like, my eyes should clap on my mom's and hers on mine and there should be some weird biological key that fits into a lock.

That didn't happen with Steph. But it didn't *not* happen, either. Which means I'm probably going to need to restrategize.

"Inconclusive," I say, before the Twizzler turns into drool in my mouth. "I think I've got to figure out a way to spend actual time with each of these random ladies."

"Well, I've been hard at work with my human geocaching, and apparently Beth lives like three blocks from here."

I un-pretzel myself from the chair, sitting upright. "Wait, legitimately?"

"Yup," says Teddy, scrolling down on his phone. "Down by the tea place you kept dragging us to when you went through your British phase."

"Their scones were amazing. Also, shit."

"Yeah. Your mom could have been, like. Living a rock's throw away the whole time."

I try to wrap my head around that. At first it won't compute, and then it computes a little too well: the idea that I might have been in the same aisle of Trader Joe's, or listening to the same musician in Washington Square Park, or simply walking past my actual mom any day of the week without even realizing it.

"So . . . stakeout?" I ask.

"Or we could go the significantly less creepy route of going to the musical theater enthusiast meetup she hosts at her apartment building's rec room every two weeks."

*Now* Teddy has my attention. I yank Heather's laptop from his lap, and sure enough, there's a public event for the "Broadway Bugs," which happens to be tonight. I skim the text, catching on the most recent update, which Beth posted an hour ago: A reminder that today's meetup is Newsies-themed! Light bites and non-stop streaming of baby Christian Bale provided, costumes encouraged. Can't wait to Seize the Day with y'all!

"Oh my god."

"I already RSVP'd for us."

"*Us?*"

"It's weird," says Teddy. "Her Facebook is like, *locked down* like nobody's business, but she's inviting a ton of nerdy strangers to her building."

"Musical theater isn't nerdy."

"Oh, it is. I'm allowed to say that because I self-identify as a nerd. You guys are nerdier than actual nerds, you just fly under the radar because you're all hot."

I flip my hair back. "Shucks."

Teddy rolls his eyes. "Anyway, yes, *us*. I'm coming with you."

I know his interest in musical theater is zero percent, if not in the negative percent, so he's only doing it because he thinks I need moral support. And he's not wrong. I might be more extroverted than the sun, but after this morning, I know better than to walk into another Potential Mom situation on my own.

"You might have to put on actual pants," I warn him.

"I will. But only because I love you. And also because there's free food."

Which is how we find ourselves, approximately three hours later, standing outside Beth's building, with me in a newsboy cap I stole from Teddy's dad and Teddy clad in a pair of suspenders that I accidentally-on-purpose stole from the school after playing the role of "Male Stripper" in *Cabaret*. (Yet another casting decision I blame on Oliver, and in my defense, I more than earned them.)

"Ready?" I ask.

Teddy starts humming "Mamma Mia" under his breath in response. I nudge my shoulder into his to clam him up, but he just gets louder.

"Look at me nowwww, will I ever learn—"

"Apparently *not*."

"I'm sorry," he protests. "I don't know how, but I suddenly lose control!"

I yank the back of his suspenders and he cackles, stumbling backward like a very tall noodle, and that's when the door to the lobby opens and a woman who can only be Beth holds it for us.

Weirdly, it's more like I recognize her from a feeling than any of the badly cropped photos Teddy was able to find on Facebook. There's this innate kindness to her that's giving off a real "hobbits being neighborly in the Shire" vibe, a reference I can make only as a hazard of being Cooper Price's daughter. Her eyes are warm and already a little crinkled from laughter, her honey-brown hair so thick that it's bursting out from under her newsboy cap, her cheeks full and dimpled. She seems like the kind of person who likes tea more than coffee and has multiple go-to blogs for DIY projects and gives really good hugs.

"Do I spy some fellow Newsies out on these here streets?" she asks in an exaggerated New York accent, putting a hand on her hip.

Teddy, having refused to watch both the theatrical and movie versions of *Newsies* despite the fact that they are both masterpieces and readily available on my Disney+ account, becomes instantly useless.

"Uh . . . yeah. Yup. We, uh—" I reach for a reference. "We smelled a headline."

I can hear Teddy holding his breath in an effort not to mock me, but the smile on Beth's face is big enough to knock a moon out of orbit.

"Welcome, welcome," she says, ushering us in. "You're the first to arrive. New Bugs?"

"Yeah," says Teddy, following me in.

"You picked a good day to join, my friends. *Newsies* is in my top five favorite musicals. We're pulling out all the stops."

Beth leads us on a short walk from the lobby to the building's rec room, which is basically a testament to 1899 prepubescent newsboys who can also casually do backflips and tap dance for reasons never explained in the plot. There's a video screen playing the movie version on silent while the original Broadway cast album plays "Watch What Happens" from an iPhone speaker in the corner, and on the table there's an array of themed snacks—a chip-and-dip station labeled "Seize the Lays," a chicken app dubbed "Wings of New York," a cake that just has the word *STRIKE!* written on it in giant red lettering.

"Oh my god," Teddy mutters. "It's like walking inside your brain."

He's not wrong. But I'm too distracted to fully appreciate it, following Beth close behind so I can compare little bits and pieces of myself to her. We're both short. We're both obsessed with musical theater. And I've already decided I like her, which has nothing to do with how alike we are but everything to do with me hoping to find out more.

"I'm Beth, by the way," she tells us. "The host of these little shindigs. And y'all are . . . ?"

"Millie and Teddy," I answer for him, because somehow there is already half a slider in his mouth. "I'm a Broadway fan, and he's . . . really into free food."

Teddy gives her a thumbs-up, amping up the incorrigible tall-boy charm that he figured out how to use on adults as far back as trick-or-treating, when he'd scam extra candy out of half the block.

"Well, you're both in the right place, then," Beth chuckles. I can tell she's going to ask us some more hospitable questions like what brought us here or what school we go to, but I cut her off before she can.

"So how long have you been doing these?"

"Broadway Bugs meetups? Hmm, probably a few years now," she muses, unwrapping a set of napkins to lay out. I see some plates and utensils next to them and start unwrapping them with her, which earns me another wide smile.

I try my best not to make it sound like an interrogation, but I figure we've got five minutes before the people *not* dropping in to sniff out their biological moms start to flood the place. "Are you like—in the industry, or . . ."

"Oh, heck no," says Beth, with a self-deprecating laugh. "I'm a social worker. I just love Broadway, is all."

"And you never wanted to perform?"

"In community theater, sure," she says. "There were some groups in college I did for a while. Lots of them come to these little meetups now." She leans in like she's letting me in on a secret. "Meetups are more fun for me than rehearsals, anyway. More time to chitchat, find some buddies to see shows with. It's a good excuse to bring people together. Speaking of, what brought you here?"

"Um . . ."

"Oh, look who it is! Right on time," says Beth, her eyes flitting back toward the door.

There is an overall-clad, braces-faced teenage girl standing there, her long dark hair still swaying like she was just in motion before skidding to an abrupt halt. For a moment I'm relieved to see someone in our generation here—she looks close in age to me and Teddy—but before I have any notions of her making this less awkward, she stares at us and then back at Beth with what I can only describe as panic, self-consciously shifting the newsboy cap settled on top of her head.

"Chloe, this is Millie and Teddy. Y'all, this is my daughter, Chloe."

Teddy's eyes are already on me before I find them. *Daughter?*

"Hi," Chloe squeaks, her eyes so wide on us that she looks like one of those squirrels in Central Park that scamper out into the bike path and don't know whether to flee or stand their ground.

Beth straightens the newsboy cap on Chloe's head with the

grace of someone who is used to smoothing over awkward situations. Someone who laughs easily and fills up silences and knows how best to fit herself to make a cluster of people into a group.

And then, weirdly, I'm not thinking of either of them. I'm thinking about my dad. How there must have been a once upon a time when he was one of the people Beth put at ease. He doesn't have a ton of friends—he's the textbook definition of an introvert—but it isn't hard to imagine her drawing him out the same way. It isn't hard to imagine him falling for her.

It *is* a little hard to imagine him thinking it was socially acceptable to put a song from *Armageddon* on a mixtape for her, but there's only so much of these parental blasts from the past I can be expected to swallow.

Beth nudges Chloe over to the snack table, where Teddy and I are standing. "So you and your dad had a good time with your—"

"Yes," Chloe blurts, anxious to interrupt her. "We had a good time, um—"

"You should have seen her," says her dad. "The fastest kid on the—"

Chloe turns around and blurts something in rapid Spanish to cut off the man who walked in behind her, just in time for him to share a knowing look with Beth. Through the haze of the word *daughter* swirling all over my head like a storm, I manage to connect the dots that he and Beth must be married.

Or *were* married. Because once Beth makes her way over, the vibe seems much more friendly than romantic.

"You're welcome to stay, Javi," says Beth, gesturing at the room, which truly does look like a *Playbill* threw up on it.

He gives her an apologetic smile. "I've gotta jet and feed Seymour. But I'll see you at the picnic tomorrow?" he says, leaning in.

She stands on her tiptoes to kiss him on the cheek, the gesture automatic but not without affection. "I'm bringing mac and cheese."

"Good. I've gotten no less than five texts from my sisters asking about it." He leans down to kiss Chloe on the top of her head. "See you tomorrow, kiddo. Don't forget to bring the Frisbee."

"Bye, Dad," she murmurs, her cheeks visibly red.

Javi playfully salutes us all on his way out. Chloe can't stop staring at me, which is deeply inconvenient, because I'm trying to stare at *her*.

"Oh, shoot," says Beth, interrupting our stare-off. "I just realized I left the lasagna and the pizza rolls warming in the oven. Chloe, could you . . ."

"We'll help grab them," I volunteer.

Beth turns to me. "That'd be lovely."

She gives me a look then that seems to be half apology for Chloe's shyness and half a clear signal to go ahead and try to push past it. I know I've done nothing to earn this quiet responsibility, but it still feels kind of nice.

"Millie's a big musical theater fan," Beth calls to Chloe on our way over to the elevators. "You should show her your room!"

Chloe looks like she'd rather die. But Chloe's dignity is a small price I'm going to have to pay to check off the next part of my agenda: figuring out if this girl just pulled Beth out of the Millie Mia by existing or might have thrown an even *bigger* wrench in it by . . . being my half sister.

The thought is momentarily paralyzing. Teddy has to shove his shoulder into mine to get me in the elevator. What follows then is thirty seconds of bone-crushing silence that almost make me *miss* the elevator ride with Oliver yesterday, in which Chloe is staring at me so openly that I'm starting to feel like a science experiment.

The elevator pings to let us know we've reached the four-teenth floor, and just as the doors open Chloe bursts, "You're Little Jo!"

I freeze. So does Teddy. The words *Little Jo* have been banned from our apartment building for nearly five years now. If I were one of those sleeper assassins, they'd be the trigger words for me to black out and go full Black Widow.

"From that viral video," says Chloe. "It was you, wasn't it?"

At first I think she's making fun of me, but then I get a good look at her beaming face under the newsboy cap, and it's worse—she's praising me.

"Oh my god. I'm, like—*obsessed* with that video," Chloe gushes, leading us down the hall to her apartment. "You were so freaking good. What happened after that? Why didn't you upload anything else? I love that musical so much, I've always wanted to see it but there haven't been any off-Broadway pro-ductions close enough, I can't *believe* Sutton *Foster* has seen you *sing*."

And I can't believe this scrawny punk *recognized* me. What have all my carefully curated, painfully executed Millie phases been for if not to stop this exact scenario from happening? I've spent so long outrunning that stupid video that it didn't even oc-cur to me that someone might have the wherewithal to keep up.

But even though Teddy is all too aware of the horror playing out on my face, Chloe barrels on like a leaky faucet. "I've tried to sing that song a bajillion times, but I can never hit that one note at the end, you know? It's like, *wow*, so freaking high for a belt, I can't even sing it in my mix sometimes, and believe me, I've tried."

She unlocks the door to apartment 14G, which seems innoc-uous enough when we first walk into it. There's a homey little kitchen with mismatching pastel appliances that peeks out to a living room with cozy furniture all draped in giant blankets and soft, worn-out pillows. There's a song playing from a speaker somewhere that I vaguely recognize and can tell from the way Teddy's eyebrows lift that he knows it, too.

"My mom and dad keep saying I can do voice lessons if I want, but like, even then—*how*?" Chloe talks over it. "You have to be born with it to be able to do that kinda singing, you know? Your lungs must be enormous. Can you hold your breath for a super long time?"

I get the impression from the rate of the words spilling out of Chloe's mouth that she sure can.

"What other roles have you played? Do you have any more videos on your phone? Are you auditioning in the—"

"Is this your room?"

Thank god Teddy's sense for personal boundaries is as loose as his standards for the free food he inhales, because he stops Chloe from putting me on an extremely undeserved pedestal by snooping down the hall. She sucks in an embarrassed breath, but it's too late. We've both followed Teddy into the veritable Broadway abyss.

Heather may tease me for going in too deep re: my musical theater room decor, but if my room is a tribute, Chloe's is a full-on shrine. There's a whole wall of signed *Playbill*s all in a row above Chloe's bed. Her bedsheets and pillowcases are covered in musical notes, and the covers are a collage of Broadway musicals. The closet door is littered with stickers referencing shows—THINK ABOUT THE SUN and I GOT TEARS COMING OUT OF MY NOSE! and FIVE HUNDRED TWENTY-FIVE THOUSAND SIX HUNDRED MINUTES. Lin-Manuel Miranda's *Gmorning, Gnight!* pep talk book is lying open on the bedside table, and—

"Oh *shit*," Teddy exclaims, stumbling back.

My heart leaps into my throat, too, but it's not an actual person who has snuck up on us. It is, in fact, a life-size cutout of all three Schuyler sisters from *Hamilton,* mid-snap.

"I got it for my birthday," Chloe tells us gleefully.

I clear my throat, prying my hand off my chest. A near heart attack isn't enough to derail me, though. "Which is . . . ?" I prompt her.

"April," she tells us, rubbing a smudge on Peggy Schuyler's dress.

"And you're gonna be a freshman?" Teddy guesses, clearly catching on to me.

Chloe shakes her head. Now that she's actually talking to us, I can see the resemblance between her and Beth: her little button nose, her full cheeks, her strange kind of magnetism. I can't help getting sucked into whatever she's saying, even if the whole "Little Jo" bit makes me want to lie down on her carpet and die.

"A sophomore," says Chloe. "You too?"

"Junior," says Teddy, thankfully taking the reins on the conversation as I do some quick math against my will.

April and a rising sophomore. I'm July and a rising senior. So it would still work out that Beth could have had me, hit pause on procreation for a year, and then popped out this small, very excitable bean with someone else. In fact, didn't my dad mention in that post there was another guy in the picture?

The timeline makes sense, but I'm almost disappointed that it does. It was already grim enough wondering why my mom ditched me. It's even grimmer to think she might have ditched me, but not a different kid.

"What school?" Chloe is asking Teddy.

"Stone Hall."

Chloe's eyes go wide. "I heard that place is intense."

"Yeah, I guess," says Teddy, shifting uncomfortably.

His parents are rich on account of the whole surgeon thing, but he's never quite known how to be a Rich Kid. He gets along just fine with the other kids at his fancy Upper East Side prep school, but I know he's never quite fully felt like he's belonged—between his dyslexia and the fact that his parents aren't really in any of the circles their parents are, he's always felt separate from the hypercompetitive legacy types he shares locker bays with. Mostly he hangs out with me and my friends, or kids he meets on the GeoTeens app.

But Chloe is practically tipping over like a teapot with excitement. "I heard the valedictorian last year snapped over a grilled cheese recipe and started working at a deli—"

Teddy waves his hand at Chloe. "She's fine. She's at Columbia. But she makes a mean blondie, if you're into desserts."

"Wow. Yes. So wow." She turns to me, her eyes just as adulating. "You guys are like . . . rock stars."

I once watched Teddy Febreze his own armpits and I frequently lick microwave dinners so intensely that remnants of them end up caked to my nose, but we'll both take it.

"Sorry," Chloe says, misinterpreting our silence. "Sorry, sorry, I'm . . . a lot."

"Nah. Millie's a lot," says Teddy, tilting his head at me. "You're a normal amount."

"Excuse you," I protest. But Teddy knows better than to think I'm actually offended. I *am* a lot. On purpose. And Chloe is . . . a lot, and maybe less on purpose. But I can see she's growing on Teddy, and even though she may be a breathing red flag that my biological mom for some reason didn't want to keep me in particular, she's growing on me, too.

Chloe smiles shyly. "Kids my age almost *never* come to these meetups. I hope you guys come back. They're, like. Only kind of dorky."

"Food's sure great," says Teddy.

"Amen to that," I agree. The lasagna's been wafting into my nostrils since we set foot in the apartment. It smells so good it should be a crime. "Should we get back down to the shenanigans?"

"Yeah!" says Chloe, like she can't quite believe her luck. "You'll have to tell me everything about Stone Hall. *And* everything about your singing. And Millie, oh my gosh, you should *definitely* be the one who does Katherine's song, we do sing-throughs of the whole show, if you don't do Katherine I'll *die*."

Teddy and I exchange a bemused glance over Chloe's head, and that's pretty much the theme for the rest of the night. I get maybe within five feet of Beth a few times, but that's about it. Chloe orbits us both like an inexhaustible moon, alternating between entire monologues of excitement and listening to our answers so raptly that I'm a little worried she's forgetting to breathe. Teddy eats with great gusto everything that all Beth's friends bring and wins over all three dozen of their hearts. I sing a few of the Katherine solos with Chloe, reveling in the praise of a bunch of strangers who have never heard me sing before, sticking my tongue out at Teddy when he rolls his eyes at me from the other side of the room.

When it's finally time to leave, I'm stunned to find that four hours have passed. Usually time is only ever that slippery to me when I'm in the middle of the run of a show. Beth sends us off with extra lasagna, and Chloe puts her number in both of our phones, and we are hugged by too many people in newsboy hats to count before we deposit ourselves out onto the street, stumbling happily back home.

"Thank you for doing that with me," I say to Teddy, pressing my nose into his shoulder. "Promise you're off the hook for the next one."

Teddy wraps an arm around me, pulling me in to his lanky frame. "Are you kidding me? I'm already signed up to bring the chips and guac for it. This is my *scene*."

Or perhaps a testament to the fact that Teddy and his family mostly live off Seamless takeout and cereal, but I keep that to myself.

"Also, the timing was nuts. That song must have been some kind of sign," says Teddy cheerfully.

"What song?"

Teddy pulls out his phone with his other hand, and I groan at the URL before the page even fully loads. It's the infamous LiveJournal page. Before I can decide what kind of gagging noise to make, Teddy clicks on the post with the track list of the mixtape my dad made for Beth.

"Some Avril Lavigne song," he says. "'Things I'll Never Say.' That's what was playing when we walked into the apartment."

I scrunch my nose, walking on my tiptoes to squint at his screen. "That was on the playlist?"

"Sure was."

The thrill that runs up my spine might be hope and might be something else. "Weird coincidence."

"Less of a coincidence that the song that followed it up was 'Stacy's Mom,' which was, chronologically, the exact next song on Coop's playlist." Off my disbelieving look, Teddy says, "What? I made a Spotify version. They're my new geocaching jams. I can send you the link."

I shudder into Teddy's arm. Some parts of the inside of my dad's lovesick coed brain I was never meant to experience. "No and thank you," I say as Teddy taps the page off his screen. Only then does it fully hit. "Wait. You think she's still listening to his playlist after all this time?"

Teddy shrugs. "Sure seemed like it."

I stare out at the traffic beyond us, trying to fathom it. "But it's been a bajillion years."

"Your birth certificate begs to differ," Teddy reminds me.

"Well—does he post about her again? Like at all?" I ask, staring back at his phone. "Like, did she just disappear off the face of Coop's earth, or—"

"Nah. No more Beth posts; I checked. But is it weird that I

low-key am rooting for her to be your mom?" he asks. "She's the bomb. And Chloe's a riot."

I almost miss a step, coming back to myself. In all the excitement of the party and the LiveJournal sleuthing, I'd forgotten the full implications of why we were there and what it might mean. Now it cinches tight in my chest, grounding me back in the truth of what I'm doing, what I've already done.

"Yeah. They're chill," I agree. It doesn't quite erase the look of hurt on my dad's face last night from my memory, but it helps.

Teddy squeezes me closer to him. There are very few things that one of us feels that the other one doesn't absorb right up like a sponge.

"You still wanna do this?" he asks.

We stop at a light, for once not bullheadedly jaywalking the way we usually do. "Yeah," I say. I'm not even sure where the conviction is coming from. Maybe the idea that Chloe really *is* my sister, and that the mere fact of that means there's more to unpack here than I ever imagined. "Yeah, I do."

Teddy watches me for a moment, waiting me out. "In that case," he says, just as we get the walk signal, "I have the perfect 'in' for you to meet Farrah."

"Oh yeah?" I ask. "And what's that?"

"She's a dance instructor," says Teddy, jangling his building key. "And she just happens to have a Broadway Boot Camp class that starts . . . this week."

"You're kidding."

Teddy tosses his keys in the air and catches them, the closest thing to coordination he and his overly tall body are capable of achieving. "Nope. So if I were you, I'd take up Cooper's offer for dance classes. Two birds, one stone."

"And one *flawless* human geocacher," I say. "Seriously. Thank you."

He pauses just outside of our building, phone still in hand.

"You're welcome. But also, I can think of *one* way you can repay me."

I already know where this is going, but I humor him. "What's that?"

Teddy's eyes are bright, his eyebrows rising into his messy flop of hair. "Just got a GeoTeen push. Someone tucked some used DVDs into a corner of the Highline. I've got coordinates."

I don't bother reminding Teddy that neither of us even *owns* a DVD player, and we are subscribed to so many streaming services between our two households that we collectively own every movie ever made. A new cache is decidedly less about the prize and more about beating other people to it. And if there is one thing Teddy can count on me for, it's crushing the competition.

I pull his phone from him, glancing at the numbers. "We can get there in ten minutes if we run."

Teddy grins. "Last one there's a rotten Newsie!"

We take off into the night, two newsboy-clad dweebs darting in and out of the way of other New Yorkers, whooping and leaping up to tap street signs, dragging each other by the arm whenever one of us pulls ahead. I'm half gasping, half laughing, and fully out of my own brain—there are no versions of Millie to be, no moms to dissect, no lingering guilt or confusion or things lurking under them I don't know how to name. There is just the one person I'll always know how to be: the West Village's biggest dreamer, New York's noisiest human, and Teddy Granger's best friend.

# CHAPTER SIX

I pride myself on my lung capacity, but it's nothing compared to Oliver's. When he sees me walking into the waiting room of Check Plus Talent the next morning, he lets out a sigh long enough to blow up an entire pool floatie.

"Good morning to you too, sunshine."

I'm in a weirdly good mood, courtesy of several Eggo waffles slathered in peanut butter and jamming to the *Anastasia* original Broadway cast recording on the way here. (Number six on my List of Dream Roles to Get Before I Die, so it's important to keep it fresh.) That, and the high of beating the seventeen other GeoTeens in pursuit of the DVD collection, which means we made off with a copy of *Deadpool*. (We did end up spending another hour cleaning up litter all over the Highline, as is the GeoTeen way whenever there's a new cache hidden by one of the app's supervisors. But at least we were semi in character for it.)

In any case, even the sight of Oliver looking annoyingly put together and handsome in his khakis and pale blue button-down shirt isn't enough to burst my emotional balloon.

"I was hoping I hallucinated you yesterday," he mutters.

I glance around the room, wondering where Steph is. "No such luck," I tell him, shrugging off my bag and depositing it on the chair next to him. "I'm gonna pee. Watch my stuff."

"That's not my—"

I put a hand on his shoulder and then pat it, making him glower. "Thank youuuu!" I singsong, darting down the hall to a dark green door that can only be the restroom. I walk in more with the intention of making sure all my curls are somewhat tamed and my eyeliner hasn't smudged than actually emptying my bladder, but there's already someone in front of the mirror.

"Oh!" Steph's face brightens at the sight of me, but not fast enough. Her hair and makeup are as immaculate as yesterday's, straight out of an Instagram beauty tutorial, but even that isn't enough to un-redden her eyes. "Good morning, Millie."

"Morning," I say back, embarrassed at how pleased I am that she remembered my name. "How's . . . life?"

I ask it in that way that makes it abundantly clear that I know she was crying, and to her credit, she doesn't try to bullshit me. She tilts her head at my reflection in the mirror and says wryly, "Oh, you know. Little of this, little of that."

"Is the . . . 'that' okay?"

"Yeah. Yeah," she says, her voice stronger on the second one. "It's not anything important. I'm being a drama queen."

As the crown princess of drama, I can't help getting sucked in. Not necessarily because I want to collect gossip (although that is a known hobby of mine), but because of the Millie Moods. Because maybe this is something else we have in common—getting swept up in things other people brush off. Making mountains out of molehills.

In my defense, I'm five foot four. Molehills are slightly larger to me by default.

"Been there," I say breezily. "What about?"

Steph hesitates. I don't move a muscle, planting myself to the floor the way I was trained to do for auditions—no "traveling," as Mrs. Cooke says. Sure enough, Steph's mouth twists to one side, and I know I've got her.

"Just—there was this audition. And I didn't go. I don't even . . . I was just tired, I guess." There's a rueful look in her eyes, and then she elaborates, "I thought they were going to cast it much younger. And then an old friend of mine from school got it. And I'm just—upset with myself, is all."

"Because you're better than she is?"

Steph lets out a genuine laugh. "I guess that wouldn't be polite of me to say."

A *yes* if I ever heard one. I smirk at her in the mirror.

"Well," I say, "that's good, right? More motivation to get out there next time."

The smile on Steph's face softens. "I think I'm starting to run out of 'next times.'"

"If someone who looks like you is saying that, we're all screwed."

She holds herself a little straighter, that pageant-girl poise coming back to her. "Aw, hon. You better be careful or I'll keep you in my pocket." She winks at me. "But you better skedaddle. Georgie will be here any minute."

"Right." I linger for a beat, not even sure why. It's not like I can say anything worth saying in the five seconds we have. But Steph shoos me toward the door and I head back out, stopping short of the waiting room when I hear the lash of Georgie's tongue.

"I said to be here at nine."

Oliver is in full damage-control mode. "Yes, Miss Check—"

"Georgie," she corrects him. "What time is it?"

"Um—eight fifty-five A.M."

I don't move a muscle, don't even breathe. Bless this ridiculously oversize potted plant for hiding me and the big full-skirted dress I paired with Heather's boots today.

Because here's the thing. That intimidating vibe I felt in Georgie's office yesterday? Apparently was fully warranted. I did a quick Google search of her last night, and she's catapulted enough of the most recent generation of Broadway performers into stardom to fill a calendar. She wrangled connections to get clients into famed writer and director Gloria Dearheart's workshops before anyone could have ever known she had two shows bound for hugely successful runs at the Public Theater, for one thing. She plucked Broadway's most recent Cosette out of a crowd at Marie's Crisis on a weekday night (rumor has it she has a debut album on the way). She's also single-handedly responsible for putting baritone heartthrob Baron Levait on the map.

In other words, if the Broadway industry is made of puppets, Georgie is definitely one of the people holding the strings.

"Oh, good," says Georgie. "You can read a clock."

"Do you—want us here earlier?" says Oliver carefully.

"I believe nine A.M. is what we discussed."

"I, uh—I brought coffee—"

I'm wincing even before Georgie cuts Oliver off.

"If I want coffee, I'll ask for coffee." There's no meanness in Georgie's voice, not a hint of a threat. But the bluntness of it is jarring just the same. "This is an internship. I have no intention of taking advantage of either of you. So from here on out, you'll do only the tasks I assign, during the hours you're meant to be here. Am I clear?"

"Of course. Right," says Oliver, in this dazed voice like he was just murdered and now he's a ghost, standing over his own body. "I'll just, uh . . . wait here for five minutes."

Georgie doesn't answer, unless the click of her office door shutting counts. I tread out quietly, grabbing my bag up from the chair, doing a very poor job of hiding my smirk.

"Don't," he warns me.

I slide the bag back on my shoulder, shaking my hair out from under the strap. "Wasn't gonna," I say, eyeing the coffee in his hand. "But since you're just tossing that anyway . . ."

"In what universe do you think I'd possibly give you this coffee?"

"Waste not, want not. And you're an English Breakfast–guzzling snob, and I know you won't," I say, plucking it from his hands. He lets it go so easily that I can't help but be wary, until I get a look at his face. "Oh, don't be so surprised. You've been inflicting your presence on me for three years."

He shoves his hands in his back pockets, one eye on Georgie's door, the other on me. "Didn't think you noticed things past your reflection."

"I got rearview mirrors, baby," I say, taking a pull. It's still hot. "Mmm. Pike Place roast."

"Enjoy your wet beans."

"Leave it to you to make coffee unsexy."

We both settle uncertainly in the lobby, watching Georgie's door, checking our phones. There's a text from my dad: Knock 'em dead! I told him about the internship last night. I may have left out some key details, like that I was technically competing for it, and I'm planning to use the money to fund the first semester of Madison against his will, and that I'm high-key stalking a woman who might have abandoned me at birth, but he's in the loop on the rest.

Not necessarily because I wanted to tell him. Mostly because I was afraid if I didn't fill up the silence with something, we'd veer too close to the shit show of what I said to him before he left—which, incidentally, I have not apologized for.

And I am sorry. I *am*. But I don't know what extent of sorry, and I have a feeling I won't until I have at least one shred of context on what happened. And unless I figure it out for myself, the only other person who can give me context is *him*.

At least he said we could wait to let Madison know if I'm coming. His answer is still technically no, but it's not *not* yes. In a sense. Which is more than I had yesterday.

The door to Georgie's office swings open so fast that Oliver flinches.

"These are your Check Lists," she says. They're handwritten on pages that are attached to clipboards. "You're expected to complete each of the tasks on them by five P.M. sharp. Some you will do on your own, and some are important enough that they will be shared tasks—those are highlighted. When you arrive in the morning, your lists will be on Steph's desk. Don't lose them. I don't keep electronic files."

We take them from her cautiously. Mine has about ten tasks on it: *Pick up Eataly catering order for 11 A.M. meeting. Pick up Baron Levait's dog from Fun Fur All Daycare and bring him to Broadhurst.* Highlighted: *Assemble new bar cart for waiting room.*

Oh, great. One of us is going to die today with IKEA instructions shoved down their throat.

"I want you to return to have Steph check things off your list and confirm they were done between each task," she continues. "That way I ensure you have singular focus on the task at hand. Field any questions you have to Steph."

I nod, but I'm already doing the only kind of mental math I'm equipped to do, which is figuring out which subway and bus lines are going to get me to all these places the fastest without too many transfers. It'll be tight, but it's doable. Where there's a will, New York usually has a way.

"Well?" Georgie's eyes cut to the elevator sharper than a knife. "Go."

# CHAPTER SEVEN

After Oliver takes a picture of his list, he stashes it so deep in his backpack that you'd think I was threatening to pull it out with a fishing rod. I tap the elevator button to go down, and only when it pings and opens does he acknowledge me.

"So," he says. "*Now* are you ready to call it quits?"

For the splittest of seconds he's looking at me with the same intensity he was looking at his Check List, and it feels like stepping out into a spotlight. There's this heat in his eyes that I've never noticed before, embers in the dark of his pupils. The warmth settles somewhere in my chest, and I have to huff out with an indignant breath.

"Over a little list?" I ask, folding mine in half and sliding it neatly into my shoulder bag. "What makes you think that?"

"Your track record of being allergic to any kind of work." Before I can protest, he points right at me and says, "Last time we had to strike a set, you hid for like, three hours."

I take a step so close to him that he has to retract the finger. "I wasn't *hiding*, I was organizing the *costume* rack."

Oliver leans back on the elevator wall, staring at the doors like they can't possibly open fast enough. "Seems like more of those costumes ended up on Instagram than they did in the storage racks."

I flip my hair back, just barely avoiding his face. "I can't help that I'm the perfect muse."

In my defense, I'm not actually this insufferable in real life. Our costume designer did end up using me as a human mannequin, but only to start mapping out ideas for a production of *Bye Bye Birdie* she was helping out with at a rec center over the summer. Which is to say, I'm an extremely vain individual, but not so much about my own looks.

It's just that Oliver is a specific level of annoying, and I can't help that my own levels of annoying are constantly rising up to meet his.

He's too distracted by the lists to take the bait this time, though. The elevator doors open up and he wastes no time leaving me behind. "Well, even if you've got it in you, you're screwed," he says on his way out the door.

"And why's that?"

Even in his deep and unmistakable irritation with me, he can't help holding the door open. I glide out of it with a brief nod of thanks.

"Because, Your Majesty," says Oliver, pausing for a moment so he can unlock his bike and jam his helmet onto his head. "Unlike you, I know parts of this city that aren't just Broadway theaters and the inside of a Sprinkles cupcake shop."

"Oh, Oliver. I almost feel sorry for you." I slide my Metro-Card out of my back pocket just as the M23 bus rolls to a stop in front of me.

Oliver swings his leg over his bike seat and lets out a laugh so sharp that a bona fide New York pigeon actually moves out of his way. "And why's that?" he asks, repeating the words with a mocking tone.

I hop on the bus. The driver knows me, so I give her a nod and she holds up on asking me to sit down, setting the stage for my mic drop of an exit. "My best friend is a GeoTeen," I tell

Oliver. "Which means I've seen every corner of this glorious trash island, and I know all the fastest ways to get to them." I wave at him with four dainty fingers as the bus doors close. "Toodle-oo."

The look on his face is so simultaneously confused and intimidated that I close my eyes for a moment so I can burn it into my brain forever. And then I do what I do best—I get impossible shit done.

Because although Oliver has zero to no faith in my work ethic, I am nothing if not a hustler. Talent like mine isn't the kind you're born with. It's the kind you fight for, the kind you run all over the city and wait in auditioning rooms for a bajillion hours for, the kind you sweat and bleed and cry for. Minor tasks like this are *child's* play compared to trying to make it in musical theater.

So I'm back with the full catering order hooked in two enormous bags under my elbows within twenty-five minutes, so fast that Oliver with his measly first task of "take a Boomerang of the Highline for client's Instagram stories" is laughably stunned to see me hand my list over to Steph right behind him.

"Where the hell are Ripley-Grier Studios?" Oliver mutters. "There are like, four of them popping up."

I snort.

"What's so funny?" he asks.

"I used to live inside those studios." Back before my Millie Makeovers began and I put myself on lockdown until the worst of puberty was over, that is. "The real question is where the hell is Fun Fur All Daycare. It's not showing up on Google Maps."

"Upper East Side. Eighty-Fourth and Lex," Oliver says without missing a beat. I raise my eyebrows at him. "It's where we board our dog when we go away."

I scowl. "You don't live up there." In fact, I know his precise cross streets, because we have an unfortunate mutual affinity for the bakery in between our apartments. It takes expert strategizing to make sure I don't run into him.

"No. My dad does."

"Oh."

"Divorced," says Oliver, waving me off. But his eyes skirt away from mine and back to his list with this extra jilt to them, like he's not really looking at anything at all.

"Well." I begrudgingly look over at his Check List. It mentions an audition for the next tour of *The Lion King*, which I know for a fact is being held in the Thirty-Eighth Street location. "She means this Ripley-Grier. Here. I'll AirDrop it to you."

"You don't have my number."

I roll my eyes. "You're our stage manager. Of course I have your number."

He shields his screen from my eyes, but not before I see that he has "Millie Price" in his phone as a contact, too, with a cookie emoji next to it. I'm about to ask, but we're cut off by a delivery driver rolling his bike up on the sidewalk and dinging his bell at us.

"Thanks," he says. "I guess I'll, uh . . ."

My body is here, but my brain is already mentally calculating the time it will take me to get on the Q train to get uptown, and whether or not my bag will be big enough to smuggle said dog on the subway to get back.

"See you for the IKEA reckoning?" I ask wryly.

"Yeah," he says. It almost sounds . . . friendly. "See you then."

It's not that I'm surprised. I know, objectively, that Oliver is a good person. Well—good to people who aren't named Millie Price, at least. He volunteer tutors at the junior high down the street after school and makes a point of learning all the freshmen's names and seems to have an actual arsenal of spare pencils that he is prepared to give anyone at any given moment.

And objectively speaking, I'm not the worst either. Cornelia Arts & Sciences' theater department was an overly competitive hellhole when we first started high school—like, someone genuinely ripped the sheet music out of my binder ten minutes before my *Seussical* audition while I was touching up my makeup freshman year—and it's been my aggressive mission to make it more collaborative ever since. I was the one who started setting up the mentoring program between upperclassmen and new theater freshmen, the one who suggested we start double-casting musicals—essentially making two versions of the show with two separate casts—so everyone would be able to get a chance to be onstage without getting cut. It was no easy feat to get a school as traditional as Cornelia to pivot, but somehow we pulled it off, and I'd argue we were all better for it.

Well, maybe not *all* of us. The *Mamma Mia* debacle between me and Oliver freshman year was just one of a zillion other moments we've been at odds. I think maybe what it comes down to is that we both like to be leading the charge, and even when our agendas match up, our ways of going about them almost never do. A scene transition will be weird and I'll insist it's a sound cue issue and he'll insist it's the actors' timing. We'll be tasked with fundraising for the department and I'll say we should sell singing-grams for Valentine's Day and he'll counter that we should bump up the price of tickets by a dollar. At one particularly memorable cast party we ended up arguing over where we should get pizza delivery from, at which point everyone went over our heads and ordered from a third spot without telling us.

Sure, we could compromise. But there's just always been this friction between us. Like we're not just challenging each other but challenging each other's authority. At some point it stopped feeling so personal and started to feel like keeping score—like every time he undermined me in front of the chorus and theater kids, I had to shoot something back to undermine him in front of the band and crew. It's almost become an expectation. I feel like if either of us were going to give it up now, it would be admitting defeat.

Mrs. Cooke doesn't mind it. Actually, sometimes I feel like she encourages it, since we keep each other on our toes. Very little slips through the cracks in the Cornelia theater department, with the two of us scrutinizing each other's decisions under a microscope. Looking out for our classmates seems to be the only thing we agree on, even if it's begrudging and we've never actually acknowledged it out loud.

That said, when it comes to having each other's backs, we'd sooner pull a Javert and simultaneously nose-dive into the Seine.

And maybe some of that is my fault. Before the *Mamma Mia* thing even happened, our cringeworthy first encounter was . . . well. Not my finest moment. And as determined as I am to blot it out of my mind, it hasn't changed the dynamic that's evolved ever since. The one where Oliver is determined to outdo me, and I am determined to not be outdone.

Hence, his patented Stage Manager Scowl, and me taking a little too much pleasure from doing whatever I can to knock it off his face.

But if this reflection on our past might have led us down any slightly more peaceful roads, all that is out the window within thirty minutes, when I am actively plotting Oliver's murder. Fun Fur All Daycare is not at Eighty-Fourth and Lex. Only after an SOS text to Teddy that leads to him sending out a blast to his army of GeoTeens do I find out that it is a full twenty blocks south of that, which means I've wasted time on both ends of this trip.

Bless ur ridiculously dorky soul, I text back to Teddy, alongside an indiscriminate mess of praise hands, magnifying glass, and clown emoji.

Don't bless me. Bless ParticularlyGoodFinders, he texts back, referencing the girl on the GeoTeens app I have teased him for having a digital crush on for weeks. She's the one who knew where it was.

By the grace of my only acknowledged god Patti LuPone and the GeoTeens, I have one tiny elderly Maltese named The Artful Dodger ("Dodge" for short) tucked into my tote bag and smuggled onto the Q train to get us back down to the Broadhurst Theatre. He asserts himself every few stops by licking my elbow, which is the only thing keeping me from pulling up Oliver's contact information in my phone so I can either deafen or psychologically scar him with my rage.

Except it's not rage, really. It's something ickier than that. I reluctantly recognize it as embarrassment. As hard as I've tried to make sure that particular feeling on the spectrum of emotion can't affect me anymore, there it is anyway: I trusted him. I did him a favor, thinking he'd done me one too. But he'd really just taken the very first and brutal opportunity to screw me over faster than that rampant case of mono that shut down our unrepentantly horny band section in *Cabaret* two years back.

"How should I get my revenge?" I ask the very crusty Artful Dodger as we clamber into the oppressive heat of Times Square.

Dodge answers by lolling his tongue out at me, then trying to make a snack out of the emergency Nutri-Grain bar in my bag.

"Hey, no stealing," I say, pulling it out of his teeth. "Except . . ."

Dodge is a genius. Theft it is.

I'm still so peeved at Oliver that it sucks half the magic out of doing something I never imagined I'd get to do this soon: walk backstage in the *actual Broadhurst Theatre,* to meet a legitimate Broadway star I've been stalking since before I got my first zit.

"Thank you, thank you," says Baron when security leads me

over to the open door of his dressing room. Dodge clambers sloppily out of my arms and into his, immediately licking the bejeezus out of him. "Nice to see you too, you rascal."

He's so handsome in real life that even the fact that he's clad in mismatched denim and enough hair gel to be a one-man Slip 'n Slide can't detract from it. Tonight's his last night playing Sky in *Mamma Mia* before his replacement takes over for the last month of the run. I'd be lying if I said I haven't been manically refreshing *Playbill*'s site in an effort to figure out what exactly he's leaving the show *for*, but whatever it is, it's intense enough that he had to board his dog for the rehearsals leading up to it.

"You're Georgie's new intern?" he asks, flashing me that same broad "leading man" smile that landed him a stint as Fiyero two years ago.

"Millie Price." I extend my hand out to him. "You were phenomenal in The Playhouse's *Little Shop of Horrors*."

He raises an eyebrow, taking my hand with a firm shake. "That's a deep cut."

I know. It's not even mentioned in his *Playbill* bio. "I swear I'm not a stalker," I tell him candidly. "I just go to every show I can. Best way to learn is to watch the experts."

He smiles appreciatively as Dodge wriggles in his arms, his tongue still lolling out and making him look more like a sock puppet than a dog. "Well, you've got a name with some star power, so you're halfway there."

It's a good thing I have an urgent revenge plan to hatch right now, because it's the only thing keeping me from spontaneously combusting from joy. I clear my throat.

"Well, it's no Artful Dodger, but I guess it'll do."

Dodge's ears perk up despite being conveniently out of commission when I asked him to stop gnawing the handles of my bag earlier.

"Maybe we'll see you here in a few years, then," says Baron. It's enough to make my ego swell like I swallowed the sun—that is, until he adds, "If you survive Georgie, of course."

"Right. I better get going." I blow Dodge a kiss on my way out the door, and Baron calls after me, "Godspeed!"

I thought it might be difficult to pull off my revenge, but once I get back to the office I see Oliver made it too easy. His bike is propped next to the building—*unlocked*, which is a true testament to how distracted he must be right now—but I don't need to steal the whole bike. If I've got the helmet, I'm golden. Oliver is obsessed with road safety. Not only did he bully our principal into letting him be ten minutes late to homeroom so he could be a volunteer crossing guard, but I've seen him yell "Wear a helmet!" at strangers in the bike lane outside our school more times than I can count.

I pluck the helmet off his bike seat, carefully placing it behind a dumpster in the alley by Check Plus Talent. A rat immediately scurries out of the trash, squeaking indignantly.

"Don't judge me," I tell it. "He started it."

I race back up to the office and get Steph to sign off on my Check List, and barely get two words in with her edgewise before I have to sprint down to Sweetgreen to get Georgie's Guacamole Greens salad off the preorder shelf. Oliver isn't back by then, so I guiltily ask Steph what he's up to and she tells me he's picking up a client's dry cleaning across town and dropping it off at a rehearsal space.

Okay. That's like, a solid two miles round trip, which means we're about neck and neck. I head downstairs and pull his helmet out from the alley, intending to put it back on his bike, when instead I am accosted by none other than Oliver himself.

"You *stole* my *bike helmet*?"

Oliver's shirtsleeves are hiked up to his elbows, his once-slick hair now dripping with sweat.

"I had to hand Gloria freaking *Dearheart* an updated contract looking like *this* because you *stole my helmet*?"

For a moment I forget to be mad altogether. Gloria is in a tier above regular humans. One of her shows at the Public was about a bunch of reincarnated Greek gods living in the same coed college dorm (Dot, a.k.a. Aphrodite, is obviously one of my dream roles), and it was so phenomenal I not only dragged half the theater department to see it, but *also* my dad and Teddy, whose interest in live theater of any kind is approximately none. Anybody who knows anything in the theater world is teeming with excitement over the show's move to Broadway next week, especially since they'll be debuting three entirely new songs.

Naturally, Georgie sent Oliver, whose acting aspirations are on par with a sponge.

Oliver moves to yank the helmet from my grasp, but I shove it at him before he can. "You sent me on a wild goose chase through the Upper East Side," I shoot right back. "Do you know how many old people and strollers I had to dodge sprinting down Lex?"

"Do you know how many *insufferable hipsters on their phones* I just had to dodge sprinting through the East Village?" he snaps, looping his helmet strap back onto his bike handlebar.

"Oh, boo-hoo," I say, still trying to bite down the jealousy that is practically steaming out of my pores. "You could've taken the crosstown bus."

"I don't know the bus system because usually, there aren't deranged Kristin Chenoweth wannabes *stealing my bike helmet*." He walks away from me, but I'm hot on his heels and he knows it. He angles back for just a moment to point a finger at me. (This is becoming somewhat of a habit of his.) "If this is how it's gonna be, then game on."

The nerve of him. "What game? *You're* the one who gave me bogus cross streets," I remind him.

Oliver stops on a dime, so fast I almost barrel right into him. "Well if I did, it wasn't on purpose!"

We're so close that I can practically feel the heat of his sweat like it's my own. Any person in their right mind would back up, but if Oliver won't, I'm sure as hell not going to first. "Oh, good. In that case I *accidentally* hid your helmet behind some trash," I say through my teeth.

Oliver throws his hands up in the air, just barely missing yet another insufferable hipster on their phone. "You're impossible."

"Well *you're* hypocritical."

"You're *both* going to be in a whole lot of trouble if you don't take care of the next task on your Check Lists."

We jolt to attention on the sidewalk, where Steph is standing with her arms crossed and faint amusement on her face. The heat of my humiliation is so immediate I wince like I'm stepping back from a fire.

"Sorry," says Oliver quickly. "I . . ."

"I get it. First day. Getting in the groove. And Georgie sure didn't make it easy, pitting the two of you against each other like this," she says.

Shit. *Shit.* Now this woman who might be my actual legitimate mom thinks I'm an actual legitimate brat. I stare down at Heather's boots, trying to pull myself together, but I can't do it fast enough.

"Take a breather. You're both doing a great job." Steph pauses for a second, clearly waiting for me to look back up, but I can't. If I do I'm going to do something stupid like cry, and make the whole thing even worse. "And then once you're ready, you can head down a few blocks to get the bar cart—they accidentally had it shipped to my building. It should be right in the main hall. Here."

I hear the jangle of keys. Out of the corner of my eye I see Oliver take them from her, along with a piece of paper that must have an address.

"It'll be heavy. A two-person job. And you're probably going to have to sneak past our very protective landlord." She takes a step closer to us. I tip my head up just enough to see the earnest look on her face. The way she's acknowledging I helped her with a moment of weakness this morning, and now she's trying to help us with ours. "But from what I've seen, the two of you are more than ready to handle it."

"We're on it," says Oliver.

I purse my lips and bite down on them before my eyes can sting with the stupid tears that are clogging my throat. "Yeah. We got this."

She smiles at me, and only me. "Good. See you in a bit."

I know deep down that she's not judging me for what just happened, but it doesn't matter. She saw it. And she doesn't have the context of the last three years of what Mrs. Cooke dubbed "The Oliver and Millie Show," so she doesn't understand that I'm not *actually* like this, that I'm only like this when it comes to *him*.

"Millie?"

It's Oliver. I can feel a Millie Mood rising like a tide behind my throat. I blink, hard, letting myself squeeze out exactly one tear, and then scratch at my face to get rid of it as if there were an itch on my nose. "Yeah. Let's go."

I take off, but he touches my arm. For a moment we're both so still that it feels like the entire day of running around just crashed into us from behind. He must feel it, too, because it takes a second for him to speak.

"Uh . . . it's the other way," says Oliver.

I don't say anything. Just nod and start following him down the street, then across it, and down the next one he leads us down. It's ten minutes of silence and me thought-spiraling into a hole where Steph decides she hates me. A hole where I've already convinced my mom not just once but a *second* time that I'm not worth being in her life.

"You're being really quiet," says Oliver.

I don't dignify this with a response. At least, I'm trying not to. The thing is that "being really quiet" isn't exactly in my repertoire.

"I don't like it," Oliver mutters.

He probably thinks I'm scheming. I *wish* I were scheming.

"I just . . ." I don't know why I'm saying it, only that it spills out anyway. "I want Steph to like me."

This takes him visibly off guard. "Georgie's the one in charge of us," he says, pulling out Steph's key to let us into the building.

"Yeah." I shake my head. "I don't . . . Let's just . . . get the package and go."

He pauses, his hand still midway to the apartment building's front door. "I really didn't mean to give you the wrong cross streets. I guess I just remembered wrong." I don't have to be looking at him to know that there's something else he's going to say, something waffling between us. "I . . . don't spend as much time up there during the school year."

I take a breath, and just enough of the Millie Mood goes with it that I can look him in the eye. It's something I don't appreciate that much in Oliver, even though I know—he's honest. By the book. Not just about the little things, like cross streets and bike safety. But about the way he feels. He's never been the kind of guy who's hidden stuff out of pride. Hell, I saw him crying during English once when the sub got lazy and made us watch *Dead Poets Society* a third time. For someone who is careful not to let me know too many details about his life, he's never been anything but honest about the ones he does.

Which is how I know for a fact that he doesn't just dislike me. He means it.

And how I *also* know that the whole cross streets thing really was an accident. Even if it was a shit one.

"Well," I say, hedging some line between comforting and insulting. "Anything above Fourteenth Street that isn't a theater is overrated anyway."

Oliver shakes his head, but I catch the small smile. "The princess of the West Village."

"The *queen* of Lower Manhattan," I correct him as he unlocks the door.

This earns me an eye roll. "Let's just—agree to stay out of each other's way, okay?"

I elbow him in the side. "So you do acknowledge I'm worthy competition."

"I acknowledge that you're annoying as hell," says Oliver, which is to say yes.

I'm brightening considerably as we stroll through the main hallway of Steph's building, a typically cramped entrance not all that different from mine. Before I can start imagining her living in it, and by some extension imagining me there, too, we're interrupted by the sound of a door rapidly opening.

"Hey! That package is not addressed to you."

Oliver looks over at the slippers-clad, gray-haired, stooped-over man who just poked his head out of the first-floor apartment in alarm. Lucky for him, the generation above baby boomers happens to be one of the key demographics susceptible to my Millie charm. I offer him the brightest smile I can muster.

"We're picking it up for Steph. She gave us the key."

He squints at me, his voice gruff. "You her niece or something?"

I can already tell "we're the interns" isn't going to cut it with a guy like this. So before Oliver can open his mouth to tell the truth, I reply without missing a beat, "Sure am."

The landlord's brow uncreases considerably, searching my

face. He gestures up to his own eyes. "You got the same . . . look."

I cling to the words like Saran Wrap. "Yeah?"

"Yeah. That look like you're gonna cause some trouble," he says, but with some marked affection in it that makes me think Steph's probably lived in this building a long time.

Oliver lets out a scoff. The landlord turns to him. "And you are?"

Might as well have my cake and annoy the hell out of it, too. I grab Oliver's hand, squeezing it tightly enough to crack my knuckles. "My boyfriend," I say, beaming up at him.

Oliver's eyes widen just enough to let me know that whatever quasi-bonding moment we had out on the front steps is effectively over, and I am dead to him once more. "I'm not your—"

"Well, technically we just started dating, but he's been *begging* me to go out for so long, and you know what?" Oliver's stare is burning with such intense annoyance that I probably need sunglasses, but at least he doesn't let go of my hand. "He finally wore me down."

The landlord cackles. "That's a Fedotowsky girl if I've ever seen one. You tell that Steph to quit working so much; I haven't seen any of those boyfriends of hers around for a while. Used to get a big kick out of 'em mooning after her."

I flash him another grin and flip my hair back, untwisting Oliver's fingers from mine. "I'll be sure to let her know."

"And you take care of her, young man!"

"Duly noted," Oliver grumbles, lifting his side of the package.

I grab my side merrily, Steph's landlord waving me out, Oliver giving me murder eyes. The instant the door closes behind us, he mutters, "So much for our truce."

"Truce?" I flash him a wicked smile. "We said we'd stay out of each other's way. Not that we wouldn't have any fun."

Oliver stares at me, then out into the middle distance of the street, like he's trying to glance into the future. "Jesus," he says, evidently having seen it. "This is going to be the longest summer of my life."

# CHAPTER EIGHT

"Heather. I love and appreciate you. But I do not need a chaperone for the L train."

My aunt takes an aggressive bite of her egg-and-cheese bagel, still blinking herself awake. It's five thirty P.M. on a Thursday, but basically breakfast time for her. Our fellow commuters, who are dodging sesame seeds left and right, do not seem to appreciate Heather living this particular truth.

"I feel like if you're physically leaving the island of Manhattan, I am at least somewhat obligated to make sure you don't end up getting kidnapped by anyone who puts oat milk in their coffee," she says through a mouthful of cheese.

"I'm going to a dance class that's, like, three feet from the station," I remind her. "Besides, it's Brooklyn. I'm not cool enough to be kidnapped."

Heather scowls. "You're plenty cool. You're wearing my boots."

"You're right. I take it back. The oat milkers may steal my shoes."

"Speaking of, you got your jazz shoes in your bag, right?"

"Yup." By some small mercy, I remembered them after sleeping through my alarm this morning. It's only day two of the internship and I'm so wiped out that I'm pretty sure if I let myself blink too long I'll fall asleep. "Brought my tap shoes too, just in case. I'm not really sure what to expect."

"Yeah, that's the other thing I'm nervous about," says Heather, pausing her bagel consumption. "This 'Farrah' woman doesn't have any kind of online presence."

"Uh, Heather, the website for the Milkshake Club is basically a graphic from before I was born. And Dad's a computer nerd who could probably fix it like *that*," I say with a snap of my fingers.

Heather pouts. "I love that little graphic."

I roll my eyes. "You only love it because what's-her-face made it."

Heather raises a warning eyebrow at me. In my defense, "what's-her-face" is a much kinder nickname for her ex Jade than the ones she probably deserves after yanking Heather around all these years—saying she didn't want to be exclusive but accusing Heather of cheating and pitching a fit when Heather's college roommate was staying with us for a few days. Asking Heather to move in, then saying she had to "find herself" before up and moving to Europe—without Heather.

That was a few months ago, and Heather told me and Dad that she was officially finished with Jade. Heather's phone screen (and email inbox) tells an entirely different story. I'm about to mention the several texts I've seen pop up with Jade's name on them, but Heather seems to anticipate this and beats me to the punch.

"My point is, at least we *have* a website," she says quickly. "Where did you find this dance class anyway?"

My eyes cut to Heather's boots. "Uh—Teddy found it."

Which is technically not a lie, even if he was more looking for my mom than an affordable dance class option. Farrah seems to do most of her advertising for classes on her personal Facebook page or by word of mouth, so it's not like she's *completely* off the grid. But Heather's right. A casual Google search won't really pull her up. And trust that I've tried.

"Leave it to the GeoTeen," says Heather fondly. Just then the L train finally spits out into Brooklyn, and she starts wrapping up her bagel before we reach our stop. "Listen, I know you're probably still bummed about this whole precollege thing, but I'm glad you're taking Coop up on this."

I nod, too guilty to say anything.

"You should give him a call when you get back tonight. He's been dying to know how the internship's going."

"'Course," I say. "Yeah. I will. Just been . . . busy."

The doors slide open, and I scamper out before Heather can call bullshit on that. Aside from the internship, I guess I'm not actually busy. Or I shouldn't be, at least. But between the working hours and the hours I spend geocaching with Teddy and the hours I'm secretly getting my stuff together for the precollege despite what every adult in charge of me has said about it, there really isn't much time to spare.

Plus the whole looking-for-my-mom thing. Enter: this dance class.

The address takes us to a little studio above a chicken-and-doughnut place that smells so good it's a miracle we even find the staircase through the haze. Still, I can see Heather scrutinizing every corner of the building, from the flimsy, handwritten BROADWAY BOOT CAMP sign duct-taped to the wall to the flickering light at the top of the paint-chipped stairs.

"Okay, we're bailing," says Heather.

"I'm sure it's fine," I say quickly.

"I'm afraid if I breathe too hard the stairs will cave in under us."

I reach the top before she does, stubbornly opening the door to "Farrah's Dance Studio" before she can get another word in edgewise. I skid to a stop, stricken by what I can only call aesthetic whiplash—the creepy staircase has given way to a sweeping, gorgeously lit studio with immaculate hardwood floors and walls with giant spotless mirrors. There's a little prep area on the side for dancers to leave their stuff and change their shoes, with pretty pale pink painted benches, fairy lights, and a hand-painted glittery message that says DANCE YOUR HEART OUT.

"Wow," says Heather. "It's like walking into a Pinterest board."

"Well, thank you. Or, I guess—thank my mom. She's an interior designer and did this one on the house."

We both turn to see a woman in a bright yellow leotard with fluttery sleeves and built-in shorts and a pair of worn-out beige LaDuca dance shoes, the kind with the flexible soles that I've mostly seen only on well-trained, serious dancers. Her strawberry blond hair is pulled up into a bun spilling with thick tendrils and wisps that frame her face, still glowing with sweat from the class that must have just let out before us. There isn't a speck of makeup on her, but with her striking brows (*thick* like mine) and the pop of freckles that fan out across her pale cheeks (*just* like I get in the summer), she radiates all on her own.

"I'm, uh . . . my name's . . ." My aunt clears her throat, evidently winded from that one flight of stairs we just walked. "Heather," she finally says, extending her hand.

"Heather," Farrah repeats, taking Heather's hand between both of hers and squeezing it warmly. "Welcome. Is this your first dance class, or—"

"No. Oh, god, no, I'm—an aunt. Millie's aunt. This is Millie," she says, laughing this nervous laugh I haven't heard since that time we saw Anne Hathaway on the sidewalk in the East Village. "I can't dance."

Farrah lingers for a beat before letting Heather's hand go. "Well, I'm sure *that's* not true."

The laugh again. And oh. My god. Oh *no.* I know what that laugh is, because it's the same laugh from when Jade first came to the Milkshake Club and started flirting with Heather when she was working the ice-cream bar. The laugh that means she is supremely, irrevocably, in one fraction of an improbable second in love.

"Millie, right?"

Farrah has turned her gaze over to me, and for a moment I forget that Heather has thrown an incredibly awkward wrench into this "Are You My Mom" plan. There's this pulsing energy in Farrah's eyes that makes me certain she's one of those people who will be every bit as energetic in her nineties as she is right now in her thirties—something almost birdlike about her, in her sprightly steps on the floor and the light way she carries herself.

I recognize that energy. That tirelessness. It's electric in my own bones, even if mine aren't half as nimble as hers.

"Right," I say. Teddy signed me up with a fake last name so it wouldn't give me away. Thank god she doesn't remember it and say it in front of Heather, or I'd be sixteen thousand kinds of busted.

Farrah purses her lips into a sly smile. "You're the last-minute sign-up!"

I smile back broadly, trying to make it look like I'm *not* inspecting her head to toe looking for every potential similarity between us. "That's me."

Heather steps forward and nearly trips. "Glad you could, uh . . ." The moment Farrah turns to look at her again, Heather seems to forget that she started a sentence in the first place, let alone that it needs finishing. I accidentally-on-purpose step on Heather's foot. "Fit her in!" she manages.

"Of course!" says Farrah brightly. She leans in closer to Heather. "There are still a few extra spots, you know. Plenty of space." She gestures out to the studio.

Heather's cheeks turn pink. "I . . ."

"Have to get back to Manhattan," I remind her, before she

mom-blocks me. As thrilled as I am that she's looking at any living thing that isn't Jade, this is decidedly not the time, profoundly not the place, and *extremely* not the woman.

"That I do," says Heather. She rocks back on her heels, angling herself toward the door but still lingering near Farrah. She does, at least, remember to look at me when she says, "Pop into the Milkshake Club after so I know you're back?"

"The Milkshake Club?" Farrah asks, her face lighting up.

And just like that, Heather's not angled at the door anymore. "You've been?"

"Nah, I've only ever seen it on Instagram. It looks sick."

"Heather's the owner," I say for her, partially because I am proud as hell of her for running it on her own, but partially because her tongue looks too tied to say it herself.

"Get out!" says Farrah, hip checking Heather. "A club owner, huh? And you say you can't dance?"

"Well—uh . . ."

I blink, hard, because if I don't then I am going to think about things like the fact that my biological mom might be flirting with my aunt and I'm pretty sure there isn't a type of therapy in the whole world that could cure me from it. I clear my throat loudly, which prompts Farrah to look at the pretty blue clock on the wall.

"We've got day classes, too, if you ever want to give it a spin," she tells Heather. "As for us . . ." She pauses to clap her hands, the other dancers' heads turning at attention. "Two more minutes until warm-ups, my stars!"

Oh, right. I actually have to dance.

Shit.

My relationship with dancing is—well, not complicated. It's actually pretty simple: I suck at it. I have impeccable rhythm when I sing, but it's like my bones never got the memo. I've managed to compensate by videotaping the student choreographers for our shows and then doing the routines at home so many times that our downstairs neighbor is one sloppy jeté away from calling the police. But that's high school theater. You have time to fake it. Time that you definitely don't have in dance calls in the real world, where you can get cut before you fully buckle your character shoes.

It's not like I haven't *tried* to get better. I've taken dance classes the same way I took classes for acting and singing. It's just in the other classes, I started out bad and then I got better. Dancing . . . I started out bad and *stayed* bad. And if there's one thing in this world I'm worse at than dancing, it's being humiliated in public.

Hence, why I have avoided taking any dance classes this past year.

I know. I *know.* There's no way to make it in musical theater these days when you're not a triple, if not quadruple threat (mental note to self: learn how to play the guitar at some point). So really, these classes are long overdue. I've just been too busy clinging to my last shred of dignity to pencil it in.

"All right, my stars, I'm so happy to be seeing all your beautiful faces for the next few weeks!" says Farrah, beaming at all of us in turn. She stays at the front of the room but paces back and forth across it, occasionally giving a little skip. Only now that it's quiet do I hear "Voulez-Vous" from *Mamma Mia* in the background. "A little bit about how these classes will go: every day we'll do a dynamic warm-up and get our blood pumping, and then we'll learn a full routine from a Broadway number. The first week of classes will be modern musicals, then jazz, then ballet, then tap, then a MegaMix week where we infuse all of them into different numbers."

Farrah breezes through the studio so nonchalantly as she announces this that it takes a few seconds for the information to fully process in my brain, and along with it, the sheer idiocy of what I've just done.

This is not a "two birds, one stone" situation, like Teddy thought it would be. This is just one incredibly stupid bird, who is about to look like an idiot in front of a woman she is desperate to impress.

The thought takes root in my stupid brain and just about short-circuits half the synapses, and by the time I look back up, Farrah's already leading a warm-up and I'm still standing like a kid who wandered into a circus ring, about to get trampled by everyone jumping and stretching around me. I catch my reflection in the mirror as I join in: my stubborn legs, my furrowed brow, the way my feet keep landing half a beat after everyone else's and never fully stick to the floor.

The next hour and twenty-eight minutes are, perhaps, some of the most excruciating in my life. I find a spot in the back left corner, farthest away from the fairy lights and the eyes of my fellow Broadway Boot Camp "stars," but it does nothing to mitigate the situation. I can't spin fast enough, and the girl on my immediate right can't help but huff in annoyance when she ends up nearly barreling into me the fifth time. There's just an unprecedented amount of hip thrusting, and while everyone around me looks sassy and demure, I can't ever figure out which leg to shift my weight onto.

By the time we're doing the full choreo we've learned at the end, I'm basically a puddle of humiliation. I can't even look at myself in the mirror. I only hazard a glance at it because I can feel someone staring at me, and I'm prepared to scowl back at them—like, *I'm bad! We get it! If you're that bored, go watch some Netflix when you get home!*—until I realize that the person staring is, in fact, Farrah.

The moment she dismisses us I want to beeline it the hell

out of here like my life depends on it, but my uterus chooses that precise moment to betray me. There's the telltale "yikes" sensation that can only be my period starting. I book it to the bathroom, grateful that Heather has a habit of tucking pads into the inner pockets of all my bags (apparently I inherited the "unpredictable Price flow," according to Heather and my grandma), and pause for a moment to look at my sweaty, red-cheeked face in the mirror.

"What the *hell* is wrong with you?" I ask her.

Not that anyone's keeping score here, but since the beginning of this week, I've: one, gotten into a pissing match with Oliver in front of Steph; two, proved myself utterly incompetent at moving in a straight line, let alone dancing, in front of Farrah; and three, not even managed to have one meaningful conversation with Beth.

Even if any of these women are my mom, would I want them to know? For someone whose literal future job will depend on making good first impressions, I've basically sabotaged my chances with each of them at every turn. What's the point in finding my mom at all if I'm just going to disappoint her?

I grip the sink and bite down, hard. This is *not* the time for a Millie Mood. There's too much to think about, too much to do. I swipe at my eyes, take a breath, walk out of the bathroom—

And immediately run into Farrah.

"Hey—great work today, starshine."

Her words are so earnest and genuine that I want to close my eyes and let them bounce off me, because I sure as hell don't deserve them. Instead I look her dead in the eye and say, "I'm pretty sure I almost decapitated someone."

To her credit, she doesn't do that phony thing adults do when they're scrambling to bolster your self-esteem with a bunch of lies. Instead she gives me a close-lipped, knowing smile. "Very funny," she says. "But you know what my advice is?"

"A leg transplant?"

The smile quirks slightly. "To relax." She puts a hand on my shoulder. "Enjoy yourself. Don't take it so seriously."

I bite my lip, the words coming at me from an unexpected angle. Or maybe not the words so much as the fact that I have Farrah's whole and undivided attention, and I'm not sure what that means to me.

She squeezes my shoulder before she lets it go. "You're a perfectionist. I can tell."

"From *that*?" I say, gesturing back out to the studio.

"From the way I could see you beating yourself up during class." She takes a sip from her water bottle but doesn't break eye contact with me. "I know that look. I used to have the same one."

I don't mean to sass her, but I also don't mean to blink, and my eyes go ahead and do it all the time anyway. "And then dancing fixed you?"

This doesn't faze her. "Nah. Dancing let me know something needed to get fixed in the first place." Before I can ask what this particular brand of millennial-pink wisdom means, she explains, "I think dancing is about honesty. You can feel stuff when you're honest with yourself. And perfection? It's not honest."

"I want to make it on Broadway," I say, trying to keep my voice even. "I can't *not* be perfect."

She seems almost satisfied to hear me say this, like it confirmed her diagnosis. "That's my homework for you: let yourself get a little messy. You know the show, right?"

I'm living the show. "Uh. Yeah."

"Listen to it on your own and just dance the way you want to dance to it. Shake it loose. Even if you're just jumping up and down and flailing like a noodle," she says, making a funny face and doing the wave with her arms to demonstrate. "You gotta figure out how your body works before you make it do stuff."

I crack a smile despite myself.

"Let me see you do it."

I raise an eyebrow at her. She raises one right back, so uncannily in rhythm with mine that it's like a delayed mirror.

I sigh but do a halfhearted wave with my own arms.

"Good. For now." Then, despite being someone who seems so chill and go-with-the-flow-y, she fixes me with a look. "I'll see you next class."

My throat tightens. I hadn't even fully let myself think the thought yet, but we both know I was thinking of bailing. Newbies can get a refund for the whole thing after their first class, so money wouldn't be an issue.

But there's this tug in me, something deeper than the usual one: it's not just that I need this class to survive out there as my post–"Little Jo" self. It's that even without knowing all that much about her, I don't want to let Farrah down. And maybe that new tug is just rooted enough in me that I have to listen to it, have to consider that it means more than just dancing jitters—that maybe this was meant to make our universes collide all along.

"See you then."

I dart down the stairs, my heart still pounding like it has embarrassment aftershocks all the way to the subway platform. The entire ride feels like I'm marinating in self-hatred. My only solace is catching my reflection in the window of the L train and knowing that my sweaty curls at least had the decency to frame themselves cutely around my face. It's enough to buoy me so when I finally reach the West Village, I feel some of my mojo returning.

That is, until I turn the corner to my building and barrel right into none other than Oliver.

"What are you *doing* here?" we both ask at the same time.

He must have changed since we wrapped up for the day,

because now he's in faded jeans and a drama department T-shirt from our freshman year. It's clear that I've caught him off guard, because for once he looks away faster than I do.

"I was . . ."

He gestures back, the door to the Milkshake Club swinging shut behind him.

"Were you just in there?" I ask.

"Yeah." His eyes are back on me again, taking in the sweaty hair and the unitard and the leggings like maybe he just caught me off guard, too. I stand up a little straighter before he lets himself think it. "But don't worry, I'm leaving."

"Wait, why?"

He shoves his hands into his jeans pockets. "What, you want to hang out?" he deadpans.

I stick my tongue out and make a *blech* noise. "No. It's just . . ." The thing is, the Milkshake Club is so much a part of me that I'm pretty sure if something cut me, I'd bleed mint chip ice cream and punk rock beats. Some of my earliest memories are of Heather putting noise-dampening headphones on my ears and my dad hoisting me on his shoulders so I could watch the early sets of up-and-coming New York rock bands. "You didn't like it?"

"The Milkshake Club?"

It's weird hearing those words out of Oliver's mouth, like watching two planes of my existence collide. But I still have to know.

"I— Yeah, I like it," he says, shrugging. "I mean, I have fun there."

"But not tonight," I prompt him.

"Well, I guess not. I mean . . ." He stops himself, shaking his head like he's surprised he said that much. "Doesn't matter."

"Tell me."

He looks genuinely puzzled. "What do you care?" he asks.

There's no hostility in it. Just genuine curiosity. And then I feel bad, because I don't really care about *him* so much as I care about the club.

I think.

It's just, in the last few days, we've mostly behaved ourselves. Oliver because he wants to use Georgie as a reference and me because I'm desperate to redeem myself in front of Steph, but behaved nonetheless. And it's hard to spend that much time with someone and *not* pick up on their little moods and tells.

Like for instance, the way his lips just twisted to one side, the way they always do when he's weighing whether or not he should say something. Or maybe when he's just weighing whether or not to say something to me.

"I'm allowed to care. It's not a crime."

Oliver sighs. Looks back at the closed door to the club, and then down the street, and then finally back at me. He seems surprised that I'm still standing there, like I should have lost interest by now.

"My brothers . . ." He starts the sentence reluctantly but finishes it anyway. "They're in a band."

My eyes widen. I'm about to say *Get out* and ask a thousand questions, but by some miracle he doesn't notice and keeps talking.

"I was trying to see if I could get them a slot to perform. But it's all booked up for the next few months anyway, and they don't have enough exposure to even really be considered, so." He shrugs. "Guess I'll just have to try again later."

Woof. He may think he's up against some odds, but they're probably worse than he thinks. Carly, the woman who books talent for the Milkshake Club, is one tough egg to crack. She likes to scout talent on her own. Her nights are split between the club and roaming all over Manhattan to smaller gigs and open mics to find acts for the eight P.M. set, and most acts for the ten P.M. set are already well-known enough in the city that they're drawing in their own crowds.

It's not necessarily a dealbreaker if they're not, but one thing's for sure: Carly doesn't like to be told to book anybody. Carly likes to tell people she'll book them.

"What's the band's name?"

Oliver opens his mouth and then closes it, narrowing his eyes at me. "Nice try."

Only then does it occur to me that it might be something embarrassing. "Six Seconds of Autumn?"

"Oy," he says, his shoulders loosening up a bit.

"None Direction?"

That might be a hint of a smile.

"The Tweetles?"

He rolls his eyes, but not in an annoyed way. In this knowing way, like he's got his own version of an eye roll especially for me. A slight improvement from the scowl especially for me. "I've gotta get home," he says, aiming himself back down the street.

"You want exposure?" I call to his turning back. "I've got the biggest mouth in Manhattan!"

He shakes his head at me, the barest of laughs in the words: "Good *night*, Millie."

I'd be madder about it, but there's something gratifying in knowing I got that laugh out of him, so instead I blow him an exaggerated kiss. "See you bright and early."

After I check in with Heather, I pull out my phone to check in with Teddy by sending a stream of salsa dancer and barfing-face emojis. Both his parents were off tonight, so they decided to get Artichoke Pizza (I'd anticipate leftovers if I wasn't sure Teddy would eat them on the way home). But before I pull open my texts I see a notification for an email in my inbox from the meetup site Teddy used to find Broadway Bugs.

No—not just an email. An email from Beth herself.

> Hey Millie! So glad you and Teddy RSVP'd to our next shindig—can't wait to see everyone in their Wizard of Oz finery! I was wondering if you have any time in the next week or so if you wanted to grab a muffin and chat? Teddy mentioned you lived nearby!

Cancel the barfing-face emoji. This is shocking enough that I might legit barf. She left her phone number at the end of it, and a bunch of times she's free tomorrow and the next day, which can only mean one thing, right?

She knows who I am. No—she knows who I am to *her*.

And just like that, the search narrows itself down from three to one. The summer of *Mamma Mia* is over, the "mamma" part of the mia fully accounted for.

Teddy picks up on the first ring.

"Why are you physically calling me?" he asks in alarm.

"Because," I say, only then realizing that I'm so winded from shock that I have to suck in a full second breath. "I think we found my mom."

# CHAPTER NINE

Because I apparently feel like playing fast and loose with both my nerves and my bladder, when Beth meets me the next morning before the internship, I order a Venti iced Americano and then immediately drop three packets of sugar into it.

"What are the odds we'd have the exact same order?" says Beth at the self-serve counter, plopping her drink next to mine and grabbing three sugars of her own.

My heart is pounding somewhere too loud to be my chest. "Must be a West Village thing," I joke. But it really could just be a genetics thing. I've always loved dessert, and Cooper Price thinks apples are too sweet. I had to have come from *somewhere*.

And maybe Beth's about to tell me exactly where that was.

Beth finds us a table in the back, positioning us away from the rest of the morning-commute crowd and leaning in just enough that it's clear that whatever she's about to say isn't something she wants broadcast to the rest of the café. I'm so nervous I feel like I'm going to do something stupid, like start drooling, or spill my entire drink. It's not a feeling I'm used to having anymore.

"So, I wondered if I could pick your brain."

I brace myself. She's going to ask about my dad. She's going to ask how much I know. She's going to ask—

"Mostly because of—well, you met Chloe."

I blink. "Yeah. She's great."

And possibly my half sister, which is super casual and normal and not at all a thing I'm *sweating out the pits of my dress* wondering about right now.

Beth smiles one of those gentle smiles at me. "Well, you might have noticed she's on the shy side."

"Oh. Well. A bit," I say, taking a gulp of my coffee. "But, uh—I guess my gauge for that is probably a little off, considering I could talk to a wall."

Beth's eyes light up, like I'm saying exactly what she wants to hear. "It's *so rare* for her to start talking to people like that so fast, but you and Teddy really just seemed to pull her right out of her shell. It's part of why I wanted to meet with you—I guess I was just . . . You seem so well-adjusted, so . . ." She searches for the word and settles on, "Confident. And I just want that so badly for Chloe. For her to feel like she can be herself around *anyone*, and not just me and her dad and her cousins."

I take another swig of my coffee, which suddenly tastes a whole lot more bitter than three packets of sugar should.

"Oh . . . uh . . ."

It feels like my grip on reality is tilting. This isn't what I expected. What I'd spent the last twelve hours preparing myself for. It's so far from it that I can practically hear the universe laughing at me, and for a moment I can't help the stupid, babyish thought that swells up in me like a balloon: *I want my dad.*

I bite down on the inside of my cheek, willing it to go away. I'm supposed to be mad at him.

And I'm supposed to act like a normal person in front of Beth right now, so if I'm going to have a meltdown about this, it needs to happen some other time.

By the time I set my coffee back down, I've gotten ahold of myself. I square my shoulders and look Beth in the eye and summon Audition Millie, the one who grits her teeth and does whatever it takes to get through it. She's not the best version of me, but she's the closest I can get without letting myself feel all the things I shouldn't let myself feel.

"I used to be shy, too," I find myself confessing. "Like, really anxious. I mean—for a little bit. When I was younger than Chloe."

Beth nods encouragingly. By the mercy of the Starbucks mermaid, she doesn't mention the "Little Jo" incident we both know happened right around that time.

"I guess what drew me out of it was musical theater. I just loved it so much, and I knew that's what I wanted to do, so . . . I just kind of pretended to be confident until I actually was?"

As I'm saying it, though, I realize that's not strictly true.

"Or maybe it was more like—I knew I loved it, so then I found other people who did. And made a lot of friends because of it. And then it was easy to feel confident because I knew there were lots of people who had my back."

Godammit, Audition Millie and her unintentional wisdom. Just like that I feel myself aching for my school friends all over again. The truth is, I haven't even told them about the precollege thing yet. Between everyone ducking in and out of the city to see family and my hours at the internship, I haven't seen any of them since the end of the school year.

But maybe that's just an excuse. Maybe I haven't told them because I know it's not going to happen. That I'm never going to find my real mom, and I'm never going to convince my dad to let me go, and I'm not even sure if I—

"That's what I want for Chloe," says Beth, nodding at me. "For her to make friends with people who love the things she loves. I mean, you've met her. When she loves something, she *loves* it. And I love that about her. How passionate she is." She looks me right in the eye, so carefully that I almost hold my breath. "And it's why I wanted to talk to you—you seem the same way. Like you throw yourself into things you love. Just hearing you talk about all the classes you were taking, and that internship . . ."

I can't help the happy flush in my cheeks that she remembered. I didn't even get to talk to her that much the other day, but I must have left an impression.

"You just seem so in command of yourself. Unapologetic. I wish Chloe could push past enough of that anxiety to see the things she loves that way, too."

There's an idea I wish I could ignore right now in this deeply inconvenient moment, because it aches up my throat. The idea that maybe Chloe and I don't just happen to be "the same way" because we're both passionate. Maybe it's because we're both *Beth's.*

I squash it down.

"Well—you probably don't want her to be *fully* like me," I say. "I can be, uh . . . a little dramatic."

Beth takes a sip of her coffee. "What's life without a little drama?"

I wince, thinking of the way I left things with my dad. "Well . . ." I shake my head. "Sometimes I feel like I traded in anxiety for being a diva."

"Well, to that I'd argue that *being a diva* is its own form of anxiety." Beth gives me a mirthful look. "God knows I drove my mother up the wall with it growing up."

"I can't imagine that."

But I want to. And it surprises me just how much. Like maybe it would give some rhyme and reason to the Millie Moods, to have someone who gets it—the push and the pull of them, the way it sometimes feels like my heart is leading louder than I am, and how it never checks where it's headed until after I've already crashed.

"Oh, you don't have to imagine it. My mom's coming to the next Broadway Bugs meetup, and she'd be *delighted* to regale you with tales of my teenage antics," she says wryly. "I think she was secretly hoping Chloe would turn out the same way to give me some of my own medicine."

I have to physically curl my toes into Heather's boots and dig my heels into the floor to stop myself from interrupting, because it's not *about* me, but in some ways it kind of absolutely is. Maybe she did get a kid who turned out the same way. Maybe it's me.

"Sometimes I wish she were," Beth admits. "Then I'd know how to help. It's just been so hard on her, I think—especially now that she's transferring schools."

"She is?"

Beth clutches at her coffee with both hands, like she's bracing herself for something. "Javi and I . . . Chloe's dad," she elaborates, even though I remember every single detail of her shindig like I'm some kind of Beth historian. "We got divorced a few years ago."

Something in my expression must shift, because Beth waves her hand at me.

"We were high school sweethearts and then some stuff in college bungled everything and then we were . . . well."

She pauses to think, and it's only a second, really, but for me it might as well be an eternity. *Some stuff in college bungled everything.* Some stuff like getting involved with my dweeby, ridiculously earnest, Tolkien-stalking dad?

"Anyway, we married young. Too young."

She shakes her head like she didn't mean to say that much, and I guess I'm not surprised. That's always been a weird quirk of mine, and Heather's, too—people just start confiding in us sometimes, without even really deciding to. Must be something with our faces.

"And we're still on great terms and everything, but I ended up moving back down here to be closer to my mom, and for a while Javi was still in our Hell's Kitchen apartment, so it made sense for Chloe to stay at her school in Midtown . . . but he's moving to New Jersey, so she's transferring this year."

"Transferring where?" I ask.

Beth tilts her head out the window toward downtown. "She got into the student lottery for Cornelia Arts and Sciences."

Thank god I don't have any coffee in my mouth, or I'd have choked on it. "Oh my god. That's *my* school."

Beth's eyebrows disappear into her bangs. "Really? I thought you two went to Stone Hall."

I lean forward, her excitement contagious. "Nah, that's just Teddy. I was supposed to go to the public school down the street from CAS, but I got into the lottery, too." That's the whole deal with CAS—it lets students specialize in an arts or science track from the start, but it's still a public school. Admissions isn't based on where you live in the city, but a random drawing every year. "It's a great school; she's going to love it."

At least, love it the way it is now. My own excitement for getting into the student lottery in eighth grade could never have prepared me for the veritable Hunger Games we walked into at the start. But it's a much more Chloe-friendly zone now.

"Oh, this just makes my *day*," says Beth. "You wouldn't mind looking out for her, would you? Maybe showing her around campus?"

"I'd love to. I'd—I'm . . ."

A rock drops in my stomach.

"I'm not actually going to be there next year, I don't think."

Beth tries to keep it off her face, but I can see the quick flicker of disappointment. "Oh?"

"I got into Madison Precollege."

Beth doesn't react the way I'm hoping she will. In fact, she doesn't really react at all.

"For musical theater," I elaborate. "It's this competitive program—it blends the last year of high school with the first year of college, so you can get out even earlier."

"Oh!" Beth perks up. "Well—that's fantastic. Congratulations."

And *there's* what I was hoping for. I have at least one potential mom in my corner on this.

"But I've got so many friends at CAS who would love to meet Chloe," I say quickly, before I can let that thought derail me. "Some in the theater department, in chorus, in dance—"

"Chloe loves to dance. She'll only take classes her cousins sign up for, though." Beth runs a hand through her bangs. "It's great that we have family so close. But I wish I could get her to branch out more."

"Well . . . this summer I'm in a dance class," I tell her. "It meets in Brooklyn twice a week. There are still openings, and it's totally Broadway-themed. Chloe would probably like it a lot."

"You wouldn't mind if she joined you?"

I don't even let myself think it fully through. "Of course not," I blurt, so desperate to be in Beth's good graces that I entirely forget the point of the dance classes is to get into *Farrah's*.

Okay. Well. It'd be a complication, but a small one. And if Chloe really is my sister, then it's basically my job to help her out, right? I mean, I've never been anyone's sister before, but it can't be all that hard. Just make sure she doesn't get eaten by anyone on the L train and pack an extra snack.

"Besides," I say, "I could use an ally in there. I'm not the best dancer."

Beth blows out air. "You're telling me. Two left feet," she says, pointing at herself. Then she unexpectedly reaches across the table and squeezes me on the arm. "Thank you so much, Millie. I can't tell you how relieved I am."

I wish I could tell what I was. It's all churning in me at once—my own relief. But also the lingering disappointment. And also the guilt that's been churning just under the surface since my dad left.

Or maybe it's all the caffeine and sugar jumping rope with my organs right now.

"Let me get your number," she says. "What's your last name?"

I could tell her. I could drop the name "Price" and see if it makes her flinch. I could ask her point-blank if she's my mom— the same way I could ask any one of them.

The idea makes me shiver. I tell myself it's because I don't have time right now, anyway. I have to get to my internship.

"Queller," I tell her. It's Teddy's mom's maiden name, and the fake one he put down for Farrah's dance class.

"Millie Queller," she says. "It's got a nice ring to it."

It does. But then again, so do all the new personas I've taken on over the years. I've been chameleoning so nonstop since the "Little Jo" debacle that it almost feels natural to make up one more version of me.

But as we say goodbye and I finally get some distance from her, that gnawing guilt takes a bite, and I know exactly why—the personas were lies I told myself. Now it looks like I'm willing to lie to everyone else, too.

# CHAPTER TEN

"You *angel*. How did you know how desperately I needed this?" says Steph, taking the iced vanilla latte from my hand and then slurping through the straw like it's an IV.

I'm early. And I'm also technically not supposed to be bringing Steph coffee unless it's been noted on my Check List. But the first week of the internship is almost over, and I've barely spoken two words to Steph that weren't "hi," "bye," and "does this say *macaron* or *macaroon*?" (Georgie has *highly* specific taste in desserts.) If I'm ever going to have a chance to get to talk to Steph, it's going to have to be off the clock.

"Late night?" I ask, plopping on the green chair closest to her desk.

Steph eyes the elevator, but Georgie hasn't come in yet. She leans forward conspiratorially, the blue in her eyes soft against the pale yellow floral of her dress. "Kind of."

I raise my eyebrows.

"Excuse you," says Steph through a smirk. "It was a business dinner."

"What kind of business?"

"A friend of a friend who's kind of a . . ." I can see her deciding whether or not to name-drop, because I know that face. I've watched enough YouTube clips of interviews with performers to spot it a mile off. "Kind of a known name," she settles for, "is trying to get a show off the ground, and wanted to cast some people for the table read."

My emotional investment in Steph's performing career might be misplaced, but I can't help it. Not when she might be the closest I'll ever get to squinting into a crystal ball and seeing my future. "And?"

"And," says Steph glumly, "he wanted me to read for the *mom* part."

My brain latches onto the word *mom* like a dog with a bone. "Okay, but like . . . what kind of mom?"

"The mom kind," she says, setting her coffee down.

"No, I mean, like—there's a spectrum." I extend my arms out to demonstrate the two ends of it. "Are we talking young, sporty mom of toddlers or mean, chain-smoking mom of adult children who fled the nest?"

Steph's nose crinkles. "I don't know. Honestly, I tuned out after that." Off my look, she says, "I should have some kind of established career before the biggest part on my résumé is *mom*."

The universe might as well have served me this opportunity on a silver platter. All it would take is a wheedling question: *Why is the idea of playing someone's mom so bad?*

I flinch, the thought rubbing at something a little too close to my chest.

"So it could be a big show, you're saying?" I ask instead.

"Yeah. Probably."

"Then why don't you—"

Let it be known that if Georgie Check weren't managing half the Broadway talent in New York, she would have made one hell of an assassin. Steph and I don't even notice her enter until she's fully in front of us, peering at me suspiciously. She's in another variation of what I've come to recognize as a uniform of sharp, jewel-toned fitted pieces and statement jewelry—today it's a sleeveless, waist-hugging emerald-green dress and pear-shaped purple drop earrings, her hair tucked into a twisted low bun.

"Oh, hey, Georgie," says Steph.

"Hey," she says back, her eyes still trained on me.

"I asked her to come in early," says Steph.

Georgie is still considering me. She caught me sitting casually, with my legs crossed and my coffee in hand, and I thought it was best not to snap to attention and look like a small animal that just spotted a lion at the watering hole.

Mercifully, we're interrupted. "Uh—am I . . ."

Georgie's gaze cuts away from me and over to Oliver, who must have just emerged from the other elevator. I watch his expression waffle from confused to nervous to suspicious so fast that to everyone else in the room it probably didn't happen at all.

Then Steph's phone rings and Georgie sweeps out of the room and into her office, presumably to get our Check Lists.

"What are you doing?" says Oliver through his teeth.

"Drinking coffee. Sitting. Staring at the bike chain oil on your khakis."

"What?"

Oliver immediately looks down, tilting his ankles to stare down at his perfectly pressed, stain-free pant legs.

"Made you look."

He goes very still. "Some higher power is testing me."

"Patti LuPone?"

"Seriously," says Oliver, sitting on the chair next to mine so fast that even I'm surprised by the sudden closeness. "Why were you here early? What are you trying to—"

Georgie emerges from her office and Oliver's mouth snaps shut. "Your Check Lists," she says, a select three of the handful of words she says to us every day (my particular favorites are "take your lunch break" and "go home," because although Georgie is by all accounts terrifying, she is also very strict about adhering to child labor laws). "No need to check in with Steph at the end of each task today; send me proof over text when they're complete."

She hands them to us so indiscriminately that I've started to realize there really is no rhyme or reason to which of us gets assigned what tasks. As reluctant as she was to hire me, I'm pretty sure when she comes out here each morning she doesn't see me or Oliver so much as two amorphous teenage blobs. This only seems to up the stakes, though. How are you supposed to prove yourself to someone who barely grants you object permanence?

And the stakes are actually high now, because with summer already in full swing there's no way I'll be able to get a job anywhere else. If I have a prayer of paying for Madison, I have to see these shenanigans all the way through.

I glance down at my Check List, and just like that, all my resolve goes out the window.

"My life is a joke," Oliver says flatly.

Our Check Lists for today are the punch line. They're fully highlighted from top to bottom, meaning that everything we're doing today is a "shared" task.

The first is picking up two massive sheet cakes and hand-delivering them to a wrap party for an indie movie musical that one of Georgie's clients landed a lead for. After that we have to go to the tech rehearsal for a charity gala at Carnegie Hall and be stand-ins for Saundra Donald and Phil Fenton, a Broadway power couple who are busy in rehearsals right now for an upcoming off-Broadway revival of *The Last Five Years*. The third is to help post on the Instagram of an older client by taking photos of her at a rally scheduled for later today, which I assume will just be the whipped cream on the "Millie and Oliver Kill Each Other" sundae.

Objectively, all these things are really, really cool. Conditionally, we're doomed.

"Well," I say, bouncing up to my feet, "let's hop to it, sunshine."

The bakery is nearby, so as we power walk over to it I amuse myself by asking him ten times what the name of his brothers' band is and he amuses himself by pretending I don't exist after the fifth. Collecting the sheet cakes is easy enough, at least until it comes time to leave.

"Hold on, I'm grabbing us an Uber."

Oliver props his sheet cake on the bakery's counter. "You're kidding."

"I am carrying a sheet cake as large as my actual wingspan. No, I am not kidding."

"We'll never make it in this traffic." He stares out the window, his brow creasing. "What is even going on out there?"

"It's Pride weekend," I remind him.

"No it's not. Pride weekend's at the end of June."

"It *is* the end of June."

To be fair, I'd probably have lost all sense of time and space in this internship, too, if the Milkshake Club hadn't been decked out in rainbows the whole month. This last weekend of the parade and rallies draws in enough crowds that I usually find migrated glitter in our apartment well into July.

"Well, *I'm* taking the train," says Oliver stubbornly.

For all this resolve, I notice that he doesn't actually move, waiting for my cue.

I sigh. It's too early in the morning for us to self-destruct.

"Fine," I say. "But only because I get carsick anyway."

"Thank you, Your Majesty," says Oliver.

I roll my eyes and say a quick prayer to Patti LuPone that we don't end up dropping these sheet cakes into the bowels of the 1 train as a sacrifice to the rats.

"Hold on," says Oliver once we reach the station. "I'll ask the station guy to buzz us in through the emergency exit."

I wait at the turnstile dutifully, then spot a group of Pride revelers in matching sparkly rainbow shoes and temporary tattoos. By the time Oliver turns back around, a group of men have eased the cake out of my hands and through the turnstile and proceeded to carry it down the stairs to the platform, making sure it's firmly in my arms before blowing me a kiss and taking off.

Oliver shakes his head in disbelief after he catches up. "Your life is some kind of warped Disney movie."

"I imagine yours is like living inside a call sheet."

Oliver sighs.

By some miracle we make it to the wrap party with the cakes unscathed. Less miraculously, they don't let us actually see any of the actors or the set, so Oliver has to half drag me out of there before I can go snooping by falling back on my go-to: pretending to need to use the bathroom.

"I've seen you chug an entire Hydro Flask of water and not pee once through the entirety of *Jersey Boys*," he says. "Nice try."

So instead of breaking in to set and getting a sneaky pic of a famous person to show off to Heather later, we're right back on a packed 1 train car, the two of us clutching the same pole but doing a very good job of not making eye contact. Or at least *trying* not to. It's hard to find anywhere else for my eyes to settle, so they keep snagging on things they shouldn't. Things like the curve of Oliver's bicep, or that slight sheen of sweat on his brow, or—

The train jerks to a stop so suddenly that my hand slips off the pole, and then the second-most embarrassing thing that can happen to a New Yorker (aside from getting caught ordering Domino's pizza) happens to me: I fall on the subway.

Or at least, I start to. My feet physically leave the ground and I pinch my eyes shut, already bracing myself for the ten thousand apologies at whoever's lap I fall into, when instead I fall backward into a firm chest and feel the very same bicep I was just staring at wrap around my waist and hold me there.

A beat passes, and everyone else around us starts grumbling and righting themselves. But Oliver and I are completely still, his grip still tight around me, my hands reflexively clinging to his forearm.

"You okay?"

I swallow thickly. "Yeah." He eases me up to my feet, looking me up and down like he's accounting for me. Weirdly, I can't seem to look at him at all. "Thanks."

The train starts back up again and I reach out and grab the pole before we get too much momentum, but Oliver still hovers. Or maybe I'm the one hovering. We're definitely close, close enough that I can feel the heat of his chest against my bare arm, but I can't tell if it's an accident or yet another unspoken competition where one of us is waiting for the other to move first.

Well. I'm not one to lose a challenge, no matter how silent, potentially nonexistent, or patently absurd. I lean in closer. Oliver doesn't back away.

"You two make a cute couple," says the older woman sitting in front of us.

I'm so distracted by the smell of Oliver's shampoo that I don't react fast enough. Instead Oliver says, "Thanks. If only I could get her to stop cheating on me."

I splutter indignantly as the woman's jaw drops in shock.

"Oh, look, our stop," says Oliver, pulling me out by the arm.

"Hey!" I protest, following him out. I lean back at the woman. "I didn't cheat on him!"

The doors are already closing, but now half of the Fifty-Seventh Street station is staring at me like I've grown an extra hand. I pull my arm loose from Oliver's.

"What was *that* for?"

"Karma for Steph's landlord."

He's actually smiling, and it's this cheeky, full-throttle kind of smile. It makes me think he must have been a really cute little kid.

"Fine," I say, tossing my hair back. "But for the record, I cheated on you with Tom Holland."

"I'll shed one single tear every time I see a *Spider-Man* billboard."

And then, within the next few minutes, we're someplace I wasn't planning to be in at least five years, four if I was lucky: backstage at Carnegie freaking Hall. After security clears us, we walk in through a side door that leads to a narrow hallway running parallel to the theater, all the way back and back until we're in a holding room backstage.

I can see Oliver's head turning to stare at all the stagehands and crew members rushing by in organized, choreographed chaos, his eyes following the equipment and the highlighted clipboards and PAs muttering things into headset mics. My eyes are fixed on the door that leads out to the stage wings.

We both stand still for a moment, suspended in this world of things we know we are and things we aren't quite yet, and breathe out the word *Wow.*

Our eyes snap onto each other's in surprise, and I wonder if he also feels himself yanked back just as fast—back to three years ago. Almost to the day.

I'd just finished junior high, just gotten my braces taken off, and, most importantly, just convinced my dad to let me dye my hair. It had taken a solid year of wearing him down in the post–"Little Jo" aftermath, and the timing couldn't have been more perfect: that summer they were letting the incoming freshmen come in waves for an orientation day based on whatever their primary interests were. Now when I showed up for the theater one, no prospective new classmates would recognize me from the viral video that was getting me laughed out of every audition in town.

I remember exactly what I was wearing, because I was midway through the hippie phase of my Millie transformations and Heather had just gotten me a fringe vest as an early birthday present. I was wearing it over a loud tie-dye dress I'd paired with a thick headband and Heather's boots and I felt unstoppable. Brand-new. Brave, even.

Brave enough to walk up to the cluster of nervous-looking freshmen waiting for our guide outside the school's theater and take charge.

"Let's go around and all say our names. I'll start. I'm Millie."

I turned to the girl next to me, who introduced herself. So did the kid after that, and the kid after *that*, but the next kid didn't. Instead he was staring at me.

"Do we know each other from somewhere?" he asked.

Coming out of another boy's mouth this might have seemed like a line, but even in a group of mismatched theater kids in various degrees of puberty, he had a self-possession that set him apart. It was something in the unselfconscious way his eyes met mine, the assured posture of him, even the way he was crossing his arms. Like he'd already figured himself out and was so fully confident in it that it had never once occurred to him to be any other way.

It's what I wanted, too. What every Millie transformation was attempting to achieve. And unfortunately, it was clear from the way he was frowning at me that I had not transformed *nearly* enough.

"Nope," I said quickly. "You are?"

"Oliver." He narrowed his eyes at me. "Huh."

I gritted my teeth. "Nice to meet you," I said firmly before turning my attention to the next kid in the group.

By the time the guide showed up I had one eye on her and the other on this Oliver kid like he was some kind of time bomb. I wasn't egotistic enough to assume he recognized me from the video, but I *was* paranoid enough. Until I knew for sure, I had to keep as much distance between the two of us as possible.

But once they let us into the theater all bets were off.

The other kids started following the guide to see the dressing rooms and the prop closet, but I lingered to get a better look, and so did Oliver. For a few moments we stood there on the stage, me looking out at the audience, Oliver staring up at the rigging above us, and both breathed out the word *Wow.*

Our eyes met. I was grinning so hard my cheeks hurt, and then he was grinning back, and even then I knew it wasn't something he did often. That I was witnessing something rare.

And it sounds dumb, but for a second I forgot about the fringe vest and the dyed hair and the shiny new teeth. I forgot about first impressions and the casting directors who'd patted me on the head and the impossible distance still standing between me and making my dream come true. For a second, I could already see it. Out in the sprawl of empty audience seats, in the glare of stage lights, in the faded glow-in-the-dark tape at the edge of the stage: not just a dream, but a promise. One that I knew how to keep.

Then Oliver opened his big dumb mouth on a stage in front of *all* our future peers and said, "Oh! You're the girl from the 'Astonishing' video."

He could have physically shoved me off the stage and it would have hurt less. "No, I'm not."

He nodded. "You are. You're—"

"Shhh," I said, less walking over to him than sprinting.

"—'Little *Jmmmf*'!"

Which is what "Little Jo" sounds like when you reach up and shove your hand over a strange boy's mouth in a desperate attempt to get him to *shut the hell up* before he destroys your entire high school reputation. Which, yes, may have been a little extreme. But tell that to a thirteen-year-old girl clinging to her last shred of auburn-dyed dignity.

Oliver tore himself away from me, his face the picture of shock. "What the *hell*?"

It was that precise moment that the school guide and our future physical education teacher poked her head out from behind the wings.

"Excuse you, young man. Mind your language," she snapped at him.

Oliver's mouth dropped open, but right then I was a little too preoccupied by my own horror to appreciate his. "Of course," he stammered. "I just—"

By then the school guide had already walked away, leaving us on the stage with a handful of classmates trying to figure out what had caused the commotion. Oliver turned to me, and the first iteration of his Stage Manager Scowl was born—the tight lip, furrowed brow, blazing scowl that would go on to be aimed at me more times than I could count.

"What is the matter with you?" he hissed.

I cut a glance back at the other kids. "*You're* the one flapping your big mouth about the 'Little Jo' thing."

"I didn't realize it would be a crime to recognize someone from the internet," he said, taking a cautionary step back from me and rubbing his sleeve over his mouth.

"I don't *want* people to recognize me."

Oliver was incredulous. "What, you think you're some kind of celebrity or something?"

No. I didn't *think* anything—I *knew* things. And what I knew was that I'd been memed and cheek-pinched and made fun of all through the musical theater corner of the internet. What I knew was that there was a tweet roundup about me on a website for theater geeks. What I knew was that if this Oliver kid blew it for me now, I'd never be able to outrun it.

But by then I was in the full swing of a Millie Mood, and it didn't leave me any room to explain. I was mad, Big Mad, mad at this stupid blabbermouth boy with his stupid smug confidence and the way he was looking at me right then like I had just lost my last marble.

"Yeah, that's it. I don't want people asking for my autograph," I sniped at him. "It's such a burden trying to avoid all my *fans*."

Oliver was apparently immune to sarcasm. "Wait, seriously?"

"No. God," I said, gesturing wildly in some combination of exasperation and sheer disbelief. "I'm not *that* much of an egomaniac."

"Well, whatever you are, just—stay away from me, okay?"

The Millie Mood was already shifting in that whiplash-y way it always does, like a big tide just got swallowed by an even bigger one. It pushed all the anger right out of me, ached all the way up my throat, stung at my eyes. Oliver would say it himself later: *You just need people to like you. Like, all the time.*

Oliver noticed I was starting to cry before I did, because he muttered a low "Shit" and seemed to drop some of his guard. But it was too late.

"No problem," I spat out. I wasn't very adept at comebacks then, Oliver being my first actual adversary and all, so that's all I said before I pointed myself toward the back of the theater, stalked up the aisles to the exit doors, and left.

And that was the first of the encounters that would come to define all subsequent ones over the next three years: me pushing too hard, him pulling too fast. An unstoppable force and an indestructible object. Our spats are now so legendary I've heard rumors that some of the underclassmen started to unofficially choose "winners" and tally up our scores.

Except now the tallies are anything but unofficial. Now we're neck and neck for an actual internship, and everything counts.

Usually one of us looks away first. That's how we can tell who's winning and who's not, without a sophomore marking it down in the Notes app on their phone. But this time neither of us does, and it feels like we're hovering in between the kids we were then and whatever we are now—like this moment was a bookend to that one, the universe seaming itself back together after we spent the last few years tearing it apart. A quiet ending. A second chance.

It's the first time I feel a pang of regret about the internship. There's no way we don't blow it all over again—and I don't need any kind of Millie Mood to know that the fallout will feel much worse.

# CHAPTER ELEVEN

I'm afraid to blink, to miss even one moment of staring out at the expanse of Carnegie Hall from the stage. I've been here before, way up in the highest balcony seats to see the New York Pops two Christmases ago, but nothing really prepares you for the enormity of it—the sweeping gold ceiling, the blaze of endless glittering lights, the height of the audience seating. It feels like you could throw out a note here and have it echo into eternity. Like the entire hall is still pulsing with years and years of music suspended in its walls.

"Okay, Saundra stand-in over here."

I wander over to where the woman pointed, still gaping out at the theater as she gestures to clip a body mic to my dress. I lift my arms to let her.

"And Phil stand-in over there," says someone else.

"Wait, no," says Oliver, ducking away from a crew member. "We're stand-ins, we're not getting mic'd."

"They just need us to talk into them for sound," I remind him.

Oliver runs a tight ship between the cast and the crew at Cornelia. He must know that's going to be a whole part of the process. But Oliver's always been stage-shy—he notoriously refuses to do the before-curtain speeches introducing the shows, leaving it to one of the other kids.

But then the other crew member dealing with Oliver turns back to me. "What? No. We need you to sing."

If a heart could salivate at the idea of something, I'm pretty sure mine just did. "Seriously?" I ask, half convinced someone is playing a trick.

Oliver, on the other hand, goes so pale I'm pretty sure the blood just evaporated out of his body. "Absolutely not."

The crew member dealing with Oliver looks just exasperated enough by this response that I know it's not a joke.

"Sing what?" I ask, pulling my hair out from under the body mic wire. Honestly, they could tell me to start freestyle rapping my own Social Security number and I wouldn't flinch.

"'Lay All Your Love on Me,'" says the tech micing me.

I gasp. Oliver lets out a sharp laugh.

The crew guy blows out a frustrated breath. "It's a tech rehearsal. We need to be able to gauge the sound, or—"

"This is not happening. Nope."

The tech guy sighs. "Look, we're on a tight schedule, kid. We don't need you to win a Tony Award here. Just sing."

"This isn't our job!" Oliver protests. "Find someone else."

"There *is* no one else."

"I'll do it."

Four pairs of eyes flit over to Baron Levait, who is, as usual, so handsome that even the piano accompanist pauses her hands on the keys to turn and stare. He walks onto the stage from seemingly out of nowhere, like the heavens opened and dropped him into our laps.

"Hey, Millie," he says, nodding at me. "What do you say? We closed the show last night, but I think I can still remember the words."

He punctuates it with a wink, and I'm dead. I hit my head on that subway fall and died and this is the place you go after you bite it in plain view of the noon commuters on the 1 train.

"She's in," Oliver answers for me.

The stagehand gives me a quick rundown of the blocking so the light tech can follow our paths. "Doesn't have to be anything fancy," says the crew member who mic'd me, but Baron shoots me a smirk over her head as someone mics him back up.

Then the pianist starts playing, and within a second, we're not Baron and Millie anymore—we're Sky and Sophie, playful and cheeky, darting up and down the stage like a game of cat and mouse. It's Baron's verse first, and he sets the tone, circling me on the stage and then taking a quick run to slide on his knees at me for "And all I've learned has overturned, I beg of you . . ."

I don't miss a beat, extending my boot out and pretending to push him back. He bends to my imaginary force just in time for me to flip my hair and walk away for the beginning of the chorus, and by then we're on such a roll that I don't feel like I'm playing a character at all. I've never worked in a theater with such a pure sound, or with a scene partner so experienced and quick on their feet. I'm just in it, fully in it, the way I don't usually get to be until we're so close to the show that it's more of a relief than anything else.

It's like if you ate oatmeal for breakfast your whole life, and then someone gave you your first egg-and-cheese bagel. Like that moment you get off the Q train in Coney Island after being surrounded by buildings for months and are gobsmacked by the open space of the water. It's understanding that the things I've been doing are *good*, but there's a whole other world out there with the potential to be *great*.

We finish the song facing each other in the middle of the stage. The piano fades out, and there's no applause, no fanfare—it's just a tech rehearsal—but I don't need any. Because Baron Le-vait grins at me, raises his hand for a high five, and says, "Damn, kid. You're about to take this scene by storm."

I have zero memory of how I got off the stage, if I walked or I floated or got shoved by a PA. I'm still living in the haze of it, like someone blew dream dust into my eyes and now the real world is something that doesn't apply to me anymore. The first moment I blink myself back into it is when I catch Oliver's eyes and see something in them that almost stops me in place.

It's not admiration or surprise or anything you hope for when you get off a stage. But it's something better than that. It's familiarity. Amusement, even. Like it's nothing he didn't already expect.

"Holy *shit*," I whisper. My skin is tingling. "I can't believe I just did that."

Oliver lets out a laugh. "*I* can."

I'm rushing up to him mostly because my whole body is flooded with adrenaline, but then he takes a few steps forward to meet me and for a fleeting second I almost think I'm going to hug him. Then a crew member walks in between us and we both come to an awkward stop, me beaming like I swallowed the sun, Oliver smiling a quiet smile.

"I just wish . . ."

*My dad had seen*, I almost say. I don't need a video to remember that feeling, but I wish I had one to send him. I glance at my phone, thinking to text him at least when I get a chance, and notice two missed calls from a number I don't recognize.

Then Oliver's phone buzzes in his hand. "Georgie says to take lunch."

"Oh." I'm suddenly so hungry I could have taken one of those sheet cakes we delivered to the face. "Wanna go to Big League Burger?"

Oliver tilts his head at me and I almost laugh it off and pretend it was a joke. But then he shrugs. "Yeah, all right."

A few minutes later we're both sitting at the window of a BLB, me switching between grilled cheese and a mountain of fries and Oliver opting for a cheeseburger and a side salad. We could make small talk, I guess, but that seems too boring after the kind of day we've already had. So instead I do what Oliver and I do best: cut straight to the chase.

"So why are you so scared of the spotlight?"

Oliver scoffs. "I'm not *scared*."

He says it more dismissively than defensively, so I decide to believe him.

"Then what? I mean, you're fine with big crowds of people and you're hot."

Oliver nearly chokes on a piece of lettuce.

"What?"

He keeps his face neutral, but I don't miss the pointed blink. "You just called me hot."

I scowl. "It's an objective fact. So what is it?"

He clears his throat, still recovering. "I'm just . . . I don't like singing, and I'm a bad actor," he explains. "I never saw the point in doing stuff I'm bad at."

I glance at our reflections in the window so I don't get caught staring directly at him. It's weird, having something in common with Oliver. But I guess that's one thing we always will—we both hold ourselves to a high standard and won't settle for anything less.

"How does a person not 'like' singing?" I scrunch my nose. "That's like . . . saying you don't like eating, or breathing."

He snorts. "To you, maybe."

"Plus you've got brothers in a band," I say, switching over to the second half of my grilled cheese. "How does that add up?"

Oliver groans. "I knew you weren't going to let that go."

"Obviously not. And if you don't just tell me their name, I

can text my friend Teddy right now and he'll probably find it in less than thirty seconds."

"Then why haven't you?"

I pivot on my chair to face him. "Because then I wouldn't have the pleasure of annoying the hell out of you."

"Ha ha," Oliver deadpans. But I can tell I've worn him down when he braces himself and says quietly, "They're called the Four Suns."

"Like sons in a family, or suns in the sky?"

A bit of the tension eases from Oliver's jaw. "Kind of both," he answers, pleased that I asked. "Our youngest brother wrote something for a school assignment that our mom wanted a daughter, but got 'four suns.' My parents got a kick out of it and the joke always kind of stuck. Anyway, it beats Power Yangers, which for some ungodly reason was on the table."

I let out a snort. "Yeah. Bullet dodged." Our eyes meet, both smirking. "But the Four Suns—I like it."

His eyes linger on mine for a moment before we both look down at our meals. "I'll let them know it's Millie-approved."

I take another big bite of fries, and then, because I inherited my eating habits from Heather, say, "Three brothers. No wonder you thrive in chaos. Where are you in the lineup, anyway?"

Oliver waits to swallow before he responds, since he is not a monster. "Third. First Hunter, then David, then me, then Elliot."

I rib him. "Nice of them to include you in the 'four' part of the band name, even if you have stage fright."

"I don't have . . ." Oliver waves me off. "I'm still pretty involved."

"You play the triangle?"

Oliver's fork hovers over his bowl. "I'm their manager. At least, for now."

"What, too busy being in charge of our whole theater

department and the road safety club?" Which, let it be known, Oliver spearheaded and would probably be the lone member of, if the underclassmen girls weren't determined to find excuses to talk to him.

"No, it's not that. It's that . . . they're good." He doesn't just turn to me this time, but turns his whole body on the chair, like he really wants me to understand. "They only started this about a year ago, but they're really starting to get some buzz around the city, and they're putting together a demo. They're getting approached by other people now."

"Oh. Shit." I tread carefully—an unfamiliar feeling, since usually the *goal* is to piss Oliver off. "And you . . . don't want that for them?"

Oliver frowns. "I mean—I want them to succeed. But I don't agree with these other managers' visions for them. They want to package them a certain way, craft this whole bogus narrative— like, Hunter as the silent, mysterious one and David as some kind of punk rebel kid and Elliot as a regurgitated Disney Channel wannabe, and I think they should just stick to what they already are."

I put my elbow on the table and prop my head on my hand. It's fun watching Oliver get worked up, even if I'm not the one doing it. "What's that?"

"Just . . . themselves." He picks at the edge of his bowl, making a tiny tear in it. "And not playing characters, like the Chinese Jonas Brothers."

"So what is their 'thing,' then?"

Oliver leans back in his chair, a small smile playing at his lips. "Honestly? They're all dweebs."

"Your brothers? Dweebs?"

Oliver gives me a familiar eye roll. "But I think that's the whole point. People like them. They're awkward and funny and real. And Hunter agrees with me, but the others I think are just so excited they're getting noticed that they're more focused on the short term of like, getting signed and getting more exposure than the long term of what the band would actually have to look like if they don't keep the original concept."

I almost don't want to ask it. I already know what the answer is and already know it's going to make me feel like an asshole. "Is that what you want this internship so bad?" I ask anyway. "So you can manage them?"

"Well, that, yeah." He's still looking out the window, sitting completely still. "I just . . . I want to keep us together. Things are already so weird, with the divorce. We get shuffled back and forth every other weekend. But we're always together. And I just want to keep it that way."

When he looks back at me there's something uncertain in his expression, and I realize there must be something uncertain in mine, too. We've never talked like this. And it's not that either of us minds it—it's just that there isn't a regular rhythm to follow anymore.

"That makes sense," I say, picking the beat up for us both. "But there's still one thing I don't get. Everyone else in your family's in a band, but you're the only one into theater?"

Oliver reaches over and helps himself to one of my fries, dipping it in the vat of ketchup by his burger. "Not the only one. My mom's always been into it."

I perk up in my chair. I've always liked Oliver's mom—at least peripherally. She always brings candy for us to eat at intermission and takes sneaky videos of our performances with her phone that are actually decent, unlike the ones my dad takes with half his thumb in the frame. But that's about as much as I know of her, since it's hard to get to know someone when you're otherwise occupied shooting the occasional death glare at their son.

"Does she do theater at all?"

"Used to. She took it as a minor in college and did it semiprofessionally—like, even after we were born. She was always blasting soundtracks in the house, especially right before her agent would send her out on something."

I feel a reluctant pang, wondering what that would have been like: listening to musical soundtracks with your mom. It's not a pang that I'm used to having, but I guess I'm not used to having possible faces to put to a mom, either.

"That must have been fun," I say quickly, cutting my brain off before it can go there.

"It was," says Oliver. "Even if rehearsing sides with six-year-old me may have been, uh, less than helpful to her process."

There must be something in the ketchup, because I can't remember Oliver ever being this willing to tell me things about his life. "Did you really?"

Oliver's trying not to smile, looking away from me like he's afraid he's going to catch mine. But a smile sneaks up on him anyway, and when he looks back and realizes I am very much expecting to hear more, he leans back with an accommodating sigh.

"I could read faster than David and was apparently insufferable about it. Somewhere in the Yang family blackmail vault is a video of me shouting half the lyrics to 'Love Song' to prep for some off-Broadway audition for *Pippin*." He raises his eyebrows at me. "She got the part. I didn't."

"Aw. You would have been a cute little existentially fraught Pippin." I avenge my stolen fry by snagging a crouton from the top of his salad. "I wonder why she stopped."

"Yeah. I wondered for a while, too."

He stares down at what's left of his burger, quiet for a moment, like he's followed that *Pippin* memory further down than he wanted to go. I brace myself for him to clear his throat and change the subject, for us to pick up our regularly scheduled snark-and-forth, but instead he frowns.

"I mean, mostly it was because other things got in the way. She's big on the choir scene, and she had all four of us, and at some point the band started taking a front seat. But I think part of it was just the industry in general." He presses his fork into his bowl, making little dents in the paper lining. "Sometimes she was frustrated because a few of the bigger casting directors weren't considering her for roles that weren't some tokenized Asian thing."

"Wait, seriously?" I ask. We've had classes in musical theater history at Cornelia that have touched on some of the racism of early Broadway shows and issues with casting that went on for years after that, but it was always something I assumed was just that—history. Something we learned about so it wouldn't happen anymore. Especially not by now.

Oliver shrugs. "She'd get called back for stuff, but not the parts she went out for. People in the industry are always saying it's super inclusive, but when it comes down to it, it's just not there yet."

I think of my list of dream roles, the rotation I've kept in my head for so many years that going through it every night is basically my version of counting sheep. The question was always whether or not I was talented enough to do it. I've never had to wonder whether or not there were other factors that might get in my way.

"That's so messed up."

Oliver nods. "Yeah. I mean, Broadway's come a long way. But parts of it really need to catch up still." He stares out the window at the street like the conversation has reached its natural end, but then he pulls in another breath. Like he's already said this much to me without planning to, so he feels like he can tell me the rest. "And I know stuff like that could happen to my brothers, too. I think that's why my mom's always been on board with me trying to manage them. I think maybe that's why she told me about all that in the first place, because I don't know if she ever told them."

I don't doubt that's part of the reason, but I think it might be more than that. Oliver's always had this way about him—he's easy to talk to, easy to trust. It's why Mrs. Cooke basically told him every secret of the inner workings of the arts department before sophomore graduation, why all the freshmen come crying to him when there's a problem. He doesn't just tell people how to fix problems. He makes them his problems, too.

I guess Oliver and I have been too busy being each *other's* problems for me to really appreciate that. But seeing he's the same way with his family doesn't surprise me one bit.

"What's your mom doing now?" I ask.

Oliver blinks, pulling himself out of a thought. "Actually, she got so busy with the Midtown Chorus that it just kind of took over."

I shove my tray to the side, leaning in so fast that anyone who didn't know me so well would flinch. "Your mom's in the Midtown Chorus?"

I'm not big into choir stuff, but the Midtown Chorus is legendary. They have a three-month season in the city every year with performances every weekend, but scalpers descend on the ticket sales so fast I've never been able to so much as hit "Add to cart." Their arrangements are so tight and their soloists so breathtaking that it gives you chills to listen, and that's *without* all the ethereal lighting and stage smoke I hear go into their shows.

"Wait," I realize. "Is your mom on my *Spotify*?"

Oliver can't even pretend to be exasperated by my theatrics, biting down a proud smile. He pointedly pulls my tray back before my grilled cheese makes its acquaintance with the floor.

"Probably. She's one of the co-presidents now. And she loves it. It's a lot of international travel and performing in cool venues, so she always invited us to come backstage, and I just . . . it blew me away, everything it took to bring her shows to life. My brothers always wanted to sit in the front row with our dad, but I always liked watching from the wings."

I can hear an echo of that awe that was in his voice at Carnegie Hall, at Cornelia the first time. It's just that this time I don't only hear Oliver in it. I hear some of myself, too. In that way you can love something so much but never fully explain it no matter how hard you try.

"Huh. So that's your origin story," I muse, using his ketchup to dip another one of my fries. "Where this whole stage managing thing began."

Oliver's been staring out the window, so I'm not prepared when he turns and the full force of his passion is directed at me. He's looser, less guarded. A little less like Oliver the Adversary and a little more like the Oliver he was when we first met.

"I know people don't like the idea of all the work that goes on backstage because it kind of takes the magic away from it all. But I've always thought that was the best part," he says. "Getting to see the end result and knowing everything and everyone that went into making it happen."

Only after he finishes does it seem to occur to him that I might use this as ammo, the way we historically have with any information we've gleaned about each other's lives. He stiffens almost imperceptibly. But now I'm as caught up in what he's saying as he is—the rush of it all. The satisfaction of the lights coming up and seeing everything we've worked on for weeks come together in a few hours. We may be on opposite sides of the stage when it does, but looking at him right now, it's impossible to imagine that we aren't feeling the exact same magic. That we haven't been all along.

"Bet that's going to feel a whole lot better once you have a budget that isn't largely based on hawking cupcakes to parents during intermission," I say.

Oliver loosens up, letting out a laugh. "Yeah. Even just see-ing Carnegie Hall for a few minutes was pretty wild." He stares down the street in the direction we just came from. "My mom's gonna flip when I tell her about it tonight."

I shoot him a wry smile. "That must be nice," I say, swirling my drink with my straw. "I'm pretty sure my dad thought Car-negie Hall was an arcade before I brought him up to speed."

"Yeah." Oliver is still for a moment. Reflective. "I mean—I know your situation is different. Since your mom is . . ."

He lets the sentence trail off like he isn't sure how he's sup-posed to end it, or if he regrets bringing it up in the first place. To be honest, I'm a little surprised he did. We know a lot of things about each other by virtue of hearing about them from our ocean of mutual friends, but we've never actually talked about them before.

"Oh." I shake my head. "Well, uh—it's not a situation, really. I never knew her."

"I'm sorry," he says quietly.

"She didn't like, die or anything. She just sort of, uh. Pulled a Dumbledore and dropped me off at my dad's door and pretty much took off."

The joke is tired, because I've told it a thousand times now. I figured out at a young age that saying "my mom abandoned me at birth" will bring most conversations to an awkward, shrieking halt. But this greases the wheels on it a little bit. Makes people less uneasy and gives them a chance to laugh through the awk-wardness of it all.

But Oliver doesn't laugh. He doesn't even do the thing most people do, flashing one of those nervous, sympathetic smiles. He's just watching me, like he heard what I said and what I didn't say, too.

"I never knew that," he says after a bit. And by now I know him well enough to hear what he didn't say, too—that he's glad to know. That he understands it's more complicated than whatever it looks like on the surface.

"I mean—I've got my dad. And my aunt. We make a good team." I take another very large bite of my grilled cheese, so I can fill my mouth with cheddar instead of any unintentionally revealed secrets.

Oliver nods thoughtfully, a quiet acknowledgment that this particular topic has reached its end. After a moment he shakes his head, blinking himself out of some train of thought.

"So . . . why do you want the internship?"

I can't begin to explain why, but there's this moment when I suck in a breath that I think I'm going to use it to tell him the truth. And the jarring thing isn't that I might tell it—the jarring thing is that I think I might want to. Maybe it would even be a relief. I'm flying blind out here, but Oliver is nothing if not a boy with a plan. That, and he just trusted me with some piece of his history. It feels natural to trust him with mine.

The trouble isn't really whether I trust Oliver with it, though. The trouble is I'm not sure if I trust myself.

"The, uh—the industry experience, mostly," I say, staring down at the last remnants of my fries. "And the money. So I can use it for the precollege."

Oliver doesn't say anything for a moment, but I can feel him watching me. "I don't believe you."

The words aren't heated. More curious than anything. Enough that I look back over at him, curious myself.

"Why's that?"

He smiles that barely smile again. "You're a great actress, Millie, but a pretty bad liar."

"Ha!" I exclaim, seizing the words like candy out of a piñata. "You admit I'm a great actress."

Oliver rolls his eyes, leaning in. "It's an objective fact," he says teasingly.

The tips of my ears burn. I always thought getting a genuine compliment from Oliver was some kind of white whale, but now that I actually have one, it's like it doesn't know where to settle in me.

"Well," I mumble, "it wasn't always."

I'm not expecting Oliver to say anything. It *does* sound like compliment fishing, after all, which would be precisely on brand for me. But instead he takes a sip from his fountain drink.

"Look, I know you're sensitive about that whole . . . 'Little Jo' thing."

Neither of us has uttered those words one time in the past three years. I'm surprised he even remembers enough to say them.

"Am I?" I ask, my eyebrows flying up in warning.

He puts his hands up in mock defense. "I guess I'm just wondering why you never did anything after that. You're all talk at school, but have you ever actually gone out for anything in the city?"

"I did when I was a kid, but now I have to bide my time," I say defensively. "Wait until the smoke has fully cleared from the meme aftermath."

"Screw that," he says. "Embrace the meme."

"Embrace it?" I scoff. "How?"

"Get on TikTok." I'm expecting this to be a throwaway suggestion, but when I raise an eyebrow, Oliver doubles down. "You're not just a good singer, Millie—you're funny. And you've made enough bizarre costume changes in the last few years that I'm pretty sure your closet is bursting with clothes and props. You could do so much with everything you already have." He's on a roll now, so impassioned that he's not even looking at me but just past me, like he's seeing something all fall into place. "Like—that semester you dressed all emo? Or that other one you dressed like you were on the track team? Make them characters or something. Have them sing in their own styles. Make it a whole series or start the next *Ratatouille: The Musical*. It's open season."

It's weird—every time I was making all those "costume changes" I was counting on the fact that people were noticing them. They were a flashy distraction. A way of making my actual self invisible in plain sight.

But Oliver wasn't just noticing them. He was seeing past them, down to the person I was even before we met. And for some reason, it doesn't feel half as mortifying as it probably should.

"What?" he asks.

I realize I've been staring at him. I shake my head.

"Nothing," I say. "Just . . . you're gonna make a good manager, is all."

He looks back down at his burger wrapper, but not before I see the smile quirk on his face. "Tell that to my brothers."

"Sure. Right after I force them to fork over that *Pippin* video so I can AirDrop it to half the school."

Oliver groans, grabbing both of our baskets and trash. "You're the worst."

I hop off the chair, following him to the counter. "You love it."

Oliver sighs, which is the closest thing to a concession I'll ever get.

# CHAPTER TWELVE

The running list of things Teddy drags me along to find that weekend include and are not limited to: a piece of paper with a code on it to get free GeoPoints; a shiny piece of fool's gold; a keychain with a corgi's butt on it; and a heap of free kids' Clif Bars so large I had to physically drag Teddy away from them before he took more than five (GeoTeens is *here* for that sponsorship money).

By Sunday afternoon, our feet are aching, we are both slightly sunburned, and we are wrecking our dinner by eating Clif Bars on the High Line.

"I should go," I groan. I think we've gotten enough steps to break Heather's Fitbit. I'm so tired I could curl up under the gelato counter behind us and take a nap. "I've gotta get to Farrah's dance class."

"You know, I think my money's on her."

"Why's that?"

He whips out his phone, revealing not just that a LiveJournal app has the audacity to exist, but that he has fully downloaded it.

I gasp. "Teddy, *no.*"

"Teddy, *yes,*" he says, clicking it and pulling up my dad's page. "So there are pretty much no posts after the whole

Smirnoff Ice debacle, but what we *didn't* look at were posts from before. Like, posts from the summer."

I scoot over closer to him, squinting at the screen as he scrolls.

"There's really just a few. Like, some nerdy stuff, another one mooning over Beth, and one about how he and Steph got into a fight over whether they should watch a bootleg DVD of *Rent* or some horror movie about aliens called *Signs*."

"That all tracks," I say, my sigh implied.

"But he doesn't really mention Farrah. She's out of town most of the time, right?" says Teddy. "So like, of all the people to disappear off the face of the earth and surprise your dad with a kid . . . she's kind of in the best position for it."

I bite down on my lower lip, trying to remember everything we read in the initial posts. "I guess so. But . . ."

But so many things. But the way I feel like Steph and I understand the tug of our ambitions in a way that very few people do. But the way I talk to Beth so easily, like we've known each other for years. But the way Farrah could instantly cut down to the heart of my dancing woes before I could begin to articulate them myself.

"I dunno," I finish, at a loss.

But Teddy's already distracted from his phone, his eyes skimming the park. "Hmmm."

I straighten up, trying to follow his gaze. The GeoTeens staff who were overseeing the Clif Bar stash have long since left, so there's nothing but tourists and skyline. "What are you looking for?"

He turns to me, the phone forgotten. "It'd be weird to try to, like . . . geocache a fellow GeoTeen, right?"

I raise an eyebrow. "Isn't that just stalking?"

"Technically, no. Legally, probably." Teddy blows out a

breath, leaning back on the bench and forgetting that he is perilously tall until he almost seesaws himself right off of it. "I haven't seen ParticularlyGoodFinders on the message board for days."

"Ah. Right. Your GeoCrush."

Teddy's too distraught to remember to protest.

"I take it she hasn't been messaging you, either?" I ask.

"No," he says glumly, biting off the end of another Clif Bar with his back teeth. "Maybe I'm just a big GeoGeek."

"Aw, Teddy," I say, wrapping an arm around his shoulder. "You're just a regular geek."

He doesn't lean into me the way he usually does, all tense and gangly. "A regular geek with no friends."

"What am I, chopped liver?"

"You're chopped precollege," says Teddy miserably. "You'll go off to California and forget all about me."

"Theodore Rex Granger, please."

I'm expecting him to make some kind of *blech* noise the way he usually does when I use his actual name—only his grandparents call him Theodore, and he's scarred for life from the week they babysat him as a kid and refused to let him eat sugary cereal—but he doesn't say anything. When I turn to fully look at him, there's something wobbly in his expression, some line crossed between rambunctious dog and sad puppy.

"Teddy . . ."

My phone buzzes in my lap.

"It's Coop," says Teddy.

I move the phone toward my bag. "I can call him back."

Teddy plucks the phone from my hand. "You can't avoid him forever."

"I'll call him—"

"I hogged you the whole weekend. It's Coop's turn." Before I can get another word in, Teddy swipes the phone to answer the call. "Millie's phone, this is *Theodore* speaking."

I groan and extend my arm out for him to give it back.

"Ah, yes, I think she can squeeze you in between appointments. Here she is now!" he says to my dad before finally forking over the phone.

"You're a terrible assistant," I tell him.

Teddy salutes me. "Catch up with you after class?"

I hold the phone away so my dad doesn't hear me say, "If I haven't broken my legs and possibly Chloe's in the process, sure."

As Teddy bounces off I consider the phone for a second, watching the seconds tick by on the call. It's been almost a week since I last talked to my dad. I've never gone that long without talking to him in my life.

"Hey, Mil-a-mille."

I immediately feel my chin start to quiver. It's his nickname for me, the one that he only ever uses when it's just me and him and Heather—a play on my actual first name, Camille, buried so deep in the History of Millie that I'm pretty sure even Teddy's forgotten.

It makes me feel like a little kid again. The thoughts that have been swirling like a tornado in my brain over the last week are settling, and now I'm standing in the eye at the loudest thought in the center of it all. I really, really miss my dad.

If it were a normal Sunday, we'd be making pasta right now. It's Heather's only night off from the club, so she makes the sauce, and I head over to Chelsea Market for fresh bread, and Dad boils the water because he can't be trusted to do much else without daydreaming and accidentally setting the apartment on fire. Then he and Heather have red wine while I have cherry soda and we go around the table and talk about everything we did that week.

I clear my throat and blink hard. It's probably for the best he's gone right now. There's nothing I could tell him the truth about anyway.

"Hey, Dad," I say, my voice bright. "How's Chicago?"

"Uh—sunny?" There's a beat. "I think?"

I frown, pushing myself off the bench and grabbing my dance bag so I can start heading toward the train. "Are you holed up in your hotel room avoiding all of humanity again?"

"I'm on the phone with you, aren't I? You're still humanity."

Typical Cooper Price. Without me or Heather, he'd probably never leave our apartment for anything other than the occasional *Lord of the Rings* trivia night.

"Dad. Go outside! Go make some friends!"

"I went to the museum," he protests.

"Some friends living in *this* century."

"Touché. So? How's the internship going?"

"It's going," I say, narrowly dodging a group of kids on their skateboards as I walk down the stairs from the High Line to the street.

"Setting new standards for budding audition monitors everywhere?"

I wince. It's become clear over our texts this week that my dad thinks I'm interning with a casting agency, and I haven't exactly corrected him. I figured on the slight chance that he *has* kept tabs on Steph over the years, he might put two and two together and figure out I'm up to no good before I can get up to anything at all.

"Just, uh, doing my best," I say noncommittally. "But walking over to dance class now."

"Right! Heather mentioned you'd already had your first class."

"Did she mention I nearly grapevined into a group of dancers like a human wrecking ball?"

"She did say *something* about your habitual use of hyperbole, yes," says my dad with a laugh. "But you're powering through?"

"One poorly landed jeté at a time." I bite the inside of my cheek. "But yeah. I think it'll help get me up to speed. So—thanks for, uh . . ."

"'Course," says my dad. "And hey, it looks like the class will wrap up just in time for college auditions to start."

"Oh?"

"Yeah. I checked the admissions schedules for NYU and Pace and Marymount—you might want to start figuring out which weekends you want to do which, so we can space them out."

This is the closest Cooper Price will ever get to being a certified Stage Dad™, and only because he loves himself an organized itinerary. It would be sixteen kinds of precious if there weren't a rock plummeting in my stomach.

"Well, I mean . . . if I'm going to those auditions," I say carefully.

"I thought those were in your top five?"

"I mean, yeah, but—the precollege."

"Oh." My dad doesn't say anything for a moment, and I can practically see that bewildered Dad face he gets sometimes from all these miles away. "So you're . . ."

I stop walking and hover on the edge of the sidewalk, out of people's way. I press the phone a little closer to my ear.

"I mean, I thought we were leaving it open for now, right?" I don't want to fight with him. I'm not even particularly sure *how* to fight with him, considering the one time I tried we ended up having a blowout in the middle of the Milkshake Club. So I keep my voice even, try to stave off the Millie Mood. "Since we don't have to decide yet?"

I'm not used to long pauses in conversations with my dad. We don't have a ton in common, maybe, except that once we're in a conversation we're both *fully in it*. Sometimes Heather comes back from the Milkshake Club at two in the morning to me ranting about the sheet music not being available for a song I want in my audition book or my dad on an hour-deep wormhole about the historical accuracy of the movie *Tolkien* and she has to physically drag us to bed.

"But Millie . . . have you really thought about it?" my dad asks. "What it's really going to mean, moving out in two months and starting all over?"

What he's not appreciating here is that I've spent the better part of my young adolescence starting all over. I've hit reset on myself more often than a hairdryer. "What, you don't think I can do it?" I ask.

"I know you can. I just think . . ." He lets the sentence hang there and I can feel us both wincing in the aftermath of it. "Anyway."

It's the Cooper Price version of "Let's drop it," and for now, at least, I'm happy to. I'm not ready to go to bat with him on this. Not over the phone, and certainly not before I have someone else in my corner.

"I also just wanted to . . . I mean, the way we left things . . ."

And here's the conversation I dodged during our last phone call, sneaking up on me from behind.

"I know I haven't always been—entirely forthright about . . . things with your mother."

Even hearing him say the word *mother* feels foreign to me, like when you're in a dream and someone starts speaking gibberish. You somehow understand what it means, even if you have no context for it in real life.

"And I wanted to be clear that I—I wasn't doing it on purpose. It's just . . . I thought it was easier, I guess."

He's not wrong. It was easier. The less any of us talked about it, the smaller it was, until we spent my whole life with it tucked into a closet or swept under a rug. Not just the truth of what my mom did—but why she must have done it. It can only be because whatever she wanted out of life, it didn't include me.

"There are a lot of questions I really don't have the answers to, but when I get back, I'm ready to tell you what I can. If you want to."

"Uh . . . yeah. I mean—actually, I've gotta go, Dad, I'm hopping on the L train in a second."

"Oh—good. Good. Well—have fun tonight."

"I will." Another lie, but really, who's counting? "Love you."

"Love you too. I'll be home before you know it."

After we hang up I spend the entire train ride so preoccupied by the churning of guilt and self-pity that I almost forget to get off at the right stop. I'm slammed unceremoniously back into reality when I walk through the door to the studio and find Farrah in an animated conversation with Beth, and Chloe hovering behind her in a pair of athletic shorts and a *Fun Home* T-shirt.

"Millie! Hi!" Chloe squeaks, her eyes so wide she looks like a pair of headlights is coming at her. She rushes up and then hesitates when she's halfway to me, so I take charge and hold my arms out to hug her. She squeezes back with an earnestness that kind of reminds me of Teddy, then says, "I can't believe you go to Cornelia!"

"Well—*went* to." Maybe if I keep saying it I can manifest my dad letting me go to the precollege into existence.

"Yeah, but still!" says Chloe.

Farrah's eyes sweep over to us, and I realize that I didn't just fail to do her "homework assignment," but that I actively forgot it existed. She smiles at us and I have to force myself to smile back, feeling suddenly like there are spotlights coming at me from all sides—the side that wants to impress Farrah, that wants Beth to like me, that is supposed to be listening to whatever Chloe is saying to me right now.

Right. Shit.

I blink and backtrack. She asked me if I'm much of a dancer.

"Because I'm not," Chloe blurts. "I mean, I like to dance, but—"

"Then you're a dancer," says Farrah before I can answer. She puts a hand on my shoulder and squeezes it. "And so is everyone here."

She claps her hands again to get the class's attention, and Beth waves and mouths the words *thank you* at me before ducking out into the stairwell. I position myself in the back row to keep out of people's way, and Chloe follows me like a ponytailed duckling, watching me every bit as vigilantly as she's watching Farrah.

We get through the warm-up without incident, but then Farrah starts to teach us the first combo for "Waterloo"—a mess of hand gestures and thrusts that both Chloe and I trip during—and says a combination of words I dread more than most in the English language: "All right, let's switch rows so everyone gets a chance in front of the mirrors."

Translation: *Let's put the kids hiding in the back front and center so everyone can get a 360-degree view of just how awkward they are.*

I square my jaw and get ready for five minutes of humiliation, then notice I have lost one neon green scrunchie in my periphery. I turn back and see Chloe's still frozen in the back row.

"What's up?" I ask out of the corner of my mouth.

"Um. I'm just. Gonna stay back here." She fiddles with the bottom seam of her shirt so aggressively that it looks like her shoulders are caving in on themselves.

"Uh . . ."

"Make haste, my sunbeams!" Farrah claps.

Crap. Now Farrah's going to think I'm a delinquent on top of having the grace of a limp noodle.

"C'mon," I say, tilting my head.

Chloe's answer is so quiet I almost don't hear it. "I'm not good enough for this."

It's like she ripped the words right out of my brain. When I turn back to Chloe I see the same embarrassment crawling under my skin written all over her face, like I'm staring at a reflection of myself from two years ago.

I swallow it down. "Yeah, well, neither am I. We'll suck together."

Chloe shakes her head. "I don't believe that."

"Yeah? Well, seeing is believing, and you gotta come up front if you want the view," I say, hooking my arm through hers. I wait for her to take the first step, and when she does we scramble up to the front under Farrah's watchful eye.

If this were a movie, Chloe's faith in me would magically turn me into a *Footloose*-worthy dancer who doesn't miss a beat. But because this is real life, what happens instead is that I miss the first combo so prolifically that I almost end up careening straight into the mirror in my attempt to catch up.

Chloe hasn't moved and is watching me in said mirror like she's watching a car crash that's also about to slam into her. I meet her eyes and stick my tongue out. Chloe lets out an accidental snort.

"That's the spirit!" says Farrah. "Now let's break down the combo and go again."

"See?" I tell Chloe. "You're perfectly fine. And if you stick next to me, you'll look even better."

It's not quite Farrah's homework assignment for me, but maybe it's better. The more I focus on helping Chloe keep her cool the easier it is to forget I'm supposed to be losing mine. Soon enough we're released from the hell of the front row, but we stick close, goofing up half the moves and laughing at each other, catching each other's eyes in the mirror every now and then like we're in our own class separate from everyone else.

By the time class finishes, Chloe's right back to talking in that animated, mile-a-minute pace from her apartment the day Teddy and I met her, smiling so broadly and riffing off a dance move so enthusiastically that she knocks someone's sweater off the hangers at the front. I swipe it from the ground and hang it back up before she notices.

"That was so freaking fun," says Chloe, her cheeks rosy and her eyes bright. "I just gotta pee, and then I'll be ready to go."

"I'll be here," I say, gathering up my shoes to leave.

"Hey." Farrah's tone is so abrupt I'm worried we're about to get in trouble for being disruptive, but when I turn around she's got a sly smile on her face. "Great work today."

I can't help grinning back. "I didn't take anyone's eye out."

"And you nailed the last sequence, if you didn't notice," she says. "See what I mean? Sometimes you just gotta shake a few screws loose." She does a little shimmy to emphasize it, and I laugh and do one back. I open my mouth to say something else—I'm not even sure what—but then Chloe's back and showing me a musical theater meme on her phone, and we're off.

We stop at the doughnut place under the studio on the way out, because it seems like the potential-half-sisterly thing to do, and pick up extras for Heather and Beth. We're about to tuck into them on the L train when I notice three things in rapid succession: one, that this may be the most beautiful old-fashioned sour cream doughnut I've ever laid eyes on; two, that Chloe is approximately a foot from my face and looking very anxious; and three, that Farrah is *also* on this train, and just spotted us and started milling her way over.

"Are you and Teddy dating?" Chloe blurts.

I'm so stunned by the question that I laugh. "What? No. God, no. We're best friends."

Farrah sidles in next to us, and Chloe is so surprised to see her that she jumps and I have to grab the doughnut bag from her hands before it gets sacrificed to the L train floor.

"Fancy running into you two here," says Farrah.

"You live in Manhattan?" I ask. It'd be unlike Teddy not to know that.

"Nah, I'm just grabbing a late dinner with a friend." Farrah deftly pulls her hair into a messy bun without holding onto any of the subway poles, moving with what I'm guessing is years' worth of dancer's grace and MTA savvy. Then she looks at each of us in turn. "So. Who's Teddy?"

Farrah, I'm coming to understand, is a lithe mover, but one very blunt conversationalist. From the curve of her close-lipped smile, though, it's more than intentional.

"He's Millie's . . ." Chloe looks at me to fill in the blank.

"Friend," I emphasize.

There's a beat when Farrah seems to be taking the temperature of the conversation. "Well, don't rule it out," she says, mischief in her eyes. "Some of my best and messiest relationships were with friends."

I feel like I've just unintentionally hit a pressure point. "Messy?"

"Ugh. College," she says almost nostalgically.

Screw pressure points. I may have just hit a tectonic plate.

"What was messy about college?" I ask. "I mean . . ." I backtrack, trying to sound less like a journalist on a deadline, but even then I can't help myself. Farrah's the potential mom I know the least about, and any time I can get alone with her is in perilously short supply. "Messy in a good way?"

"Messy in all the ways." Her eyes flit to the side, and the words are just cryptic enough that I'm wondering if I could have been one of those ways. "But maybe that's a 'me' problem. I'm usually friends with someone before I'm with them, so I just sort of ended up . . . well. For better or for worse, being with friends," she says, when she realizes she's veering into a PG-13 zone. To be fair, Chloe looks about twelve.

But Farrah's not looking at Chloe. She's looking at me.

"Well, believe me, Teddy and I could never date," I say. "It's not even that we're friends. We're like siblings."

"Fair enough," says Farrah.

"So he's not dating . . . anyone?" Chloe persists.

I snort. "His parents' coffee machine, maybe."

"Sounds like someone has a crush," says Farrah.

I'm about to laugh again, but then I look over and see that Chloe has clapped her mouth shut and gone redder than a tomato.

"On *Teddy*?" I exclaim.

Okay, it's not that Teddy isn't crush-worthy. He's smart and he's funny and when he's not stealing the last sleeve of Ritz crackers out of your apartment and pretending it was a ghost, I'm sure he'd be considered a catch. But as far as I know, Chloe's only met Teddy once.

"Is that stupid?" Chloe asks, her voice wobbly. "I mean, I know he's a year older, and way cooler than I am, but—"

"I'm gonna stop you right there, because Teddy's idea of 'cool' is talking like a pirate whenever he gets a good cache on that GeoTeens app."

"But what do I *do*?" says Chloe miserably.

Farrah answers before I can get past the idea that my Polly Pocket–size maybe half sister wants to make out with my best friend—yet another thought I never anticipated having before this summer began.

"Well, how well do you even know Teddy?" Farrah asks.

"Not super well," Chloe admits. "And I guess I could text him, but I just . . . get nervous."

"Try being friends with him first. See how that goes," says

Farrah encouragingly. The train rolls to a stop at Union Square. "I gotta bounce. See you later this week, my stars!"

She flits out of the subway, leaving me on the train deciding how to play this. I wish I could say something to Teddy first, but whipping out my phone and texting him in front of Chloe would be about as subtle as yelling at him from across a crowded street.

"It's dumb," says Chloe, blowing it off before I can get a chance to think. "Sorry. I didn't mean to . . ."

I weigh my options, but with Chloe looking at me with those sad puppy eyes so weirdly reminiscent of Teddy's, I don't really have any.

"It's not dumb," I assure her. "It's . . . well, maybe Farrah's right. Just—hang out with us. We're coming to Broadway Bugs again. And Teddy's hosting some kind of GeoTeens shindig at his place next week. You can be my plus-one."

"Yeah?"

"For sure," I say. I figure this can go one of two ways: it doesn't work out and Teddy and Chloe become friends, or it *does* work out and I end up third-wheeling my pseudo-brother and long-lost half sister for the rest of my life. But at least with the two of them, I'm relatively certain it wouldn't end badly. They're both such cinnamon rolls that I can't even imagine them in a pillow fight that didn't start and end with profuse apologies.

"Thanks, Millie. You're the coolest."

Chloe beams at me, and I feel this unexpected ache blooming in my chest. The idea that I might have had a lifetime of "the coolest"—of being the kind of big sister who took Chloe out for doughnuts and listened to her bubble over about crushes and tried to make the scary things seem less scary.

But I guess there was no world where that was going to happen, whether Beth really is my mom or not. It was always going to be just me.

We've just reached our stop when my phone buzzes in my pocket. A text from Steph that she must have sent to me and Oliver while I was in the tunnel. How did the "stand-in" gig go? I heard there was a . . . mixup, she wrote, with a winky face.

Ha, Oliver wrote back. I take it that was on you?

I might have fed some incorrect info to the tech team about Miss Millie to see if we could get her a little action.

I grin like I've just gotten a Tony nomination. I wish she'd still been in the office so she could see the look on my face when I got back that day, but Oliver and I ended up working so late taking pictures of Georgie's client at the rally that she was out by the time we came back. Well, mostly working. I guess we didn't need to be out as long as we were, but time just got away from us.

Oliver responds again before I can. Well, she rocked it. But her actual Carnegie debut better include this.

He's attached a GIF of the dancers in *Mamma Mia* hopping around in their giant flippers on the dock. I laugh out loud, the sound of it getting swallowed up by the station.

"So how do *you* talk to your crushes?" Chloe asks, hot on my heels.

"Pfft." I wave a dismissive hand, flipping my hair over my shoulder. "*That* I can't help you with. I can confidently say I've never had the time."

But even then, my laugh at Oliver's text lingers in the back of my throat the rest of the way home—and for the first time in the history of ever, I fall asleep looking forward to seeing him the next day.

# CHAPTER THIRTEEN

Before bed last night I texted Steph back profusely thanking her. She wrote back with a wink and said, I know you didn't take this internship to perform, but just a reminder from one actress to another—take all the chances you get! You never know where they'll lead.

I'm still staring at the text and trying to stop myself from screenshotting it for posterity the next morning when my phone rings.

"Is this Millie Price?"

"Sure is," I say, admiring my reflection in a coffee shop window. My summer outfits have taken on a degree of lawlessness, now that I'm not seeing my classmates every day. Instead of making them fit a theme, it's been a little of this and a little of that—Heather's boots, a cute sleeveless black dress that survived the goth phase, a scrunchie from the nineties grunge phase. I'll have to figure out what the next one is before my first semester kicks off, but I don't mind the hodgepodge for now. "What's up?"

"This is Becca from the New York branch of the Madison admissions office."

"Oh—hi." I pull the phone away from my face. It's eight forty-five on a Monday morning. "The deadline for the deposit isn't for another two weeks, right?"

"Well, yes. For people who have confirmed their acceptance. I was calling because it seems as though you tried to reverse your decision to decline acceptance."

When we were little kids Teddy and I did the ice bucket challenge in the middle of Washington Square Park with enough ice to reasonably concuss someone. Even that wasn't half as jarring as this. I stop dead on the sidewalk.

"Decision to what?"

"I have here in my records that you declined your acceptance last week when you were contacted about the deposit."

"I wasn't contacted."

"Well, nobody picked up at your primary number, so we called the secondary one on your form."

Shit. *Shit.* I made my cell phone the primary number, but I put my dad's down as an emergency contact.

"In any case, we received a message last night asking us to reverse the decision . . . and I'm afraid the circumstance is a little unusual."

About as unusual as an otherwise healthy sixteen-year-old girl forgetting how to breathe in the middle of a busy sidewalk, and yet that's happening, too.

"I didn't—I'm not—I'm coming," I blurt.

"Be that as it may, I'm worried someone has already been in touch with whoever's next on the waitlist."

This conversation is veering so quickly into disaster territory that my brain can't keep up.

"But they might not have been?" I ask, swallowing down the molten panic threatening to rise all the way up my throat along with the Eggo waffles I ate for breakfast.

"I need to check with the secretary when she gets in tomorrow. I just wanted to verify with you first, before I pursued the matter any further."

My dad must have really thought I wasn't going to go. He

must have just said no without asking me and then tried to fix it before I found out.

I don't know what feels worse: the fact that I might have completely lost this opportunity I worked so hard for, or that my dad really doesn't know me well enough to understand how much it means to me.

"Well, I—I'm coming." I blink and already there are big thick tears streaming down my face, like the few drops of rain that tap the ground before the sky erupts. "Can you let me know as soon as you can?"

"Of course. We'll be in touch."

It's not a Millie Mood. It's a full-on Millie Meltdown. I'm crying on the street like a walking cliché, except it's not the understated, dainty "girl in a rom-com" kind of sniffle. It's hiccup-y, snot-nosed, red-faced crying, the kind where you forget where you are or that you did a perfect cat-eye this morning or that you are standing smack-dab in the middle of the most crowded and least empathetic city on earth.

Someone grabs my shoulder so firmly that if my wits were about me I'd assume I was about to get murdered. What happens is much worse: I look up and through the stream of tears, make out Georgie Check.

"Off the street," she says, steering me into the building.

"I—I can't just—"

I'm trying to tell her I need to get a handle on myself first, but that's obviously not going to happen anytime in this century. She's not listening to me anyway, continuing to nudge me forward past lobby security and into a miraculously open elevator. I try to muffle my crying but then it comes out in these big gulping noises that make me feel like a beached sea creature.

It's fine. It's fine. Actually, this makes things easier. If there's no precollege there's no reason to have this internship, and this spares me the trouble of figuring out how to tell Georgie and Steph that I'm out. Georgie will fire me and I'll just slink away, pretend all of this never happened, give up this ridiculous stupid search for my mom and—

"Are you okay?"

Somehow we are in Georgie's office, and I'm sitting in her chair.

The words are clipped enough that I can tell she wants to know if something colossally terrible has happened, like I've witnessed a crime or gotten kicked out of my apartment, which would maybe be reasonable circumstances to justify this brand of tears. So I nod, because I am technically physically okay, even if I *emotionally* want to crawl under Georgie's desk and use her carpet as a Kleenex.

"Here." It's my Check List clipboard, but Georgie moves today's list under several blank pages before handing it to me. "Just write it down."

"Write what down?"

"Whatever it is that did . . . *this* to you," she says, gesturing at the general space I am occupying. When I continue to stare at her like she's just asked me to play the piano accompaniment in a Sondheim number, she taps a firm finger on the clipboard. "Writing will help."

"B-but my Check List."

She sighs. Then she takes the clipboard and writes at the top of it, *Write until you stop crying.*

"There," she says, setting it back down in front of me.

It is a true testament to the absurdity of this that I have to bite my cheek so I won't laugh. When I do open my mouth, all that comes out is a wet "Okay?"

Maybe Georgie was going to say something else, but my eyes cut to the office door.

"Steph's out today," she says before I can ask.

The smallest, most microscopic piece of mercy the universe has offered me in the past few minutes, but I'll take it.

"You won't need to report to her when your tasks are done. Text me instead," says Georgie. "I'm in client meetings most of the day."

"Okay," I say again, because apparently it's the only word I know how to say.

Georgie clears her throat and waits until I look up at her. Her brow is as steely as ever, but there's something soft in her eyes. Something that examines me, only this time not to size me up. Maybe to understand.

"You will not be embarrassed about this when it's over. It will be business as usual. No need to explain." She pauses. "Unless you want to."

I've never heard a human command another human not to be embarrassed before, but with an iron will like Georgie's, I'm not entirely convinced it won't work. I nod at her, and she nods back, first at me and then at the clipboard.

"Writing will help," she says again.

Then Georgie takes Oliver's Check List from her desk and sweeps out of her office, closing the door behind her.

The office is so quiet that I might have just imagined the whole thing.

I stare down at the empty pages attached to the clipboard, or at least what I can see of it through my steady stream of tears. *Write until you stop crying.* Trouble is, knowing me, that could be five minutes or five hours. Once I'm in the grips of a Millie Mood, it's like the brakes get cut loose in a speeding car. I don't get to stop on my own. Something else does it for me.

I pick up the pen and for a moment my hand just hovers there. I'm not really a writer. My idea of catharsis is singing in the shower or going full Éponine and humming to myself walking along the Hudson.

Dream Role #3. Yet another dream that went from being a thousand miles away to a million in ten minutes flat. My eyes sting and my vision blurs, then all at once, I'm not just writing—I'm tearing into the paper, the words pouring out of me like lava. It starts with my dad and the precollege, but it doesn't stop there. It's everything. It's the years I've spent trying to recover from "Little Jo." It's the exhaustion of keeping up with all the different versions of myself I've been since. It's the bajillion times I've watched my reflection perform in a mirror and wondered if the girl staring back at me was good enough. It's the fear that maybe I never will be.

It's the rare but punctuating moments in my life that despite everything—despite a dad who loves me enough for two people, and an aunt who taught me everything I know, and a happy life in a nice apartment in the greatest city in the world—I still lie awake at night and wonder, *What was wrong with me? Why would my mom decide to have me and then walk away?*

I put the pen down. I'm not crying anymore.

I pull the pages out and read them back to myself, my heart finally slowing in my chest. Then I fold the pages in half, hold them to my chest for a moment, and take a breath.

It's all still there, heavy as ever. But it feels like it's a little easier to lift now.

After I put the pages in the trash I get to work on my Check List, picking up a rare piece of sheet music from a library at Pace for a client's audition, grabbing Georgie's dry cleaning, picking up paper towels for the office. Usually the Check Lists feel like a pain, something I have to race through to beat Oliver, but today there's something soothing about it. Something to tell me where to go and what to do. Simple. Easy. Distracting.

"If you're . . . behind at all, I don't mind taking something from your Check List."

I frown, straightening up from where I was stashing the paper towels under the sink. I didn't hear Oliver come in.

"I'm . . ." *Not behind*, I'm going to say. But then I meet his gaze. See the caution in it. The concern. And it becomes abundantly, painfully clear that he witnessed some of the shit show from this morning.

"I mean, not for credit," he says quickly. "It's just—I'm in good shape on my own. It'd be easy for me to grab something."

I walk over to him, searching his face. He shifts his weight between his feet, wary, but lets me come right up to him, until I'm close enough that he has no choice but to search my face too.

His reminds me of a few months ago, when we were opening *Jesus Christ Superstar* and one of the freshman girls in the ensemble burst into tears just before curtain, too scared to go on. How Oliver lowered the backstage mic strapped to his ear and pulled her aside, his entire demeanor changing at the drop of a hat. How he probably had a hundred thousand things to be doing and a dozen people shouting in his ear, but for those two or three crucial minutes, all that mattered to him was making sure a stranger was going to be okay.

I reach out and put a hand on his shoulder. "You're a good guy."

I'm expecting him to shrug me off like he usually does, but we both go very still. "Sometimes," he says, his voice low.

I smile, and it feels different. Not just because it's the first time I've smiled all day. But because Oliver's smiling back at me.

"Thanks," I say, pulling my arm away. "I'm good, actually, but—thanks."

Oliver clears his throat. "Well, if you . . . let me know if you change your mind."

When Georgie comes to collect our Check Lists at the end

of the day, she doesn't say anything about the meltdown. She just nods and says, "I'll see you tomorrow," which is about as close to friendly conversation as either of us have gotten with her. Oliver waits for me at the elevator, and for the first time we leave the building together on purpose, walking down the street until we have to split off to get home.

"This morning," he says suddenly, just before the light changes for me to cross. "Is everything . . . I mean, are you . . ."

I shrug, trying to play it off. The truth is I can still feel the weight of what happened this morning sinking like a stone, but it's more than just the precollege now. It's too many things to count. It's Steph and Beth and Farrah and all the in-betweens and uncertainties, all the little lines I've crossed and the ones I'm still trying to define.

"You know me. Just being a drama queen."

I can tell he doesn't believe me, but he doesn't press the point either. Instead he says, "Hey. If I'm not allowed to call you that, you're not, either."

I let out an unexpected laugh. "Fair enough."

The light starts counting down for me to cross, so we wave goodbye. But instead of going home, I head to the Milkshake Club, where they're just setting up for the night. I make myself a shake and then make a second one with banana, sea salt caramel, and chocolate fudge sauce, which I plant in front of Carly at the desk where she keeps her calendar of bookings.

She takes it from me. "What's this for?"

"I want to show you an act we should try out."

Carly narrows her eyes at me from under her blunt, edgy bangs. "For the last time, Millie, I can't pull in the Broadway cast of *Six*."

"We'll revisit that later," I say cheekily. I pull out my phone and text her a link. "I think they'd be a good opener, or fun to test on a weekday. Just have a peek."

Carly sighs, watching her phone screen light up. "Only because you remembered my rainbow sprinkles," she says, taking a sip of her milkshake.

The call comes in a few minutes later—Madison hasn't contacted anyone on the waitlist, so they're holding my spot at the precollege. The relief hits me so hard that I sit on the stairwell in our apartment building just before our floor, waiting to reach some kind of equilibrium again. Waiting for it to fill up the empty this morning left behind.

A full minute passes, and it doesn't change anything. My dad's still going to say no, and I'm still working on borrowed time. But whatever this empty feeling is suddenly feels so much deeper than that, deep enough not to follow it down.

# CHAPTER FOURTEEN

"So . . . Coop's dead to us," says Teddy, power walking through the East Village later that night, the GeoTeens app open in his hand.

On the long list of "Moments Teddy Inconveniently Forgets He Is Tall," attempting to keep up with him on a city street might be in the top five. "Coop's definitely testing me."

"But he did try to reverse it."

"Yeah, but . . ." I purse my lips, which is a mistake, because I am half jogging to stay on his tail and need all the air I can get. "You didn't hear him on the phone. I really don't think he's going to cave on this. And I've only got two weeks to get him on my side."

"So maybe it's time to—y'know. Get someone else on your side. Figure out which one of them is your mom."

"I don't know yet," I grumble.

Then Teddy says out loud the very words I've spent the last week trying to avoid. "You could just ask."

It's true. There are so many moments I could have ripped the Band-Aid off all this. I could have used my real last name and watched to see if they'd react. I could have filed something on the internet to get a copy of my birth certificate. I could have just said to any one of these women, point-blank, *I'm looking for my mom, did you happen to drop a baby with a Cancer sun sign and a Leo moon off at the doorstep of a deeply nerdy college junior in the early 2000s?*

"I just . . ." I pick up the pace and it's less like I'm trying to keep up with Teddy and more like I'm trying to outpace my own thoughts. "I thought I'd just *know*, you know? And it's weird that I don't."

"Well, let's recap." He glances at his phone and takes a sharp turn onto Twelfth Street, so fast my hair flies behind me like a whip when I follow. "All three of them knew your dad."

"Yeah. And all three of them are *arguably* kind of like me. Like—Steph's an actress and even went to school for it, and is also, like. You know. Vain like I am. But in a cool, harmless way."

"Tell that to the tube of your lipstick that exploded in my backpack when you stashed it in there last summer."

"And Farrah—yeah, she can actually *dance* and I can't, but I feel like we share the same bluntness, and her hair is the exact color of strawberry blond that mine would be if I didn't dye it. And Beth *loves* musical theater, and she was a super moody teen, and she has a kid who is just as bad at dancing and weirdly passionate about things as I am—"

"Hey, how did the dance class with Chloe go, anyway?"

"Oh!" It's a good thing Teddy is navigating, because I'm thinking out loud so fast he could lead me straight into a subway tunnel and I'd mosey on in. "Chloe has a crush on you."

Teddy looks at me bewilderedly. "On me?"

"Yeah, you."

"Huh."

"Is that a bad 'huh' or a good 'huh'?"

"That's a 'why would someone have a crush on *me*' huh."

Teddy's concerning level of self-esteem aside, this is at least a somewhat promising reaction.

"Like, ParticularlyGoodFinders? *Completely* ignoring me now," Teddy laments. "Hasn't answered any of my messages. All I can think is she figured out who I was at one of the meetups and now wants nothing to do with me."

"First of all, that's ludicrous. You and I are the best-looking GeoTeens at those meetups and that's a fact."

Teddy sighs.

"And maybe . . ."

He waves a hand at me. "We're getting sidetracked. The mom thing. You've hung out with them all at least once, and you said earlier all of them at some point seemed to reference something weird about college, and even with that you *still* don't have any idea?"

I bookmark my Teddy-shaped pep talk in my brain for after we find the geocache, when he'll actually absorb it. "No," I admit. "But like, in my defense—none of them have recognized me, either."

"Does that bother you?"

I scrunch my nose. "I don't know." Teddy's slowed down enough for me to think straight, which prompts me to say something I haven't really considered yet. "I guess I'm . . . relieved, a little. That they didn't recognize me right away. I used to worry that whoever she was, she saw that stupid 'Little Jo' video."

Teddy gives me a knowing look. "Would that be so bad?"

Now that I've said it out loud—this private, embarrassing thought I've kept to myself for so long—I'm not so sure. Somewhere along the way I got so focused on trying to settle on some version of myself that I actually liked that I lost sight of the reason why I was doing it in the first place. If I was doing it to lose something or find it. Parts of me that aren't a part of Cooper, or

Heather, or anyone I know. Things that maybe could only have been a part of *her*.

I blink the thought away. "I want her to see me as my best self, and that wasn't it." I say it firmly, pushing past it, but the next part still comes out unbidden. "I guess if I'm being honest, maybe I'm upset none of them have recognized me after getting to know me. Like, as Millie. Their kid."

The worst part is I'm not even sure where to aim the frustration—at them? At myself? Instead it's just kind of loose and shapeless in me, weighing me down but not giving me any sense of where to go.

"Well, maybe it's time to just . . . pick one. And ask."

I bite the inside of my cheek. "I want to get to know them, though. So I can be sure. Like, what if I'm wrong?"

Teddy shrugs. "Then you don't have to see any of them again after this summer. What does it matter?"

Oof. It feels like the words skip my ears and go straight for my solar plexus.

"Maybe I . . . do want to see them again."

"All of them?"

"Is that weird?"

Teddy stops short in the street. We're at least two blocks from the geocache and we're on a timer, so I know when he looks me in the eye and commits to the stopping, he means business.

"No, I don't think that's weird. But now the rest of it might be. Do you really think any of them would want to get tangled in this precollege business?" Teddy asks. "And if they did—do you really think it would change Coop's mind?"

The truth is, for all the bullheaded planning I've done to orchestrate all these meetings—the internship, Broadway Bugs, the dance classes—I've never really thought the scenario all the way through to its end. I got as far as figuring out which one of them is my mom and just skipped ahead to the part where I got to go to the precollege.

I also skipped the part where I suddenly know who my mom is for the rest of my life. And the part where maybe two of the other women who *aren't* my mom don't get to be in it.

"I don't know," I admit.

"I don't either. Which is why I think you're not trying to find them for that, or you would have just asked them by now." Dammit. Between hunting for knickknacks and shoveling Goldfish into his mouth like it's his last snack on earth, Teddy is eerily perceptive. "You're a lot of things, Millie, but subtle's never been one of them."

It is perhaps a little on the nose that I am wearing a pair of glittery rainbow bangles so bright they could blind passersby right now.

"It's just . . ." I take a breath, and it's like the words I wrote this morning breathe right back out of me. "Maybe it's true. That I need people to like me. And maybe I have to be sure that—whichever one of them she is—she *likes* me."

"What do you mean, maybe it's true? Who said that?"

Oliver did. And probably other people before him, but for some reason things Oliver says to me always stick longer than most. And anyway, just because it was a cheap shot doesn't make it any less true.

"I mean, it would track," I say quietly. "I know it started out as a way to get into the precollege, but I think . . ."

I pull myself back from the end of that sentence like I've gotten too close to a fire, but it doesn't matter. Teddy knows exactly what I meant to say.

"Hey," he says.

I tug on his arm. "We're gonna miss the geocache."

"Let someone else beat us to the punch for once. Listen."

He puts his hands on my shoulders, holding me in place. "You don't have a thing with being liked. Trust me, I'd know if you did. Half of Stone Hall is still terrified of you from when you bit their heads off for making fun of my tie at homecoming freshman year."

"I hope they see me in their nightmares."

Teddy cracks a grin. "See what I mean?" He lets go of me but leaves the big puppy dog eyes on mine. "I'd say you're ambitious. That's different than needing to be liked. You kind of go through the world like you've got something to prove."

He says it like it's a fact, like it's something he's proud of. But maybe he shouldn't be. Maybe he's just hit the nail on the head: whoever my mom is, I want to prove her wrong about me.

"I think there's something else behind this."

"Maybe," I concede.

But even as I say it, I know it's more than just a maybe. It wasn't just the precollege that changed things. It's like something took hold of me once I saw those LiveJournal entries— once this imaginary gray figure in the back of my head became a living, breathing entity. Not a possibility, but a reality. One close enough to touch.

Teddy tilts his head like he's trying to think of something comforting to say, but neither of us is really good on that front. We're just good at being there for each other.

Speaking of: "C'mon." I yank him by the arm. "We've still got two minutes to beat those other kids to the geocache, and I'm going to spend them all yelling into your ear about why you're entirely crushable."

"You really don't have to do that."

"You're very tall and also symmetrical!" I yell, taking off.

Teddy's eyebrows shoot up in alarm, scrambling to keep up with me.

"You always share your Reese's Puffs!"

"*Millie—*"

"YOU ONLY SNORE MEDIUM LOUD!"

"Curse your impressive lung capacity," Teddy grumbles, and then we're off, and for a little while leave the rest of it in our wake.

# CHAPTER FIFTEEN

I'm up early the next morning, determined to put yesterday behind me. I blow out my hair and find a bright red flared dress in the back of my closet, throw on Heather's boots, and march myself over to the CVS, where I spend the next fifteen minutes deliberating over which notebook and set of colored pens to buy. If this whole "writing stuff down" thing can stop one Millie Mood in its tracks, it's worth the future investment to see if it stops others.

I settle on a sparkly one, deciding that if I'm already being slightly reckless with the internship money, I might as well treat myself. I reroute myself to the bakery I love so much, wondering if I'll run into Oliver there. When someone calls my name, I don't even blink, whipping around like I expected it—only it's not Oliver. It's Chloe.

"Hi hi hi," she says, running up to me, her phone extended in her hand. "Good morning! What are you doing up so early?"

"My internship," I say, barely muffling an *oof* as she throws her arms around me. "What are *you* doing up so early?"

She presses a finger to her phone to dim the screen and shoves it in her pocket. "Just, uh—it was nice out, I wanted to go for a walk," she says quickly.

It feels weird to just "hi" and "bye" her, even if we did see each other two days ago. I tilt my head toward the bakery. "Wanna split a croissant?"

"Um, *yeah.*"

I keep an eye on the time as we stand in line, getting a croissant, an iced Americano for me, an iced vanilla latte for Steph, and a frozen hot chocolate for Chloe. She slurps it so fast it's a miracle she doesn't get a brain freeze all the way down to her toes, and tells me about the flying monkey costume she's putting her dog Seymour in for the *Wizard of Oz*–themed meetup.

"Why do I have a feeling you named that dog after seeing *Little Shop of Horrors*?" I ask, splitting the croissant.

Chloe, right on cue, says, "Feed me, Seymour," as I hand over her half. I laugh and she goes bright red, pleased with herself.

"So . . ." Chloe frowns at her hot chocolate, that nervous expression back on her face. I brace myself, thinking she's about to ask about Teddy, but she says, "Is the musical theater department at Cornelia like, super competitive? I've heard some things."

My shoulders relax. "Nah. It's actually pretty chill now." I pause. "Well, *I'm* not, obviously, but the whole vibe is." I point a finger at her. "Except our stage manager, Oliver Yang. Best piece of advice I can give? Get on his good side."

"Because he's mean?"

A few weeks ago I would have said that's exactly why. As well as Oliver and I have been getting along these days, it doesn't magically erase the last few years of him pulling the strings against me with casting. But that had everything to do with our dynamic, and nothing to do with the way he is with everyone else.

"Nah. He'll look out for you," I tell her. That much I know is true.

Chloe scrambles to open the Notes app in her phone.

"Oliver . . . good side," she mutters to herself. "I looked at the school website, but it hasn't been updated with what next year's play and musical are going to be. Have they told you?"

I lean in, cutting a glance at the window as if Oliver's going to overhear me from two blocks away and Hulk in through the glass. "Well, officially I don't know," I tell her with a smile. "But unofficially my friend has been doing the costuming, and based on the absurd number of overalls she added to a Pinterest board I'm assuming it's *Mamma Mia*."

Her eyes light up like I just told her she won a game show. "Holy crap. That's one of my favorites." She deflates. "But they've probably already cast for it, right?"

Oh, shit. I hadn't thought of that. We get transfers at Cornelia Arts & Science, but I've never really dealt with the logistics of it.

"They did auditions, but they don't announce the cast or anything until we're all back at school," I tell her.

"So I probably can't be in it."

I munch on my croissant, trying to think of some way to cushion the blow more effectively than filling her up with more dessert. The costuming team would probably welcome the help, and we always need extra hands with publicity. If she couldn't be *in* the show, she could at least be adjacent to it.

Unless . . .

"Well—make a video." I say it before I can overthink it or the light groveling I may have to do. "We'll give it to Oliver, and he'll give it to our teacher."

Chloe blinks at me. "Make a *video*?"

"Yeah. Just pick a thirty-two-bar cut."

Her voice is so quiet it nearly gets swallowed up by the sound of the coffee grinder. "Of *what*?"

I shrug, trying to keep the conversation casual. By virtue of being a dramatic person myself, I have discovered that if you rise to someone's level of panic then it'll just keep bouncing between you both like a feedback loop and nobody will get anywhere.

"You sound great doing 'Watch What Happens,'" I remind her.

"I . . ." She shakes her head. "No, I don't."

I lower my chin and stare her down. "Yes, you do," I say firmly. "You have a beautiful voice."

It's the truth—her voice is distinctively hers, sweet and quiet with a fast vibrato like a little bird. I'd say so, but her chin goes wobbly enough that I know it already sank in and I'll only embarrass her if I press the point.

"I wouldn't even know how to film it," she says.

That part, at least, is easy. "Teddy'll do it. He tapes for me all the time," I say, pulling out my phone.

Chloe leans forward so fast the chair makes a skidding noise from under her. "Oh—no, you don't have to bother him—"

"Trust me, he has nothing to do today except create a Teddy-size hole in his parents' couch and chase after things on his GeoTeens app."

I tap out the text asking him before Chloe can talk me out of it.

"But then I'd have to *sing* in front of him."

"You already did, remember? No pressure." I reach out and pat her hand, the one she was no doubt extending to try to take the phone from me. "Besides, Teddy listened to me screltch all through puberty. Even if you mess up a take, I promise he's seen eighteen thousand times worse."

Chloe swallows hard. "Okay. Well. Even if I did do it . . . what should I wear?"

I wave a hand at her. "You're fine with what you have on," I tell her. She glances down at her floral tee and jeans, and then back at me uncertainly. I pull a hair tie off my wrist and hand it to her. "Just make sure to pull your hair back so we can see your face."

She accepts it so preciously that I might have just handed her a diamond. Then she looks back up at me. "Do you think I'll get cast?"

Thanks to our efforts to make the department double-cast all the shows, there's no chance she won't be. But I figure there's no point in stealing the magic from her when she makes the list. I reach out and grab her hand, squeezing it.

"I'm absolutely positive."

She holds my eyes there for a moment like she's waiting for me to qualify it with something. When I don't, she starts yanking her hair back into a ponytail, using my hair tie to secure it. "Thanks, Millie," she says with a shy smile.

"No problem." I glance at my phone. "I gotta go. But sit tight, Teddy says he can meet you here with his camera." I pull my purse off the chair and brush the crumbs off my dress, pausing to look down at the table. "And eat that croissant before Teddy gets here, or he'll eat it for you."

I sweep out of the bakery with my drink in one hand and Steph's in the other, positioning myself to nudge the door open with my hip, but someone reaches over my head and opens it for me.

"Oh, yikes," I say before I can stop myself. In my defense, Georgie was basically conjured in midair. "Uh—I mean—good morning."

Georgie juts her chin out to the sidewalk to remind me to keep moving. I do, but not before shooting a glance back at the bakery, wondering how I missed her when I was the one sitting facing the door. Was she chilling at one of the other tables the entire time?

We start walking down the street and I take a very long sip

of my coffee to do something to fill up the silence. For once, Georgie fills it herself.

"Was that your . . . mentee?"

The subject of "What Chloe Is to Me" is such a gray area at this point that I just go ahead and nod, falling into step with her. "She's going to my school next year, so kind of."

Georgie nods back solemnly. "Mentoring is important. It's why I do this internship."

Huh. A hot take for someone who thinks my first name is "My lunch order is ready for pickup" and Oliver's is "Go ask Steph," but I guess this is technically the first job I've had where I wasn't reporting directly to my aunt.

Off my look, she says, "The second part of the summer is more hands-on."

Our strides are almost completely matched, neither of us lagging or pulling ahead. "So you're hazing us."

She raises an eyebrow at me. "A healthy work ethic is important." She turns her gaze forward again, but she says out of the corner of her mouth, "As is the ability to collaborate with your peers."

After a split second of debating whether or not to, I say, "Oliver and I have stopped trying to kill each other, if that's what you're getting at."

This earns me the tiniest little uptick of her lip. I get the impression she rarely gets sassed, but I figure after yesterday, it's not like I can embarrass myself any *more* thoroughly.

"A wise decision on both of your parts."

"Probably," I agree, even though it was less of a decision and more of something that just kind of happened on its own.

We walk in mutually non-awkward silence for the next block or so. I figure we must cut a somewhat intimidating picture from our bright outfits and the way we're carrying ourselves, from the eyes we're attracting from people passing by. One woman even does a double take. I sneak a glance at Georgie in her purple blazer and her loose, wild hair, and even though she has the same unaffected expression she wears 90 percent of the time, I can tell she feels the stares, too.

Just before we reach the office, I pull out the notebook. "Also, uh . . . I got my own to write in."

"Well." She eyes the glitter on it, so bright that it's casting a translucent shadow on the ground. "You'll never misplace it."

"Not a fan of glitter?" I ask, pushing the door open for her.

"I'm in show business, Millicent." She tucks her hair behind her ear and flashes one of her oversize earrings at me so casually that it might have seemed like an accident if she hadn't added, "Glitter's in my blood."

I don't even bother correcting her on the "Millicent" bit, grinning at her back as she walks toward the elevator. After she taps the button she turns to me.

"I trust the issue yesterday was . . . resolved?" she asks, so discreetly that she might have been asking if I'd successfully committed a murder.

I brace myself for the wave of embarrassment, but oddly, it doesn't come. She told me not to be embarrassed, and I'm not. Maybe Georgie really is that powerful.

"It's ongoing," I tell her candidly. "But you were right. Writing it down helped."

She nods, then her phone trills in her hand and she slides it open to her email. When the elevator lets us out and we walk into the office waiting room together, I stop short of Steph's desk. It's empty again.

"Don't worry. Steph will be back tomorrow, and the two of you won't have to deal with me."

"I don't mind dealing with you." I let my lips curl into a smile. She raises the eyebrow again but lingers just enough that I know this is the precise amount of cheekiness I can get away with. It's not necessarily a whole new Georgie Check, but it is a far more interesting one. It makes me wonder what's in store for whichever one of us makes it to the "second part of the summer."

"I don't suppose you want this, then," I say, referencing Steph's coffee.

Georgie eyes it. I can tell she doesn't want to take it, but only on principle, not because she doesn't want it.

So I just hand it to her. "Maybe there's glitter in your blood, but there's also a ton of caffeine."

She lets out an appreciative noise that might have been a laugh, taking a sip. "Not bad," she says. Then she walks into her office and shuts the door.

Oliver sweeps in from the second elevator a beat later and immediately narrows his eyes at me.

"How do you keep beating me here?"

"Because I drink coffee like a real New Yorker and you drink tea like the American Revolution never happened." This would usually be the moment Oliver makes a crack about me paying attention in a subject other than theater, but instead he's patting down three of his pockets before finally finding his phone in the fourth. "You seem stressed."

"Uh, yeah." Oliver checks his screen and sees we still have a few more minutes before Georgie reemerges and gives us our Check Lists. "There was a cancellation at the Milkshake Club. They're letting my brothers open for another band, *tonight*."

Even I'm surprised to hear that. Normally if an opener cancels, Carly just lets it go. "Well, fancy that," I say. "Are you assembling the troops?"

"I'm *waking up* the troops. None of them are ever conscious before noon." He taps something into his phone. "I'm going to have to call my mom to wake them up. They're gonna think she's pranking them. I can't believe this."

Oliver's in prime Stage Manager mode now, when he's all hyperfocused and worked up and clearly loving every second of it. I lean back on Steph's desk.

"You're staring at me," he grumbles.

"Just trying to decide what I'm going to yell into the phone when your mom picks up."

"You wouldn't."

"I'm debating between pretending to be a pot dealer and yelling 'Has anyone seen my underwear.'"

"Millie, I swear to— Hi, Mom."

Oliver's tone is Well-Behaved Son but his eyes are blazing a warning. I bite my lip, biding my time as he rattles off instructions to her, taking a step closer. Then another one, then another, until I'm right next to his face, and I can see him torn between trying to scowl at me and trying not to laugh.

"Yeah. Thanks, Mom. Love you too—"

I reach forward and tweak him in the side so he yelps out a laugh just as he's hanging up. I throw my head back to cackle, so I entirely miss him taking a quick step forward and reaching out his hand to do the same thing to me. I let out a full-on squawk and Oliver tries to shush me, but by then we're both laughing so hard that we nearly bump heads.

"You're a menace," he says, but he's grinning through it.

I pick up the long skirt of my dress and flick it at him like I'm in *West Side Story.* "And *you* need to relax. Your brothers are gonna be fine."

Oliver looks down at the fabric. "And how would you know?"

"Because I stalked the hell out of them online, obviously," I say, crossing my arms.

"What?" Oliver's head snaps back up so fast I swear I heard his neck crack. "When?"

"Like, the minute after you were out of my sight line on Friday," I say, with a "duh" eye roll.

"Oh," says Oliver.

"I'm a particular fan of 'I Only Came to Meet Your Dog.' Party banger."

"Yeah?"

Then he goes very still in that way he does when he's about to overthink something. Usually that leads to him combing through all the lighting cues and driving the techies up the wall, or readjusting the placement of so many props that he ends up tangled in stray feather boas. I shudder to think what he'll do if I let it happen now.

"Take a breath, Oliver. You've already put in the work. Now it's up to them."

He scowls like he's not going to listen to me, but he takes the breath anyway, so I consider it a win. Then he stares down at the skirt I flicked at him, then back up at me, and says, "Huh."

"Excuse you?"

He blinks, shaking his head. "Just trying to figure out what the next Millie phase is."

"Oh." I glance down at myself. "I'm not sure."

"Well." Oliver raises his hand in this sweeping, endearingly awkward gesture and says, "It looks nice."

For a moment I'm too surprised to respond, half bracing myself for a punch line. But there isn't one. There's just Oliver and his eyes so unwavering on mine that my cheeks flush and I do something I almost never do—I look away first.

"Thanks," I say, tossing my hair. "It's going to look even nicer while I'm running circles around you today."

Oliver straightens up like he's rising to the challenge. "We'll see about that."

Georgie comes out to hand us our Check Lists, but each of them has a ticket attached to it. I gasp before Oliver even registers what's happening, seeing the words *Greek Life*—the name of Gloria Dearheart's show—in familiar bold font. Just under it is this week's Thursday premiere date.

"You're not required to attend, but you have the option," says Georgie curtly.

"Not *required*?" I blurt. I'd sell my own kidney to get into this theater. "How is this even happening right now?"

She raises an eyebrow, and if I'm not mistaken, almost seems pleased that we're out of the loop on something. That she gets to be the one to clue us in. "It isn't public yet," she says, "but Tyler Dean Bassey was offered a pilot. So Baron's taking over the role of Poseidon for the Broadway run."

"Holy . . . *shoot*," I say, catching myself just in time.

She turns away, but not before I spot the little smirk playing at the edge of her mouth.

"Well," says Oliver, "this just turned into the least boring day of our lives."

I haven't been this excited since our school got those discount tickets to see *Hamilton* on a field trip freshman year. At least this time I managed not to scream.

"Tell me about it."

We finally glance down at our Check Lists, and I'm almost disappointed to see that there isn't anything highlighted on them. In fact, after all the commotion of the morning, I barely run into Oliver all day—he skips right past his own lunch to leave as early as he can to help his brothers set up.

I head home and knock on Teddy's door, but he doesn't answer. It occurs to me that he might still be with Chloe, so I decide not to text him just in case. Heather's also out, with a note saying she stocked up on my favorite frozen pizza and that she's downstairs in the club if I need her. For a moment I just stand in the kitchen and soak in the rareness of having a moment all on my own.

Usually I feel like these moments are stolen. I use them to belt my face off or practice a really weird monologue and savor the fact that nobody's around to see me make a complete ass of myself. But right now all I can think about is how quiet it is and how loud my brain feels. Like the emptiness of the apartment left too much extra space for me.

I open up Heather's laptop, going back to the Madison admissions page. I stare at the rosy-cheeked faces of the students in the pictures. A girl standing under a spotlight as Olive in *Spelling Bee*, her mouth open in song and her arms wide with feeling. A group of students caught in midjump dancing onstage. The tagline you see under the school's logo before you even scroll down the page: *Become the person you're meant to be.*

A little grandiose for an undergraduate program, maybe, but the words have stuck in my head since I first saw them. I know I'm impatient. I know I don't have the answers yet. But that's the kind of thing you don't find out until you leave your old life behind, right? How am I supposed to know who I am if all I've done the past few years is figure out what I'm not?

The sun is starting to set outside, and I'm itching. Restless. I keep glancing over at the desk in the living room where my dad usually works during the day, the quiet nucleus of the apartment. At the chair where Heather curls up with her knees to her chin and has stashed so many blankets that I'm not entirely certain what color the chair is anymore. At the spot in the middle of the couch that's mine, right between Dad and Heather, anchored between them as far back as my memory goes.

I get up abruptly, without even really thinking about a where or a why. A minute later I walk into the Milkshake Club and slide my way back behind the ice-cream bar, in a little spot where I can see the stage and some of the crowd, but nobody would think to look back and see me. My timing is spot-on—Carly just finished her final quick mic check and nodded at someone. I glance over and see that the "someone" is none other than Oliver, flanked by all three of his brothers. They huddle together in this incongruous bubble, all four of them dressed so differently from one another that you'd never guess they were part of the same band, let alone brothers. Then Oliver nods and the light in the venue shifts and people start looking up from their ice cream toward the stage.

Elliot hops up first, wearing mismatched denim and hauling an electric guitar that just about dwarfs his scrawny fourteen-year-old self. He reaches for the mic before the other two even fully get on stage, grinning unabashedly, his eyes bright like he's already sucking up energy from the crowd.

"Get your SPF fifty ready, because we're the Four Suns," he announces.

The crowd gives out a few whoops—the Tuesday-night opening act is a notoriously tough slot, particularly at the last minute—but Elliot doesn't miss a beat, and neither do his brothers.

"I begged you not to introduce us that way," says David, the lead singer and the brother a year older than Oliver. He just graduated from Cornelia, so I recognize him from the halls, and also from the trademark bright colored cotton joggers he always seems to be wearing (tonight's are neon blue).

"Well, guess you got *burned*, bro."

David tries to swipe the mic from him, but Elliot ducks. Then their oldest brother, Hunter, a sophomore at Marymount Manhattan tall enough to make Teddy look regular-size, puts his hands on the top of both of their heads and pretends he's going to bop them together. They both protest, and Elliot puts up a hand to shield his eyes as if the sequins on Hunter's jacket are blinding him, but it's clearly all part of the routine.

"Please excuse these numbskulls," says Hunter, his voice low and quiet but somehow all the more commanding for it. I can see the calculation in his eyes, the intensity in them—it's more subtle than Oliver's, but they're clearly birds of a feather. "They really do love each other. In fact, we're going to start out tonight with a number that truly represents the heart of our band—a celebration of brotherly love. This is called, 'You Ate My Taco Bell, Prepare to Die.'"

The club laughs. Hunter takes his seat behind the drums, leans forward, and deadpans into the mic, "That wasn't a joke. One, two, three—"

Then Hunter jerks his head forward in a nod and they kick off, the younger two following Hunter's beat, Elliot jumping up and down and in the occasional circle with his guitar as David walks up and down the tiny Milkshake Club stage, delivering lyrics to his brothers and to the audience. Elliot joins in for the occasional harmony, and Hunter adds low, ironic commentary in the middle that people often miss and then laugh at a second later when it lands.

"Blood may be thicker than water, but not as thick as a cha-lupa," David half sings, half says into the mic. Elliot punctuates it with his guitar and jumps in on the harmony for "I am my brother's keeper but not if he keeps my chalupa!"

After the opener loosens everyone up, they transition into a less absurd but no less engaging number, this one an upbeat pop song called "Time Off Your Side." Then they move seamlessly into a more thoughtful rock ballad, "800 Miles," which I get so swept up in that it only occurs to me when it's over that it was one thousand percent inspired by David's girlfriend, who's going to Northwestern in the fall. Once they've gotten enough of the crowd's attention that a hush has fallen over the club, Elliot kicks it into high gear with the catchy, flippant "Love at First Spite."

My phone buzzes in my hand. A text from Carly: That Four Suns band is on tonight. They're legit, it reads.

I smile to myself, tucking the phone away. They are legit, but they're more than that. They're magnetic. Fresh. Surprising. They all talk into the mic in turns, sometimes talking over one another but somehow still managing to keep the feeling of it so intimate and relatable that any person in the crowd might think they were talking directly to them. It's like they've got everyone's attention suspended on a tightrope, but it doesn't waver even once—not during the songs or in the beats between them.

Still, even with all eyes on the Four Suns, I can't keep mine from straying to a quiet corner to the left of the stage. Oliver is standing there still as a statue, watching the audience's reactions like a hawk, only moving to give his oldest brother a silent signal at the wrap of every song. But there are a few moments he loses himself in it, too. He starts to bop his head to the beat in this dorky, earnest way, or catch a grin from Elliot shot at him so fast that nobody else could have noticed it. And those are the moments something flits in my chest—something unfamiliar, something I can feel taking shape faster than I can make room for it. I've always known there are a lot of people I'll miss when I leave for Madison. I just never thought Oliver would be one of them.

# CHAPTER SIXTEEN

Steph is out again the next day, which means Oliver and I are so busy keeping up with the new tasks on our Check Lists that I don't even get to talk to him until we're both walking out of the building. I'm expecting him to update me about last night, but instead he seems very preoccupied by his phone screen.

"How was the show last night?" I ask, never one to be bested by Instagram.

"Good," says Oliver. I stayed for all five of their songs, including the quirky, truly Netflix-movie-soundtrack-worthy "I'm Not What You Don't Think I Am," which had half the club dancing by the end, so I know he's underplaying it. I raise my eyebrows and he relents. "They were great. The crowd loved them. The band they were opening for wants them to do a few gigs with them in the city."

"Would you look at that. Maybe you don't need this internship after all," I say innocently.

"Nice try," says Oliver. "Also, speaking of performances, I got that video of the transfer student?"

"Oh shoot. I completely forgot about that." I glance over at his phone reflexively, and he pulls it out of my view. I'd rag on him for trying to hide the five-minute yoga app I've definitely seen on Heather's phone before, but I'm too concerned about Chloe. "How was she?"

"She sounded good," he says. "I sent it over to Mrs. Cooke. Do you have an email for her or something?"

"I'll get you one." I walk a little faster, a skip in my step. "She'll look just darling in a pair of bell bottoms."

"I never said we were doing *Mamma Mia*," says Oliver, begrudgingly speeding up to match my pace.

"Who said anything about *Mamma Mia*?" I ask, flashing my teeth. "Anyway, thanks for doing that. She was nervous about it."

Oliver shrugs but looks like he wants to say something else. Probably about me pulling strings, or abusing my position as a senior, all the usual hits. But instead he asks, "So, uh—who's Teddy?"

I blink. I'm so used to thinking of Teddy as an extension of myself that I forgot Oliver doesn't already know him. But I gave him Oliver's email to send Chloe's audition over once they wrapped up, so I guess now he does.

"He's my best friend," I say, even though it feels like an understatement.

Oliver clears his throat. "Oh," he says, scratching the back of his neck. "Well. He seems nice."

"Yeah, he's got that going for him," I say, searching Oliver's face.

He notices me staring and snaps himself out of whatever weird trail of thought he must have just gone down. "But you might wanna check in with this 'best friend' of yours, because he's definitely been asking me for embarrassing stories about 'School Millie' he can rub in your face later."

"Luckily I've never done an embarrassing thing in my life."

"Luckily," says Oliver drily. "Wait, I thought you lived that way."

I pause on the sidewalk. "Yeah, but I think I'm gonna go to a coffee shop for a bit," I say, pointing in the opposite direction. I told Teddy I'd meet him at the Milkshake Club for a sundae tonight, but knowing him he won't be done GeoTeening for at least another hour.

"Oh—I just . . ."

I know the full repertoire of Oliver's faces. There's the patented Stage Manager Scowl. There's the look he gets when he's so focused I'm pretty sure even a stage curtain catching fire wouldn't break his stride. There's the small, reluctant smile I can wheedle out of him with my theatrics, and the bigger, genuine one that sometimes pops out like the sun on a cloudy day.

But I haven't seen this one before. I'd say it looks like confusion, but there's this weird top note of desperation in it, like his eyes are quietly screaming.

"Actually, there was something I wanted to talk to you about," he says quickly.

"With the internship?"

Oliver glances down the street. "Yeah, sure." He starts walking across the street toward my block. I follow him, too flummoxed to not, but then he doesn't actually say anything—just looks back to check if I'm still walking.

"Well?" I prompt him.

"Oh. Uh . . ." Oliver is not a stammer-y person, so I've gone from mildly annoyed to highly intrigued. "I just wanted to . . . make sure there'd be no hard feelings."

Back to mildly annoyed. "When I get the internship, you mean?"

Oliver lets out a laugh. "When either of us do."

"Sure," I say, glancing back at the coffee shop. I wanted to have some time to write in the notebook I bought. I know I have to call my dad tonight, and I've been feeling on edge about it all day—I still haven't brought up the whole admissions snafu with him yet. "No hard feelings."

"Good," says Oliver, without breaking his stride.

"Is that all you wanted to talk about?"

Then Oliver does something distinctly un-Oliver-like. He reaches out and grabs my hand.

"No, there was—something else."

I stare down at our hands, but more out of surprise at myself than at him. He may have been the one to grab mine, but I was the one who intertwined our fingers without even thinking. Now we're just standing at a dead stop on the street looking at each other.

I'm about to make a joke out of it, scrambling for a way to play it off like it was just another thing I did to irk him. Then Oliver goes crimson, and my own cheeks are so hot that it feels like we caught each other's fires. I can't tell what it is, if we're annoyed or confused or just stunned, but whatever it is, I know we're feeling it exactly the same.

*What else?* I'm about to ask. But I don't need to. The *else* is already there in between us. It's loud and it's steady, pulsing stubbornly between our fingers even before the thought can fully form in my head.

"Just . . . c'mon," says Oliver, tugging for me to follow.

And I do. Our hands are still intertwined, and I don't know if it's because we want them to be or because we're both too proud to be the one who pulls away first. But this much I do know: whatever it is Oliver's about to say, I'm not ready to hear it. Not when I've already got one foot out of this city, far away from him or anything I can do about it.

Then he turns us down my street. "This isn't the way to your place," I say.

"Yeah, I . . . think I left my jacket at the Milkshake Club last night."

"You didn't have a jacket," I say out loud, like an idiot.

Mercifully, he doesn't notice, pressing on. "You mind if we just go in for a second to check the lost and found?"

I blow out a breath. There is no lost and found so much as a "This Is Carly's Now," and whether or not you get it back entirely depends on what direction the wind is blowing that day.

"Yeah, sure." I swallow, my throat thick. "And then we'll . . . talk about whatever it is you wanted to talk about?"

"Yeah," says Oliver.

But he lets go of my hand. It takes another second for it to hit me: I was wrong.

It feels natural to be embarrassed. Is my ego really so swollen that I thought, even for five seconds, that *Oliver* might have feelings for me? He'd sooner make out with his Check List. And *I'd* sooner make out with a pole on the 1 train.

What doesn't feel natural is the disappointment. It's vague enough that I can't pinpoint the root of it but heavy enough that I can't ignore it, either. Which is stupid. It's not like I have feelings for *him*. And even if I did—which again, I do not, could not, and will not, so long as I have any say in the matter—it's not like I could do anything about it now. Not when two months from now I'll be in California, and he'll still be here.

So why am I feeling anything at all? And why does it feel like such a—

"SURPRISE!"

I gasp so sharply I choke on my own spit. Every human I've ever met is screaming at me, which is very alarming until I realize that the words they are screaming are, in fact, "HAPPY BIRTHDAY!" The second wave of it is somehow louder than the first, and just about knocks me right out of Heather's boots.

I blink, staring out at the little crowd clustered at the front of the Milkshake Bar. Half the theater department is on one side, all of them blowing into colorful noisemakers. Next to them are Teddy and Chloe, both hollering and jumping up and down. Then there's Teddy's parents and some other neighbors from our building, wincing from the noise but smiling, and Heather with the confetti cannon she liberally abuses all summer between Pride and the Fourth of July. All these people I love beaming and shouting at me, but even in all the hullabaloo— even before it hits that I just walked into a legitimate surprise party celebrating *me*—there is a tinge of disappointment, knowing that my dad's not here, too.

Except when I sweep my eyes to the corner of the room, there he is, beaming that close-lipped, bright-eyed Dad beam so familiar to me that for a moment I'm knocked back in time—back to when I was a little kid, and when my dad picked me up from kindergarten I'd be so overcome realizing how much I missed him that I'd burst into tears. How I'd cling to him all the way to the apartment, and if Heather was there I'd refuse to walk a single step if I wasn't holding both of their hands. I've grown up in a city too big to measure with dreams too big to hold, but I've always had that tether keeping me safely on the ground.

He's hovering a few feet away from the rest of the crowd, the way he always does. He hates attracting any kind of attention to himself. That's too damn bad.

"DAD!"

I run at him so fast that my bag clatters to the floor, and he doesn't brace himself because he knows by now there's really no point. He lifts me up and squeezes me, and I get one whiff of his shaving cream and just like that I'm five years old again and trying not to cry.

Only this time it isn't just because I missed him. This time it's so many things that I don't know how to feel them all at once. It's the anger of what he did to me, the guilt of what I did to *him*, both of them raw and scratching just under the surface of the ridiculous, overwhelming relief that he's home again.

"What are you *doing* here?" I exclaim. "What about the rest of your trip?"

"There is no rest of the trip." He's grinning harder than that time we got front-row tickets to see *Infinity War* in one of those movie theaters with the chairs that shake you around. "It wrapped up this morning."

I whip my head over to find Heather, because as much as I love my dad, I know he barely had a hand in this. The words *surprise* and *party* would probably rub together and start a fire in his unsuspecting introvert brain. "How long have you been planning this?"

Heather smirks. "A few months." Teddy knocks into her from behind in his excitement to get over to us. "With Teddy's help."

"Except I had *one job*," says Teddy, breathless from all the shouting, "and that was to get you *here*. And apparently I had to recruit your archnemesis to drag you."

Before I can get another word in edgewise with my dad, I get swarmed by our theater friends into a giant group hug, a sweaty jumble of Cornelia kids that reminds me of countless cast parties and delirious tech week rehearsals and that one especially trippy sleepover we stayed up all night watching the first season of *Glee*.

I squeeze my eyes tight in the thick of it, holding them for an extra beat like I'm holding them in place.

Oliver takes a step back from us. "Well, I'm probably just gonna . . ."

"Hey," I say, about to pull him into the mess of limbs.

"Favorite ice-cream flavors?" Heather interrupts. "Also, hi, I'm Heather. Aunt of Millie, dispenser of ice creams."

The knot of theater kids untangles, and I crane my neck

looking for my dad, but he's laughing about something with Teddy's parents, no doubt at mine and Teddy's expense. Birthdays are their favorite times to pull out their phones and unearth embarrassing pictures of us.

"What can I get ya?" Heather asks, starting with Chloe.

"Um—I'll have—whatever's easiest," she says quickly, planting herself in between me and Teddy and looking very much overwhelmed.

Heather does that scary game show buzzer impression and Chloe full-body flinches. "Wrong answer."

Chloe looks at me in alarm, so I nod at her encouragingly. "Um . . . do you have any strawberry?" Chloe asks.

"Girl after my own heart," says Heather, flashing her a grin. "And you?"

She turns to Oliver, but he has angled himself toward the door and looks ready to bolt.

"Uh . . ." He looks away from Heather, his eyes skimming the theater kids before landing on me. I'm so used to seeing Oliver in his element this summer that it doesn't occur to me until just now that he's very much out of it. I don't know if he's really ever interacted with a ton of the theater kids outside of rehearsals. He tends to run with the tech and band crews.

So I snap my fingers at him. "Ice cream, Oliver," I command. "You're stuck here now."

He tilts himself back toward us a few degrees, and I try to pretend I don't notice the other rising seniors who have watched us duke it out for three years staring at me like I've grown a second head.

"Mint chip, if you have it?" he asks.

"Finally," I say, throwing my hands up in the air. "Something we can agree on."

This earns me a sliver of a smile from Oliver, enough of one that I know he's going to stay. It softens some of the disappointment from earlier. In fact, I probably just imagined it in the first place.

Heather salutes us. "Coming right up." Then she bops me on the nose. "Happy early birthday, punk."

I smile at her, my heart rate finally at a normal-enough human rhythm again to appreciate how much work she must have put into this—getting Teddy to corral our friends, keeping this all a secret, exerting enough self-control over last weekend to save one of the confetti cannons for me.

"What about Teddy?" Chloe asks as Heather walks away.

"Oh, he's got his own milkshake," I explain. "Heather just dumps whatever ingredients we have the most of into a vanilla milkshake and swirls. We call it 'The Teddy.'"

"Last time there were gummy worms," Teddy says cheerfully.

Chloe, to her credit, doesn't gag. Instead she glances over at the cluster of theater kids and asks, "Do they all go to Cornelia?"

I'm about to cut in and introduce Chloe, but Teddy raises his hand just slightly at his side to stop me. I look up at him and he tilts his head for me to let Chloe do it herself. I narrow my eyes at him teasingly, because it definitely seems like I have missed some kind of memo about the two of them in the last twenty-four hours, and I'm absolutely going to rib him for it when we're alone.

Sure enough, I've got nothing to worry about. Chloe joins the group in the middle of someone's rant about off-Broadway shows not releasing cast albums and after a few awkward beats, introduces herself just fine. Judging by our department's mutual affection for newcomers and habit of showing off how much we know whenever we can, they'll have her up to speed in no time.

"Wait, so . . . your aunt works here?"

Before I even turn to Oliver, I realize I'm about to get busted.

"Her aunt *owns* here," says Teddy, one eye on us and the other carefully trained on the milkshake bar, watching the progress of the milkshakes.

Oliver's eyes widen. "So when the Four Suns got fast-tracked . . ."

My first impulse is to lie, and I'm not even sure why. It's just a gig, really. It's not a big deal.

"I may have nudged the booker," I admit.

"Millie, I . . ."

For the first time in recent memory, Oliver appears to be speechless. His mouth opens and then closes and then opens again, and in those brief seconds my stomach drops. He's furious. And he's probably right to be. He's spent the last three years ragging on me for being a busybody, and what did I just do if not become the busiest body of them all?

"Thank you," he says. "I . . . wow, Millie. Just—that was a really nice thing to do."

I don't even realize how much I care until the relief surges through me. "Yeah, well." I clear my throat. "It was chill of you to send over Chloe's audition, so."

He smiles despite himself. "Look at us, looking after our clients. I guess we're both good manager material after all."

I smile back, nudging him with my elbow. "Georgie would be proud."

"Speaking of—isn't that the girl from the video?" says Oliver.

"Yup. That's Chloe."

"She really did a great job," says Oliver. "I'd say you should watch your back, if you weren't ditching Cornelia."

I beam like a proud older sister, which there's a 33-ish percent chance I very well may be. "If I've got a mini me starting at Cornelia, I'm pretty sure *you're* the one who should be watching their back."

"There's no such thing as a mini Millie," says Oliver, shaking his head. "You're one of a kind."

I brace myself for the snarky remark that's supposed to follow, only it doesn't. Oliver's eyes are so sincere that for a second time tonight I'm worried I'm going to lose the silent game and look away first.

"That video we sent was literally the first take!" Teddy brags on Chloe's behalf, sparing me the awkwardness.

"One take, huh?" I say out of the corner of my mouth. "Then what were you two up to the rest of the day?"

I'm expecting Teddy to flush at least a little bit, but it seems that Teddy is every bit as guileless about potential crushes as he is about all things in life. "Turns out she has a real knack for GeoTeens. And finding good bodega snacks."

Heather comes back with ice cream then, in bright pink plastic cups with tops and glitter straws so we can hit the dance floor with them. Right on cue, the volume of the music kicks up, and the sound of Stevie Nicks's "Edge of Seventeen" thrumming through the walls. I scan the room to find my dad, and he's already looking over at me, anticipating it.

He jerks his head toward the dance floor. "Go get your groove on," he says, doing an attempt at what may or may not be the robot. "We'll catch up."

I grab a few of our friends by the hands and holler at the rest of them to follow. I'm shameless and Teddy basically dances like a drunk noodle, so between the two of us everyone loosens up pretty fast. By the second chorus we're all jumping up and down and using our milkshakes as fake microphones. The next song that comes on is Alessia Cara's "Seventeen," and by then I'm extremely onto Teddy, who must have curated this aggressively on-theme playlist. Sure enough, "Dancing Queen" comes on next, and we all collectively lose our marbles—there's this moment when I'm breathless and sweating and jumping surrounded on all sides by my friends, and I'm both in it and on the outside of it at the same time. In the here and now of this happy little bubble, and somewhere just beyond it, trying to bottle it so

I can make it last after it's over. After summer ends and I leave them behind.

The song finishes, and we all stop jumping to catch our breath. "A little preview for when you knock Donna out of the park," says one of my friends. She notices the frown starting to crease on Oliver's face and quickly adds, "Not that, uh, we have the rights to *Mamma Mia* or anything."

Oliver shrugs. "Well, I guess it doesn't matter, since Millie isn't—"

"Going to tell anyone," I interrupt quickly. I fully turn my back on our friends so they won't see my face which, thankfully, Oliver interprets as a *shut up shut up shut up*.

"Right," he says warily.

Nobody seems to have missed the weirdness, though. The dancing dies down just enough that I can see more than a few curious looks pointed in our direction, and I can sense Teddy and Chloe about to turn around and notice, too.

I grin broadly before all the socially awkward dominoes can fall. "Be right back—I'm just gonna grab some water real quick!"

In my defense, that part isn't a lie. It turns out sweating bullets on a dance floor and downing frozen dairy products don't mix (bodies are, first and foremost, scams). I head to the back and pour myself a glass of water, yanking my damp curls into a ponytail, but even after I catch my breath I have no idea what I'm going to say to our friends. Or if I'm going to say anything at all.

But I can't think about that now. People are going to notice if I'm gone too long. I sweep out of the kitchen, then abruptly stop, my breath hitching with surprise—Oliver's standing by the door to the kitchen, clearly waiting for me.

"Just so we're all on the same page—did you not tell anyone about Madison?" he asks.

Just then "Seventeen" from *Heathers* the musical starts playing over the speakers.

"Oh, I love this song," I say with forced enthusiasm, starting to walk away.

"Millie—"

I slide past both him and the question, angling myself toward the main room. "I gotta dance."

"Fine," he says. He doesn't offer his hand so much as he just takes mine and pulls me in, and this time there's nothing hesitant or ambiguous about it. He looks me right in the eye, putting his hands on my waist. I am suddenly so still that all I can feel is the heat that blooms in my chest and spreads itself out so fast that I might have imagined it.

Oliver's the one who starts to sway, just as the song's pumped-up intro gives way to a ballad. For once, I follow his lead, surprised at how easy it is. I've never actually slow danced with anyone before. Well, not with anyone I wasn't on stage with.

But this doesn't feel like dancing, really. It feels too natural for that. Like it's something I've always had the rhythm for, and it was simply a matter of finding someone who had the same one.

That fleeting thought is dashed the moment Oliver opens his mouth. "Why haven't you told your friends?"

I purse my lips. "My dad might not even let me go."

I'm expecting Oliver to ask why. Almost dreading it, because then I'll have to go through my dad's list of reasons all over again and remind myself that there's definitely going to be at least one more fight about this ahead.

But Oliver doesn't seem surprised by this in the least, a thoughtful expression on his face. "Are you even sure you *want* to?"

I roll my eyes. "Why does everyone keep asking me that?"

"Because I know you." The pressure of his hands around my waist tightens slightly on the *know*, so I don't just hear it but feel it. "You're competitive as hell."

My cheeks flush. I can't believe I'm now defending this choice to Oliver, who probably has more reasons to want me to go than anyone else I know.

"Hence why I'm going to a competitive program," I say, leaning in closer. "I'm going to be a year ahead of everyone else, and in Broadway years, that's like, a decade."

Oliver's lip quirks. "Yeah, but after that year is over you're going to miss being a part of the action here, and you know it," he says, before I can open my mouth to protest. "You've always wanted to be the best. I think after a year you're going to set your sights on something better. Something in New York."

In this moment my sights are so set on him that it's blotting out everything else. I take a breath, full and deep, and feel his hands moving with it.

"You think I'm settling for Madison, then."

Oliver doesn't answer, his eyes still trained on mine. I want to hold on to my frustration with him, pressing myself closer to him like I'm daring him to say it.

"I think . . ." His eyes are so close to mine that I can see something brewing under the surface of them. For a moment, I'm not breathing at all, suspended on whatever's at the other end of that sentence. "I know if you waited, you could get into any of the big-name schools in the city. I'm not sure why you're in such a rush."

I'm not used to my voice sounding small. It usually announces my presence long before I walk into a room. "I've waited so long already," I say.

Then it's not just my voice that goes quiet but both of us.

Our rhythm slows even as the song picks up, until we're not really dancing at all, but just holding each other. Even the club itself seems to still.

The world is quiet, but the thought that interrupts it is all too loud: *kiss him.*

There's so much charge in the air between us that it seems like an inevitability. Like there can't be this much electricity without it collecting, without it ending in some kind of lightning strike. I wasn't wrong before, I realize. There's something here. Something so fully formed and rooted so deep that maybe it's been here longer than we knew.

"Well . . . it seems like you've made up your mind, then," says Oliver, his voice lower than I've ever heard it. "And if there's another thing I know about you, it's that once you've made up your mind, there's no stopping it."

I want to smile, but I can't. The song comes to an end and Oliver doesn't let me go.

"I'm going to tell them," I say quietly. "Just not tonight. I don't want us all to be thinking about how much we're going to miss each other. I want to enjoy this."

Oliver considers the words, then says, "Okay. I won't say anything." I duck my head in relief. "But Millie?"

The question hovers in the air, but I don't answer it. I'm trying to figure out when it was that I got used to Oliver calling me by my name instead of "Your Majesty." I'm trying to figure out why, in this moment, I like the way he says my name more than anyone else.

"I'm gonna miss you, too."

One of the regular shift workers shows up early for the club's opening and nudges past us. Oliver steps back and so do I, and before I can say anything, we're interrupted by "Seventeen" by MARINA blasting from the dance floor. Oliver nods, and so do I, even though I'm not sure what we're nodding about—whether it's an acknowledgment of the secret I asked him to keep or the secret I suspect we are both keeping.

But both of them are too big to tackle tonight. I let him go first, then I follow him back out, grabbing my milkshake from where I propped it up on the bar. We all dance for a few more numbers, and every time I look up into one of my friends' faces, I try to stamp the memory of it in my heart—but it's all happening so fast, the night slipping out from under me before I can grab on to anything I can hold.

# CHAPTER SEVENTEEN

Eventually Oliver has to leave because he and his brothers are staying with their dad this week and he needs to get uptown. We all follow him out to say goodbye, and he seems surprised and then genuinely touched by all the fuss, waving before he disappears at the end of the block.

"Hey, gang," says Teddy's mom, holding her own version of what appears to be The Teddy. Despite being doctors, you can always count on his family to maximize their dessert horizons. "I'm being told to assemble the crew for cake in five."

We file in and I scan the room for my dad, knowing he has a way of wandering away from crowds. When I don't immediately see a tall head with slightly askew sandy hair I head over to the greenroom.

To be clear, the greenroom is anything but. It's actually just as smack-you-in-the-face pink as the Milkshake Club itself, only instead of looking like Hello Kitty's living room it looks like Hello Kitty threw a rave. I'm pretty sure there isn't an inch of it that doesn't sparkle. I find my dad standing in the corner, by the wall where the bands who headline get to sign their names. On the very edge of it is a height chart, two dozen little markers with scribbled dates that go all the way up to five foot four and then abruptly stop.

This is one of the rare moments I keep my voice quiet on purpose. My dad has a tendency of getting so lost in his thoughts that he doesn't hear people walk into a room.

"What are you up to?"

My dad still flinches, but he's smiling by the time he turns to see me. But when he follows my eyes back to the wall, he lets out a sigh. "Just trying to figure out why we let you grow up."

I walk up next to him, resting my head on his shoulder. "I'm stubborn that way."

He wraps an arm around my shoulder and squeezes it. "I missed you."

"Yeah. Me too," I say.

For a moment neither of us says anything, and that is the inconvenient moment the guilt of what I've been doing starts to work its way up my chest and all the way to the space between my ears, where it feels like it's suddenly roaring. Like if I don't say something about it *right now* it'll just come bursting out of me anyway, whether I want it to or not.

But then my dad takes his hand off my shoulder and sits down on a sparkly pink blow-up chair. "Listen," he says, and then it becomes clear that he is planning to have a heart-to-heart in said sparkly pink blow-up chair. I take a seat in the one next to him. "I know the admissions department contacted you."

I nod. "You told them I wasn't coming."

"I hope you know I wasn't trying to be sneaky about it. I didn't realize telling her I didn't want to put a deposit in that day meant that they might give up your spot." He fiddles with his glasses, something else still working its way out. "And anyway, I thought when you started taking the dance classes that maybe you were reconsidering the whole thing."

In his defense, I hadn't really planned on taking them. I wouldn't have if it weren't for Farrah. A huge perk of the pre-college is knowing that I got in already, even without the dance skills—I might not be so lucky up against legitimately trained dancers at the bigger-name schools.

"I . . . I still really want to go."

"Okay. Well—how about this weekend, we take them up on one of those virtual admissions tours. Talk to some of the teachers."

"Really?"

"I'm not saying yes. I'm just saying we'll check it out. Get a feel for things." He pats a hand on my knee. "I appreciate you being patient with me on this. And not . . ."

*Overreacting* is the word he's looking for, but my dad's too easygoing to ever come right out and say it. That's Heather's job. And if she were here right now, she'd know from one quick glance at my face that *overreacting* is exactly what I've done.

"Well," I say hollowly. "It's important to me."

"I can tell." He gets up abruptly then. "And I'll try to keep an open mind. I hear cake helps with that."

"Oh yeah?"

He opens the door to the greenroom for me. "Yeah. Plus, I heard a rumor a friend of Heather's found a bakery that does Nutella between the layers."

My mouth starts watering. "For real? What kind of—"

I see it the split second before my dad does, but not fast enough to process it. He walks out, sees Heather and Farrah pressed up against each other in the middle of one extremely passionate kiss in the back hall, and his jaw drops so fast I swear I can hear a clicking noise.

I yank him back and close the door. The two of us stare at each other with identically wide eyes.

There's a knock at the door. "Millie? Are you in there?"

My dad and I continue to stare at each other, frozen. He finally nudges me to talk.

"Uh—yes?"

The door creaks open, Heather sheepishly stepping in front of it.

"So." She touches a hand to her lips, like she's half talking to us and half still out canoodling in the hall. "Farrah and I . . . are kind of a thing."

"You are?" my dad and I ask at the same time.

Heather nods, so dreamy-eyed from the kissing that she doesn't register our mutual surprise.

"Since *when*?" I ask.

My dad turns to me. "You know Farrah?"

Heather is apparently so far gone that she doesn't even make the connection that my dad has, in fact, said Farrah's name out loud.

"She's Millie's dance teacher." After Heather says that out loud, it seems to rattle her back into the reality of what I have just witnessed with my bare human eyes. "I meant to tell you. It all just kind of—happened the past few days. I hope you don't mind."

"Uh," I squeak. I blink, hard, but it does not erase the image of what very well may have been my aunt making out with my mom.

"She was only here because she left her MetroCard . . . but is it okay if she stays?"

"Of course," I manage, because what am I supposed to say? *Hey, good for you for finally getting over the manipulative asshat who's been jerking you around for years, but maybe don't do it with my potential* mom?

Heather bops me on the nose with her finger. "Excellent. We'll go get those candles ready."

She leaves us standing in the open doorway, my dad just far enough behind me that I can't see his face but can still feel his surprise. I close my eyes, but I don't turn around. I know the moment that I do I'm going to have some kind of answer—I'll see it in his eyes and know whether or not Farrah is my mom without having to ask.

But when I turn, his eyes are crinkling like he's on the verge of laughing.

"You okay?" I ask.

"Yeah." He shakes his head. "Except no. Because now I have to figure out how to tell my sister we've made out with the same woman without laying on the floor and hoping the elements take me."

Let it be known that my flair for drama was not created in a void.

"*Dad.*"

He shakes his head again, more aggressively this time. "Nope, nope, I should not have said that." He smiles, clearly waiting for me to tease him, and that's when I know for sure: Farrah's not my mom.

He sees my face fall before I even realize it's falling. I don't feel it. I just feel kind of numb.

"I mean . . . it's not that big of a deal," my dad says quickly. "Is it weird for you, though? Since she's your teacher?"

"No. Uh, no."

"She's really nice. Or at least she was when I knew her. We took first-year seminar together." My dad sucks in a breath through his teeth, then lets out a nervous laugh. "Well, never a dull moment, huh?"

I'm reeling as we walk out to rejoin everyone for cake, and I'm not sure why. Because Farrah's not my mom? Or because it means that Beth or Steph *is* my mom? I try to figure out what I was hoping for, and that's when I understand—maybe I'm not ready to know at all.

There's a pit in my stomach a mile wide. It didn't feel real before now. It felt like a game. Human geocaching. Something intangible enough that nobody could get hurt.

What if she *had* been my mother? What if we'd been having an entirely different conversation right now, one where my dad was the one reeling right now instead of me? One where I suddenly had to explain right on the heels of him telling me how well I was handling this that I actually went nuclear and started stalking three adult women I don't know behind his back?

I don't want to have that conversation. I don't. I have to end this, somehow, before this gets out of control with Steph and—

"Beth? Beth Dunne?" my dad stammers.

I whip around and see my dad staring at Beth like he's just seen a very friendly, cardigan-clad ghost. She's carrying her purse slung over her shoulder, and it occurs to me unhelpfully that she's probably here to pick up Chloe, and it occurs to me even less helpfully that I am officially fucked.

Then Beth's eyes light up with unmistakable delight. "*Cooper?*"

Chloe detaches herself from Teddy, her face bewildered. "Mom?"

"Shit," I mutter under my breath.

For a moment Beth and my dad are both so stunned that all they can do is stare at each other, until Beth finally reaches out and hugs him. There's a split second where my dad goes completely stiff, and I see something flash in his face—an undefined kind of hurt, like he's too surprised he's even feeling it to let it happen—before he finally loosens and hugs her back so hard that something aches in me just watching them.

"You . . . you look great," my dad stammers.

"You look just the same." Beth says the words so fondly that even though they are objectively not a compliment, they sound like the kindest thing in the world.

My dad responds by staring at her moonily. I almost feel bad for being here, like we weren't meant to see something so personal, even though literally all they're doing is staring.

Chloe clears her throat loudly.

"Oh! I was just picking up my Chloe," says Beth, stepping back and ushering Chloe forward. Chloe looks at me, chagrined.

"Is this your . . . This is my . . ." My dad reaches out for me with sloppy enthusiasm, putting his hand on my shoulder like he's never felt a shoulder before. "We have daughters!"

"They've met," says Beth, with a smile so wide I'm worried her face can't contain it. Her eyes are legitimately watering from excitement. I don't even have to look at my dad to know his already are, too—he's got that Big Geek Energy radiating off him so hard right now that it's bouncing off every wall in the club. "We've all met, I just—I never had any *idea* that . . ."

"How the heck do you two know each other?" Chloe blurts.

"Oh," says my dad. "Uh, hi, I'm—" He extends his hand for her to shake and then shakes it way too hard, like there's too much energy in him to be contained. "I'm Cooper, I uh . . . I went to school with your mom."

"You were friends?"

Beth is still staring at my dad so intensely that he might be a piece of art in the Met instead of a thirty-seven-year-old man whose glasses keep sliding down his nose. "No, we were—" She blinks, stopping herself just in time. "Yes, we were friends."

They're talking to us without tearing their eyes off each other, like they can't see anything beyond the feet of space between them. Chloe cocks her head, a clear *Let's leave them to it.* And we should. But my feet are frozen in place. I can't pinpoint the exact moment in the conversation it became clear, but it doesn't make it any less true: Beth is obviously not my mom, either. She seems genuinely happy to see my dad, and my dad, for his part, looks like he just tripped on a stool and fell into his dweeby undergraduate self.

But he doesn't seem like a man who just ran into the mom

of the kid who got dumped on him almost seventeen years ago. Which can only mean . . .

"Okay, they *definitely* dated," says Chloe.

I feel wobbly. "What makes you think that?"

"'Cause I read my mom's journals from college, and she talked about a 'Cooper' she used to study with like, a lot."

This temporarily snaps me back to reality. "Chloe!"

She shrugs. "If your dad just left his journal from college out in the open, wouldn't you read it?"

Touché. I clear my throat. "Well." I feel dizzy. Like I'm going to be sick. "Wow."

"Yeah. Is it weird that I kind of ship it?" says Chloe. "I mean like, gross because it's my mom. But also like, she wrote really bad poetry about him, so I'm pretty sure she was obsessed."

I nod, and some part of me is absorbing this information, but not a helpful part of me. The helpful parts of me are too busy ringing every alarm bell in my system, my heart hammering, my palms breaking out into a sweat.

"Hey. If they *did* date and then like, get married, we'd be sisters."

It's the first time it occurs to me in a very real way that this means that we aren't. I'm surprised by how tight my throat is, not even realizing how much I liked that possibility until it was off the table.

"Yeah. Yeah, I guess we would be," I manage. I need an escape route, but that's the thing about your own surprise birthday party: you can't exactly disappear from it. I never thought there'd come a day when I *didn't* want to be the center of attention, but as I am learning in the past ten minutes, there's a first time for everything. "I'm just gonna . . ."

"*Cooper?*"

This time it's Farrah. She's trailing behind Heather, who's holding a cake full of lit candles and has just opened her mouth to start singing "Happy Birthday." Within a second, the whole room has followed her lead—the room except for my dad, who is staring at Farrah, and Beth, who is staring at my dad staring at Farrah, and Teddy, who meets my eye and just about sums up the entire situation by mouthing the words *Holy shit*.

It's like something out of a dissonant horror movie trailer, everyone cheerfully singing in six different keys that eventually resolve themselves, while I watch my ill-conceived summer plans get unraveled so fast that they're strangling me in the process.

Then the singing stops. The cake is in front of me.

"Make a wish," says Heather.

I close my eyes, blow out the candles, and think to myself, *Please let my dad not figure out what I just did.*

Except after all the candles are blown out and I look around the room, my dad is nowhere to be found.

Heather takes the cake to start cutting and serving it, and I feel someone yank my elbow. By the time Teddy has pulled me out to the back hallway I'm so thrown that it feels like this is happening to someone else. It reminds me of one of the first and few times I ever had stage fright, about a year before "Little Jo." Just before I was supposed to walk out it felt like my soul had just peaced out from my body. It's like that, except my fingers and toes are tingling, like the blood doesn't know how to flow through them anymore.

I push past the hallway and out to the back alley, but the humid air does nothing to help.

"I swear I didn't invite them," says Teddy. "Well, I invited Chloe, but I was going to walk her home, I didn't think—"

"I know," I say, pacing up the alley. "Farrah's dating my aunt, apparently—"

"*What?*" asks Teddy, following close behind.

"And my dad's already spotted both of them, and I'm so busted, but—"

"Does Coop *know*?"

"Not yet, but Teddy," I say, stopping abruptly and reaching up to grab him by the shoulders. "Do you know what this means?"

"Murphy's Law is real?"

"Steph is my *mom*."

Teddy's eyebrows fly into his mop of hair, and he sucks in a breath like he's going to ask me how I know that. But then the wheels turn in his head and it becomes all too evident how I know.

"Is that . . . is that a good thing?"

It is and it isn't. I take a step back from him and try to catch my breath, try to settle the atoms in my body that feel like they're crashing into one another. It's not that I don't want it to be Steph, or that I didn't want it to be Beth or Farrah. It's that when I didn't know, it could have been any of them, and this feeling in me . . . whatever it is. It could be dispersed. My mom couldn't disappoint me, because she was all of them and none of them at the same time. I could see myself in all their good qualities, maybe, and just choose to ignore any of the bad.

The bad primarily being the fact that, for whatever reason, she didn't want *me*.

I itch at my face, catching the unexpected tear that wells up in my eye before Teddy can see it.

"Yeah." I put a little more force behind it, trying to convince myself as I say it. "Yeah. This is good."

"You seemed to like her," says Teddy. "Plus, she's an actress. So maybe it all makes sense."

Maybe it does. If I were in her shoes—if I'd gotten into Tisch, and was taking classes at NYU, and had my whole future ahead of me—what would I have done if I suddenly found out I was having a kid?

It's a simple enough question, until I press down on it and it explodes into a dozen more, each of them heavier than the one that came before it. Like why she had me in the first place. If she knew she didn't want me before or after she had me. If she's wondered about me at all ever since. If she's ever looked at me, Millie, and wondered even for a second if I could be the "Baby Price" she left with my dad seventeen years before.

I turn away from Teddy, pretending it's to fix my hair. "So maybe it's for the best." I grapple for something to focus on, something to pull me out of the spiral, and when I find it I latch hard: "If there's anyone who can get my dad on my side about Madison, it's Steph."

Teddy lets out a very un-Teddy-like scoff. I turn to look at him, and even he seems surprised at himself. But then he holds my eyes, and I see something defensive in them, like he doesn't want me to call him out on it but he's daring me to at the same time.

I can't remember a time Teddy was ever feeling something I didn't already understand. I can't just let it go. "What?"

"Does everything really have to be about this precollege?"

I grit my teeth. "Well, that's why we started this whole thing in the first place, isn't it?"

Teddy gestures back at the club door. "So that's it, then. You're just gonna pull Steph into this and go."

"I don't . . . I don't know that." Honestly, even as it's coming out of my mouth, it's the furthest thing from my mind right now. "But you always knew I was going to go. You've known for months."

"You only *thought* you were going to go then."

"What, you didn't think I was going to get in?"

Teddy rolls his eyes. "*Please* don't make it about that right now."

I dig my heels into the cement. My patience for Teddy may be fairly infinite, but given the already ridiculous circumstances of this doomed party, he sure is testing it right now. "What are you trying to make it about, then?"

"This whole thing—was it really just a means to an end? These other women aren't your mom, and it's just . . . over?" Before I can even wrap my head around what he's accusing me of, he adds, "Like, what about Chloe?"

I shake my head, incredulous. "What about her?"

"She's not your sister anymore, and you just drop her?"

"Who said I was going to do that?" I demand. "Did you not just see me introducing her to new friends? Getting her audition to Oliver?"

"Yeah, for now. But you're leaving, and once she gets to that school, she'll be on her own."

"You've known Chloe for like, a week," I remind him, the frustration reaching its boiling point.

"I'm just saying—"

"Are you worried about *Chloe* not having any friends when I'm gone, or are you worried because you never bothered to make any of your own?"

Teddy looks so stricken that I know I've cut right down to the heart of it, sliced it clean through. It's a problem I've never really had to consider before—that you can know someone so well that you know exactly how to hurt them. Until now, I've never had a reason to try.

First it was my dad. Now it's my best friend. I bury my face in my hands, all at once madder at myself than I am at him.

"Teddy—"

I'm interrupted by the sound of Heather snapping her fingers, appearing from behind the door back into the club. The *open* door.

If she heard any of what we just said, she doesn't acknowledge it. "C'mon inside," she says. "I saved you both corner pieces."

The idea of eating cake right now makes my stomach churn. But Teddy looks all too relieved for an excuse to end the conversation, and after a few seconds pass and Heather is out of earshot, he starts making his way to the door.

"Teddy, I'm sorry," I say, immediately going after him.

Teddy's always been a notoriously fast walker, but it turns out even then he was holding back. I have to run to keep up with him as we make our way back down the hallway, my boots slapping the ground so loudly they have their own echo. He seems to remember that we're about to make a scene before I do, and stops.

His eyes are watery. He knows I mean it. It just isn't enough to undo what I just did.

"Just . . . leave me alone for a little bit, okay?"

I've known Teddy since he was two days old. That's sixteen years and forty lost baby teeth and two *Les Mis* Broadway revivals and at least four hundred boxes of Reese's Puffs. That's countless sleepovers and late-night YouTube wormholes and pranks on our parents and secrets under his phone's flashlight. That's a whole lifetime of being directly in each other's faces, and never once has either of us told the other one to "leave them alone."

But I let him push ahead of me. I follow a few feet behind, keeping my distance, and proceed to put on the best performance of my life: smiling through the rest of the party even as my heart sinks so far down into my chest that it feels like it could mop the floor.

The next hour passes in a blur of cake and thanking people for coming and cleaning up so the club can open to the rest of the city for the night. Teddy makes himself scarce, my dad is completely AWOL, and even Heather won't seem to make eye contact with me for more than a second. I feel like an island in the middle of the room, reaching out with nobody left to touch.

I wait until we're climbing the stairs back up to the apartment to ask, steeling myself.

"Where's Dad?"

"Home," says Heather. "So thankfully he didn't hear any of this conversation about you deciding to look for your mom without saying anything to him about it."

I stop on the stairs, my heart slamming in my chest but the rest of me going very still. There are a hundred thousand things I could say to her right now, but the first thing that comes out is "Are you going to tell him?"

Heather stops on the landing above me. When she turns to look at me, she isn't angry. Isn't disappointed. More than anything, she just looks sad.

"Tell me you weren't really going to pull some woman into this precollege thing and rub it in his face."

My whole life I've always felt like we were a team: me, Dad, and Heather. I've never given much thought to what they were before I existed, but I'm seeing a flash of it now: of a woman who isn't just my fiercely protective aunt but was my dad's fiercely protective older sister first.

"I don't . . ." Her mouth goes tight, ready to catch me in a lie. "I thought I would," I admit. "At first. But I wasn't going to."

Heather watches me like she's trying to decide whether or not to believe me. The worst part is I don't even know how much of *myself* I believe. A few weeks ago I couldn't have imagined a night like this. If I could let it escalate this fast, how much further could I have gone?

Finally Heather sighs, leaning against the railing, running a hand through her hair. "It's one thing to be curious about your mom, Millie. That I can understand. But you could have just asked. Had a reasonable conversation about it."

"Asked *who*?" I don't mean to raise my voice, but just like that it's reverberating through every floor in the building. I gesture at the empty space between us. "You don't even know who she is, and my whole life Dad's acted like it was some kind of untapped land mine."

Heather's mouth makes a tight line, nodding curtly to acknowledge this. But it doesn't soften her. "Your dad was going to talk to you about it. I know he mentioned that to you, because I told him to."

She's watching me steadily. I know only because I can feel it, because my eyes are trained on the floor.

"I didn't know," I say quietly.

"Millie, look at me."

I do. Slowly. Defensively. But Heather seems to be expecting that.

"I don't know why you started looking for your mom," she says. "I don't know who this Steph woman is, or how you found her, or what you and Teddy have been up to . . . but I just thought that if you really needed anything, you knew you could always come to me."

I'm about to protest, but she scratches at her face in that exact same way I do when I don't want people to notice me crying, and it stops me in my tracks.

"I know I'm not your actual *mom*, but. Well."

She gives this tiny shrug, but it isn't enough to shake off the very real hurt I see in her eyes. It isn't enough to make the words settle after they land right on my chest, so heavy that it hurts to breathe.

"Heather . . . it doesn't—I didn't mean for it to have anything to do with you," I say pleadingly. There's the part of me that feels rotten, and then a part of me, maybe, that *is* rotten—the part of me thinking that this just isn't fair. That I should be able to ask for something this simple, something most kids I know never even *have* to ask, without it hurting everyone I love.

"Yeah, well. You're my whole world, Millie. There's not a thing you do that doesn't have something to do with me."

It occurs to me then in a very real way how much I've messed up. That there won't just be consequences, but that they'll be worse than the ones I'm used to—they'll be quieter and last longer. They'll cast a shadow that I can't just walk away from.

I say the only thing I can, the only thing I know that I mean, even if I don't know what parts I mean it for: "I'm sorry."

She nods, then right on cue I feel the telltale rumble of the bass kicking up downstairs for mic check. "I've got to go back down for the night," she says. "We'll talk about this later."

She passes me on the stairwell without bopping me on the nose or scratching my shoulder or even looking at me at all. I walk up to the apartment, the lights dim, my dad's bedroom door already closed, and wait for myself to fall apart.

But for once, there is no Millie Mood to give in to. There's just me—careless, stupid, thoughtless me, and no relief from it. I walk into my room, kick off Heather's boots, and lie down staring at the wall, waiting to cry, and discover there's something worse than falling apart—knowing that you've broken something, having no idea how to put the pieces back together.

# CHAPTER EIGHTEEN

That night I barely sleep. I open up my glitter journal and I write and I write and I write, until everything is written out of me, until there's something close enough to clarity that I can close my eyes without seeing it all on a reel: Teddy's shock, my dad's wide eyes, my aunt's deep and unexpected hurt. I write long after I hear Heather come home, long after I hear my dad's door open and murmured voices in the kitchen, long after New York has gone so still around me that for once, all I can hear is my own breathing.

The next morning doesn't feel like the blank slate I'm hoping for, but at least I know what I want to do. I want to keep going to Farrah's dance classes. I want to keep meeting up with Beth. And even though I know it might just make things worse, I want to continue the internship. I've pulled the thread too far now not to follow it all the way to the end. I want to know Steph, really *know* her, now that she's not just my potential mom but my actual, legitimate mom.

For some reason, though, I'm nervous as the elevator pulls me up to Check Plus Talent. It's not like stage fright or dread or any other kind of feeling I've felt before. I pull out my notebook and hug it to my chest, like all the words I wrote in it can steady me.

I open the door and there's Steph, her curls immaculate, her signature matte lipstick firmly in place. She sees me and her face crinkles into a smile—a genuine one, deeper and brighter than the ones on all the glossy headshots on her acting website, or the ones she flashes clients when they walk in through the door. Like I've dug in deep enough to be trusted with it.

And just like that, I'm not nervous anymore.

"Hey, honey. How's it going?"

"It's . . ."

I stare at her and give the universe one last chance for something earth-shattering to happen. No—not even earth-shattering. Just something to happen at all.

"Good," I lie. "How was your vacation?"

"Oh." Steph pulls a face, sticking out her tongue. "I was actually in the audition process for that project I was telling you about."

I glance toward Georgie's office door, but Steph doesn't seem overly concerned about her hearing us. "How'd it go?"

She blows out a breath. "Well. They pulled the rug out from under us a little bit. A new producer got involved, and he thinks the story would be better adapted for television."

"Oh." I choose my words carefully, because I don't want it to seem like I'm assuming she can't do it. "And you don't like camera work?"

"No, I just don't have any experience with it. I assume that takes me right out of the running."

"But you're still gonna try, right?"

She smiles, and at first I see her usual sass behind it. But then something softens. "You're a funny kid, Millie. Worrying about me when you've got your whole future ahead of you."

I raise an eyebrow at her. "A wise woman told me to take all the chances you can get. That you never know where they might lead."

"Well, she sounds like a trip," says Steph, even as she beams, clearly pleased that she made an impression. "But yeah, I'm gonna try," she says. "Not because I think I can get it. But because I anticipated this conversation and had a feeling you were gonna kick me in the butt if I didn't."

She smiles at me again, and I smile back, twin smirks pressing into our lips. It occurs to me that if I'm going to say something to her, this is the perfect moment. We're alone. We're on some kind of common ground. At this point I know enough about her and she knows enough about me that the conversation might be even easier than I thought, like talking to some version of my future self. The more I get to know her, the more it seems like maybe I could understand.

But I like this, whatever it is. There's room in my life for it. Maybe it doesn't have to be anything more than this. Maybe it can just be these conversations with this person who wants the things that I want, who knows the world I want to know. Maybe I already am understood in the way I always wanted to be—just not as mother and daughter. As something like friends.

"Hey, maybe I wouldn't make such a bad manager after all," I joke. And just like that, the moment's gone before I can think of everything else that might go with it.

Steph straightens up in her chair. "Speaking of, fingers crossed for both of you."

"Why? Is something particularly harrowing on the Check List today?"

Steph tilts her head at me. "Well, you have your one-on-ones with Georgie," she reminds me. "Since the trial period is almost over and all. She's deciding which one of you to keep on tomorrow."

I try not to look surprised. It's a few days early, but this shouldn't have snuck up on me. Even with everything going on, the internship's been top of mind. I've just been so busy in the thick of it day-to-day that I never really looked beyond it, to the part where it might not exist anymore. Where I might not have a solid excuse to see Steph or get her advice about the industry or text her funny audition memes I screenshotted from Instagram anymore.

"Right. Of course." I lean back into the arm of one of the chairs. "If I don't get it, can we still . . ."

I don't know how to ask because I'm not sure what I'm asking for. A casual coffee run every few weeks? A mentor? A mom?

But Steph doesn't wait for me to figure it out. "I've got your number and you've got mine. We theater gals have to stick together."

We share another smile just as her phone rings. She rolls her eyes at me, then flips back her hair to answer.

"Hey, you." Somehow Oliver has materialized next to me. When I turn he's smiling this smile that I'm not sure how to classify. It's quiet, but not in that guarded way it usually is. There's a stupid moment when I try to file it away the way I do the others—the Stage Manager Scowl, that "in the zone" look he gets during shows, that little-kid grin that sometimes breaks through—but all I can think is that it's *mine*.

The kind of smile that has distracted me from the coffee he's holding out for me, which, given my caffeine habit, is no easy feat. He also has a cookie from the bakery in between our apartments. "Are these for *moi*?"

"I figured you'd be tired after all the ABBA last night," he says. "Also, I didn't get you a birthday present, so."

I take them from him solemnly, splitting the cookie and offering him half. To my surprise, he actually takes it. "This is arguably the best one I'll receive."

"Just don't use all the energy to shout *Avenue Q* lyrics out the window at passersby."

"That was *one time*. And in our defense, we were not hopped up on coffee, but all those Twix bars that fell out of the vending machine in the band hallway."

"Duly noted."

I take a bite of the cookie, which I have discovered over the years is a true breakfast of champions—a belief I have asserted by showing up to first period with one more often than not.

"Is this why you have a cookie emoji next to my name in your phone?" I ask. "Because I like cookies?"

To my surprise, the words make Oliver go very still. He stares down at his cookie half and says, "Uh, no. That was for . . . well. I realized after we first met I hadn't just recognized you from the 'Little Jo' video. I recognized you from the coffee shop."

"Oh." It makes sense. We're neighbors, after all. We'd probably been walking past each other for years. "I didn't realize."

Oliver shrugs. "Sometimes when my parents needed to talk with us out of the apartment, Hunter would take us out. You probably don't remember, but the first time we were there Elliot held up the whole line trying to pick a treat, and you butted in to tell him to get the cookie."

I don't remember, but only because I have such a habit of making other people's business my business that it'd be impossible to retain it all. "That sounds like something I'd do."

Oliver smiles to himself, half here and half in that moment all those years ago. "Yeah, well, the cookie was so good we ended up making that our spot whenever my parents needed some space to talk things out. We'd go and split one four ways. It made the whole thing a little less . . . well." The smile fades a bit but is no less sincere. "It was nice to have somewhere to go with my brothers that was just ours. And I guess we kind of owed that to you."

I smile quietly back at him, sensing that uneasy tension you feel in the aftermath of saying something more than you meant to say. "Well, I'm glad for that," I tell him. "And I gotta admit, 'Cookie Girl' is a much better legacy than 'Little Jo.'"

Oliver winces. "Once I made the connection, I tried running into you again that summer after we met. To apologize, I guess. I mean, I did some digging into the whole 'Little Jo' thing and read through the comments, and—"

"La la la," I singsong, my fingers moving toward my ears. I've seen enough snippets of myself in YouTube compilations of girls yelling "Christopher Columbus!" at the end of that song to last me a hundred lifetimes.

Oliver shoots me a rueful look. "Yeah, well. It put your whole reaction in perspective. I just wanted to clear the air."

I lower my hands. "So you put that emoji in there as a reminder of where to find me?"

At this, Oliver's lip quirks upward. "At first. But I left it there as a reminder to *avoid* you, actually." He moves his foot forward, nudging his shoe against my boot. "It became pretty clear after that whole *Mamma Mia* argument freshman year that we were probably not destined to be friends."

"So that's when the chance of us ever being friends went up in smoke? Because you sabotaged my ABBA dreams?"

I lean back on a chair leg so he knows I'm only teasing—it's all water over the Holland Tunnel at this point—but Oliver takes a step closer, closing the distance.

"That's just it. I was trying to *help* you, Millie. That was before Mrs. Cooke put us in charge of all those fundraising efforts. We didn't have the budget. At least not the budget to make it decent, the way we do now."

This, at least, we've always had in common—high standards for ourselves and what we put into the world.

High standards that led us to get more money for our theater department than they'd seen in years. We may have disagreed on how to do it a thousand times before we reached an idea we were both satisfied with, but hosting the monthly talent shows with bake sales outside the theater was the double punch we needed to get enough money for elevated sets and period costumes for every show we did afterward.

I take a sip of my coffee. "We did crush those fundraisers."

"And nearly each other," says Oliver wryly.

It's quiet for a moment, Steph listening to whoever is on the phone and taking intense notes, the two of us both watching each other.

"Weird to think how much more we could have gotten done if we hadn't been jerks to each other," I finally say.

"I think we still kind of did," Oliver counters. "I mean, why else would Mrs. Cooke team us up so many times? We push each other."

"Off cliffs, maybe," I say, snorting.

But Oliver isn't laughing. "I was actually on board with a ton of your ideas, you know," he says. "Like that mentoring program between the upperclassmen and freshmen. Just—sometimes things take time. And someone has to help execute them."

"Wait, you had something to do with that?"

Oliver looks unexpectedly self-conscious, like he hadn't anticipated me picking up on that so fast. "A bit."

"But . . ." I blink, that year coming back to me in pieces. How we were told there were too many clubs and extracurriculars to get space for the mentoring program, and right before I was about to unleash the full throttle of a Millie Mood on the faculty, suddenly we had somewhere to go. "You got us the space booked for the mentoring program."

I feel stupid for not realizing that before. One of the first things Oliver did freshman year was join student council, which basically made him our only advocate in getting the theater kids space in a school full of overachieving nerds.

"Yeah." He clears his throat. "I also was the one who showed Mrs. Cooke how we could rotate the schedules to double-cast stuff without her having to spend extra time at school."

I forgot how resistant she was to that at first. How she'd really refused to even entertain it. Now that we do double-cast all the shows, it's almost a time-saver, if anything—we all rehearse together for the first two months and separate for the last two weeks, and if someone misses a rehearsal or needs extra help, their cast double can teach it to them later. Not only did it help a ton more students get featured and make the whole spirit of Cornelia less cutthroat and competitive, it's gotten to the point where none of us can even really remember a time when we *didn't* have that to our advantage.

And I guess we owe it to Oliver.

"I had no idea," I say. I can't even muster up a thank-you, because I don't know if it would come close to covering it.

The lilt of his shrug tells me he understood it anyway. "You were right. The school needed a change."

"Yeah, but you actually changed it."

Oliver shakes his head. "*You* changed it. I just closed the deal."

I wish I'd known. I'd gotten a lot of the credit for spearheading the new initiatives and cemented a lot of friendships while we were pushing for them. Friends that Oliver might have made, too, if we hadn't been so busy undermining each other anytime we had an audience.

I swallow down the guilt, taking my half of the cookie and raising it to the air to cheers it. He lifts his up, too, our knuckles grazing, our eyes locked.

"Well, who knew?" My cheeks are just a little too warm. Probably from the coffee. "Turns out we make a good team."

"Yeah, we do." Oliver pauses, mulling something over. "Actually, I wanted to talk to you about that."

Before I can even try to guess at where that's going, Georgie opens her office door, looking at both of us in turn.

"Which one of you is first?"

I glance at Oliver, but he doesn't miss a beat. "Millie should go."

I open my mouth to ask why, but Georgie's already walking back into her office, the door open so I can follow. My eyes are still on Oliver's, waiting for him to say something to psych me out or explain why he's insisting on going second. But he's still smiling the way he was before.

"Break a leg."

I don't realize I'm smiling back until it follows me all the way into the office, and Georgie seems momentarily disarmed to see it. No, not momentarily—fully disarmed, like I walked in with a baseball bat instead of a smile. She blinks at me, then down at her desk.

"Should I sit?" I ask warily.

"Yes. Yes, please sit."

By the time she looks back up she's entirely composed again. I sit in the chair opposite her desk, setting my bag and my notebook on the floor, and face her the same way I did at the interview when I first bullied my way into this gig. Back then I was all full of nerve and fire and a little bit of fear, but now all that seems muted. Like I've had some kind of metamorphosis, left that version of myself behind.

It takes me off guard, the ache I feel. I've turned myself inside out a dozen times over. It's that this time, I didn't mean to; it's that this time, the change isn't my clothes or my hair or my attitude, but something quiet, something bone-deep. Something I can't change back, for better or for worse.

Georgie folds her hands on top of each other on her desk. "Obviously both you and Oliver are more than capable of the tasks required in this internship. You have both done exemplary jobs, and demonstrate a crucial understanding of the industry and a drive to learn more."

Ordinarily I thrive on praise like a plant converting sunlight into energy. But this praise is so unexpected and resolutely stated that it feels more like someone just accidentally hit me with something.

Georgie pauses. I can tell she doesn't want me to say thank you, so I don't. This earns me a faint smirk.

"By virtue of that, the purpose of these one-on-one meetings is less about what you can do for me and more what this internship can do for you. What are your plans?"

I'm ready for this the same way I'm ready for any kind of audition. Every conversation with someone who has more power than you is an audition if you squint.

"Like, the next year, five years, or my whole life?"

The smirk deepens. "Let's start with the next year."

"Well, hopefully—" I cut myself off. Georgie does not need to know the exhaustive details of the back-and-forth with my dad. "I got into Madison Precollege for musical theater, so the immediate plan is to start there in the fall."

I'm expecting this to at least warrant a bemused look, if not an impressed one. Instead Georgie scowls. "Madison?"

"Yes," I say firmly.

Georgie's scowl stays locked in place. I feel the air in the room start to shift, the crackle of energy just before a storm, and sit up a little straighter in my chair.

"You're not going to Madison," says Georgie, shaking her head so definitively that she might have just willed it like it was a decree.

I choke out a laugh. Georgie doesn't budge.

"You don't think I could get in?" I press.

Georgie seems insulted that I'd ask. "Of course you got *in*. I saw that video Oliver sent to show you'd made it to the tech rehearsal. You're phenomenal." This would mean more to me if Georgie weren't saying it through clenched teeth, or if she didn't immediately follow it up with, "And it's not what I think. It's what I know. And what I know is that Madison Precollege pushes its students way beyond reasonable training and will set you further behind in your career than you can imagine."

For so long Madison has been the kind of dream that only lives in snow globes, some other world I could touch but never reach. In one fell swoop Georgie just smashed it.

"Madison had produced some of the biggest names on Broadway," I persist, leaning forward, my scowl every bit as unyielding as hers.

"And has one of the highest dropout rates."

"All musical theater schools have issues with retention," I argue. "If it were easy, everyone would do it."

"There's a difference between challenging your students and ignoring their needs. And trust me, that place has no regard for its students' mental or physical well-being. They only want results."

I scoff. "Isn't *Baron* one of their alums?"

"And did you see Baron booking any roles worth having in his early career?" Georgie fires back. "He hated the whole industry by graduation. He left the city for years. Thankfully he had the raw talent to recover when he decided to come back, but it took *years* to retrain and undo the all-or-nothing mindset he got at that institution—"

"Or maybe *you're* just a shit talent manager."

Georgie abruptly takes her hands from the desk, pushing her chair back and narrowing her eyes at me. "I think we're done here, Millie."

I grab my bag from the floor, too angry to see straight. The words poured out of me like lava, but I can tell that they're just the beginning. That if I don't get out of here and *fast*, the words that come after them are going to be my own personal Pompeii.

It doesn't even register that I've left her office until I'm passing Oliver and Steph in the waiting room. I duck my head and don't meet their eyes, but it doesn't matter. I feel them trailing after me, so wide with shock that I can practically feel them chasing me out to the main hall, where I slam the down button. The elevator is mercifully still there, and I practically throw myself into it, waiting for the doors to close so I can shove my face into my bag and scream.

But just as they're about to shut, Oliver jams his arm in between them and lets himself inside.

I don't say a word. Just stare straight ahead like he isn't there. I can't talk to him right now—I'm so worked up that my tongue is practically licking a flame, waiting to spit something awful back out.

"What just happened?"

I focus on our blurry reflections in the elevator doors. "Nothing," I say stubbornly.

"Millie—"

"I screwed up, okay?" I snap. "You should be happy."

"Yeah, well, I'm not."

Oliver's blurry reflection moves closer to mine. I suck in a breath because I catch the smell of his shampoo and for one sweet and horrible moment, I'm reliving last night—the pressure of his hands on my waist, the warmth of his body pressed against mine. The moment when for the first time, I could feel myself giving in to a feeling that was more quiet than loud.

"Millie, whatever happened—just go back in there and apologize."

I crush my eyes shut. He needs to stop. Every single word that comes out of his mouth is a reminder that I haven't just messed up, but messed up in the kind of colossal, irreversible way that is going to follow me forever. "But I'm not sorry."

"Don't you want the internship, though?"

Yes. But there's too much *want* in me now, and I'm exhausted by it. I don't know where the want ends and I begin. I *want* to go to Madison. I *want* to keep my friends. I want to go back to two weeks ago before I bulldozed every important relationship in my life, but I also want those two weeks to at least *mean* something, and now they don't. It's worse than square one. It's square zero. I found Steph, and now she probably thinks I'm a monster. Which all tracks, I guess, because I'm pretty sure my dad and my aunt think I am, too.

In fact, the only person I haven't seemed to shake off yet is standing next to me in this elevator, which is why the loudest *want* of all is for him to get the hell away from me before I ruin this, too.

"Don't *you*?" I burst, finally turning to look at him.

His eyes are so unexpectedly earnest that it splinters the last part of me that was holding itself together. "Yeah, but hear me out. I've been thinking—"

"Stop trying to *help*, Oliver," I finally explode. "I didn't even want this stupid internship, I just took it to make enough money for precollege and get back at my dad."

Usually after I lash out like this, there are at least five seconds of relief before the regret hits. A few beats where I've gotten the poison of my frustration out of my system and it's not a part of me anymore, but a part of someone else. But somewhere along the way hurting Oliver and hurting myself became the same thing.

He goes very still. "What?"

It's only a tiny truth living in the shadow of the much bigger one. But what could I say to him? That I took this internship to meet my mom? That I'm not only the world's worst friend, but the world's worst daughter, too?

The elevator doors open.

"Millie, what is that supposed to mean?"

I push my way out the front door, and Oliver is still hot on my heels, clearly hoping against hope that I'll say something that undoes what I just said. *Good*, some part of me thinks. This is it, then. I'll cut him out of my life clean and easy, and there will be no missing him at precollege, no wondering what might have happened if I stayed.

"It means I'm exactly what you always thought I was. A brat. A diva. Pick one of the above."

But Oliver doesn't take the bait, following me all the way out to the curb. "If you were really here just to piss your dad off, you could have taken any job in the city. Why was it this one?"

There are precisely ten dollars in my pocket, which is enough to hail a taxi and get at least ten blocks away from this place before it spits me out. I throw my hand up and see a driver signal his way over to the curb.

"Do you really hate me that much?"

I can't answer him, because if I do, I might tell him something worse than what I already have: I might tell him the truth. I might tell him that I did hate him. That I don't know if it was the last two weeks or the last three years, but something has shifted, and now I couldn't hate him if I tried. I can't answer him because if I do, it will only make this harder than it has to be, when I can put a stop to it all right now before it is anything at all.

The taxi pulls up to the curb, and I open the door.

"Millie—"

"I'm sorry," I cut him off. That much I can tell him. But I already know before I watch his face disappear in the taxi window that it's nowhere near enough.

# CHAPTER NINETEEN

The taxi driver, who seems very disinterested in my drama, is more than happy to drop me off at the piers so I can moodily walk up and down the Hudson until I've decided what exactly it is I'm going to say to explain myself when I get home. I don't know how long it's going to take to un-burn down my brain, but I've got the whole day now. I pick a direction, put my headphones on, and walk.

But I don't even make it through the opening number of *Next to Normal* before I glance ahead and see a man in khakis squinting at the water, his hands in his pockets, his glasses already sliding down his nose. I should have guessed it. My dad was the king of moody river walks long before I was born.

I walk up to him and he startles before he realizes it's me, and then he startles all over again. For a moment neither of us says anything. Then my dad's lip twitches, and I feel the dad joke coming before it even fully enters his brain.

"Huh. You look just like my daughter," he says. "But *she's* supposed to be at work."

"Yeah," I say. "Funny story. So's my dad."

"Well, then. I'm glad they're both putting the hours in," he says. Then he tilts his head at me. "I don't suppose you came out here to follow me?"

I wait for the rest of it to come—the volcanic eruption. The tidal wave. The Millie Mood to end all Millie Moods.

But my dad's here, and that's enough to stop it. Like all that chaos just rolled over his back before it could hit mine.

"No," I say. "Just . . . taking in the view."

He blows out a breath. I brace myself for whatever's coming next, like my dad's spinning a wheel of "Disappointing Things My Daughter Did." Will it land on the fight we had before he left and never resolved? The shit show of last night? The fact that I am unrepentantly playing hooky right now?

In the end, it's none of the above. "Some summer we're having, huh?" he says instead, looking out at the water.

"That's . . . one way of putting it."

He cocks his head toward one of the benches. "Should we sit?"

The sun is already high enough in the sky that it's beating down on us, making me feel like every inch of me is exposed. He picks a shady spot, but when I meet his eye I see that same flicker in them—that same wariness, like something is about to get opened that we can't put back.

"So." He clears his throat. "Heather tells me you've been trying to find your mom."

I don't bother trying to deny it. Instead I just nod, staring down at my legs. It's a conversation I should have been anticipating all summer, but now that it's happening, it's almost excruciating—the push and pull of wanting to know so much, and suddenly being scared to know anything at all. Steph is real to me now. A living, breathing person to hold myself up against like a measuring stick. Someone who can understand me or disappoint me. Someone who could just as easily fade into the background of my life and be nothing at all.

I pick at a hangnail, mostly just so I don't have to look at him. Mostly so I can have a few last seconds to think about her on my own, before my dad says anything that might change it.

It happens faster than I think it will.

"She said you mentioned a woman named Steph?"

It's humiliating to have to ask. Like screeching to a halt some train that was already moving full speed ahead in my brain. "It's not Steph?"

My dad shakes his head. "I don't know any Stephs. Certainly not any who could be your mom."

I want to push back. He's friends with her on Facebook, so he must know her. But then again, he only logs on every few months and doesn't seem to bother with much beyond hitting "Share" on the pictures Heather posts that I'm in. He doesn't exactly use it to keep in touch with people from his past.

And even if he did—he's telling the truth. Or at least the truth as he knows it. If Steph were my mom, I'd know by now. I'd have seen it in his eyes before I heard it in words.

"Is that— Are you okay?" my dad asks.

I probably shouldn't be. I almost *want* to not be okay, because then it would give me a concrete thing to feel. But mostly right now I'm just tired. Tired and sorry and confused.

"I don't know."

I'm so used to being full to the brim with things to say that we're both expecting there to be more to it than that, but there isn't. For once, my dad's the one who has to take the reins of the conversation, keep pushing it to whatever place it's about to go.

"I don't know how you found this woman—or Farrah or Beth, for that matter—but I'm sorry that you felt like you had to do it on your own," he says.

Ah. So Heather did very much connect the dots on the Millie Mia. My face burns, partially out of embarrassment for what I did, and partially out of shame that my dad seems so willing to forgive me for it.

"I'm sorry, too," I mumble. "I should have talked to you."

My dad sighs. "I know I haven't made that easy. I haven't exactly been . . . vocal about her. And part of that was because she asked me not to be." Out of the corner of my eye I see him fidgeting the same way I am, his hands flexing and unflexing. "But some of that was just me not really knowing what to say."

I'm afraid he's going to fall back on that now and handle it the same way he has for years. By brushing it off, or pretending not to remember that much, or distracting me with a milkshake.

"So how's this," he says instead. "I can't tell you some things, but—you can ask me whatever you want."

"Why didn't she want me?"

The words come out of me faster than I can think them, so unflinching and so immediate that it feels like they've been coiled in me for years.

"Oh." My dad blinks, momentarily stunned. It occurs to me that Heather probably walked him through everything I might ask, and that this wasn't one that she prepared him for.

"I think, uh. She did want you. In the sense that she had you." My dad is choosing what to say so carefully that I can tell he knows what it means to me. How it'll slide under my skin and stay there, an invisible part that I'll always feel even if I can't see. "From what I understand, she didn't necessarily want to be a mom."

But even with the words settling in the air between us, they don't quite land. I keep waiting for them to make me feel something—anger, maybe, or relief. Some way I can frame this, spin my own story to myself so I can finally have some concrete feeling about it. But I'm nearly seventeen years on the other side of her choice, and even knowing this, it feels like it's too far back for me to reach.

"You knew her well?" I ask.

My dad's throat bobs. "Yeah. I did."

I try to imagine it: my dad and this woman as friends. Try to imagine the world the way it was before I existed, a world where my dad had his nose buried in a comp sci textbook but his heart tangled up in a world's worth of drama. Try to imagine this girl who maybe loved to sing and had a soft spot for a boy with his own personalized goblet from the Prancing Pony in *Lord of the Rings*. A time where one thing led to another that led to another that led to—well. Me.

But in my head, she can never really take shape. She's Beth and she's Farrah and she's Steph, all of them and none of them at the same time. She's like smoke, and I can't hold on to her, even in my imagination.

"And she never wondered about me?" I can't help but ask.

This, I can tell, Heather did prep him for. I can see it in the way his eyes go up and to the left like he's trying to remember how he's supposed to answer. But a few moments later he lets out another breath, and it's clear that he's just going to say it however best he can.

"She actually . . . for quite a few years . . . we were in touch about you."

It takes every fiber in my overly talkative being not to interrupt. There's so much I want to ask, but I'm afraid if I start asking that he'll get overwhelmed and hold back.

"I sent her pictures. I emailed her about what you were up to. And—and you were right. She is a theater person. She loved that you were, too. We didn't talk much about anything other than you, but I think it—I think it made her happy."

It feels like I'm wringing my heart out, but I have to know. "And then what?"

"And then she—I suppose she asked me to stop." He purses his lips, and I wonder who he's thinking of in that moment—if he's trying to explain it just for my sake, or hers, too. "I think it was painful for her. You're—a lot like her, in some ways. And I think that became clear when you started to grow up."

"In what ways?"

My dad smiles. "You sure didn't get any of that gutsiness from me."

That's one truth I've always known. My dad may be a homebody, but I was born loud and I've stayed that way. And there were so many moments this summer I looked for that gutsiness outside of myself, tried to find it in someone else. In Beth's way of bringing people together. In Farrah's confidence. In Steph's drive. But the gutsiness has never been the mystery; it's just the surface of so many things about myself that I don't fully understand.

It's what is under it, what sets everything in motion—the tides of me that can become tidal waves in the blink of an eye. The way it feels sometimes like I'm holding myself so tight that I splinter like glass. The Millie Moods that get the better of me far more often than I can get the better of them, so fast and so full that I can't explain where they come from, let alone how to stop them from coming.

And it's only now, on the other side of everything I've done, that I understand what Teddy was getting at when he said he thought there was something else behind this, some reason I felt so compelled to find her in the first place. I wanted her to be able to explain this to me. I wanted someone to understand. Because for all the times my dad has tried, for all the times he's forgiven me for it—for all the times like this moment right now—I don't know if he ever will.

Or maybe he does. If he really did know my mom as well as he says he did. I want to ask, trying to figure out how, but my dad speaks before I can.

"In case it wasn't clear—I wanted you." He says it very slowly, like he wants this to be the part of the conversation I remember most. "I didn't know about you until you were already here, but—I did."

What my dad doesn't understand is that I don't need to remember this, because I've always known it. It goes back further than I do. I can't remember the first time he told me about my mom, but I do remember the feeling of it, because it's never changed—a feeling that I was supposed to be exactly where I was. That I've always been ridiculously, unequivocally, infinitely loved.

I smile so he knows I'm teasing. "You were twenty years old, Dad. You didn't want a kid."

"'Course not. I didn't want any old kid," he says, knocking his shoulder into mine. "But you, yeah. You, I did."

This time the asking doesn't seem as scary. "Because you loved my mom?"

"I still do. I always will," he says. "She gave me you."

I want to pull a face and tweak him the way I usually do when he gets overly sentimental. But it catches me by surprise. Not the sentiment, but how unhesitatingly he says it.

He shakes his head. "But that's not why I wanted you. I wish I could explain it. Maybe one day if you have kids of your own, it'll make sense. But she handed you over to me and you just scrunched your face at me and screamed, and I knew you were mine."

I laugh out loud, making him jump. "That's—that's a *terrible* story, Dad."

He scratches the back of his neck, sheepish. "Is it? I don't know. You're the storyteller, not me." He backpedals, then smiles ruefully to himself like he's there again. A kid with a kid. "It's just—I heard that little wail and it was like you were mad at me for taking so long. Like we'd both been waiting to meet each other and you were giving me a piece of your mind."

Something catches in my throat, then, because I know that

feeling. That crying-in-the-car-seat-after-kindergarten, choking-up-after-a-long-business-trip kind of feeling. There are some things, maybe, he does understand. Things he understood long before I did myself.

And just like that, there's a little voice in my head saying not to go to Madison. It's not my dad's. It's not Oliver's, or Teddy's, or even Georgie Check's. It sounds an awful lot like mine.

I rest my head on his shoulder. "You're a really good dad, you know."

He doesn't say anything for a moment, but I can feel the split second when he doesn't breathe, the words cementing themselves between us. I don't look at him, because I get the sense he'd be embarrassed if I did.

"That's what all the Father's Day cards you gave me said," he finally says, the slightest wobble in his voice.

I laugh, and we just sit like that for a little while, watching the boats go by on the water and the bikes go by on the path. At some point down the line there will be decisions to make. About this summer and precollege and whether this is the end of my search, or if I'll pick it up again somewhere down the line. But it feels a little bit like an ending right now, or at the very least a reminder—there will always be something I'm looking for, the same way everybody does. But I already have what I need.

"So, should I . . . be taking you back to an internship?"

I pinch my eyes shut. "About that."

"You . . . *do* have an internship, right?" my dad asks, that good old-fashioned parental alarm finally kicking back in. "You haven't just been, like. Running all over the city since I've been gone?"

"Well, yeah. For the internship. That I had. Past tense." I let out a sheepish laugh. "I might have . . . gotten into an argument with my boss."

"Never a dull moment, huh?"

"Not a chance." I sigh. "Is this the part where you tell me I should go back and apologize?"

"Seems like I don't have to tell you," he says. "But how about we grab some lunch at home?"

I hesitate for a moment. I know if we stand up right now and leave, a window will close. That I might be able to ask him about this again, but it will never be as open, as plain as it is in this moment now.

So I take a breath.

"If I hadn't gone looking for her, would you ever have told me any of this?"

It's easier now for him to answer, like all the other questions knocked down enough walls to make the answer to this one more clear. "I don't know. The truth is, I wasn't really sure how to tell you. It was easier to just . . . let it go."

I nod, letting this sink in. I might understand where he's coming from, but it's not enough. There's something still itching at me, something I need to know before we seal this up again and set it back on a shelf.

"I might still want to know who she is someday," I tell him. "Will you be okay with that if I do?"

"Of course I will be. It's *you* I worry about. Whenever that happens—I know it'll be a lot to take in." He puts his hand on top of mine. "But whatever you decide, I'm with you every step of the way."

I nod quietly. "Thanks, Dad."

At that his stomach grumbles, and we both laugh, grateful for something to break up the silence. Even then he waits me out, letting me decide whether or not I want the conversation to end. I reach for anything else to say, any other questions to ask, but I'm out of them. The only ones left are the kind I have to answer for myself.

So I stand up from the bench, swiping at the mascara under my eyes.

"Sandwiches?" my dad asks, following my lead.

We fall into step with each other, pointing ourselves home. "Can we pick up a box of Reese's Puffs first?"

# CHAPTER TWENTY

The second stop on Millie's Apology Tour is across the hall. My dad tells me he'll knock in a few minutes when lunch is ready, so I steel myself, doing something I don't often do without immediately bursting in right after: I knock on Teddy's door.

It takes a few seconds for him to answer, and I hear voices in the apartment, so I know he's not alone. I steel myself as the door swings open, but Teddy looks so relieved to see me that for once, he doesn't even notice that I'm holding food.

"I'm sorry," we both blurt at the same time.

I shake my head. "I'm the one who—"

"Yeah, but I—"

"Wow," I laugh. "We're really bad at this."

Teddy runs a hand through his hair. "I guess we haven't really had to apologize for anything before."

I hand him the Reese's Puffs box. "A . . . peace offering."

"Oh, thank god," says Teddy, accepting it. "I was down to my last three."

"That's dire."

Teddy swings the door all the way open to reveal that Chloe is on the couch, a pair of giant headphones on her ears, frowning into Teddy's laptop screen. There's a Spotify playlist titled

"Teddy's Party Mix" that she seems to be carefully curating. She glances over and her whole face lights up when she sees me.

"Oh, hi," she says, shutting the laptop. "Are you guys all good now?"

"Uh . . ." I usually have no trouble speaking on Teddy's behalf—or anyone's, really—but I want to hear it from him before I assume. Also, I'm not actually sure how much of this Chloe's in the loop on.

"Yeah," says Teddy. He looks at me sheepishly. "So, uh, Chloe knows about—"

"The Millie Mia," she says, propping Teddy's laptop on the couch. "He told me. And like, not because he was mad or anything, but because I told him about my mom's weird Cooper love poems and I know you guys had some kinda fight last night because the energy was super weird and anyway, it all just kind of came out, so don't be mad at Teddy, it's mostly because I had a lot of questions."

I blink, trying to process. I can see Teddy tense, his hand halfway in the cereal box, waiting to see how I'll react.

"I mean, the whole thing's kind of out in the open anyway," I finally say. "Heather told my dad about the, uh—Millie Mia."

"Yikes," says Teddy, in a way that makes it clear we are going to dissect that whole conversation later.

Chloe hikes up her legs on the couch to make room for me to sit next to her. We've never sat three people to Teddy's couch before, but I don't mind it. We all seem to fit just fine.

"Wild that you found your mom, though," says Chloe.

"Oh—I . . . actually, I didn't."

"What?" Teddy asks, his cheeks somehow already full of Reese's Puffs.

"It's not Steph."

There's this quiet beat where nobody says anything, and Teddy swallows his Puffs. "Well, shit," he says. "I'm sorry."

I shrug. "I don't know if I am."

Teddy tilts his head at me in acknowledgment, and I know we're both thinking of that conversation we had about it the other day. How I could have ruled them all out much faster if I'd wanted to know. How I still could.

"And it's not my mom, either." Chloe seems surprisingly invested in this whole thing for someone who was just brought up to speed on it, but a second later it's clear why. "For what it's worth? It would have been all kinds of weird, but I wish she had been. Then we'd be sisters. I always wanted one of those."

I never really needed siblings—I have Teddy, and even if I hadn't, I never had any trouble making friends. But there is a part of me I haven't had any time to really feel yet that's disappointed, too.

"Well," I say, "good thing we only children know how to stick together."

Chloe's chin quivers for a second, her eyes shifting from me to Teddy and back like she can't quite believe it. Then Teddy grabs a Reese's Puff from the box and flings it at her face.

"Welcome to our weird club," he says. "You've officially been hazed."

Then the buzzer to Teddy's apartment goes off, and Teddy bounces up from the couch. "That'll be your mom," he says to Chloe, pressing the button to let her in.

I jump up from the couch, too. "Uh—my dad's going to be out in the hall to come get me any second."

A hand grabs my wrist. It's Chloe. Her other hand is wrapped around Teddy's to stop him, too, but her eyes are focused on the door, steely with determination. "Let it happen."

I shake my head. "He'll die. Of introvertism, if nothing else. It's bad enough that we sicced a whole party full of humans on him yesterday—when he ran into Farrah and Beth, he literally *fled the scene*."

"If I can survive going to a brand-new dance class, and meeting like, ten different new people last night, *and* having to transfer schools without losing my marbles, your dad can handle talking to my mom for five minutes," she points out.

I hear the click of my own front door opening and pinch my eyes shut.

"Don't. Move," Chloe whispers.

Sure enough, we hear a telltale *"Cooper?"*

"Beth!" my dad exclaims.

My eyes are still clamped shut like it's happening to me instead of him. Or at least, whatever the Millie version of this would be. Unlike my dad, I would probably be able to walk up to Idina Menzel in the flesh and ask what's up without batting an eye.

"Wow. Twice in one week!" says Beth.

Chloe, her hands still clamped to Teddy's and my wrists, slowly backs us up from the door. Their voices are muffled enough that we can't hear what they're saying, but not so muffled that we can't tell that they are, in fact, pleased to see each other.

"If my dad explodes into a million pieces like the Eye of Sauron out there, it's on you," I tell Chloe.

She squeezes my wrist harder. "Do you wanna be stepsisters or *not*?"

I sputter out a laugh, because this seems *deeply* optimistic given the circumstances—not only has my dad managed to avoid dating for my entire human life, but his method for wooing women before that seemed to be mixtapes and brooding about them on LiveJournal. It'd take a miracle to make something happen now.

But it'd be nice if something did. I make a mental note to

drop an unsubtle hint to my dad that I'd be okay with it, just to grease the wheels. Before I can start thinking of the long game, though, there's a knock on the door, forcing us to answer it.

"C'mon, ParticularlyGoodFinders," says Beth, jerking a thumb toward the hallway. "If you want to find that cache today we better get going before it's time for your dad to pick you up."

The room goes very quiet, Teddy gaping at Chloe, Chloe glaring at her mom, and me desperately trying to hold back the giggle threatening to erupt out of my mouth. I've forgotten how delicious it is to be in the middle of some good old-fashioned wholesome drama that has zero to do with me.

"*Mom*," Chloe hisses.

"What?" She finally assesses the approximate level of teenage embarrassment and gives Chloe an exasperated look. "Oh, come on, Millie and Teddy know you're on GeoTeens, right?"

By then Teddy has already opened the app on his phone, pulling up an old conversation. "Chloe, are you—"

She grabs his phone from him. "No. Yes." She throws his phone on the couch. "Shoot."

"Chloe, what has gotten into you?" Beth asks, mildly alarmed.

I gently start shutting the door on Beth and my dad, who are both still standing in total bewilderment in the hall. "Just give us one hot sec, okay?" I say with a wink. My dad's eyes are screaming. I pretend not to notice, clicking the door closed.

"Chloe, *I'm* FindingTheodory, I'm the one you've been—or you *were* talking to," says Teddy. He's trying not to seem as bent out of shape as he's actually been about it, which might be more effective if it weren't for the chronic puppy dog eyes betraying him.

"I know. I know," says Chloe miserably, putting her face in her hands.

I should probably do the same, because the physical effort

of not butting into this conversation may actually cause me to combust.

"Why did you stop messaging me?" Teddy asks, picking the phone back up from the couch and staring at the screen. I know he's just about memorized the last few messages he sent ParticularlyGoodFinders, so there's really no point. "Did I say something? Did you . . . I mean, I really thought we . . ."

"I have to go," Chloe squeaks, scrambling for her bag.

"Nuh-uh." In one deft motion I grab her wrist the same way she grabbed mine. "You can't throw my dad into introvert hell if you can't take the heat, too. All the introverts in this building are going to suffer right now."

Then *she* flashes me puppy dog eyes. For a split second I see my future, now full of not just one hapless, adorable goon to account for, but two. They're lucky I know how to wrangle them.

"Out with it," I say.

Chloe's eyes flit over to Teddy's. "The truth is—the truth is I had a really, *really* big crush on the boy from the app. FindingTheodory, I mean. And on the app you were—you seemed to like me, too, and—"

"I did! I do! I—"

"And then I met *you*," says Chloe. "And I had a big crush on *you*, and I felt like a total *jerk* because how could I keep talking to FindingTheodory about meeting up when I suddenly had a big crush on this other guy named Teddy?"

Teddy's face turns a truly lawless level of red. He knows full well Chloe was crushing on him, but I guess this is what it took for him to actually believe it.

"And then I figured out you *were* FindingTheodory, but by then it was too late, I'd already been ignoring him, so I just— thought if I never said anything—that maybe it just wouldn't matter, and then I realized it *would* because at some point we'd run into each other at geocaches, and anyway that's how this whole thing got super awkward and I'm really, *really* sorry," she finishes in a rush, as if she has been trying to close the lid on the words for days and they all just finally burst out of her.

To my credit, I don't say anything. Partially because of the age-old theater rule of "If you don't have any tea to spill, don't say anything at all." And honestly, no tea in my arsenal is going to be as strong or as weird as this.

It takes Teddy a second to catch up to us. "Wait," he says, the hurt lifting from his face. "You were worried about having a crush on me . . . because you had a crush on *me*?"

Chloe's back to being bashful. "Yeah."

"Oh," says Teddy, just as unhelpfully bashful. "Wow."

If the two of them are just going to blush and stare at his parents' carpet all day, I figure I officially have license to cut in. I clear my throat loudly. "Okay. Well. I, for one, am glad we talked this all out. Teddy, thoughts?"

Teddy steps over to Chloe. It's the moment in the rom-com where the tall, lovable goofball is supposed to surprise everyone by saying something swoony, but what happens instead is arguably much more entertaining. "Do you maybe . . . wanna . . . geocache together sometime?"

Chloe takes a breath that might be the first one she has taken in two full minutes. "Yeah."

I let go of Chloe, but only so I can nudge Teddy in the ribs.

"I mean, uh—in a romantic way," says Teddy.

There's a beat where she looks so frozen that I wonder if I'm going to have to grab a hairdryer to thaw her back out. Then the hesitant smile on Chloe's face just about bursts. "Yeah," she says again.

After letting the two of them moon over each other doofily for a few seconds, I clap my hands together. "Well, in that case, my work here is done." I turn back to Teddy. "Please just promise me you're not going to give her the coordinates to Panera and call it a date."

Teddy frowns. "But the mac and cheese."

"We'll workshop this," I say, gesturing widely at them. "In the meantime, I'm going to bail out Cooper Price before he dissolves into the carpet."

Except by the time I reach the door, it's clear he doesn't need my help. They've both burst into laughter over something— Beth with this big, open guffaw I haven't heard from her yet, and my dad with that quiet wheezing laugh he usually has only when we're watching something go terribly wrong on *The Office*. And then a few words that have me matching Chloe's grin, ear to ear: my dad finishing his wheeze and saying, "Yeah. Yeah, I'd like that. I should be free Tuesday night, too."

# CHAPTER TWENTY-ONE

After an hour of eating ham-and-cheese sandwiches and ribbing my dad within an inch of his life about the "casual coffee" he's getting with Beth that is "not a date, Millie," emphasis on "I don't even know what 'shipping' means," I have reapplied my makeup, squared my shoulders, and headed back to Check Plus Talent. I'm braced as if Oliver, Steph, and Georgie will be lined up and glaring at me in the waiting room like my own personal firing squad, but it's quiet when I walk in. Just Steph, right at the desk where I left her, finishing up a salad.

"Hey, hon," she says sympathetically. "You okay?"

I nod on reflex, but oddly, I am. Something pops up on Steph's computer screen and distracts her for just long enough for me to get one last weird glimpse into what my life might have been like if I'd been right. If she really were my mother, and if instead of coming here to make nice with Georgie, I was coming here to salvage a relationship with Steph instead.

But there's nothing to salvage, really. Steph turns to me with those bright eyes that I thought looked so much like mine, and it's clear she still feels the same way about me that she did this morning. That she's not going anywhere. And from the looks of it, Beth and Farrah aren't, either.

Everything in the last two weeks may have changed, but it's nice to think that this, at least, probably won't.

"So . . ." I start carefully, sinking into one of the chairs, an eye on Georgie's office. "On a scale of one to 'she'll set me on fire with her eyes,' how's Georgie?"

Steph laughs. "Actually, she left for an errand this morning and hasn't come back yet."

One small mercy. At least I have a few more minutes with Steph before I get the boot. "Am I totally fired?"

Steph puts her fork down and looks me square in the eye. "I'm guessing not."

"You . . . heard what went down, right?"

"Yeah." Steph checks the hall, and when she's sure nobody's coming, she leans in with a wink. "But I have it on good authority she was looking for a way for you and Oliver to split the internship for the rest of the summer, too."

I almost lose my grip on my bag. "Wait, actually?"

"She thinks you've got 'spunk,' so. You've got that in your favor."

I'd just dismissed the internship altogether at this point—really, it seemed like collateral damage to all the other things I'd metaphorically set on fire in the last few days—so I'm surprised by how relieved I am. Oliver actually wants to do this with his life, and he's more than proven he'll excel at it. At some point the internship just became his in my mind, before this deadline snuck up on us. But I was going to miss the routine of it. The little insights into a world I wasn't fully part of yet. The kind of smiles on Oliver's face that I've never once gotten to see at school.

Still, I'm going to have to deliver one hell of an apology to get off Georgie's shit list and back on her Check List after this.

"Have you ever gotten into an argument with her?" I ask.

Steph waves her hand at me. "Plenty of times. But to be fair, she *is* my cousin."

"Huh," I say. "I didn't know that."

"Oh, yeah. Why else do you think I'm allowed to skip out for auditions?" She pushes her salad away, looking over at me with a gleam in her eye. "Speaking of . . . I got another call today. They still want to see me for that project."

I jump up in my seat. "The one they want to turn into a TV show?"

She nods, her lips pursed but a smile still sneaking its way through them. "Yeah. The producer's in town with a casting agent this afternoon. They want to meet at a studio uptown. The whole thing's kind of nuts."

I hit the desk with my hand. "Steph!"

"We'll *see*," she says, as if my excitement is contagious and she's trying not to catch it. "It might be nothing."

"It might be *everything*," I counter.

She shakes her head, laughing at my enthusiasm. "Well, if it's anything at all—thanks for bullying me into it. I needed a good kick in the pants."

I sit back in my chair, satisfied. "Any time."

Oliver walks in then, holding his Check List for Steph to sign off on. When he sees me he stops short, but only for a split second. After that all I get as he hands the notebook over to Steph is a curt nod.

Steph signs his task list. "You can go on lunch now," she says, looking between the two of us with clear curiosity.

"Cool," he says.

I ease myself up from the chair, taking a step toward him. "Mind if I join?"

He doesn't say anything. Just cocks his head toward the elevator for me to follow.

"So . . . what's your deal now?" Oliver asks as we reach the ground floor. He's clearly still on his guard, even as he holds the door open for me and tilts his head again to indicate he's heading over to the bodega to grab a sandwich.

I follow. I don't know when I decided I was just going to go ahead and tell him the whole truth, but apparently at some point it was decided. I grab on to the strap of my bag to steel myself, then say, "This is going to sound ridiculous."

At first he just keeps walking. Then when I catch up enough to sneak a peek at his face, he's softened by just an imperceptible degree that I know I've got an in.

"It's Millie Price," he says. "How ridiculous can it be?"

"Oh boy," I say as we walk into the bodega. "You're gonna regret asking that."

Oliver lets out a sigh that does not conceal the mild amusement under his exasperation. "Let's find a place to sit."

A "place to sit" ends up being Washington Square Park, where we find a bench and Oliver lays out his sandwich and I pop open my seltzer. I wait until we are both somewhat plied with pastrami and LaCroix before I cross my legs and clear my throat, diving in with both feet.

"First of all, you were right."

*That* sure gets his attention. Only he looks more startled than smug. His back straightens and his eyes narrow at me as if he thinks I've been body-snatched.

In both of our defenses, I am rarely wrong.

I give him a rueful smile. "I shouldn't have taken this internship," I concede. "But I want you to know it wasn't just to get back at my dad. It was . . ." I bite the inside of my cheek, trying to figure out where to start, what order to tell it. "Well, first of all, it had nothing to do with you. And I'm sorry I made it sound like it did."

"I didn't say you shouldn't have taken it," says Oliver. I raise an eyebrow at him, and he stares down at the half of his sandwich still left. "You're—well, you hold your own."

I have about ten retorts lined up, but I figure now's not the time. "Well—that aside. I was only really in the office that first day because I was looking for my mom."

I wait for a beat for the justified bewilderment, but Oliver's just watching me, seemingly on board with this harebrained scheme before I can even spell it out. Then again, after three years of prolonged Millie exposure, I'm guessing it will take a lot more than that to faze him.

"Is she . . . one of Georgie's clients or something?" he asks quietly, as if someone in the park is going to overhear us.

I fiddle with my hair, pulling it back into a ponytail without actually committing to it. "No. I, uh—I'd narrowed it down to three women, actually."

Oliver's eyebrows arch in alarm, his sandwich hovering a few inches from his mouth. "No."

I drop my hair down again with a wince. "Yes."

He sets the sandwich down. "Did you legitimately, actually go *this* method to get a part?"

I pick up the plastic fork he's not using and point it at him. "So we *are* doing *Mamma Mia!*"

"We are *way* past that, Millie," he says, his eyes still just as disbelieving.

"Don't let anyone ever tell you I'm not at the top of my game," I say, trying to joke off some of the tension. Except it doesn't work. I lower his fork back down and we both stare at it for a moment before Oliver breaks the silence.

"So . . . what happened?" he asks quietly.

"Well," I say candidly, "it's not Steph."

"Steph? You thought *Steph* might be your mom?"

He leans back on the bench for a moment, like he's trying to piece something together. Maybe superimposing my face onto hers the same way I did a thousand times this summer with all three of these women. Something that was only mildly embarrassing at the time but seems prolifically so in the aftermath.

"Yeah," I mumble.

"I mean . . . jeez." He puts a hand to his forehead, vexed. I brace myself for an Oliver the Stage Manager–level scolding, but instead he says, "I had no idea. I wish you'd have said something—I mean, no wonder you were so upset that day she caught us fighting."

"Well. Yeah," I say, almost self-conscious at how fast he summoned that particular memory. Like it's been weighing on him ever since.

"And all those times you showed up early . . . you weren't trying to one-up me. You were trying to talk to Steph?"

I wince. "Kind of."

"Millie, I . . . I mean, I guess it makes sense you didn't tell me." He shakes his head. "I just wish I'd . . ." He trails off, and when his eyes meet mine again there's something cautious in them. Something apologetic, even. I'm so caught up in the unexpected weight of it—the way he seems to understand the real depth of what this meant to me, even as I try to brush it off—that it takes me a moment to snap back.

"Hey, wait. You're still fully supposed to be mad at me," I remind him. "I did give you hell all this time for an internship I technically didn't even know existed before I got it."

Oliver doesn't take the bait, though, his eyes still solemn on mine. "So did you find her?"

He's still holding my gaze, and I understand then why it's always been so unnerving to have Oliver's eyes on me. He's never really looking at me. Not my rotating outfits or my flashy entrances or the little things I say or do to avoid the big ones. He's always seen deeper than that, whether I wanted him to or not.

"No," I tell him.

Oliver opens his mouth like he wants to say something comforting, but doesn't know what. But that in and of itself is comforting enough.

"It's okay," I say. "Like—good things came out of it. We had fun, didn't we?"

He puts his hand on top of mine. I've gotten surprisingly used to what his hand feels like, but it doesn't stop the slight flutter that starts somewhere in my chest and ends everywhere else.

"Yeah, but . . . are you okay?"

I may never find someone who can explain the Millie Moods. I may never have an explanation for a lot of things in my life, whether they have anything to do with my mom or not. But at least I have people who will ride it out with me. And right now, I'm mostly just glad to know Oliver is one of them.

"At this specific moment? Yeah. But thanks."

"For what?"

"For caring, I guess." Before he can say anything to that, I add, "And for not killing me through all this."

I smile firmly so he knows I'm good. Like, actually good, and not that theater-kid version of good where we pretend we are and then end up bawling four notes into someone humming *Dear Evan Hansen*'s "You Will Be Found."

He smiles back, then blinks, remembering something. "About that. I—I haven't had my one-on-one with Georgie yet, so I was wondering if I could ask you something."

I shift on the bench, twisting to sit closer to him. "Weren't you supposed to go right after me?"

Oliver leans in, too, our food long forgotten. "Yeah, but she took a few minutes to make a call, and then she had to go. She pushed it to this afternoon."

This seems unlike Georgie. I'd say as much, but I guess I'm not really in a position to say what's Georgie-like and what isn't.

"Anyway . . . if it's okay with you . . . I was wondering about asking her if there's some way we could split the internship."

I turn my head to the side for a moment to hide the smile that sneaks up on my face. Not just because of what Steph told me about Georgie planning to do it anyway. But because Oliver wanted it, too. Because despite everything—despite the years of mutual torture, the weeks of competing, and this past day where I'm not even entirely sure what we are to each other— we'd rather be together than apart.

"You're sure?"

"Yeah." He smiles one of those new Oliver smiles again. "It's like you said. We make a good team."

I smile back at him, and the feeling of it blooming on my face is distinct and easy enough that I know I must have my very own smile for him, too. "We do."

A car horn blares down the street, and I look out toward the park, knowing we'd better get back soon. I turn to ask Oliver what else is on his Check List for the day, but he speaks before I can.

"Millie—whoever your mom is? I bet she's a force to be reckoned with."

He squeezes my hand, and I'm brought back to last night, that same hand on my waist. How he didn't want me to just hear his words but feel them too. A week ago, I couldn't have imagined us speaking for more than five minutes. Now it seems like we have our own little language—now it seems like the most natural thing in the world to squeeze his hand back.

"I should hope so," I say.

Oliver doesn't say anything back. Just smirks and uses his hand to pull me up from the bench.

"C'mon," he says. "We've got a talent manager to bargain with."

We make it back just in time to watch Steph hang up the

phone, her face creased in a frown. She reaches for Oliver's Check List, scanning it with enough urgency that she doesn't notice us walk in until we're in front of her desk.

"Oh! Hi," she says, a hand flying to her chest. "Okay. Okay . . ."

The *okay*s are clearly meant for her, though, and not for us, because she seems to forget we're here as soon as she sees us.

"Everything all right?" Oliver asks.

By then Steph has already leapt up from her desk, Oliver's Check List still in hand, and let herself into Georgie's office.

"That was Georgie," she says, her voice breathy, like she's trying not to panic. "She's sick. She's . . . apparently she's not coming in for the rest of the day."

"But tonight's the *Greek Life* premiere," says Oliver, hesitating at Georgie's office door.

"And your audition," I say, barging right in after her. "You're going to be late."

"Yeah, but there's no way I'm making it now," she says miserably, running her hands through her hair.

I touch a hand to her wrist. "Your *curls*," I remind her, like the future stage mom I'm probably bound to be.

"Right." She pinches her eyes shut. "Except no, it doesn't matter now. Oliver, can you stick around until the show starts?"

"Yeah, of course—"

"And you've got me," I remind her stubbornly.

Only then does she stop in her flurry of motion, setting the papers she pulled out of Georgie's drawers on the desk and turning to face me, her lips in a tight line. "Millie, honey—I'm sorry. She also said that Oliver got the internship."

Oliver finally steps into the office. "But—"

"That's fine," I say quickly. I don't even give the information a chance to process. "He deserves it. But I'm still on the clock for today, aren't I?"

"I . . . I don't know. Maybe?" says Steph, rifling through the papers again.

"What can I do?"

She shakes her head. "Millie—"

"You're going to that audition. Tell me what you need us to do. We'll take care of it."

Steph stops again, looking straight ahead, clearly conflicted. I stare at her until she's forced to look back and see just how resolute I am. It's the kind of tough love that would probably not be super appropriate from a daughter to a mother, but entirely appropriate for what we are—two performers who know each other's overblown, ridiculous hearts all too well.

"If you're sure."

"We are," Oliver and I say at the same time. I don't even have to meet his eye to know that we're in sync for whatever she's throwing at us next.

"It's—well, Oliver has his Check List," says Steph, pulling up his notebook from the pile. "And it's about to get a lot longer, if you don't mind."

"I'm on it," says Oliver.

"But would you mind running this to Georgie's?" Steph asks, turning to me. "Her apartment isn't that far from here. I'll text you the address."

It's Georgie's outfit for the premiere. I picked it up from the dry cleaner's yesterday, which now feels like a year ago.

I open my arms up for her to drop it. "Done and done."

"You're an angel," she says.

"An angel with a watch. You've got to get uptown. Go, go, go."

"Right," says Steph, rushing out. She hands the papers to Oliver, who presumably knows what to do with them. "Thank you both. I'll text you."

I follow her, nudging Oliver to follow, too. But he's stuck at the open door to Georgie's office, looking stricken.

"Millie, I swear I didn't know. I'll still talk to her. I'll—"

"No, you absolutely will not," I say firmly. I put a hand on his arm. "I meant what I said."

"But . . ." He glances around the waiting room like he's looking for some kind of out. A way to undo what's already been done. "It won't be half as fun without you."

Steph's already out in the hallway, beyond our line of sight. I take one quick glance just to make sure, then bounce up on my tiptoes and kiss him on the cheek.

"I'll see you tonight, Oliver."

I turn on my heel with the intention of fleeing the scene, Cooper Price–style, before the adrenaline dies down and either one of us can fully contemplate the audacity of what I just did. Then Oliver's voice pulls me back.

"And after?" he asks.

I stop, turning back. The afternoon light is pouring in through the window, casting warm colors on his face, streaming into his eyes. I drink in the sight of him, doing something I'm usually not very good at: taking my time.

"And after," I say quietly.

He smiles his Millie smile, and I smile my Oliver one. We've said a lot of things to each other over the years, tossed more mean words between us than I could ever count. But making a promise only takes two.

# CHAPTER TWENTY-TWO

"Come in."

I lower my hand from the door, wondering if I have the right apartment. But the number on the door matches Steph's text, so that throaty, clogged voice I hear on the other side must be Georgie.

I close my eyes and blow out a breath. It's not that I'm intimidated by Georgie. It's just that this is going to be awkward no matter which way we slice it.

I let myself in and do what New Yorkers do best—immediately rake my eyes over every corner of the apartment they can land on, guesstimate the square footage and the rent, and judge every minor decor choice from floor to wall.

I see pale yellow interiors with little gold accents. I see a sunny kitchen with a cookbook propped open to a page for mint chocolate brownies. I see framed prints of minimalist drawings that I recognize as versions of Broadway playbills. What I don't see is Georgie.

I poke my head farther into the apartment. "Should I just . . . leave this in the front hall, or—"

"Shit. I thought you were Steph."

"No, just . . ."

When Georgie whips around to face me from her couch,

she looks like a ghost. All her makeup has clearly been cried off, her mound of curls has been yanked into a scrunchie, and she's sitting in an oversize NYU T-shirt and a pair of leggings. She looks startlingly young—at least, younger than I've ever thought of her, behind the armor of her bold blazers and jewels.

She turns away and shoves something under her coffee table, but not fast enough for me to miss it: the telltale shine of my notebook. The one I've been writing in the past few days.

The one I must have left in her office this morning on the way out.

I take a step closer to her, hovering in the open space that divides the kitchen from the living room. It feels like I'm walking in a dream, or maybe like I've stumbled into someone else's. Georgie won't even look at me.

"How long have you known?" she asks.

"Known . . . what?"

"That I'm your—that I'm your . . ."

*Mom*, my brain supplies, when neither of us will. I take a step back, stumbling on her carpet.

"I called HR to cut you your paycheck. They told me your last name was Price," says Georgie. She glances at the notebook. "I didn't mean to read it, but it fell with the pages open, and when I picked it up . . . you wrote that you found your mom." She swallows with her whole body, like she's trying to pull something back in. "How long have you known it was me?"

There are so many potential minefields here, but I can't do anything but keep walking in them. The conversation just keeps moving forward before I can catch up.

"I—I thought it was Steph."

"Steph?" she asks hollowly.

I'm still standing there in the space between her kitchen and her living room, her dry cleaning in my hands and my heart in my stomach. I can't stop staring at her. It's like I'm willing her to stare back at me, but I also don't want her to. I want all of this and none of this, and I can tell just from the way she lets out a shaky breath that she feels the same way, too.

But we've trapped each other in this moment. Unintentionally, but irreversibly. It may not be a show, but it has to go on.

"I mean, I know she's not, but . . . that's what I was doing there. My dad. He wrote about someone called Fedotowsky, I thought . . ."

It doesn't matter what I thought, because what I know is right in front of me. What I know are the things I've been seeing and looking right past for weeks. Little things that all add up to a big one. Georgie's intensity. Her competitiveness. Her honesty. Her love for musical theater, and how it carved her path in life. Her hair, the exact reddish-blond shade mine was before I dyed it post-"Little Jo."

And even if that weren't enough to seal it, it's right here. It's in the way she's looking at me right now. The way I know the feeling without ever having felt it before—that this is what it's like to be looked at by your mom.

"I'm Fedotowsky." Her voice is barely above a whisper. "I changed my name when I started the business. Check is my mother's maiden name."

I'm about to ask her if I can sit, but we're way past asking for things now. We're already in the give-and-take. I'm just not sure who's doing which.

She watches me out of the corner of her eye, so still that she doesn't move a muscle when I sit on the other side of the couch, laying her dry cleaning on the coffee table.

"I know . . . I know you told my dad not to talk about you," I say. "And he didn't. I just wanted to be clear that—this is my fault."

Georgie lets out a choked laugh. "It is very *clearly* mine," she says, as if she's offended that I might try to take the blame from her.

I stare down at my lap. I'm not sure if she means us finally meeting, or if she means having me in the first place. This seems to occur to her the beat after it occurs to me, because she straightens up and looks at me.

Except a moment passes, and then another one. She doesn't say anything. Just stares at me, like she has to account for every freckle, every hair, every limb.

"Jesus," she finally breathes. "Look at you. How did I not know?"

"Did you . . . not even know my name?"

"Of course I do. It's Camille," she says, without missing a beat. "Camille Rose Price. My mother's name and Cooper's grandmother's. Your birthday is in four days. You love mint chip ice cream and those penguins at the Central Park Zoo."

She says these facts out loud like she's guarding them, like she has held them so close to her chest for all these years that she's afraid even to say them out loud. I sit in the aftermath of it, but I'm not thinking of Georgie, or even of myself. I'm thinking of my dad, who took me to see the penguins every weekend that summer my obsession was at its peak. I'm thinking of Heather, who has probably made me more mint chip milkshakes than even Ben and Jerry themselves could count.

I'm thinking of my dad diligently sitting in front of a computer and typing this all out to her while I slept in the next room, telling the story of my life to a person who left him in charge of it.

"I haven't seen a picture of you in years," says Georgie, staring at my notebook where it's peeking out from under the coffee table. "Not since that video."

I shut my eyes. "Please tell me my dad didn't send you that stupid 'Astonishing' clip."

I brace myself for it the way I've braced for it for the past five years, every muscle in my body poised for impact. But Georgie shakes her head, still staring at the notebook as if the words didn't even fully reach her ears.

"It was a video of you on a subway platform. You were only five. A street performer was singing 'Don't Rain on My Parade,' and apparently you took it upon yourself to make it a duet."

I wait for the relief to hit, for the long-overdue exhale. That was the nightmare, wasn't it? That she'd see the clip, and that mortifying, infamous moment would be the only thing she knew about me? This is my best-case scenario, what I wanted most: to be my own person when I met her. To feel fully formed in a way I wasn't then. To be free of this thing that followed me so long.

But instead it feels oddly like disappointment. This thing I've tethered myself to, this thing I've used to define myself in so many moments she wasn't around to define herself—she never saw it. She doesn't even seem to know what I'm talking about. Her eyes are so distant in the memory of something else that for a jarring moment I'm there with her, in a world where that video never happened. In a world where all the things I did to outrun it didn't happen, either.

Then she goes somewhere further than the memory, somewhere I can't follow. It's the first time I've ever seen someone smile and wanted to look away. There's so much sadness in it that it feels like something else entirely.

"I knew I couldn't see you again," she says.

It cuts so deep that I'm not even sure if it hurts. I just know that something has happened, and at some point I'm going to have to breathe in a full breath, or get up off this couch, or walk out of this apartment, and only then will I know the extent of the damage.

"Why?"

"Oh. Oh," she says, when she hears the hurt in my voice, then looks up and sees it in my eyes. "I don't mean it like that."

She takes a shaky breath, then says half to herself and half to me, "I still can't even believe I'm talking to you right now. That I've been talking to you. And I'm just—putting my foot in it."

I twist my lips into something close to a smile of my own. "An inherited trait?"

She lets out a breathy laugh. I wonder if this morning feels the same way to her that it does to me—like it happened a million years ago, to people who don't even really exist anymore.

"What I meant is that when it was just pictures—when it was just Cooper sending things along—I don't know. You were still ours, to me. This person who existed between us." She stares into the glass of her coffee table. "But I saw that video and it was—clear that you were your very own person. A vibrant, talented, plucky little person. And that there was so much I was missing out on, the kinds of things Cooper would never be able to tell me. The kinds of things you have to be there to know. And I just . . . it broke my heart. It was easier to just let it break all the way. Ask him to stop." She swallows hard. "At least, I thought it would be."

We both take a breath then, with these uncannily similar rhythms, like we're both trying to absorb the same weight of something too big to hold. I'm not sure which one of us is supposed to say anything. I'm not sure which one of us is in charge, or if neither of us are.

"I'm sorry," I finally say. "For—crashing into your life like this. I was looking for you, but I'd stopped."

Georgie shakes her head. "I think we both know it was going to happen eventually. Even when I told Cooper . . . I figured no daughter of mine would be able to let this go."

It doesn't make me smile, but it does make me happy. The idea that someone can know you without knowing you. That there are some things that were meant to be—and how I know, even without having all the answers yet, that the whole weird journey that led us here was one of them.

"Can I ask you what happened? I've always wondered, but my dad doesn't really seem to know himself."

Georgie shifts her weight on the couch like she's getting her bearings, trying to anchor a conversation she never meant to start. It's been a week of adults being very careful about what they say to me and how, but Georgie, at least, is frank. I can tell before she even opens her mouth that she's going to tell me the truth, even if it's not a truth I want to hear.

"When I found out I was pregnant with you, I wasn't sure who your father was. It was either the ex I was hung up on, or Cooper." She purses her lips. "I didn't want you. But I loved you. Before I knew whose you were, or what you were, or . . . any of it." She shakes her head a bit. "Maybe it sounds . . . naive, but. I didn't have a lot of good in my life back then. I hadn't done a lot of good. But then there was you, and it just seemed like . . . you were something good."

It's one of those things I don't know if I'll ever be able to understand, and she seems to know that even as she explains it to me. I tuck it into some part of myself, knowing I'll wonder about it later. But the biggest question I have is one I don't have to ask. She can see it in my eyes. She's probably been answering it to some imagined version of me for years.

"I couldn't raise you," she says. "I wasn't . . . I never met my mom. She died when I was born. And my dad was . . ." She gestures vaguely, like she doesn't want to get into it. But I don't miss her slight shudder. "An asshole. Growing up, just about the only good thing in my life was the boy who lived across the hall."

It dawns on me before she gets there, like some kind of puzzle piece clicking into place. "You mean my dad?"

She nods.

"I was going to put you up for adoption. I didn't even tell anyone I was pregnant. But I took one look at you and I knew you were his. And I knew he'd take care of you the way I couldn't. I knew he'd . . . give you a good life." She looks at me and this time, her guard is so fully down that I can see past all of it, straight to the part of her that has nothing to do with me—a part that has always been and will always be just hers. "He's—he was my best friend. The best person I've ever known. I was a mess after you were born, but all I can really remember thinking is how lucky we all were that you were his."

My eyes are brimming with tears. More for their sakes than mine. I don't have to ask to know that if it weren't for me, they'd still be best friends. Maybe she'd even still be the one across the hall, instead of Teddy and his parents. It's all too much to wrap my head around at once.

Georgie knocks me out of it with an unexpected question. "Is he still a big dweeb?"

She asks it quietly, like she's not sure if she's allowed.

"The dweebiest," I assure her.

Her mouth quirks. "Does he still try to translate takeout menus into Elvish?"

I laugh, surprised at the way it punctures right through my tears. "It's worse. He even does it to fortune cookies."

Georgie laughs, too, wet and genuine, and for a moment I see it—who she must have been to him, and who he was to her. It's the way I feel about Teddy. When you know someone inside out, so well that they feel less like another person and more like an extension of yourself. All your battles, all your victories—they're always shared, always known. Always fought for side by side, whether you're propping each other up or balancing each other out.

It isn't hard to imagine them. Georgie with that no-nonsense attitude she must have used to pull my dad out of the little worlds he hides in, my dad's quiet calm comforting her from the one she wanted to escape. Life can be a scary ride sometimes, both in your head and outside of it, but it always helps to have one person who's always on your team.

They may have lost that, but it feels fated, in some way. Like the universe pulled my dad and Georgie together, and pulled me and Teddy together to fill the space they left behind.

"I think about you every single day, you know. Both of you."

I don't know if I needed to hear this, but it feels good to hear it just the same. I already have my anchors; I already know where I belong. But for the first time it feels less like I'm trying to make myself fit somewhere, and more like I'm making space for someone else. For Georgie, if she still wants to be.

"You're not gonna hate me for choosing Oliver, are you?"

I smirk, thinking of him running around the city right now like a chicken with his head cut off. "'Course not," I say, straightening up. "He actually *wants* to do all your bidding."

"That's true." She blinks at me again, and smiles back at me cautiously. "But you were just so fucking fun to have around."

I don't want to push her by saying I could still be around. That this doesn't have to be a goodbye. But it's clear that we've reached a goodbye for now, if not a goodbye forever. There's still this tug in me that's afraid to move away from this moment and afraid to stay in it at the same time, but if I start asking more questions now, I don't think I'll ever be able to stop.

I ease up from her couch, taking my bag from the floor.

She stands up, too. "And Millie—for what it's worth—I meant what I said about that program. It's a waste of your talent and your time."

I bite my lip, stopping at the edge of her couch. She's already looking at me intently when I meet her eye, but this time, there's no fight in her eyes. Just total certainty.

"You're going to be a force, Millie." She says it like she has enough power to will my future into being. "And maybe I'm not allowed to say that as your mom. But I am saying that as the best damn talent manager in the city."

I smile. "Thanks. Really. I'm . . . I mean it."

She nods. We both stand there like two people crossing each other on a bridge—hovering just a few more moments in between two different worlds that might never cross again. I might see her tomorrow. I might never see her again. Everything feels entirely possible and completely impossible all at once, and the moment is passing too quickly for me to even know how I feel.

Georgie puts some of it into words when I can't. "I feel like there's more I should tell you," she says. "Things I want you to understand."

I pull the notebook out from under the coffee table. "Write it down," I tell her.

She takes the notebook from me. Gives me a faint, wry kind of smile that wavers just as fast. "When you tell Cooper, could you . . ."

I leave my hand on the notebook just long enough for her to know that I mean it out of kindness, and not out of spite. "I don't know if I will," I say quietly. "But Georgie . . . if you ever want to, you know where to find us."

Her eyes fill with tears again, but this time there's happiness in them, too. She nods. Sets the notebook in her lap. Watches me all the way out the door, and waves back at me as I turn to go—seventeen years and two pairs of matching green eyes and one strange kind of understanding settling between us, even if we don't know what it is just yet.

It's hard to know what to feel even as I go, but maybe I don't need to know that either. Maybe it's less about what we need to know and more about what we need to understand. And that much I always will. I walk outside and feel the sun on my face, feel my feet fall into rhythm with the rest of the sidewalk, and take myself home.

# CHAPTER TWENTY-THREE

By the time I reach home, I still don't know how I feel or what I should do about it. So I don't say anything about Georgie. Instead I hug my dad and I text Oliver to ask what else I can grab from his Check List, and he writes back, All good. Meet you at the theater tonight?

My dad is working and Heather is out running errands for the club, so I spend the afternoon in my room writing in an old notebook. I want to remember this, at least, in the weird blankslate aftermath of it—when I'm still too busy processing to think of all the tiny, infinite ways this changes things and all the big, important ones that it doesn't change at all.

When it comes time to leave, there's no hour-long tortured search through my closet. I slide back on Heather's boots and a flouncy dress and a bright red lipstick. I catch my reflection in the mirror, and for once, there's no theme. No part I'm trying to play. I'm just Millie. Like the past few weeks have rattled my core enough that I've finally cracked enough surfaces of past Millies to let myself pop out.

Once I get up to the theater, there's a short carpet you can walk before you go inside. I know better than to try to get on it—not that anyone would stop me (my curls *are* immaculate as ever), but I have every intention of walking my first carpet as a star, not an onlooker. So I stop and admire it all for a few moments. The nervous energy, the sea of voices, the sharp glitz of everyone's outfits and the fierce passion in everyone's eyes. Like catching a whiff of *someday* that will make it taste sweeter when it's actually mine.

"Hey, you."

I turn and see Oliver in the same outfit he wore to the interview two weeks ago, all buttoned down and handsome with his dark-wash jeans and the swoop of his hair. Only this time my appreciation for it isn't begrudging. This time I let my eyes linger until they finally meet his, and the rising heat between us immediately crackles.

He recovers first. "It's not too late to photobomb Ben Platt."

"He wishes," I say, tossing my curls back over my shoulder. It's really just an excuse to step closer to him, and I can tell from his slight smirk that he knows it.

"Well, someone should preserve this. It *is* your first Broadway premiere."

He holds out his hand to take my phone, but I shake my head, grabbing him by the elbow and pulling him in. "We'll get one together."

Oliver doesn't protest, but he does flush as he catches his balance. "All right," he says. "Make sure to get my good side."

Then he wraps a firm hand around my waist to pull me in, and I'm the one flushing. There's no hiding it either, confronted with both of our faces in the self-facing camera—Oliver's quiet, conspiratorial smile and my wide, shameless one, both of our heads leaned in so my cheek is pressed to his chin.

We're both still smiling when we let each other go, like we're in on some inside joke that nobody else would find funny. Like we're pulling one over on the rest of the world, even though the rest of the world is still bustling around us and aggressively does not care.

"Hey, look at that," I say, pulling up the photo. "We're hot."

I'm not wrong. And apparently neither was that lady on the subway who thought we were dating. We *do* make a cute couple.

I sneak a glance at Oliver and can tell from the gleam in his eye he's thinking of it, too. "A shame you cheated on me with all those Marvel actors."

"Actors are overrated."

"I dunno," he says, looking me directly in the eye. "Some of them grow on you."

My heart flutters like I'm one of a dozen doe-eyed ingenues on my Dream Roles list. Except this time I'm not acting it, but living it. Like I finally get the sentiment behind all those sappy power ballads, where the music in them actually comes from: not from some burst of creative genius or some big, sweeping feeling. But from the moments in between. The sneaky ones. The ones where you look up at someone and your heart understands something before the rest of you does.

Then Oliver's smile falters, and he lowers his voice. "Hey. You're . . . okay with the internship thing, right?"

"More than," I assure him. "I shouldn't have been there in the first place."

He shrugs. "You had a knack for it. I'd say if the whole Broadway thing didn't turn out . . ."

I cross my arms, smirking.

"But of course we both know it will," he finishes, smirking right back.

I reach out and tweak him on the arm. "I'd save you a seat at my debut, but you'll be too busy touring Europe with the Four Suns."

He touches the place on his arm where my hand just was, lingering on it. "Yeah, well. Fingers crossed."

"They haven't made a call yet?" I ask.

He glances at his phone like he's glancing at his brothers

through it. "They're giving me until the end of the summer before we'll decide as a family. Hopefully by then some of Georgie's energy will have rubbed off on me, and I'll be able to make my case."

It's still a bit of a surprise, seeing Oliver look uneasy. Fortunately, between the two of us, there will always be plenty of confidence to go around.

"Eh, you've got plenty of Oliver energy already," I remind him. "She'll just teach you how to use it."

A cluster of people start moving toward the entrance, calling out for friends to join them. Oliver motions toward the door and we head in together. Except instead of checking our tickets Oliver flashes his at one of the ushers, who nods at us to go through.

I crane my head around to look at him. "Okay, I know we look good, but we don't look *that* good," I whisper to Oliver. "Who does he think we are?"

"Oh, I've already been inside," says Oliver. He pulls two programs out of his back pocket and hands me one, leading us down the aisle of the mezzanine. "I got our seats moved."

"How exactly did you manage that?" I say, gaping in disbelief at how close we're walking to the stage.

"Well, uh. For tonight at least, if anyone asks, my name is Georgie and yours is Steph."

"Oliver!" I swat playfully at him with my program. "Did you break a rule?"

"For good reason."

"I never thought I'd live to see the day."

Oliver stops then and gestures for me to make my way into the row. "That seat's yours," he says, pointing at one of them.

I've never been madder to have only two eyes, because they don't know for the life of them where to look. On one side of the room is the massive, gleaming stage with its thick royal green curtain pulled back just enough to see a projection of the back of Baron's head. On one side of me I am 89 percent certain I just saw Darren Criss, and on the *other* side of me I'm pretty sure I just saw a not-small chunk of the original cast of *Hamilton*.

Then I finally sit, and it hits me.

"Holy crap, Oliver," I say, grabbing his arm. "We're in the third row. We're close enough for Baron to accidentally spit on us from the stage."

"Fingers crossed," he says wryly.

Jennifer Damiano just walked past us in a pair of cowboy boots. I may not make it through the night. "For the record, this is not a 'good' reason to break a rule, it's a *great* one."

"Well," says Oliver, his voice close to my ear as he settles into his seat, "you haven't even seen the real reason yet."

Just then a very stressed-out-looking twentysomething with her nose buried deep in her phone screen starts apologizing her way down the row, her bag strap getting tangled in people's feet and her bangs blowing into her face. I can tell from her eyeline that she's aiming herself toward the seat next to me, so I pull my feet in with Oliver's to let her pass.

She trips into her seat, but with the relative nonchalance of someone who does that often.

"Hi. Sorry," she says, without tearing her eyes off her text message thread. "I promise I won't be on my phone the whole— Hey wait, do I know you?"

I clench my jaw, waiting for that all-too-familiar "Little Jo"–shaped pit to form in my stomach, but it doesn't. I don't even have to bite the urge to melodramatically sigh. Maybe there really is an expiration date on mortal humiliation. Could it be after all these years I've finally reached mine?

Then the girl snaps her fingers. "You were the intern who did the mic check for Saundra last week!"

Plot twist. "You were there?"

"Physically, yes. Emotionally? Probably asleep," she says,

looking between me and the screen of her phone in rapid succession. Finally her eyes fully snap onto mine, with enough energy in them to power a stage light. "Until you got up to sing. Who the heck even are you?"

"Millie Price."

Wow, it feels nice to get recognized and actually *asked* my name. Usually people would just call me "Little Jo" and that's that. Unless, of course, they were leaning in to pat me on the head like an overeager puppy.

"I'm Samantha, I'm Gloria Dearheart's assistant," she says. "You're phenomenal."

Thank Patti LuPone I have practiced enough breathing techniques for vocal support from YouTube or I'd genuinely forget how to do it now. "I'm— Wow. Thanks."

"You're still in high school, right?" says Samantha, seamlessly texting someone back and continuing our conversation at the same time.

That entirely depends on whether or not I'm going to the precollege, but Oliver nudges me lightly in the back. "Yeah," I say, before I can overthink it.

"Have you applied to Gloria's workshop?"

"She's doing a workshop?"

"It's like, a *little* on the DL, since she's been scouting from high school productions, but you'd be great for it," she says casually, as if she didn't just say something that has the power to capsize my entire world. "It starts in the fall."

I should probably ask for more details, but really, the words *Gloria Dearheart* and *workshop* are all I need. She could have us walking a tightrope across the Brooklyn Bridge blindfolded and I'd elbow people out of the way to be a part of it.

Before I can say anything, Samantha shoots back up from her chair like a rocket.

"Crap. I gotta take care of something real quick—just give

me your number at intermission, would you? I'll text you deets and an email to submit."

Then she's gone, like some kind of very stressed-out, highly competent, dream-bearing apparition. It's just me and the beat of my ridiculous heart and the *very* smug smile I can feel from the boy sitting next to me before I even turn to look.

When I do, I lean in so close to Oliver that we're shoulder to shoulder, elbow to elbow, pressed so seamlessly that it doesn't even occur to me to hesitate. "How on *earth* did you make that happen?"

"A good manager never reveals their secrets," he says, a glint in his eyes. "But this one wasn't so hard. She's the one who let me in to give Gloria the contract our first day at the internship. I recognized her helping out at Carnegie Hall. She really did just like, drop what she was doing to watch."

I can tell he's expecting me to crow about this, and I most certainly will at some point before the evening's out. But for right now I can't see past much of anything that isn't this boy I've known for all this time, who still manages to surprise me every day.

"I can't believe you did this," I say quietly.

Oliver shrugs, adorably self-conscious. "Yeah, well. Coffee seemed like a bad birthday present. Thought I'd give it another go."

"To think I thought all this time you were interfering with my casting opportunities," I muse.

I mean for it to be cheeky, but Oliver laughs and says, "Millie . . . of course I was. I had to, for the points system."

I blink a few times, not quite processing. "Excuse you? What points system?"

Oliver puts a hand on my knee. It's meant to be a gesture of peace, but the tingle of it makes it feel like something more than that.

"Mrs. Cooke casts on a points system to keep things fair. The bigger the role, the more 'points' you use up," he explains. "By junior year I knew we were going to get the rights to *Mamma Mia*. I wanted to make sure you'd be in the running for Donna, so—yeah. I talked her out of giving you a lead last year." His voice is markedly more quiet when he adds, "I never thought you'd be gone before . . . well."

I open my mouth to say something—about precollege, maybe, or senior year, or how I feel about all of it—but then the lights start dimming and people start filing back toward their rows.

"Well, one thing's for sure," I say. "You're going into the right profession."

I wait for another infamous Oliver quip, but the tips of his ears go red. "Thanks."

I shift in my seat, leaning in close again. "Hey, maybe one day we'll take this full circle," I say, seeing the excitement in his eyes match mine. "Me a Broadway star, you the high-profile manager who keeps me and all the next generation of Elphaba hopefuls in line."

But then Oliver lets out a laugh. "Like *that* could ever work."

Everyone's hustling back into their seats, so he misses the streak of hurt that crosses my face. The universe sure has done its best to humble me in the last twenty-four hours—like, the sheer number of things I was wrong about is impressive, even for me—but this one has its own bite. Not just because I didn't see it coming, but because I should have.

The lights to the theater start to fully dim, and Samantha distracts everyone with another squeaky round of apologies as she climbs over us again. As she passes I carefully move myself so my shoulder isn't pressed against Oliver's anymore, so my arm isn't on the shared armrest between us.

It was a fraction of the summer. That's not near enough to

undo the damage of three full years. We're lucky we can call ourselves friends at all—it would be ridiculous of me to hope for anything more. Selfish, even. One more massive overstep I've made this summer.

At least I won't trip on this one. I never said or did anything I can't take back. Just a silly kiss on the cheek. It's nothing, really. Just a passing feeling. A blip.

I press my fingers into the skirt of my dress, willing myself to believe that as the curtain rises and the music swells from the pit and people erupt into applause. I've never been this close to a Broadway stage before. My eyes start to tear up, overwhelmed by everything all at once—this dream of a night, the tangled feelings for Oliver, the shock of learning the truth about Georgie.

Then Oliver reaches out and wraps his hand around mine, giving it a quick squeeze. It feels for a moment like the chaos of it all is grounded in it, like some of it absorbed into him. Like maybe we've never been opposites, but two halves of a whole we didn't have enough distance to see yet.

I squeeze his hand back. Really, I'm lucky. Everyone's happy. My dad found Beth, Heather found Farrah, Teddy found Chloe. Oliver's my friend, and that's more than I ever thought we could be. More than enough.

I linger for a moment before I let his hand go—one last glimpse of what might have been. Then the curtain rises, and the show goes on.

# CHAPTER TWENTY-FOUR

The show is spectacular. Baron is electric, and I can feel the energy of every single person on the stage. We're so close up that I can stare into each of their individual faces—can see the pure, barely contained joy in their eyes, can imagine everything that it took for them to get where they are and how much this moment means to them now. It swells up in my own chest like I'm breathing in that same hope, that same energy. That same dream that I'll never outgrow, no matter how many old versions of myself I leave behind.

At intermission Samantha takes my number, and Oliver and I split a melted Twix bar I found in my purse, cheersing with our sticks. When the show ends we stumble out, both a little starstruck and punch-drunk from the show. All the way out of the theater I have that same weird sensation you have in the first few steps after you get off a treadmill, like I'm half floating as I walk, my eyes clouded with the future. Visions of a time when I'll be on the other side of that stage, hugging castmates and crying and peeling another night of glitter and fake lashes off my face.

Then we hit the street and a gust of warm, sweet summer wind blows in our faces, pulling me back into reality. The ache is back just like it never left. I suddenly can't look at Oliver; I need to get away from him, and fast. I need a few days to squash whatever this is out of my system, before it squashes us both.

"You don't want to stage door the cast?" Oliver asks.

I shake my head. "I'm tired. I think I'll head back, but if you want to stay—"

"No, no. I'll head back with you."

I nod, and we pivot ourselves away from the crush of bodies leaving the theater and start heading toward the subway. I close my eyes for a moment, wishing I could just will him away. I really am tired. The kind of tired I don't think I'll be able to push past, desperate to shove my headphones into my ears and let myself get swallowed up by the crowd.

"You're quiet," Oliver observes.

"That show . . . it was just amazing."

"It was, wasn't it?" says Oliver. "That plot twist in act two with Athena was nuts."

It feels like my heart is so full and confused that it's tipping over, leaking into the rest of me. It's everything. It's the precollege and the workshop, it's the heartbreak, it's the uncertainty of the life I might leave behind and the one I might keep. I don't know what to do about any of it. I only know that I need to talk to Heather.

My throat feels thick, thinking of the way we left things last night. I cast my gaze down at her boots, wishing they could just carry me to wherever she is right now. I just need her to hug me and tell me it's going to be okay.

"Millie . . . what's going on?"

"Sorry, what did you say?"

Oliver has slowed his pace, and I realize it's to match mine. I've basically been wandering blind, loosely following him toward the station.

"It's nothing," I tell him. "I'm being dumb."

An understatement. I told Chloe a few days ago that I'd never had a crush before, and it was the truth. Or at least I thought it was. This feeling, whatever it is or isn't, snuck up on me too fast to give it a name.

Well, now I have one—it's disappointment. I skipped right past crush and all the way to *crushed*. And the worst part is, I don't even know if I'm allowed to be. I had plenty of chances to fall for Oliver over the past few years. Plenty of chances to wheedle that small smile out of him, to talk about our families, to lift each other up. Maybe this is just one of those lessons I'm supposed to learn the hard way. The kind of hurt that I'm supposed to remember for the next time, so I don't make the same mistake with somebody else.

But then Oliver stops on the street, wrapping his hand around my wrist and tugging me gently to the edge of the sidewalk. I watch how his face searches mine, illuminated by the streetlamps and the taxi headlights and the glow of the bodega behind us, and that split second is all it takes for my whole body to reject the idea. I don't want somebody else. I want *this*.

"No, I think *I'm* being dumb, because I must have missed something here."

I swallow thickly.

"It's just . . ." I shake my head. "You saying you wouldn't be my manager. I just thought . . ."

*We make a good team.* We said it just a few hours ago. And maybe I shouldn't be saying anything right now. Shouldn't tarnish what is a pretty miraculous friendship, given everything that preceded it. But I can't help myself. I never can.

"Well, of course I couldn't," says Oliver, bewildered. "I thought that'd be obvious."

"Well, why then?"

He has the audacity to laugh. It's not a mean kind of laugh, but this little chuckle under his breath, like he knows something I don't.

"Do you think we wouldn't get along?"

"No, not that."

"That I wouldn't take your advice?"

Oliver just shakes his head, a smile still playing at his lips.

"Then *what*?" I ask stubbornly, my heels digging into the cement.

For a moment he just stands there, his back to the people crowding the sidewalk, my back to the wall. Something shifts in the air, and it occurs to me that Oliver isn't the one missing something here, but me. Something that's curling at the edge of that smile he only smiles when we're alone, something laughing in his eyes, something I can feel the shape of even if I can't see it yet.

I look down at the cement, sucking in a quick breath before I do or say something more ridiculous than I already have.

"Millie," he finally says, taking a step toward me. He waits, slowly and deliberately, until I look back up. Then his hand reaches out and settles itself on my cheek, lifting my face up toward his. "You want a reason?"

The word feels like it's hovering in my throat, suspended in this moment with the two of us—this moment that should feel uncertain, but in a flash, feels anything but. "Yes."

He leans in close, and I lean in closer. Our foreheads are pressed together, so close that I can't see his eyes anymore, but can feel everything else—the heat of his skin on mine, the warmth of his breath, the pressure of his other hand that has somehow made its way to the nape of my neck. We're both completely still, the same way we've always been in these few reckless moments when one of us pushes and the other doesn't immediately push back.

But this—this isn't one of our games. It's the end of one. And no matter who makes the first move or who makes the last, it's one we can both win.

"Because of this," he says.

And then he kisses me.

My whole life I have learned to have presence. To plant my feet on a stage and anchor myself there. To learn my lines and everyone else's so rigorously that I'm prepared for any and every possible mistake. To lead the charge, and above all, to lead myself.

It only takes two seconds of kissing Oliver for a lifetime of self-possession to undo itself. For a moment I'm not planted anywhere at all. For a moment there's nothing to anticipate, nothing to lead. It's perfect synchronicity. It's thoughtless and weightless and dizzying, the way I have no idea how to do this but am doing it anyway, the way I don't need a script or a reason or anything other than Oliver's lips on mine, my arms wrapped around his shoulders, his hand working its way through my hair.

We pull apart, and the world comes back in phases, but the feeling stays. His forehead is still pressed against mine, the two of us just staring in the aftermath of something that is unprecedented and unexpected and at the same time so ridiculously, stupidly overdue.

"For the record," I say breathlessly, "we can still make out and work together. Tons of theater power couples—"

Oliver rolls his eyes and cuts me off with another kiss. And then another, and another, until at some point one of us starts laughing and the other does, too, and it occurs to us that we are making *quite* the spectacle of ourselves in the middle of the theater district.

Before I can start to wonder what this is or what it means or how it'll play out, Oliver answers all of it by taking my hand. This time he's the one who weaves his fingers through mine, and this time when he squeezes them, I know what it means without having to ask.

I stop just for a second to steal another glance at his face, to kiss him just under his jaw. He pulls me in closer as we start walking, our shoulders bumping into each other, the two of us unsteady and happy on our feet.

"It's probably too soon to start calling us a power couple, huh?" I ask merrily. "Since we aren't industry people."

Oliver just smiles, weaving us in and out of clusters of other people. For once I am content to let him take the lead. If he's the one steering, I get to stare at that new smile, the one that's all mine.

"Millie, you're not a person," he says. "You're a roller coaster. My seat belt is buckled. I have no idea where you're going, but I'm in for the ride."

# CHAPTER TWENTY-FIVE

When I get home, dazed from all the kissing and the hand-holding and the way Oliver tucked a lock of hair behind my ear at the door to my building and said he'd call me tomorrow, the whole apartment smells like Heather's pasta sauce. I think my lovestruck brain is playing tricks on me until I round the corner and see Heather at the saucepan, spooning in extra salt.

There are so many things I want to say to her right now. *I'm sorry. I found my mom. I don't know what I want to do about next year, and I have to decide, fast.*

Instead what comes out is "Shouldn't you be at the club?"

"Carly's taking care of the club tonight. Coop just went out to grab pasta."

It's not Sunday, our usual pasta day. I'm trying to figure out if this development is a good sign or a bad one when she turns to look at me, then laughs so hard she accidentally flings pasta sauce on the fridge. I blink at her in alarm.

"Fun night?" she asks.

I touch a hand to my face. "Why?"

"Uh." She grabs her phone and opens the front-facing camera. My lipstick is apparently not as matte or "kiss proof"—the brand's words, not mine—as I was led to believe. I look like one of the hookers in *Les Mis*.

"Oh my *god*."

She's still laughing as I leap up to wipe it off my face before my dad gets home and I scar him for life, still grinning when I come back into the room.

"So . . . who did the honors there?"

If kissing Oliver was the cake, getting to tell Heather about it is the frosting. The thing that cements it, sweetens it, makes it feel like it really happened and it's not just some happy part of me floating into space.

"Oliver."

I fully deserve to get ribbed for this after three years of complaining about him like he was the weather, but Heather is—as usual—way ahead of me.

"Aha!" she says. "I had a feeling after he helped Teddy get you to the party. And from the way you were making eyes at him."

"I was *not*," I protest, but even I can't keep the smile from bursting on my face.

"He was making eyes, too," she teases.

Even though I'm fully aware Oliver likes me now—him saying so, and the kissing every few blocks on the way back home pretty much cleared that right up—I still feel my cheeks burn.

"Speaking of—I didn't get a chance to give you these last night." She turns off the stove, peering at the bubbling sauce for a moment before reaching under the counter for a box. "And, well—I know your birthday's technically not until Monday, but I thought you might want them for class this weekend."

I take the box from her and unwrap it carefully, recognizing the iconic LaDuca label on the box before I even see the shoes. I pull the top off, and there they are: flawless two-and-a-half-inch-heel T-strap beige character shoes with a hard sole, the same ones I've been salivating over with every other theater kid

I know for years. The kind of shoe that says you're not just in this, but all the way in it.

Heather pulls the tissue paper out of the way so I can get a better look at them, because I've completely frozen in awe.

"Farrah helped me pick them out," she says, a little cautiously. "Said these soles were best for dancers who were stronger singers and actors."

They're beautiful. They feel like some kind of talisman, like a slice of the future I can't see yet. These shoes built to last so long that they might not just see a college stage, but a Broadway one. I graze the leather with the tips of my fingers and feel the energy of everything yet to come: the auditions I'll nail and the ones I'll blow; the roles I'll play and the ones I'll miss; the path that will twist and turn whether or not I'm ready to twist and turn with it.

"They take so long to break in that I thought, you know. You'd have senior year to get them ready for college," says Heather. "But now I guess you'll have them *for* college."

"Thanks, Heather," I say. These shoes run in the mid-two-hundred-dollar range, so I know they weren't an easy purchase to make, but it's not just that. It's the faith she has in me. That she always had, before I had a lick of talent to back it up.

She pulls them out of the box, tapping their soles on the counter. "Try 'em on. Give 'em a whirl."

I want to, but there's something else I want to do more. By the time I look up and meet Heather's eyes, I can tell she feels it, too—the unresolved conversation from the stairwell last night. The apology that is understood but still unsaid. The biggest regret I have in all this, more even than going behind my dad's back: hurting Heather in the process.

"I wanted to . . . talk to you about the whole . . . finding-my-mom thing."

Heather nods. The apartment feels very quiet without my

dad here, even though he's the quietest of all three of us. Like there's so much space to fill to try to explain what happened, but there will also never quite be enough.

"First of all, I'm—I'm really sorry," I say. "For not telling you guys what I was doing, and for . . ."

I'm not even sure how to say it, because there's so much to be said. But Heather just smiles and tweaks me on the cheek.

"I know. And I am, too," she says. "For the way I reacted, mostly. What you did may have been . . . not ideal. But I don't really know what it's like to have a question like that. I've never had to wonder."

The truth is, I haven't really, either. I wonder if it weren't for the precollege if I'd have ever bothered looking at all.

But I dismiss the thought as soon as I have it. It's like Georgie said. It was inevitable, in its own way. But it was a matter of time, not a matter of anything else. I can be uncertain about everything else in my life, but never uncertain about the love in it.

"We started it and it all kind of got ahead of us too fast," I say, trying to explain. "Finding Beth, and then Farrah, and . . ."

"I know. Your dad told me."

This is unsurprising, considering I don't think I've ever said one thing to either of them in my life that wasn't immediately repeated to the other.

"And I guess I can't complain, since I *did* get a girlfriend out of it."

She looks over at me hesitantly, like I might have some objection to it. I just smirk back. "Girlfriend, huh?"

"Yeah." She busies herself with a dirty dish on the counter, but I can still see the pink in her cheeks. "And yes, she has seen me attempt to dance and is somehow still into me."

"The Cooper woman curse. Flawless in every way but our two left feet." Before she can ask, I say, "I'm glad that *some* good came out of this."

Heather sticks her tongue out at me. "Maybe more than some, if this Beth thing works out with your dad." She frowns at the dish in her hands, a different kind of quiet settling over the room. "But I'm still not sure *how* you found these women."

"Teddy helped. But Dad's LiveJournal page started it," I say, only because I know it'll make her laugh.

"His *LiveJournal*?"

"From, uh, 2003." I guess I didn't keep the email fresh on her browser. Probably for the best, because the last thing she needed was Jade distracting her mid-courtship with Farrah. "It was . . . predictably angsty."

"Oh boy. Well." She bites her lip, but that doesn't stop the laugh from coming through. "Maybe we don't mention that to him."

"Yeah, maybe not."

We're quiet for a few moments again, the two of us retreating back into our own thoughts. It occurs to me that this must have been one hell of a two weeks for her, too, with all the changes. Dad being gone, me going rogue, Farrah dancing into her life. And Heather caught in the middle of all of it, whether she wanted to be or not.

"Listen, Millie," she says, coming back before I do. "I know it's a tough subject. But I also know you. Well enough to know you were sneaking around auditioning for the precollege long before you got in."

This *is* surprising but probably shouldn't be. Heather has been able to see right through me since my very first lie, which I'm told was when at the age of four I claimed my imaginary friend changed the channel from a Star Wars marathon to our DVD of *Enchanted* while my dad was in the bathroom.

"And you've never asked about this before." She leans into the counter, watching me carefully. "You've really never seemed to care. And I don't think precollege changed that. I think something else did."

I pull my lips into my teeth. If I'm ever going to tell the truth to someone, it's Heather. And if I'm ever going to properly do it, it's right now.

"I've always been . . . dramatic."

"Expressive," says Heather.

"A handful," I concede. "And I guess—sometimes I just feel things differently. Loudly. The Millie Moods. I wondered maybe if . . . finding my mom might . . . explain it. Because sometimes I feel like it just comes out of nowhere. It's not from you, or from Dad, so I thought maybe . . . I don't know."

And I still don't. Meeting Georgie didn't necessarily make that any more or less clear. It gave me a way of coping—the writing and the journaling really does help—but I don't know Georgie well enough to know if this is part of her, or just a part that's all my own. And the way we left it, I'm not sure if I ever will.

"Well, I think I do," says Heather.

I frown at her. "You do?"

"Well, yeah. Some of that is just being a teenager. It's par for the course." She sees the frown on my face deepening and adds, "I know you don't want to hear that, because it's unhelpful until you're old enough to know it for yourself, but it is what it is."

Deeply unhelpful, in fact, but I keep that to myself.

"And the other part?"

Heather looks thoughtful for a moment, staring at the spot where my dad's whole office setup is in the living room. "The other part . . . I think you got from Coop."

I shake my head. "Cooper Price is the most emotionally stable man in America."

"He's also the most *anxious* man in America," says Heather pointedly.

"Yeah, but—that's Dad. That's not me. I make Galinda look shy."

Heather sighs. "I think for your dad, he deals with anxiety by staying close to home. That's why he's always needed people to shove him out of the nest. People like you and me."

*People like Georgie*, I realize. She would have elected herself the boss of him then the same way she does everything now. The picture is already startlingly clear in my mind, of a teenage Georgie dragging a teenage Cooper out into the streets the same way Heather and I have a thousand times.

It makes me recognize, then, that this displaced sadness I feel isn't for myself. It's for them. I never needed Georgie, but my dad must have once. I wonder if that feeling ever went away for him. I can't imagine I'd be able to fill that space if Teddy left me behind.

"But I think with you, the anxiety's different. I think it just sort of bottles up until it's got nowhere else to go. With Cooper everything goes in, and with you it all goes out." She smiles at me sympathetically. "But I think the root of it is the same."

It's the kind of realization I could never have come to on my own, but one that desperately needed making. I look up at Heather, my eyes misty. I am not such a mystery after all, maybe. At least not in the ways I need to understand. And nobody would ever have been able to make me see it better than Heather, who has always understood me best.

She tilts her head at me, lowering her voice. "I think that's why your dad's been so worried about letting you go," she tells me. "I think he's always known that."

But he had friends. He had Farrah and Beth and Georgie and maybe Steph, even if he doesn't fully remember. And now thanks to his angst-fueled LiveJournaling about it, I have them, too.

"I think he just doesn't want that to happen to you. You've

always had these big dreams, but I think he's always been relieved that they've kept you close to home. And this one wouldn't."

It's the ache I've been trying so hard these past few months to ignore. The one that kept me not just from telling Heather and Dad but from telling my friends. The one that only seems to get deeper and more pronounced as the summer goes on. The one that now feels too loud to ignore.

My voice is quiet when I speak, but it's sure. "Maybe I need some time to break in the shoes."

This time it's Heather's eyes that get a little misty.

"Good," she says after a moment. "Because you've got plenty of it."

She sets me to task, then, on cutting up the baguette she procured that morning and setting the table for a late-night feast. We talk about Oliver and we talk about Farrah, teasing each other until we're both giggling the same high-pitched giggle I can only have gotten from her. Then before my dad gets back she finishes wiping off the smudge of lipstick I missed, then ruffles my curls and says, "If Oliver breaks your heart, I promise we'll never book the Four Suns again. Or at least for a month or so. They're *good*."

I laugh, then watch as she flits over to her bedroom, almost certainly to grab our matching fuzzy slippers.

She disappears for just a moment, but in that moment, something else comes into focus. All the years leading up to this one, I've had friends ask me why I didn't wonder so much about my mom, and I've never known what to say. Now I do. Now I understand. I may not have had Georgie, but I've always had Heather. I've always had someone who knows what I need to hear, someone who knows exactly what I'm feeling before I fully feel it, someone who knows me better than I know myself.

I'm a lot of things, maybe, but chief among them is that I am her kid. I'm everything she taught me, everything she sacrificed for me. And whatever she is to me, she's mine, too. I've never had to name it to know that it's forever.

"So," says Heather, coming back with the slippers. "If you do stay for senior year, what's the next transformation going to be?"

I look down at Heather's boots still on my feet, well-worn and well-loved, lasting me through all these years. I may feel like a blank slate right now, but I've always had these as an anchor. Something that has reminded me who I really am, even when I was determined to be anything but myself.

"I think I'll try something truly radical," I tell her. "I'll just be myself."

Heather's lips soften into a knowing smile. "My favorite look yet."

# CHAPTER TWENTY-SIX

Later that night, after we've eaten our fill of pasta and gone to town on a pint of Ben & Jerry's Chocolate Chip Cookie Dough ice cream, Heather heads down to the club, and I head into my room to put on sweatpants before I let myself into Teddy's apartment. I'm still trying to decide what plot twist of these last eight hours to tell him first when there's a light knock at the door.

"Come in."

My dad's holding a thin purple box I've never seen before. For a moment I think he's also giving me my birthday present early, but when he walks in, he doesn't offer it to me. If anything, he seems to hold it closer to himself for a beat, like he's not sure how to let it go.

"I've been thinking about our conversation about your mom, and . . . well." He drums his fingers over the lid of the box. "This has some things in it. Your birth certificate. An email address. A picture of her. Enough that you should be able to get in touch with her, or just . . . know about her, if you ever want to."

Instead of handing it over to me he sets it down on my desk, like he's putting it in neutral territory. It's mine to open or mine to ignore. He offers me a small smile, letting me know he's fine either way.

"Thanks, Dad."

He takes a step back, unconsciously distancing himself from it. "I probably should have just offered sooner. You're old enough to make this decision on your own." He looks at the box one more time and then back at me. "I'm here for any questions you have. Just—let me know if you are going to get in touch with her, okay?"

He leans like he's about to turn back toward the door, but something shifts in me before he can. It's not that I need to tell him, or even that I want to. It's that I've had enough secrets this summer to know that no good can come of them.

I take a breath, but it takes a few seconds for the words to follow. This secret feels every bit as much Georgie's as it does mine. But when I follow myself all the way down to the root of it, it doesn't feel like much of a secret at all.

"Dad, I already found her."

At first he just stands there, one foot pointed toward the door and the other at me. His eyebrows lift, and after a moment he says, "Wow. Okay."

I take a few steps closer to him, my hand grazing the box on the desk. "I didn't mean to find her," I tell him. "It was—Steph, the woman I thought was my mom? Georgie's her cousin. Actually, I've been working for her this whole time."

My dad blinks a few times as he walks over, settling on the edge of my bed. There's this dazed look on his face like he's trying to decide if he just stumbled into a weird dream. "I . . . didn't see that coming."

"Neither did I." I sit down on the bed next to him, and he seems to come back to himself. "Neither did Georgie, for that matter."

He shakes his head, like he can't quite process her name coming out of my mouth, or maybe just hearing someone say it at all. "How did . . ."

"It's a long story," I tell him. "But we talked this afternoon.

And I think—I think I understand it all a little better now. Why she did what she did."

I'm expecting my dad to ask for the long story, already preparing to give him the play-by-play of the whole summer and the whole conversation Georgie and I had to boot. But instead he looks me squarely in the eye, fully back in the moment, and asks, "Are you okay?"

"Yeah. Actually—better than I thought," I say. The relief in his face is palpable. It only occurs to me then that he's probably been bracing himself for this for years. "I think we . . . get each other. We're a lot alike."

The smile on his face is every bit as heartbreaking as Georgie's, almost like he is feeling the aftermath of hers. Like he was used to feeling the things she feels and is only just remembering how.

His voice is less firm when he asks, "So she's . . ."

It's a million questions at once, and he can't seem to decide on one. Even if he could, I wouldn't be sure what to say. I might understand Georgie, but I don't know her. Not in the way he does, or the way I hope I might one day.

"I don't know," I tell him. "But I do know she misses you."

"Well," he says, the word so thick that it seems to stop the rest of what he was going to say in its tracks.

But I know what he meant to ask, even if he can't ask it. "I told her she knew where to find us, if that's okay with you."

He nods. "But if she doesn't . . . will you be all right?"

I bite the inside of my cheek, mulling it over in a way I haven't been able to yet. "I like her. I'd like to get to know her. So I'd be disappointed."

My dad breathes out something close to a sigh, something resigned and a little bit sad. He wasn't keeping this secret for her, or even for himself, I realize. This is what he's wanted to protect me from all along.

I bop my head on his shoulder. "But mostly for you and Georgie," I tell him. "I've already got everything I need."

I smile at him, and he smiles back, and we both feel it then—not quite an answer to all the questions, but an understanding that we don't need them right now. This story started seventeen years ago, and it's far from its end. But it's not just my story. It's both of ours. And no matter where it leads us next, this time we'll be ready to face it together.

# TEN MONTHS LATER

Heather glances around Washington Square Park, hugging one of Farrah's ginormous oversize sweaters to her body against the slight spring chill and looking at me, Teddy, and Chloe in turn. Farrah wraps her arms around her to help warm her up.

"Where did the two of you send Coop and Beth for this treasure hunt, the moon?" Heather demands.

"Just the Milkshake Club," says Teddy.

"And then the High Line, and then the coffee shop where they had their first date as grown-ups, then the library where they used to do their homework together in college," Chloe pipes up from her tracking app, which is, in fact, monitoring Beth and my dad's movements through the city. Admittedly, dropping a tracker into Beth's purse on her way to meet my dad today *somewhat* toes the line of acceptable teenage behavior, but in our defense, if we'd given it to my dad, he'd have lost it in the first ten minutes—and then we'd be flying the entire operation of "Fellowship of the Ring (Cooper Is Giving to Beth)" blind.

"So basically the entire island of Manhattan," Heather groans.

"We wanted to make it romantic!" Chloe protests. And I guess to them, an endless string of locations with highly specific latitudes and longitudes *is* romantic. The two of them are still so hardcore into geocaching that Teddy recently employed the help of about a dozen of the GeoTeens to set up an elaborate promposal for Chloe a month ago (what Heather dubbed the "dry run" for what we're attempting to execute now).

"We needed the extra time to set these punks up anyway," I say, messing up Elliot's already messy hair.

He sticks his tongue out at me, shaking his hair back out. "*We're* all set. We're professionals, lady."

His T-shirt that currently reads BABY YODA FOR PRESIDENT begs to differ, but logistically speaking, he's not wrong. After Oliver finished his internship last summer, the Yang family tribunal decided to give him a few months to see if he could juggle managing the band with school, and since then, they've been gigging all over the city and even landed a modest-size record deal with an indie label—one that isn't trying to mold them into anything, so Elliot's free to be his weird self, David's free to be his loud self, and Hunter is free to be mostly silent and occasionally cut in with brutally hilarious, deadpan comments at his leisure.

And just in case that all didn't seal the deal, Oliver just got into Pace, where he'll study stage management. Between that and Georgie extending his talent management internship into a part-time gig, he'll be ready for anything the Four Suns will need and then some.

"Thanks again for doing this, by the way," I say to all three of Oliver's brothers, who are currently standing by the arch in Washington Square Park with instruments at the ready.

"Anything in the name of true love," says Hunter, who, in lieu of his usual drums, is unironically chilling with a bongo strapped around his neck.

Elliot scrunches his nose. "I was told there was free food."

My back is turned, so I see the smirk on Chloe's and Elliot's faces and figure out Oliver is approaching before I even hear the footsteps behind me.

"Hey, *Ollie*," says Chloe cheekily.

Elliot snickers. He and Chloe have formed tight ranks among the underclassmen at Cornelia, which unfortunately for Oliver means that Elliot is constantly giving Chloe ammo to tease him. It's probably for the best, seeing as his mortal enemy is his girlfriend now. Someone's got to keep him in check.

"Oh, dear god," says Oliver, stopping short.

He looks between me and David, and only then do we realize we're wearing identical NYU sweaters. David just wrapped up his first year at Tisch, and last week met up with Steph so they could give me an actual tour of my future school, and not the brochure-friendly, parent-pleasing one Heather and my dad and I got the day I auditioned.

Well, as much of a tour as Steph was able to give without saying "I'm so *excited* for you" about a thousand times. I guess that was more than merited, seeing as she helped me pick my audition songs and tirelessly coached me during the break she got before the pilot of her new show, *Like Mother*, got picked up. Between her singing help and Farrah's *intense* dance help the first half of senior year, I was thoroughly prepared for anything college auditions could throw at me.

"Nice," says David, reaching his hand up to me for a high five.

I oblige, and Oliver pulls a face.

"Okay. New rules," he says, pointing a finger at his older brother. "No matching outfits with my girlfriend."

"You're not the boss of me," says David, puffing out his NYU-clad chest.

"I'm your manager; I'm fully the boss of you," Oliver reminds him.

David opens his mouth to protest, but before he can I pull

Oliver in, kissing him hello. That tense part of him loosens the way it only ever does when he's with me. I feel the slow smile blooming on his face through the kiss, fully there by the time we pull apart.

"What held you up?" I ask.

"Georgie let me sit in on a phone call where she was negotiating a client salary. It was *nuts*," he says, his eyes shining like he's still caught up in the rush. He also hands me what appears to be a Ziploc with several tea bags in it. "We also met up with Gloria. She said to give this to you."

"Uck."

As much as I profoundly, deeply, and infinitely respect Gloria Dearheart—landing a spot in her workshop and getting to work with her over the past year has done more to prepare me for the industry than all sixteen years before it combined—she insists in her ability to mix her own "mojo" teas to drink on performance days. Unfortunately most of them are about as intolerable as the already infamously bad Throat Coat tea singers swear by, but at least hers gets the job done.

He takes my hand and squeezes it. "The coffee will still be there the other three hundred sixty-four days of the year."

"I suppose." I glance behind him. "Where are—"

"Georgie and Steph are on the way, they just had to pick up the flowers for Beth first."

A sentence that would have made no sense being put into the universe a year ago but is par for the course now. Another weird consequence of my Millie Mia is that Steph, Georgie, *and* Farrah are all loyal members of Broadway Bugs and now that the four of them are all reunited from their college days have started a book club with Heather on the side. From what I can tell, though, it's mostly an opportunity for them to drink rosé and relentlessly tease my dad whenever we host them at our place. I have yet to see one book.

"We were going to leave earlier, but Steph thoroughly distracted us all with Goth Millie's newest upload," says Oliver, pulling out his phone.

I preen ever so slightly. I took Oliver's advice last summer, and once I had time freed up from the internship started using my past Millie personas for actual good. We launched a TikTok account and right now I'm rotating between 1950s Housewife Millie (her hits include a cheerful rendition of "Totally Fucked" from *Spring Awakening*), Jock Millie (who recently dribbled a basketball while performing "Memory" from *Cats*), and Goth Millie, who sings Broadway's most iconically peppy songs in monotone.

We've had a few of them go semi-viral, and one that landed on the main feed for a full day. Enough that the account now has around thirty thousand followers and is pretty well-known among the theater set. It helped that we had a bit of a hook to get them invested—the name on the account is listed as Little Jo.

"Oooh, was it the one where she sings 'Tomorrow' from *Annie*?" says Farrah, peering over Oliver's shoulder.

Chloe perks up from her own phone screen, where the little dot that is my dad and Beth is getting closer and closer to the park. "I watched that one like ten times after school."

"It was more like twenty. I'm gonna have that song stuck in my head until the end of time," says Teddy, which may very well be the case, since he's the one who's been editing the videos before they go live. "Also, Georgie and Steph better step on it. Coop's getting close."

Right on cue, Georgie and Steph spill out of a taxi, roses in hand.

"We're not too late, right?" says Steph, still managing to outpace Georgie even though she's in a pair of three-inch heels in the late-spring chill.

"Just in time," says Farrah, taking the flowers from her so she can add the musical notes on sticks she ordered online.

"Look at you in your little NYU sweater," says Steph, pinching my cheek.

"Hands off the merchandise; opening night of *Mamma Mia* is tomorrow," Georgie reminds her. She leans in and gives me a quick tight hug. "I brought the camera."

"Ooh, the fancy self-tape camera?"

"The very one," she says, pulling it out of her purse. "I figure if we're going to embarrass Coop with the video on his wedding day, it'd better be in HD."

I beam, knowing full well that the aforementioned fancy camera Georgie has on hand for clients doing remote auditions will also be capturing my run as Donna and Chloe's stage debut as Sophie tomorrow in our months-delayed production of *Mamma Mia*. Mrs. Cooke ended up taking maternity leave in October, making the usual fall musical a spring one. Chloe and I have basically spent the entirety of second semester in ABBA land.

"I see them!" Chloe pipes up.

Hunter straightens up his bongo. "Ready, team?"

David runs a hand through his hair. "As we'll ever be."

Elliot jumps up and down, his version of "yes."

Over on the sidewalk I can see them making their way over—Beth laughing about something, her hair and fluttery skirt blowing in the wind, and my dad staring at her with that same quiet affection he must have had for her for years. He's so enamored with her that despite being the one who's proposing, he fully forgets to look up over at us until he's practically at the arch, which is why his shock is every bit as apparent as Beth's.

The thing is, my dad agreed to a treasure hunt proposal that ended with me and Chloe giving him the ring to give to Beth. He was not so much counting on this veritable parade of humans, or the Four Suns breaking into a heartfelt rendition of—be still, early 2000s Cooper's dweeby LiveJournaling heart—Aerosmith's "I Don't Wanna Miss a Thing."

In our defense, they both have theater kids for daughters. He should have seen this coming.

The Four Suns start the opening chords to the song, and Chloe grins at me, pulling the ring out of her back pocket. Beth and my dad both look around in various degrees of pleased and alarmed, until Beth's eyes snap on to the ring box and her hands clap over her mouth. Chloe half skips to my dad to hand it to him. My dad looks over her head at me, his eyes wide.

*You got this,* I mouth, holding up a fist to cheer him on.

He takes the box from Chloe, thanks her, and then clears his throat, taking Beth's hand. "Beth, I—"

"Yes," says Beth, already profusely crying through her smile.

"Mom!" Chloe protests. "You're supposed to let them sing first!"

"Oh," she says, adorably flustered. "I mean—TBD!"

My dad pulls Beth in, and the proposal itself gets pretty much swallowed by the sound of Aerosmith, so only my dad and Beth can hear it. She nods at him, then nods again, then looks over at me and Chloe like she wants to get a yes from us, too.

We give her identical thumbs-ups, and then she turns back to my dad. When he slides the ring on her finger the small crowd that has gathered around us in the park erupts into cheers, but my dad and Beth don't even seem to hear them, sharing a sweet kiss and then glancing at the rest of us shyly. The Four Suns have long since abandoned their instruments to join in on the cheering. Oliver pulls me in and plants a kiss on my temple, looking every bit as pleased as I am that the whole thing went off without a hitch.

"And to think, all this came about because you went aggressively method for *Mamma Mia*," he says, smiling down at me.

"This and . . . some other nice things," I say, intertwining my fingers with his.

"I'd say so. And don't worry," he says. "I've already got my brothers learning all of ABBA's greatest hits for the wedding."

My dad and Beth head toward us, punch-drunk with happiness, immediately hugging Georgie and squeezing her hard enough to bruise. What I didn't know until this past year when Georgie reentered our lives is that she was the one who introduced my dad and Beth in the first place—she and Beth were both a part of the same community theater, since neither of them actually majored in it, and Georgie had been subtly attempting to pull the strings on her dating my dad since they were all eighteen. Beth reuniting with her high school ex might have been a bump in Georgie's grand master plan, but she got her way in the end.

"It's about damn time," she tells them both.

Beth leans in and kisses her on the cheek, and when she steps back, Georgie and my dad do a very dorky series of hand gestures that must have meant something to them in the nineties but makes no sense to any of us now. Georgie grins a full-wattage kind of grin, the kind she's been smiling a lot lately now that she's back in our orbit. The kind of smile that would have been a dead giveaway of who she was, if I'd ever seen it last summer—it's every inch as broad and unrepentant as mine.

It seems like the more I get to know her, the more moments there are like this. But maybe it's less that I didn't notice them before and more that she seems to be changing. Loosening up and coming back to some version of herself that my dad must have known. It was a little bumpy at first when she came back into our lives—she emailed my dad mid-September, a few months after I told him. After that she and my dad met up a few times to talk before Georgie started coming over for dinner every week or so, or occasionally hanging out with us all at the Milkshake Club. There are definitely some heavy moments—ones where she and my dad exchange a look over my head that I don't quite understand, or someone says something about me as a little kid that makes Georgie go stiff—but for the most part, it's been nice. Having Georgie around is a little bit what having an aunt would have been like if my actual one hadn't pretty much taken over as my mom.

And if she really has made aunt status, now I've got more family than I can count. A stepmom in Beth, a stepsister in Chloe, a somewhat-related cousin in Steph, and I suspect a soon-to-be new aunt in Farrah (who very unsubtly measured my finger the other night, knowing it's the same size as Heather's).

"Thank you all for doing this," says my dad, looking at all of us in turn. A year ago all this attention probably would have killed him on the spot, but he's found a little bit more of his footing since Beth and Georgie both came back to respectively calm and boss him around.

"Can they do the chalupa song now?" Beth asks, still crying.

"Requests are extra," says Elliot cheekily, holding out his hand.

Before Oliver can scold him, Teddy pulls out his phone and starts blasting ABBA's "I Do" through the park, setting off yet another round of cheers from strangers.

Heather whistles to round us all up. Oliver and I reach for each other's hands at the same time, falling into step with each other as easily as breathing.

"To the Milkshake Bar," Heather calls. "Millie Mias on the house!"

"That's what I was hoping she'd say," says Oliver.

Perhaps the most delicious consequence of all this is that Heather coined a new sundae on the menu based on last summer's shenanigans. It's got a scoop of mint chip for me and Georgie, strawberry for Heather and Chloe, vanilla for my dad and Beth, Nutella for Farrah, sea salt chocolate chip cookie pieces for Oliver, and Reese's Puffs for Teddy. The whole thing is a big ooey-gooey fantastic mess, but I wouldn't have it any other way.

# ACKNOWLEDGMENTS

There are just a gobstopping number of humans to thank, but first a massive acknowledgment to the theater community—from the broader community that shapes and saves so many lives, to the pockets of it that raised me, to the friends I'm gonna have my whole life. I started this book a month before the pandemic began, never imagining what would happen to the world and its effect on theater as a whole; heck, I am writing these acknowledgments at the beginning of April 2021, not even really knowing what's ahead. But I do know that our love of theater is what has helped so many of us find community and hope through this whole mess, so I will always remember writing this book as a stubbornly joyful love letter to theater throughout it. Writing it was a balm in the scarier moments, and a reminder throughout all of them that no matter what you throw at this community, it was built both to love and to endure.

On that note, thank you to every theater I've ever been part of, and especially AfterWork Theater and everyone in it. I've always had this very bullheaded conviction that New York is where I belonged, but the day I first stepped into Launch Day was when it finally felt like home. Our production of *Newsies* might have gotten canceled because of COVID, but I sure did try to bring part of it back in some of these pages, one unrepentantly dweeby reference at a time. I can't wait to come up with ridiculous backstories for our next cast of characters once it's safe for us to belt our faces off in the same room again.

Thank you to every single human being at Wednesday Books. To Alex for your support and mutual love of ABBA, and the kind of edits that occasionally make me whisper "*Yessssss*" to myself like an evil scientist at eight in the morning. To Mara for always having my back, and Meghan and Lexi and DJ for the truly bonkers amount of work that goes into bringing a whole book into the world, and to Kerri and Mar for this beautiful cover that captured Millie body, heart, and soul.

Thank you to Janna, who is here for all my harebrained ideas, even when they're essentially "I'm going to smush as many musicals as I possibly can into a book and launch it like a glitter rocket into the sun!!!" The last few years have been wild and I am grateful to you for all the coolest parts of them.

Extreme blessings to Kadeen and Suzie and Gaby and Erin and Cristina and the other Wednesday authors for all the texts and group chats and phone calls that have kept our writing brains sane; to my theater partners in crime JQ and David and Harry Styles, who has been oddly quiet in our group chat lately, even though we keep putting him in all the playlists; and to Lily, whom I have spent too many hours singing with and writing alongside to count in a lifetime, and whose brain I trust most.

A belated but very heartfelt thank-you to Reese's Book Club for choosing *You Have a Match* for its Winter 2021 pick, and everyone in the community for being so kind and welcoming online. Of all the "holy guacamole" moments in my life, getting to be part of this lovely group is one of the best.

A brief thank-you to teenage me for being extremely melodramatic when I got rejected from all those musical theater schools. As cathartic as it was to listen to "The Climb" on repeat on my iPod shuffle and cry on the floor, like, twenty times that summer, it turns out it made much more sense to channel that emotion into learning how to write novels than how to dance more than eight counts without going "WHOOPS, SORRY" to whoever was on my immediate left. I might have spent a lot of years trying to reach my singing dreams anyway, but I'm grateful for them, both because it gave me nerves of steel and because it eventually taught me something important about life: sometimes you are just meant to do things for the sake of loving them. Sometimes the privilege of finding something you love that much is really the luckiest of all.

So thank you to my mom for planting all the singing seeds in our family with your own love for it; we have childhoods full of happy music memories, my favorite of which involves all of us screaming "Defying Gravity" in the minivan and likely terrifying people at traffic lights. Thank you for un-questioningly purchasing twelve-year-old me the soundtracks to *Sweeney Todd* and *Into the Woods* that first year I was re-ally into showtunes and apparently just skipped straight to "fairy tale carnage and murder" (and thank you for all the other less murdery soundtracks we got into after that). Thank you to my dad for sitting (and occaaaaaasionally sleeping) through so many productions of *Les Miserables* between his three daughters that he could probably get onstage and play Valjean without even glancing at a script. But mostly thank you to my parents for always believing in me, whether it was when I wanted to be on Broadway or when I wanted to be a songwriter in Nashville or when I wanted to publish books in New York (third time's the charm??). You have a lot of kids with moon-sized dreams, but you always have unshakable faith in them.

And with that, my last thank-you goes to Evan, Maddie, and Lily, who were my first and forever favorite singing partners. Our lives might take us very far away from one another sometimes, but we've got a whole lot of songs between us that can pull us right back.

©The Lock & Co

Emma Lord is a digital-media editor and writer living in New York City, where she spends whatever time she isn't writing either running or belting out show tunes in community theater. She graduated from the University of Virginia with a major in psychology and a minor in how to tilt your computer screen so nobody will notice you updating your fanfiction from the back row. She was raised on glitter, grilled cheese, and a whole lot of love. Her sun sign is Hufflepuff, but she is a Gryffindor rising. *Tweet Cute* is her debut novel. You can find her geeking out online on Twitter. Find Emma there and on Instagram at @dilemmalord and on emmalordwriting.com.